Julie Caplin is addicted to travel and good food. Formerly a PR director, for many years she swanned around Europe taking top food and drink writers on press trips sampling the gastronomic delights of the continent. It was a tough job but someone had to do it. These trips have provided the inspiration and settings for her novels.

juleswake.co.uk

twitter.com/JulieCaplin
facebook.com/JulieCaplinAuthor

Also by Julie Caplin

THE LITTLE SWISS SKI CHALET

JULIE CAPLIN

One More Chapter
a division of HarperCollins*Publishers* Ltd
1 London Bridge Street
London SE1 9GF
www.harpercollins.co.uk

HarperCollins*Publishers*
1st Floor, Watermarque Building, Ringsend Road
Dublin 4, Ireland

This paperback edition 2021

1

First published in Great Britain in ebook format
by HarperCollins*Publishers* 2021

A catalogue record of this book
is available from the British Library

ISBN: 978-0-00-843123-5

Printed and bound in Great Britain by
CPI Group (UK) Ltd, Croydon CR0 4YY

For my sister, Lynda, the chalk to my cheese, funny, kind and amazingly resilient, who deserves to be nothing but happy.

Part One

Chapter One

This was going to be a night to remember, Mina decided as she perched rather precariously on a chair and draped the little piñata fairy lights over the top of the archway from the kitchen into the dining area. They were the perfect finishing touch.

'Looking good,' said her sister, Hannah, appearing in the doorway clutching a bulging carrier bag.

'You're back.' Mina jumped down from the chair with a thump, belatedly remembering the neighbours below, and clapped her hands together, excitement getting the better of her. 'Did you get a bottle? I can't believe I forgot that. I mean, seriously, a Mexican evening without tequila! Actually, maybe I should have asked you to get two.'

'One bottle will be fine. Everyone will bring booze and you've got a crate of Corona. I don't think anyone's going to be thirsty.'

'You're a star. What would I do without you?' She hugged her sister.

'I think you'd probably manage,' said Hannah, extricating herself. 'There's enough food for everyone to take home and live off for the whole weekend.'

Mina gave her a cheerful grin. 'It's going to be great.' She couldn't wait to see everyone surrounding the table, the places set with her vintage china collected over the years from charity shops, her guests replete with food and alcohol, chatting in the candlelight. She'd been cooking all day and for most of the previous evening but it was going to be worth it. An anniversary celebration. One whole year with Simon. Quite a record for her, and she had to admit she was enjoying the calm and stability he brought into her life. He was the yin to her yang, or whatever the saying was. Actually it was probably the other way round, not that she had a clue about Chinese philosophy. What she did know was that she'd invited eight friends, including Hannah, for dinner tonight. It would be a tight squeeze but everyone was used to that when they came here. In the last year she'd held a Parisienne party (extremely chic), a Danish hygge gathering (very cosy), a gin cocktail speakeasy night (brilliant 1920s costumes, including Simon's fabulous Trilby that cost a bomb), and a Thai banquet (spicy, fresh, and utterly delicious).

Tonight's table with its brightly-striped Mexican serape-style tablecloth was laid with jewel-coloured raffia mats, plastic sombrero napkin rings, and a row of candles in rustic metal votives running down the centre. She'd even bought some cactus-shaped plastic ice cubes for the water jug.

'Your parties are always great, but you don't half give

yourself a lot of work. I'd have just bought a couple of Old El Paso sauces and some salsa and guacamole from M&S.'

'That's not proper Mexican food!' Mina's eyes widened in mock outrage. 'I'm doing authentic street food. Come.' Mina darted into the kitchen beckoning furiously. 'You've got to try this.' She was already holding the spoon out.

'What is it?' asked Hannah, her eyes narrowed in sudden suspicion.

'Try it...'

Her sister took a tentative mouthful. 'Oh wow.' She blinked rapidly. 'That's got a kick. But,' Hannah went back for a second lick, 'yum.'

'Chocolate sauce made with chilli from Ecuador. It's to have with the churros for dessert. Isn't it just divine?' Mina dipped her finger and took a quick taste, her eyes closing in sheer bliss. It was lovely. It had taken her a while to track this particular artisan made brand down, and it was worth every last penny of the extortionate price she'd paid. Although she'd been equally tempted by the caramel salted dark chocolate from Madagascar and the rum flavour from Trinidad and Tobago. There were just so many gorgeous chocolates to choose from these days.

'Different. I wish I could cook like you.'

Mina laughed.

'Then you wouldn't have your big fancy job and a gorgeous apartment to live in,' said Mina, looking around at her small cramped kitchen – not that she envied her sister at all, but one day she would like a decent-sized kitchen with an open-plan diner where she could entertain without having to leave her guests every five minutes. She'd even planned the layout in her head.

When she and Simon moved in together they could combine forces and buy a better place, perhaps even a house. Despite their different personalities, both of them loved food and entertaining – it was one of the reasons they worked so well as a couple. 'What do you want me to do?' asked Hannah, looking around.

'If you could grate cheese for me, for the nachos, and make sure it's the cheddar and not my special Alpine cheese.'

'What's that for? Or shouldn't I ask? Is it a Mexican speciality that no one knows about?'

Mina laughed. 'No, we've been talking about developing a fondue recipe at work, so I thought I'd get some sneaky practice in at home. It really needs the right cheese. Amelie has been emailing me traditional Swiss recipes.'

'Ah, that's nice. How is she?'

Amelie was Mina's godmother, who had been at school with their mother, in a boarding school in France. Poor Hannah had missed out as their parents had not got around to christening her, although Amelie had, in her typically generous fashion, adopted her as an honorary goddaughter and always sent her birthday and Christmas presents.

'Good. You know she moved out of Basel and bought that little ski lodge place, which does sound gorgeous. She keeps inviting me to go and visit, and I feel a bit bad that I haven't – but it's not like hopping on a plane to the city.

Where she is now is in the middle of nowhere. It's a three-hour train journey from Zurich or Geneva.'

'Not exactly a quick weekend break, then. Now what do you want me to do?'

'When you've grated the cheese, you could help me do the margarita glasses.'

'What are you doing with them?'

'I'm going to dip the rims in lime juice and then in salt, to get a proper crust around the edges.' She waved her hand towards the shaped cocktail glasses that she'd been thrilled to find in TK Maxx. 'And look: I'm going to sprinkle a little edible golden glitter in the salt to give them a bit of pizazz.' She was rather pleased with this idea, and even more pleased by Hannah's enthusiastic reaction.

'What a brilliant idea. And that's why you're the food technologist.'

'Huh, I don't think creating a new twist on pasta sauce is that exciting.' Mina tried not to sound too ungrateful. Working in the test kitchens of a major supermarket brand was a good job, a great job... it just didn't inspire her as much as it used to these days. Catering to the common denominator, like putting a more flavoursome béchamel sauce on top of a lasagne, could be a bit dull when she was wild to try new flavours.

'Now, if you're going to be my kitchen assistant, I need you to get cracking.'

Mina hummed away as she sliced and diced onions, seasoned chicken, and chopped a small mountain of chilies, like a mini whirling dervish. This was going to be a special evening and the food just one small part of it. She wanted to show Simon just how much he meant to her. He'd become an integral part of her community of friends over the last year, and she wanted to share her happiness with them as well. Good friends were everything. She glanced over at the small tissue-paper-decorated pināta striped in pink and blue. Earlier, she'd stuffed the small pouch inside it and now she felt a little thrill of anticipation at what Simon would say when it was released.

———————

By the time six o'clock arrived, and they'd both treated themselves to a taster of the freshly mixed margarita, virtually everything was done.

'Just time to get our glad rags on.' Mina surveyed the kitchen and the neat rows of everything lined up ready. She called it Blue-Peter-style cooking, with the emphasis on 'here's some I prepared earlier', so that when her guests arrived she spent as little time as possible in the kitchen – which was a challenge when you were serving really fresh, zesty street food. Somehow she couldn't help herself, and she did a little more prep as she waited for Hannah to finish in the bathroom before she finally dashed in at twenty-to-seven. Taking the quickest of quick showers, she dragged a comb through her blonde bob, swiped a quick slick of pink lipstick over her lips, and brushed on a lightning layer of black mascara to darken her ridiculously long, pale lashes, which could have rivalled a llama. Done. She blew a kiss at her reflection in the mirror, fluttered her llama lashes, and darted back into her bedroom to pull on her new, bright fuschia-pink dress and nipped into the kitchen to put on an apron. She'd been caught out by food splatters before and this dress deserved to shine.

When the doorbell rang at seven, she was in full hostess mode. As the room filled, she was in her element, dishing out bottles of Corona stuffed with the obligatory slice of lime, or glasses of the sort of margaritas that provided a mule-like kick.

'Blimey, Mina,' said George, one of her old university friends. 'That's going to put hairs on my chest. And I'm not sure about the glitter, I'll be twinkling at work on Monday. But killer of an idea.'

'Don't be a boring old stick,' said his partner, who was also inconveniently called George, and in the six months they'd been together had become G. 'I love the glitter and that is a seriously good cocktail.' He blinked his eyes rapidly as the alcohol hit his throat. 'Fire water.'

'Oh, is it too strong?' Mina paused in the act of handing over a glass to her best friend Belinda, who'd just arrived, flashing a smile at Simon just behind her.

'It'll be fine,' said Belinda, a kissing her on both cheeks and taking the glass for a sensible sip. 'Yum. And the glitter is…' She studied her glass. 'Is it OK to eat, or rather, drink?'

'Yes. It's edible. As if I'd use something that wasn't.' Mina stopped herself from rolling her eyes. Belinda had been her friend since school days and her sensible nature had often put a break on Mina's more reckless ideas in the past, but she was a grown-up now for goodness' sake. Didn't tonight prove this?

'Of course not,' said Belinda dryly, but Mina was already swinging towards Simon.

'Hi, darling.' She wished her hands weren't full and she could give him a proper hug. 'You've made good time.'

'Yes, I finished work… a bit earlier. I gave Belinda a lift.'

'That was kind.' Her eyes sparkled at him. Belinda lived the other side of town and didn't drive. He was such a kind man. Safe and steady too. Just what she needed. 'Want a margarita? Or would you prefer a beer?'

'Just water. I'm driving later.'

'Oh, babe, aren't you going to stay?' She kissed him again on the cheek, with a mischievous grin, hoping to remind him of what he might miss. 'These margaritas are to die for.'

'I bet they are, but not with football practice in the morning. You don't want me disturbing you after a heavy night.' He surveyed the table. 'Looks like you've gone the usual mile. This looks amazing. You're so talented in the kitchen.'

She raised her eyebrows in mock reproof as if to remind him that wasn't the only place.

'Well, it is a special night,' she murmured.

His brows drew together and she shook her head. 'Simon. What are you like? You've forgotten, haven't you?' she accused him jokingly. 'Honestly. Hopeless. Men.' She included Belinda in her teasing exasperation. 'It's our anniversary.'

Simon looked mildly horrified, but then he would. He didn't like getting things wrong. That driving perfectionism was one of the things she'd fallen for. She might live her life at ninety miles an hour all the time, trying to cram as much in as she could, but she still liked everything to be just so. Hence the themed evening, which had come together perfectly. Hannah was handing around plates of nachos, made with good stringy cheese and home-made spicy salsa, and from the satisfied munching they were going down well.

Leaving the room buzzing with conversation she went back into the kitchen and began to ferry out the food. Once the plates were all arranged on the table, in a haphazard jigsaw to make everything fit, she invited everyone to come and shoehorn themselves into the seats around the fully extended table, which spanned the whole width of the room.

'This looks amazing, Mina,' cried Patsy, a friend she'd made on a fish-filleting course a couple of months back, who worked in a local delicatessen. 'I have to get the recipes from you.'

'Don't you guys ever get fed up with being around food all the time?' asked Patsy's boyfriend, James, who was a firefighter. 'Not that I'm complaining.' He slung an arm around Patsy, who nudged him in the ribs with a laugh.

As she unloaded the plates, making sure everyone had something within reach, Mina basked in the exclamations of delight and interest while she explained what everything was, and invited them to tuck in. The fairy lights, the glow of the candles, and the main lights dimmed along with the low-level chatter created a wonderful, and to Mina, a deeply satisfying atmosphere in the room.

The drink flowed, the conversation rose and fell,

punctuated by shouts of laughter, and Mina relaxed into her chair next to Simon, soothed by the happy, smiling faces around her. This was what life was about. Friends, lovers, and good company.

Once everyone had demolished the churros and the tablecloth was spattered with tiny drops of chocolate, she brought out the piñata and the wooden stick that had been provided with it. Everyone roared with laughter at its dainty size.

'I know, I know, but its only for one person. One very special person.' She looked at Simon and handed him the stick. 'Today is our first anniversary.'

'And they said it wouldn't last,' quipped George from the other side of the table. She laughed back at him.

'Good job I didn't listen to you,' she said. When she'd first started seeing Simon, in secret because they were work colleagues, George had been the only person she'd confided in. He'd tried to talk her out of it, saying that it wasn't a good idea to mix business with pleasure, especially with her track record. Her relationships tended to implode at around the three-month mark, which was how she knew that Simon was the right man for her. He was calm, steady, and just what she needed, unlike her previous boyfriends, who tended to be here today, gone tomorrow. Admittedly, while they'd been a lot of fun, commitment, financial stability, or the ability to be faithful had been in short supply. Simon offered all of those things, although he could be a little stodgy and stuck in his ways sometimes. Her spontaneity and get-up-and-go was a good balance for him. They complemented each other perfectly.

With the help of G and James, she tied the piñata to the curtain pole.

'Just don't break the window,' she said, her heart starting to thump with excitement.

To a chorus of 'give it some welly,' and 'go on,' Simon took a few tentative swipes at the tissue and papier-mâché donkey. A couple of people held up their phones to film the scene as Simon rather ineptly swiped at the piñata. At one point Mina despaired of him ever breaking open the darned thing and itched to take over his half-hearted attempt. Then with one final crack, it was torn clean in two and a giftwrapped box dropped to the floor.

With a triumphant yell, Simon snatched it up, and Mina, her pulse now roaring like an express train around her body, steered him back to the table and sat on his lap.

'I didn't know I was getting presents,' he said, fighting his way through the paper. Of course, Mina hadn't made it too easy for him, because inside the box was another box, and then another box. At last he came to the final one and she held her breath as he opened it to find a blue suedette pouch.

He wrinkled his eyebrows and gave her a puzzled look, a broad smile on his face. She smiled tremulously back at him, realising her hands were shaking a little. Everyone around the table craned forward with interest.

Simon opened the pouch and pulled out the gold wedding band, holding it up between thumb and finger. With a dazzling smile, she looked up into his face.

'Will you marry me? It is a leap year after all.'

Around the table there were a few gasps and a couple of 'ahs'.

She felt Simon's body stiffen and as she watched his face, she saw his eyes slide across the table, widening as they connected with someone else's shocked gaze. Her own gaze followed, and in a single second her world crumbled. Belinda?

In the next second, Simon stood up with horrified speed, as if he couldn't wait to get away from her, and she slipped off his lap onto the floor.

He dropped the ring on the table as if it were hot lava and stared horrorstruck at her.

'Are you crazy?' he asked in a hoarse whisper. 'What are you doing?'

Mortified, Mina's throat closed up and her skin crawled as she realised everyone was watching, with avid fascination, as the car crash unfolded. What had she been thinking? It had seemed such a brilliant idea at the time. Only last month they'd been talking about moving in together and about the future. They'd even talked about how many children they'd have one day. How had she got this so wrong? She'd been so sure of him. They'd made plans. Admittedly, Simon had been distracted for the last month, but she'd assumed it was the long hours he was working and the pressure he was under in his department, which had seen several redundancies. Now it was painfully obvious that something else – or rather, someone else – had been on his mind.

'But...' She looked from Simon to Belinda, whose face was now stained with a fierce red blush and contorted by an odd, constipated sort of expression. Simon's face mirrored Belinda's. They looked remarkably similar: two compatriots, two people in sync – a couple.

As the trainwreck finally slowed to a comprehensive halt, she remembered all her earlier hopes. This was one night she wouldn't be forgetting anytime soon.

Chapter Two

Mina hurried out of the front door and down the
steps clutching her laptop bag, huddling into her
scarf, trying to hide from the biting January wind. Despite
the icy conditions predicted by the weather forecast, she
wore high, kick-ass, black patent leather boots under slim-
fitting black trousers with a matching jacket over a scarlet
silk blouse. If there was ever a down-but-not-defeated outfit
then this was it. This morning she had to face all her work
colleagues after Saturday night's disastrous proposal,
including Simon himself.

While the rest of the guests had hastily beaten a path to
her door, she and Simon had retreated to her bedroom for a
hideous, no-coming-back-from, stand-up row.

'What did you think you were doing?' hissed Simon,
shaking his head in rare fury.

'I thought I was proposing to someone who said, less
than a month ago, that he loved me. Someone who had
agreed to find an estate agent to have our flats valued, and

had selected the name Victor for our first male child – which, I'd just like to say now, I thought was an awful name, and I fully intended talking you out of it – and I seem to recall you even suggested getting married in St Mary's near your mum's. So forgive for me being a little confused. I thought I was doing what we'd already agreed we would do?'

'Typical. So it's my fault, is it? I might have known. Not that you had to jump the gun or anything, like you always do. You're in such a hurry all the time.'

'Well, I wouldn't have done if I'd realised you were shagging – I'm assuming you are, by the colour of her face – one of my oldest friends.' Belinda had been excommunicated – she no longer deserved the title 'best' friend.

At that point Simon's mouth firmed to a mutinous line rather reminiscent of a toothless turtle.

'How long has that been going on?' Mina thrust her chin up into his face.

'She's much calmer. You want to do everything at breakneck speed. You're too much. Even your ridiculous wedding proposal is so true to character. Belinda's much… more balanced. I feel on an even keel with her.'

'So, you spineless git, you're saying this is my fault, because of my personality?' Her eyes bored into him with fury.

'We're not right for each other.' Simon's words were stiff as he refused to look at her.

'Funny it took you until tonight to say anything. You never questioned things before. You sucked it all up… must have been terrible for you. Having to go on with all those awful things I organised for us – a weekend in Cornwall, dinner at Le Manoir, ski lessons at the indoor ski slope. My memory is terrible but I could have sworn that after I booked the indoor sky diving, you said that being with me was always so much fun.'

'Fun, yes.' Simon finally looked at her before saying coldly, 'But not for keeps.'

'What?' Her heart pinched in sudden pain. *Not for keeps.*

'You can't base a marriage, or even a serious relationship, on fun.' He peered at her like a headmaster delivering a lecture, which he then proceeded to do.

Now, even with the cold wind biting at her face, Mina paused for a moment, the words from Saturday night still ringing with hurtful shrillness in her ears:

'You can't spend your life being spontaneous and going off on adventures all the time. Marriage is about being grown-up, settling down, knowing you're on an even keel. With you it's like being on a constant rollercoaster, or in a plane and I'm never sure when you're going to throw me out of the door. You're too crazy, too mile-a minute, too wanting the next thing all the time. I never know where I am, and I don't want to live like that. It's probably from your genes, and I'm not sure I want those in my children.'

'Genes?' she spat.

'Your real mum and dad. It sounds as if they were always chasing adventure. It sounds as if they were reckless and irresponsible. They didn't take the important things in life seriously. That's not what I want in my life.'

Her eyes almost popped out of her head with sheer rage

at him bringing up her long dead parents and it robbed her of the ability to say anything. Simon was oblivious and on he ploughed, 'It's a shame you don't take after your adopted parents, Miriam and Derek. I can't believe that Miriam was your mother's sister, she's so normal.'

Mina had never, ever been as close to strangling anyone as she was at that moment. Her fingers actually cramped into claws, ready to do the deed. Luckily Simon stepped out of range with one more parting salvo.

'We've had fun, but... you can't have fun all the time. At some point you need to focus on what's important. And I can't see you ever doing that. You're like a butterfly, constantly flitting about, looking for the next great thing. It's too exhausting being with you.'

With that parting shot, he'd walked out of the flat, leaving her with the debris of the dinner party, which she attacked with furious energy, imaging hitting him over the head with the frying pan as she scrubbed at it. She refused to cry, although she might have suffered a slight leakage at points as she wiped down the surfaces. At last when the kitchen and dining table were almost clean and tidy, she picked up the pan of chocolate sauce and sat down, cross-legged, in the middle of the kitchen floor with it between her knees. Dipping a finger into the chocolate, she carefully licked it clean and closed her eyes. Life might be crap, but there was always chocolate. In the world of food, as far as she was concerned, it had serious super powers. She took another mouthful. Sod Simon, he didn't deserve her.

Of course, after the event, when the chocolate had soothed her and she'd eaten the lot, she could think of a dozen witty brilliant comebacks. Chief among them: what had changed? At the time Mina had felt as if she'd been punched. The words had spun around and around her head for the remainder of the weekend like a manic merry-go-round. He hadn't even said he was sorry once. The way he'd talked, it was as if she'd deserved his cheating on her. Talking of whom, the big, fat coward (of course, she wasn't fat at all; if anything she was thin, with perfect double Ds and one of those 1950s waists, but she *was* very cowardly) Belinda, had slipped out with all the other guests and hadn't so much as texted an apology or an explanation during the rest of the weekend.

Hannah had talked Mina out of marching round to Belinda's parents' house to challenge her, quite rightly pointing out that Mina would probably slap her. The last thing she needed was an assault charge on top of looking a complete and utter dick in front of her friends. Although George and G were about to be wiped from that list, because one of them had shared the video of Simon with the piñata and the disastrous proposal on Facebook. Even if, apparently, it had been inadvertent because one of them had forgotten to change their privacy settings.

As she left the communal front garden, a man stopped her. 'Excuse me, are you Mina Campbell?'

'Yes?' she answered, with a question in her voice.

'I wonder if you would mind answering a few questions.'

'Sure.' Funny time for market research, she decided – but as a lot of her work was directed by such research, she always felt she ought to stop and do her bit.

'How did you feel when your boyfriend turned you down?'

'What?' Her head snapped up.

'You are the girl whose proposal went wrong? The piñata girl.'

She stepped away from him as he gave her an encouraging smile.

'Who are you? How do you know about that?'

'Jamie Jenkins, I work for the *Mirror*. It's all over Facebook. This is your chance to put your side of the story out there.'

'I don't want my story out there, full stop.'

'Bit late for that, love. The genie's out of the bottle. Come on, give us a couple of quotes. How did you feel when he turned you down? How long have you been together? Are you still together?'

'No, we are not,' she spat before she could stop herself. 'And I wasn't being presumptuous or precipitous, we've been talking marriage for months. Turns out, he has a new lady friend he forgot to mention… or that she was my best friend. Note the past tense. Was.' Even as she was talking she knew she should stop, but it all came spilling out, the indignation of the weekend, the feeling of injustice. Yes, she was impulsive and jumped in feet-first, but this time she really had done her due diligence. She could give a date and a time to the exact conversation they'd had about St Mary's church, tell anyone where she was when Simon had talked about having children one day. What she hadn't factored in was that Simon had started an affair, and his feet had cooled to arctic blocks since then.

Suddenly she noticed the photographer with the long black lens taking photos from the other side of the street and realised she'd told the reporter far too much.

'That's all off the record,' she said, now feeling shaky and barely able to remember what had just spewed out.

'You sound pretty pissed off with him,' said the reporter who, as she looked more closely, reminded her of a weasel, with his sharp-eyed intensity and long neck. 'What did you say to him? I'd have kneed him in the balls. What was your reaction?'

'No comment,' she said, although she wished she had kneed Simon in the balls. 'Look, I don't want this in the paper. It was all a mistake. There is no story. You're not taking photos, are you?'

He shrugged with nonchalant indifference, deliberately not looking towards the photographer.

No! Mina realised he had a tiny voice recorder in his left hand. She tried to snatch at it but he moved it out of reach very smartly, as if it wasn't the first time someone had tried to do just that.

Realising that the photographer was now taking an interest, she stopped and glared at the reporter. 'Leave me alone.'

Fuming, Mina hitched her bag over her shoulder, side-stepped around the reporter, and darted across the road to her car. The photographer, mistaking her action, took a few more pictures and then, thinking she was coming after him, took off, running down the street in shoes designed with considerably more athleticism in mind than her black boots. Although it had crossed her mind to confront him, she headed for her little navy Beetle, sending a vindictive glare towards the reporter now hovering between two parked cars. He took one look at her face, waved, and speed-walked away.

She got into her car and bashed her head against the steering wheel. 'Bloody, bloody, bloody, effing hell.' Bad enough that everyone at work would know; now it seemed the whole nation was about to be treated to the story of Mina, the dumb blonde, getting it very wrong with her man. It didn't take a genius to come up with the headlines.

'Who's the donkey now?'

'Hit me with your proposal stick.'

With a sigh she started up the engine. Time to face the music at work.

'I think you need to warn Miriam and Derek,' said Hanna three hours later, when Mina phoned her during her lunch hour.

'Warn them about what?' That Simon – who they thought was the bee's knees, on account that he'd always brought them a bottle of the same wine on every single occasion he came to the house for Sunday lunch – was actually a two-timing bastard who had been shagging her former best friend for the last four weeks, one of which coincided with Sunday lunch and the provision of aforementioned, Casillero del Diablo, red wine.

'Warn them that one of their adopted daughters might

be appearing in a national newspaper. They're going to be horrified.'

'Thanks for the vote of confidence.'

'I meant they'll be horrified if you don't tell them first. Look, why don't we both go round together tonight after work. I can give you moral support.'

'Thanks, Han. I think you might need to provide medical support. There could be heart attacks all round when they find out that Simon is not the golden boy they thought he was. I reckon Aunty M might have been knitting bootees on the quiet.'

Hannah was locking her car across the street when Mina pulled into a handy parking space after a very difficult day at work. Switching off the engine, she watched her sister approach in the wing mirror as she slumped wearily in her seat. What a day. Bloody bastard Simon had told his side of the story very convincingly to just about everyone before Mina even walked through the front door. He'd managed to make her look extremely manipulative by intimating that her proposal had been a misguided attempt to force his hand in front of everyone.

With a sigh, she grabbed her handbag and hauled herself out of the car.

Hannah wrinkled her face as she studied Mina. 'Oh dear. Rotten day.'

'The worst. Simon got in first and made out I got my just desserts.'

'Ouch, I'm sorry. I did consult a friend who works for a law firm that deals with the media to try and find out if you could get an injunction or anything. Sorry, the cost would be prohibitive and the grounds – to protect against damage to reputation – are based on very stringent principles, which she didn't think applied in this instance.'

Mina threw her arms around her sister. 'Han, I love you, and that you even tried for me. You're the best.'

'Not really, I stopped you going round and slapping Belinda. In hindsight, she deserves it.'

'You stopped me getting an assault charge, as you pointed out at the time, and just imagine what the news reporter would have made of that if I'd been arrested.'

'It's so unfair, Mina.'

'Don't worry… I'll get my own back. Just give me time to think of something.'

Hannah grinned. 'That's my girl. What are you thinking?'

'He's very worried about his receding hairline.'

'And?'

'Hair removal cream in his shampoo?'

'What if he gets it in his eyes or something? It's pretty strong stuff. You could get sued.'

Mina screwed up her nose. That was the sort of thing Hannah would worry about.

'OK, maybe I'll just fill it with lots of dead flies or something horrible.'

'Where will you get—'

Mina nudged her sister. 'Shut up. I'll think of something while I've still got the keys to his flat. I'm not speaking to him at work and I'm going to completely ignore him.' There was a leave-in hair mask he was rather partial to. Perhaps she could add to it – a leave-in hair *dye*. Blue, she'd heard, was very difficult to remove. The more she thought about it, the perkier her steps towards her adopted parents' drive became.

'Oh my God!' Hannah stopped dead, putting a hand out to stop Mina.

'Oh my God,' repeated Mina, as they both stared at the For Sale sign outside their parents' house.

'They're moving?' Hannah shook her head. 'Do you think they're having a mid-life crisis or something?'

'It must be a mistake,' said Mina. 'They'll never move. They've never even talked about it before.'

Their adopted parents were the most change-averse people in the entire universe. Derek had worked in the same office for the last forty-five years and every single person that worked with him there adored him. Miriam had worked part-time for the newsagent on the other side of town since she was sixteen, even though it was two bus rides away, which Mina had never understood. Actually there was quite a lot about their adopted parents that neither girl understood, such as their complete disinterest in food, their preference for annual holidays in Eastbourne, dedication to routine: laundry on Monday and Wednesday, the food shop on Thursday, fish and chips every Friday (there'd been mild alarm when Our Plaice had been bought out and became Oh My Cod), and a trip to the park every Saturday morning.

At the same time there was also an awful lot to love.

Miriam and Derek were the kindest, gentlest, and most generous people, even if they couldn't make a decision to save their lives. When Hannah and Mina's real parents drove off a cliff in Serbia, when they were two and three respectively, it never occurred to Miriam and Derek not to adopt their two orphaned nieces. Miriam had been ten years older than her sister, Georgie, and they were the original chalk and cheese – although from what Miriam said, it seemed that the more adventurous Georgie had been led astray by her daredevil husband, Stuart, from the minute she met him. Before having children they'd climbed the Eiger, white-water rafted on the Zambesi, bungy-jumped in Queenstown, and trekked in the Kalahari. Post-children, they'd restricted their activities to weekends in Europe, rally driving in Serbia, hanggliding in Bavaria, and mountain biking in the Pyrenees – and the childless Miriam and Derek had only been too happy to babysit.

She and Hannah stood on the threshold of the gravelled drive and looked up at the three-storey house, which she had to admit did need a little TLC these days. When had the paint on the window frames on the top floor started to crack and peel? And there were an awful lot of weeds establishing themselves in places they had no business to be.

'It's probably worth a fortune,' said Hannah. Over the years the street had become gentrified.

'I guess, but I never thought they'd move, and why haven't they mentioned it?'

They sat around the faded, pale-blue Formica kitchen table, which was so old that it would probably sell well on Etsy as a retro item. The kitchen cabinets with their cream doors and plastic wood surrounds were circa 1970 and the oldest that Mina had ever seen. A museum might be prepared to take them as they were immaculate.

'It's a lovely surprise to see you both,' said Miriam, her hands fluttering around the Hornsea pottery mug of builder's tea. 'I haven't got anything in for supper though. We were going to have a couple of chicken fillets and chips. There might be a couple of Rich Tea biscuits somewhere.'

And that, thought Mina, said it all. Biscuits should be irresistible, and you should know exactly how many you had left because they're so delicious you've been rationing yourself, and there should always be something in the cupboard you could throw together.

'Don't worry, Aunty M,' said Hannah, kicking Mina under the table before she could say anything.

Not being able to feed someone was complete anathema to her.

'It's quite useful you popping round though,' said Derek with a distinctly uncomfortable wriggle. He'd been fidgeting in his seat since they'd sat down.

'Well, there's a reason,' said Mina, diving straight in, wanting to get it over with. 'Simon and I have finished. I just wanted you to know before you read about in a national newspaper.'

'Oh no, darling. That's such a shame. He's such a nice boy. Isn't there anything you can do to patch things up? Are you sure it's over, you're not just overreacting?' Mina shot a look over the table at her sister. Why did everyone automatically assume it had to be something to do with her?

'He has been seeing Belinda behind my back,' she said, proud of her restraint. The sentence deserved at least two expletives.

'But why would he do that?' Miriam looked genuinely perplexed.

'Because he's a two-timing, cheating bastard.' Mina's saccharine smile didn't placate her mother.

'Well, that's a terrible shame.' Her aunt's fluttery hands plucked at the pattern on the mug in front of her.

Mina eyed them. Neither of them had picked up on the 'national newspaper' words.

'Actually, we have something quite important to tell you,' said Derek, as he and Miriam exchanged another one of those worried, panicky looks.

Mina stiffened. Was one of them ill? She looked with alarm at both their faces. She couldn't bear it if anything happened to either of them. Her parents were a distant memory, but Miriam and Derek were the constants in her life, unstinting in their love and support. They were her real parents now.

'We've decided to downsize. I'm going to take voluntary redundancy and we're going to move to a bungalow.'

'Wow, that's a lot of change in one go for you two,' said Mina, relief coursing through her as she ignored the warning glare Hannah sent her.

'It's time. This house is too big for us… always was, really, and we can't keep up with the maintenance.'

'And the redundancy package is very good, and I was due to retire next year anyway. With that and the pension, we can buy a nice little place.'

'But if you sell this house, you'll have loads of money.' Houses on this street, this size, in this area, must have been worth well over a million pounds – one-point-two or one-point-three at least.

Miriam and Derek exchanged another one of those diffident, uncertain glances, and neither of them spoke for longer than what was an acceptably pregnant pause.

For at least a full minute the four of them looked at each other as the clock on the wall with its loud tick counted down the seconds like a timer on a bomb.

'Oh no, you haven't been scammed by one of those equity companies, have you?' Hannah straightened, her hands clasped with sudden worry.

'No, no,' said Derek. 'It's not that.'

It went quiet again and Mina wanted to shake one of them to break free the vital piece of information that they didn't seem to be able to volunteer. Hannah gave her another warning kick under the table. Seriously, why did people always assume she was the loose cannon about to say the wrong thing?

'Anyone want another cup of tea?' Miriam reached for the tea pot, pulling off the dark brown knitted tea cosy. She was the only person Mina knew who actually used a tea cosy.

'Yes,' said Derek with over-enthusiastic eagerness.

Mina moved her legs out of range, ignoring Hannah's narrowed eyes.

'So what's the problem?'

Derek sighed. Miriam sighed.

'The thing is...' Derek tapped his finger on the table. 'The thing is... The house. It's not ours.'

'Oh.' Mina frowned in confusion. 'Have you been renting it all this time?'

'But if it's not yours,' said Hannah, 'How can you sell it?'

Miriam gave a nervous laugh. 'Well, we sort of, you know, kind of...'

'We forgot,' prompted Derek.

'How can you forget that you don't own a house?' asked Hanna, glancing over at Mina.

'Well, we just got so used to being here.'

'So the owner is selling the house and you've got to leave.' Mina sat up. 'I'm sure there are laws to protect you. Aren't you sitting tenants? They can't just throw you out. Hannah can sort it all out for you. We won't let them do that.'

Miriam laughed and patted her hand. 'That's not it at all.'

'Who does own the house, then?' asked Hannah.

'Well, you do.' Miriam smiled as if it were totally obvious.

Mina clicked her key fob and saw the flash of her hazard lights. 'I can't believe those two.'

Hannah laughed. 'How do you forget you don't own a house?'

'I suppose they've been there for so long they hadn't thought about it. It must have been a legal nightmare when our real parents died. You'd have thought with their proclivity for adventure they might have thought about having a proper will.'

Miriam had explained that when Georgie and Stuart were killed, everything had been a terrible mess and it had been easier to move into the girls' family home, which Stuart had inherited from his own parents, rather than unsettling them further by moving them into a rented terraced house on the other side of town. Hence Miriam's lengthy journey to her job. Derek and Miriam had moved in and started life as a family there, and until they'd decided to downsize, had never even thought about ownership.

'How do you feel about them insisting the proceeds of the sale come to us?' asked Hannah.

'Uncomfortable. It's totally wrong. They've paid for the upkeep of the house all these years. I think they should get enough from the sale to buy whatever they want. That only seems fair to me. There'll still be plenty left over.'

'Me too, but they're adamant it's our inheritance.'

'Blimey, the house is valued at one-point-three million. Even if they spent half on a new house, we'd still have plenty. I would far rather they bought another house and kept their savings, especially if Uncle D is going to retire. They could buy a lovely bungalow with that money.'

Hannah didn't respond. Instead her face was scrunched

up in thought. They walked a few more paces in silence until she suddenly swung around to face Mina.

'If you could do anything you wanted, what would you do?'

'What, with the money, you mean?'

'Yes. If you could give up work and go and do something completely different.'

'I don't know. Why, what would you do? I thought you loved your job.'

'I do love my job, but… even you would say it's a bit dull. I want something more. I'd really like to go somewhere to learn to cook properly.'

'I just chuck it all in together and hope for the best.' Mina shrugged.

'That's not true. You're an instinctive cook. You experiment, and you have a real flair – whereas I'm always worried I'm going to get it wrong. I wish I'd done food tech, like you did, for A level.'

'I don't think that would have helped you get a law degree. And I do get it wrong sometimes. Beetroot meringue? Remember?'

'It tasted OK,' said Hannah with a sudden laugh as they both remembered the soggy purple mess. 'But I wouldn't have had a clue where to start to even *try* something like that. I want to learn to cook properly. Everything from bread-making to pastry, patisserie to butchery… there's an amazing place in Ireland where you can go for twelve weeks.'

'Wow, sounds like you've been doing some serious thinking.' Mina was impressed. She rarely thought that logically about the future – she jumped from one adventure to the next – and just for a very brief moment she wondered what she would do if she left her job.

'Yes. It's always been a bit of a dream, the course is hideously expensive but,' Hannah's eyes gleamed with sudden excitement, 'with this money, I really could go.'

'Then this is the perfect windfall,' said Mina, giving her sister a hug, ignoring the prick of envy over her sister having such a clear vision of what she wanted to do. It always seemed to Mina that Hannah had life sussed, while she'd been the one who still wasn't sure she'd found what she really wanted. Suddenly her life seemed a little hollow, and the future a little empty. With an unhappy sinking feeling, she realised that she needed to sort herself out. A week ago she'd been bouncing along quite happily and now everything seemed to have stalled, and upon reflection, that was nothing to do with Simon dumping her. What *did* her future hold, and what did she really want from it? With an unpleasant start, she realised she had no idea, and for the first time in her life she felt a little lost.

Chapter Three

'But this was outside of work,' protested Mina as Ian Walters, the HR director, folded his arms.

'The fact remains that Simon has made an official complaint about you and...' He sighed. 'Mina, I have to be seen to be doing something about it.'

'Well, that's bloody unfair.'

'Look, if he chooses to escalate things, it could be a lot worse. And I don't know what the legal position is, but what if he chooses to take it further as a civil action? What were you thinking?'

Mina folded her arms mutinously. 'I was thinking he was a cheating sod and that blue hair would suit him.'

Ian tried to hide his amusement and failed miserably. 'You know everyone is calling it Smurfgate.'

Mina grinned. 'Are they?'

'Yes, and I'm being totally unprofessional here. I appreciate that this all took place out of work, but the fact remains that you've – I don't know what to call it, not assault or criminal damage – but at the end of the day you've harmed a fellow colleague.'

'He looked a bit patchy for a couple of days.' She shrugged before adding, 'You should see Belinda – good job she doesn't work here.' An irate Simon had shown her the pictures. Despite her bravado, Mina did now feel quite remorseful. Belinda's hair was doing a fair impersonation of mottled mermaid; her streaky blonde highlights had absorbed varying differing strengths of blue and it looked terrible. Even she couldn't honestly say that Belinda deserved it; it was going to take months and a lot of hairdressing bills to sort out.

'Mina. You need to sort yourself out.'

She flinched at the words. It was all very well telling herself that, but to hear it from someone else – someone who she respected and admired – that hit home.

'I'm saying this as a friend. You need to reign in some of your natural enthusiasm and be more commercial. Your last appraisal said it all: you're creative, a hard worker, but you have a tendency to dive off at a tangent sometimes. Heston Blumenthal can get away with weird and wonderful flavours – you can't. Our customers are not ready for orange-and-fennel-flavoured pastry in their mince pies. They want traditional, tried and tested. That's what your job is. To give them that.'

She knew that, but she couldn't stop herself arguing back, 'But that's boring. Did you try my mince pies?'

'Yes, and they were bloody delicious, but the thing is, you have to toe the company line.'

'I get that, but you have to push the boundaries a bit

otherwise we'd never move forward.' Mina couldn't understand the company's attitude. Last year their mince pies averaged a measly five-out-of-ten in the magazine and online taste tests. *Good Housekeeping* only gave them a three, and quite frankly she didn't blame them. Her recipe would have at least garnered some interest, rather than rating bland mediocrity.

'Mina. Listen to me. Simon is out for blood. You need to keep your head down. You've got a lot of holiday owing. Why don't you take a couple of weeks off? Think about what you really want? Is a career here going to fulfil your creativity? You're a brilliant recipe developer but... is this the right place for you?'

Mina stared at him. 'Are you sacking me?'

'No, not all. You're one of our best – when you stay on track. I'd hate to lose you, but I worry that this isn't what you need. Why don't you go away for a little while, think things through? Hopefully when you get back he'll have calmed down.'

'But I'm not in the wrong here—'

Ian raised an eyebrow and she shut up. Actually, a few weeks' holiday was quite a nice idea. Maybe she could do with some thinking time. There was a whole world out there; perhaps it was time to do something like Hannah and take some time for herself.

'Hi Hannah.'

'What?' asked her sister with a tone of instant suspicion.

'Why would you say that?' Mina felt aggrieved as she sat on the end of her bed eying the rather small pile of clothes she'd already earmarked to go in her case.

'Because you bothered to say hi and use my name. Normally you dive in as if we're already mid-way through a conversation. Personally I find it endearing, but when you say, "Hi Hannah", I know you want something.'

'Well, now you come to mention it. Is there any chance you could give me a lift to the airport on Thursday afternoon?'

'Wind back a sec. Airport. Thursday. What, *this* Thursday, as in two days' time? What's going on?'

'You know how you said that putting hair removal cream in Simon's shampoo would be a bad idea?'

'Oh God, you didn't.'

'No, wait. I didn't. I refrained.'

'Thank goodness for that.'

'I went for the blue hair dye instead.'

'Oh flipping heck, Mina. Why do you do these things? Seriously. Consequences. Remember consequences.'

'Yeah, well this time, HR are giving me a hard time.'

'Why?'

'Because Simon has complained about me as a colleague.'

'That slimy weasel. It's nothing to do…'

'Don't think I haven't told them that, but Simon is making a big fuss. It's been suggested I take a couple of weeks' holiday. I don't see why I *should* – but I do fancy a holiday.'

'Oooh, where are you going to go?'

'I'm going to Switzerland to see Amelie.'

'Well, that's unexpected. You've got the world at your feet, I thought you'd be going backpacking in Bali, surfing in Sydney, cruising in Croatia, or riding in—'

'Exactly: too much choice. This was easier and I could do it instantly. She's always said I'm welcome. And I thought, why not? I haven't seen her new place.' To be honest she hadn't really thought about it that much. When she'd had an email from Amelie yesterday morning, on impulse she'd invited herself.

'People say that, they don't always mean it.'

'Well, she seemed to think two weeks wasn't long enough,' argued Mina. 'Besides I need to get away from work for a while, and I booked flights. I'm flying to Zurich on Thursday afternoon, staying overnight in a hotel and then getting a train to her place on Friday. Have you got any ski kit I can borrow?'

'Mina, you are hopeless. Yes, I've got kit you can borrow. Although TK Maxx do very good-value stuff.'

'Do they? Cool, I'll pop in there tomorrow.'

'What about work?'

'Ian agreed that I could have unpaid leave for the rest of this week. I'm already well ahead on next year's Christmas recipes. It wasn't difficult, just more of the same with an extra pinch of nutmeg.' She groaned at the thought of the same old, dull formulations. 'I'll go shopping tomorrow for thermals and things. I've never been anywhere where it's properly cold before.'

'Layers. It's all about layers. There's no such thing as bad weather, just bad clothes. In fact you should go to one of those outdoor places at Cheshire Oaks. They'll sort you out with all the right kit.'

By Thursday lunchtime Mina's case was packed with virtually an entire new wardrobe, and a considerable extension to her overdraft. She also had a brand new notebook and a copy of *Moving Onwards and Upwards: Get the life you deserve, find purpose and achieve your goals* which she'd bought on a whim in Waterstones. She'd caught sight of it out of the corner of her eye, and while she didn't believe in fate or providence, it did seem to sum up what Ian had been hinting at. Reading it, she felt sure, was bound to help in sorting herself out – or at least it would feel as if she were trying. She'd always been someone with a plan, who knew what they were doing. Since everything that happened after her disastrous would-be proposal, for the first time in her life, she felt herself floundering, and not really knowing what to do about it. The book was her equivalent of a lifebelt. Reading it was a practical step that she could do straightaway.

She'd read it on her journey – or maybe she'd save it for later, she had a couple of podcasts on her phone to listen to. Who knew what Switzerland held – but she was going to make the most of these two weeks, and think about the future, not look backwards and dwell on the mess she was leaving behind.

Part Two

Chapter Four

Zurich

Zurich in mid-February brought tears to her eyes as the cold bit at her nose. Mina huddled deeper in the long down coat that she'd bought especially for the trip. It made her feel positively European among the other women wearing very similar outfits in the sparsely populated streets.

Last night when she'd arrived in the dark by train, which sped efficiently from the airport to the city centre in just ten minutes, the snow-covered roofs and spires had piqued her interest. Now in the bright sunny morning she regretted giving herself so little time to explore the city. Her train to Reckingen, in the canton of Valais, was due to leave just after lunch, which left very little time to wander the streets, checking out the inviting nooks and crannies of the little lanes and cobbled roads.

She'd done a little reading on the internet and had been

fascinated to find that Switzerland was made up of twenty-six cantons, each of which were individual states with their own distinct regional foods and dialects. It was like each county in England having its own rules and regulations, and she wondered how on earth it worked in Switzerland. Now she was here, she thought maybe she should have done more research but – she gave herself a wry smile – that was typical of her, jumping in with both feet. Besides it was more of an adventure to find things out as you went, wasn't it?

Luckily the friendly receptionist in her hotel had given her an extremely handy leaflet with a recommended short walking tour which encompassed all the highlights in one quick circuit, taking in the old Roman fort Lindenhof for an 'inspiring view of the city', St Peter's church 'to see the largest clockface in Europe', the Fraumünster with its 'must-see' Chagall stained glass windows, and, across the river Limmat over the Münster Bridge, the Grossmünster, 'a Romanesque Protestant church'. It seemed like a lot of churches to someone who really wasn't that spiritual, but the prescribed walk offered a quick snapshot in her limited time slot.

After a breathless, steep climb, the old fort did indeed afford the promised 'inspiring view of the city', providing a wonderful snapshot of the different architectural styles spread along the banks of the Limmat, from the white buildings crowding onto the river front with their pale blue, green, or grey wooden shutters and the terracotta roofs glowing in the mid-morning sunshine, through to splendid steep-pointed, gothic spires protruding from every part of the city. Taking a moment to enjoy the view, she took a few photos to share with Hannah, Miriam, and Derek on the family WhatsApp group, and then, conscious of the time and her train in a couple of hours, she walked to St Peter's Church and took another tourist snap of the enormous clock face, before hurrying on down another street following the arrows on the leaflet. She was about to take a left turn when something stopped her and she lifted her head to take an appreciative sniff. Chocolate. The rich scent filled the air and she could almost taste it. Abandoning her route, she followed her nose down a narrow cobbled lane, where the tall houses created an alley-like feeling with flags on either side of the street almost touching each other.

Halfway down, housed in an old timber-framed building, was a tiny shop which, judging from its large, incongruously contemporary plate-glass window display, sold nothing but chocolate.

How could she resist? Chocolate or churches? Was there even a choice? Without hesitation, she pushed through the door and stopped on the threshold, entranced by the even deeper and richer scent, which brought with it images of molten, sinuous chocolate. Chocolate heaven indeed. Whoever had arranged the displays had to be in cahoots with the devil, the whole place reeked of sinful decadence and Mina loved it. Ahead of her, on pale grey shelves showcased by strategically placed spotlights were matt black dishes filled with all manner of temptation, from tiny Florentines to cocoa-dusted truffles to glossy pralines. In the centre of the shop were a few well-placed pedestals upon which blocks of chocolates lined up like dominoes around tiny vases of fresh flowers. Stepping closer, she read the labels: white chocolate flavoured with rose, yoghurt, and raspberries; dark chocolate flavoured with lemon and hibiscus; milk chocolate with hazelnuts.

Like a prowling cat, she examined all the different displays, taking her time, considering the flavours and wondering, if she had to narrow it down, what on earth she would buy. And then she knew without looking at the prices, which she guessed were going to be in the extremely expensive bracket, she just had to buy some.

Sometimes chocolate was all you needed, she decided with a happy smile.

Although she'd already bought Amelie a beautiful hand-printed silk scarf as a thank-you-for-having-me present, she decided an additional box of chocolates wouldn't go amiss, and then perhaps a small taster of chocolate for herself to help the long journey…

She took her time, perusing the selection before she made her final selections. Chocolate, after all, was serious business. Churches could wait. At last she thought she'd got the perfect balance. Three small bars of chocolate, because she was intrigued by the different enticing flavours, and for Amelie, whose taste she wasn't completely sure of, a box of different-flavoured chocolate squares.

'You like chocolate,' teased the petite woman when she took them to the cash desk.

'I love chocolate, but I don't know as much about it as I'd like to. These all sound so interesting.'

'You've come to the right country. We invented chocolate

as you know it today. If you're really interested you should take a chocolate tour, there are several in the city.'

'I'd love to, but I'm catching a train today and going to stay with my godmother.'

'There are chocolate factories all over Switzerland. I'm sure she'll know somewhere.'

'I'll ask her,' said Mina, as she handed over her card, not even flinching at the astronomical number of Swiss Francs she was parting with. A tour would be brilliant, she'd always wanted to know more about how chocolate was made and what differentiated one from another. Chocolate recipes were one of her passions. Before she worked in a food kitchen, she'd experimented a lot at home and had amassed a collection of her own ideas over the years. Once upon a time she'd thought about writing her own recipe book, but then life and work had got in the way.

Clutching the ribbons of her fancy carrier bag, she walked down the street towards the river, beaming at passers-by as she thought of her purchases. Most smiled back, albeit after an initial second of reserve. See: that was the power of chocolate. It made you happy, and it made other people happy in the same way as a smile. Feeling a definite skip in her step, she crammed her hat down on her head, catching the eye of a young man walking past. He shot her a flirtatious smile, dark eyes scanning her with quick interest, and she grinned back but didn't slow her stride.

Across the Limmat she spotted the dome-topped twin towers of the Grossmünster, which according to her trusty leaflet had been described by Wagner as pepper dispensers.

She thought that was a little harsh, as she studied the creamy stone glowing in the winter sunlight. It was an imposing sight – but now with very limited time, she decided the lure of stained glass windows designed by Marc Chagall, as described in her leaflet, was far stronger. These were to be found in the rather beautiful Fraumünster church which, she decided, looked much more interesting with its dramatic, dragon-scale-like green tiles covering the steeple that draped like curtains around another imposing clock face.

The stained glass windows were every bit as stunning as her faithful leaflet had promised, and the vibrant jewel-bright glass glowed, backlit by the sun. What must it be like to create something that people revered and adored, wondered Mina and, probably like many in the church, pondered her own insignificance. If she thought about it – something she'd avoided before now – she hadn't really achieved much in her life. Splitting up with Simon had brought with it an unpleasant and rather shaming awareness that, despite all her zest for life, her life was actually quite small. She hadn't really been anywhere or done anything. According to the leaflet, Wagner, Einstein, and James Joyce had all lived in Zurich at some point in their rich and varied lives, and all had left lasting contributions to society.

Good cook, great theme nights, fun to be with – would probably be the sum total of her epitaph. It wasn't as if she wanted to change the world but it would be nice to know that she'd made a difference to someone and achieved *something* during her lifetime. She thought she'd had a positive impact on Simon, livened him up a little. It turned out she'd just irritated and frustrated him half the time. And at work her most notable success was a recipe for the company's best-selling chicken and chorizo risotto, which if she was honest was mostly a paella rip-off. Hardly that innovative.

Feeling her mood deflating, she took one last look at the windows and gave them a quick salute. Good old Marc Chagall. He'd been eighty when he'd designed the windows – surely that meant there was time for her to find something more meaningful in her life?

'Can I collect my case, please? And thank you so much for the leaflet, it was really useful.'

Mina nodded at the receptionist, who'd been so helpful earlier.

'Ah, good. I'm pleased. Does your case have a name on it?'

'It has a *Harry Potter* luggage tag on it.' She grinned, remembering carefully inscribing the very succinct address. *Amelie's. Reckingen, Valais, Switzerland.*

The woman smiled back and disappeared into the small office just off the reception area before returning with the case. Mina grasped the handle and headed out along the street and across the road to the railway station, feeling a quick kick of anticipation. On to the next leg of her holiday. Proper snow and mountains.

As soon as she entered the station her eyes scanned the

kiosks looking for one particular name and there it was. *Brezelkönig*. Unfortunately her impulsive diversion into the chocolate shop had messed up her judicious allocation of time, and she only had ten minutes to find the platform and board her train. She faltered for a second – but Amelie's last email had included an instruction: Mina 'must try a *kurbiskernen* from Brezelkönig in the station. They are the best.'

As she hesitated she caught the rich yeasty smell wafting across the concourse. With sudden decisiveness she altered her course and dashed up to the window of the kiosk. There was a fine selection of dark golden brown pretzels with their glossy, shiny skin, and also a bit of a queue – but she was here now, and she'd need more than chocolate to eat on the train. As she stood in line, her mouth began to water and her eyes homed in on the *kurbiskernen*: a pumpkin seed-covered prezel. Finally when she reached the front of the queue, not trusting her schoolgirl German, she pointed to the pretzel and held up two fingers; it was a long journey after all. The girl serving immediately answered in English which made Mina smile with chagrin. She should have at least tried. Handing over her cash, she said, '*Danke schön*,' and immediately felt a bit better for making some effort.

Grasping her paper bag, she searched the departure boards and spotted the train going to Brig, which was where she had to change to get the train that travelled up through to Goms.

Platform 32. To her horror she realised that was in the lower level of the station, and she had precisely six minutes to find it. Picking up speed, she began to weave her way through the crowd and immediately found herself caught up in a cluster of schoolchildren. It was like dodging a meteor shower as they veered in front of her from all directions. After a near-miss with a small boy, she extricated herself and dived towards the escalator going down to the lower floor.

Half dragging and half lifting her suitcase, she tried to hurry down, receiving irritated glares as she pushed past the other serene passengers who seemed in no rush at all.

Running along, she counted down the platforms, twenty, twenty-three, thirty and phew, thirty-two. To her horror the platform was empty and the doors were closing. Hauling in a dry breath, she belted down the platform heading for the nearest open door which was just being closed.

'Hey,' she called. 'Can you hold the door?'

There was a whistle and she put in an extra burst of speed, drawing level with the door. A man leaned out and grabbed her case, threw it in, and then hauled her in through the door with so much momentum that they both went tumbling to the floor, the door slamming behind them.

Before Mina had a chance to disentangle herself from the sprawl of his and her limbs, the train began moving.

'Phew, that was a close one.' She beamed in delighted triumph at her saviour who was wincing. 'Thank you so much.'

'Mmph, I don't suppose you could get your elbow out of my solar plexus.'

'Oh, yes, sorry. Of course, although I'm not sure where the solar plexus is.'

'I think you'll find it's currently at the end of your very pointy elbow.'

She shifted immediately and he sat up, pushing back an unruly mop of sunshine-highlighted curls from his face, revealing dancing blue eyes and a lopsided wide mouth, already curving into a ready smile. The slightly too-long wayward hair looked as if it had seen an extended season in the sun somewhere, and the overall impression of sunshine and happiness made it impossible not to smile back.

'Oh, I'm sorry. Are you OK?' She reached out with her hands to touch him and then stopped halfway, realising it was probably totally inappropriate on less than thirty seconds' acquaintance, but there was just something about him that made her feel at ease, as if he were in the habit of conducting conversations on the floor of a train all the time and it was completely normal.

He shot her another dazzling grin that made her feel a little fizzy inside. Probably just the adrenaline buzz after nearly missing the train.

'I'm fine. Although you do have exceptionally pointy elbows.'

She examined her elbow. 'Do you think they're pointier than most people's?'

With a tilt of his head, he studied her arm as he rubbed his chest. 'Yes, and I'm prepared to give you a testimonial if you ever need one. But it was a pretty damn brilliant rescue, you have to admit.' This time the grin on his face was decidedly cocky, but still full of good humour.

'I do. A perfect knight with metaphorical shining

armour. Although if you had been wearing armour the elbow wouldn't have been a problem. Thank you again.'

'So do I get one of these?' He held up one of her chocolate bars, which must have spilled from her bag. The sunshine streaming in through the window glistened on the golden hairs on his arms. Mina knew that finding arms attractive might be considered strange, but it was her thing, and those forearms were lovely enough that it was tempting to reach out and stroke them. That would be weird, wouldn't it?

'Hmm,' she sucked in a considering breath and looked at him, deliberately studying his face, realising that her pulse had just tripped ever so slightly. 'I'm not sure it's worth a whole bar.'

Although she wouldn't mind sharing it with him; he had a very nice face. Good strong jaw with sand grains of bristle glinting on his chin and definite laughter lines etched in tanned skin fanning out from his dark-fringed eyes, which were deep set and very blue. If they ever had babies together, they'd be gorgeous – and just as quickly she slammed that thought down.

'A rescue like that. Come on.' Now he was twinkly-eyed, encouraging her in the game.

'A quarter.'

'A quarter!' His mock outrage made her giggle. 'For heroic services to fair maidens. That's not going to keep body and soul together. And how am I supposed to battle to the death for a seat for you? I need sustenance.'

'Are seats in short supply?' she asked, alarmed. The journey was just over two hours.

'We should be alright at this time. It gets busier later as everyone heads to the slopes for the weekend.'

They both rose to their feet and he hauled up a huge rucksack and slid it onto his back before picking up an ancient suitcase which looked as if it might have belonged to his granny. This bizarrely incongruous combination puzzled Mina as he ushered her through to the carriage, which was surprisingly full. 'If you keep going, the other end of the train is usually much quieter.'

Together they swayed along the aisle as the train slunk with surprising quietness through the outskirts of Zurich, walking through five carriages before they finally came to one with several pairs of free seats.

'Mind if I join you?' he asked, gesturing at two seats together. 'You're going to want a window seat on this trip.'

'No, not at all.' The very same question had been hovering on her lips as she'd followed his cute bum and loose-limbed stride down the train. In jeans and a leather sheepskin-lined flying jacket, he embodied cool without trying too hard, but then the bright red, chunky, woollen scarf added a dash of irreverent mischief, stopping him from having that frosty unapproachability of the ubercool Instagram crowd. Besides, he seemed cheerful, upbeat, and was very easy on the eye – she had no objections at all. She got the impression that he was an embrace-life-at-full-speed, fun guy who was easy to flirt with and would never take anything too seriously. A bit like herself.

'How about I go find us a coffee to go with the chocolate?' he asked, unwinding the scarf from around his neck.

'You're not giving up, are you?'

'Well, it does look like jolly nice chocolate.' A Labrador couldn't have looked more hopeful.

'Stop with the puppy dog eyes.' She held up a warning hand even though she couldn't hide her amusement. 'You supply the caffeine and I'll supply the theobromine.'

'The what?'

'It's a stimulant found in chocolate.' She preened just a little, because she liked the sudden admiration in his eyes.

'Fancy. Are you really good at crosswords?'

She laughed. 'God no, I don't have the patience. I'm a food technologist. We know that sort of stuff.'

'Is it true they put motor oil in sauces to make them shiny in the pictures?'

''Fraid so. And white glue as milk, and mashed potato to fill pies. All tricks of the trade.'

'I think I'd better go and buy the coffee before you tell me that it's made with tar or something horrible.'

'Would you like some money?'

'No.' His mouth twisted with that beguiling lopsided smile. 'This way you'll feel beholden to share your chocolate.'

'You don't know me very well. When it comes to chocolate, I'm not beholden to anyone.' She lifted a teasing eyebrow.

He huffed out a sigh. 'Tough nut. I'll have to come up with a new strategy while I scour the train for a trolley or the food carriage.'

She watched him leave. Having an amusing travel companion would certainly brighten the journey. Sitting still for a couple of hours had never been her idea of fun. Hannah, her sister, was a world-class bookworm, but Mina couldn't keep her mind on the pages unless it was a recipe book. At Hannah's suggestion, she had tried audiobooks, but she'd suddenly find herself lost in thought and ten minutes on from the last bit she'd heard, with no idea what had happened between. With podcasts, it didn't matter if she tuned out.

At least in his absence she could give herself up to thinking about which chocolate bar she should open. It took a lot of deciding, and she was still umming and ahhing when he returned with two steaming cups of coffee.

'It's quite simple, you just open the packet,' he teased, sitting down opposite her.

'This is not just any chocolate you know. I have Ecuadorian dark chocolate, Madagascan milk chocolate with a praline filling, and a Ghanaian sea salt and almond chocolate.'

'Are you a connoisseur or something?'

She pondered the question for a second.

'An afficionado, I guess.'

'Is there a difference?'

'A connoisseur knows their stuff, an afficionado has great affection for something,' she replied gravely, as if she had the first clue what she was talking about.

He regarded her for a second, suspicion darkening his eyes, before she burst into laughter. 'I don't actually know, but I love chocolate, and I know a little about it from working in a food kitchen.'

'It's a bit late for introductions but, girl-with-a passion-for-chocolate, do you have another name?'

'Yes, Mina.'

'Nice to meet you, I'm Luke.'

'So where are you headed?'

'I'm… I'm going skiing. In Valais.' Mina frowned at the quick hesitation. She was good at spotting a lie, or at least she always thought she'd been. Clearly she'd missed a trick with Simon.

There was something about his words that didn't quite ring true, and then she realised. 'So where are your skis?'

'That is the most brilliant thing about train travel in Switzerland. You can send them on ahead.'

'Really?'

'Yup. The Swiss are big on trains. They travel more by train than any other nation in the world, and you can get one to just about anywhere in the country, which is pretty impressive when you consider most of the country is taken up by mountains. Which makes them experts at building bridges and tunnels. This journey is quicker by train than by car and takes in—' He halted suddenly and waved an apologetic hand. 'Sorry. Time to get off my soapbox, your eyes were starting to glaze over.'

Mina didn't think they were; his enthusiasm was infectious. He could probably make drying paint sound appealing.

'You sound like a bit of a train enthusiast.'

For a second his eyes slid away from hers and then he asked, 'So are you here on holiday, or do you work here?'

She recognised a change of subject when she saw one.

Uncle Derek had one serious hobby. He was a proper, full-on trainspotter and his ever-expanding Hornby railway set, which had once belonged to their real dad, still took up the entire floor area of the loft. For a moment she wondered what Derek would do with it when they moved, and whether it actually belonged to her and Hannah.

'Me? Work here? Why on earth would he think that?'

'Twenty per cent of the population in Switzerland are foreigners. Usually based in the five main cities. Financial folk in Zurich, political in Bern, pharmaceuticals in Basel, legal in Lausanne – and Geneva, where I work, is the HQ for the UN.'

'So you live in Geneva?'

'Sort of. I'm between posts at the moment, trying to decide on my next role, so I'm taking an extended holiday.'

'The UN sounds interesting.' Although he also a sounded a little flaky; wasn't 'between posts' a euphemism for being unemployed?

'It sounds a lot more interesting than it is sometimes.' He shrugged. 'But it has its pluses. I get to do a lot of travelling.'

'Lucky you. I create food dishes from all over the world – Milano parmigiana, Bombay spiced chicken, Moroccan lamb tagine. The nearest I've got to Bombay is Manchester Airport. My family were never big on travel. My parents' idea of exotic is a static caravan in Normandy – and that's a significant upgrade from our six-man tent in Eastbourne.' She wasn't going to talk about Simon and his allergy to flying; his name had been expunged from her brain. She refused to give him one micromillimetere of head-room.

'I've never been camping. It always sounded a lot of fun.' Luke sounded wistful.

'Hmm, me and my sister would rather have been having fun in Ibiza or Mykonos, but if we hadn't gone with my aunt and uncle – we grew up with them – they'd never have got the tent up. They're a bit useless sometimes.' She shook her head, 'Love 'em to bits, but they're the most dithery, indecisive people on the planet. Thank goodness Aunty M's bladder isn't what it used to be and she likes to have a handy bathroom. Hence the upgrade to caravan in France. Oops, sorry too much information.' She slapped her forehead. 'I'm sure you don't want to know about my aunt's incontinence problems.'

He laughed. 'Not really. So is this a holiday or not, then?

'More of a tactical retreat.' She rolled her eyes. 'I'm taking some time off from work. Let's say HR suggested I book some holiday. My godmother lives over here and she sent me an invite at exactly the right moment. It seemed like a good idea. I'm dying to try skiing properly, I've only ever done the indoor type. Are you a skier?'

'Yes. Downhill, snowboarding, cross-country. You name it, I love it – although where I'm headed there's a lot more cross-country skiing, which is more leisurely than downhill, but gives you a chance to take in the beautiful scenery.' His eyes glowed with enthusiasm. 'And it is a beautiful country.' He nodded out of the window and Mina gave a gasp. The train had slowed, and as she looked back she could see it was easing its way around the dramatic curve of a viaduct that seemed to have been built straight into the mountainside. 'Oh my, we're so high up.'

'Over fifty metres. This is an incredible feat of engineering.'

'It's amazing, and to think suddenly we're in the mountains, just like that.' She stared out of the window at the jagged peak edges that dominated the skyline and the snow-laden firs that crowded onto the lower slopes. Far below, a valley stretched away to the distance, a dark river meandering through the snowy banks and a tiny village straggled along the valley, the houses spread out across the river meadows.

'Imagine living there.' She pointed down at the tiny settlement. 'It feels as if we're miles from anywhere, cut off from real life.'

'That's part of the attraction for a lot of people, especially those who come at the weekend to get away from it all. The lady who runs the place I'm going to really understands that. She makes it a home from home.' He laughed. 'There are quite a few regulars who come out every weekend during the season. I get the impression she likes looking after people.'

Mina's smile dimmed. People used to say that about her, but now she felt a little abandoned. In the last two weeks, everyone at the fateful dinner party had given her a wide berth, as if they were embarrassed for her. Even the two Georges had cancelled their regular second-Saturday-of-the-month pizza night. She was grateful for the sudden distraction of the view, which had burst upon them in glorious technicolour.

She pressed her forehead to the cold glass trying to peer down the valley. The train skirted the hillside, the tracks truncated its slope at the halfway point, and below, lush green blanketed the meadows on either side of a deep blue river that sparkled and raced across the smooth boulders lacing its shores. Across the valley on the horizon, the jagged snow-covered peaks framed the skyline, the dark rock and white striking against the azure blue of the sky. The contrast of blue and white was almost blinding, and she thought the view was possibly the most beautiful thing she had ever seen, until they rounded another bend and another valley opened up before them, dominated by a brilliant jewel-bright turquoise-blue lake that reflected the mountains on its surface.

'Oh my goodness, it's gorgeous,' she breathed, her eyes scanning each and every detail, trying to commit the sheer beauty to memory.

Luke smiled with almost paternal indulgence.

'Told you, you get the best views from the train.'

'It's so beautiful. I think I could sit and watch for hours.'

'I find it quite restful, although when I get to the other end I'm always desperate to stretch my legs. Won't be time today, it'll be nearly dark when we get there. But tomorrow morning I'll be out on one of the hiking trails. Can't wait.'

'I thought it would all be skiing.'

'Depends where you go. There's also a lot of winter hiking. Until the Swiss voted against it, naked hiking was very popular.' He grinned at her. 'Imagine the frostbite.'

Mina laughed, not sure if he was telling the truth or not.

'I'd rather not, it sounds hideous.' She shivered as her imagination took over. 'I'll stick to fully-clothed activities, although I have no idea what's available where I'm going. I just booked a flight and here I am.'

'Nothing wrong with that. More of an adventure.'

'Absolutely,' she grinned at him. 'And I'm always up for adventure. I'd really like to have a go at the cross-country skiing, it always looks so elegant.'

He snorted. 'It's bloody hard work, but then when you get into a rhythm it *is* great, and you can take the time to look around and enjoy your surroundings. Zooming down a slope is all good and well, great for the adrenaline rush, but you miss so much. Don't tell anyone, but sometimes I think I prefer cross-country.'

'Your secret is safe with me. Now as well as chocolate, I also have these.' She dug in her bag and brought out the pretzels.

Luke groaned. 'I think I'm in love. Chocolate and *kurbiskernen*. You are the perfect woman.'

'You're easy. You should try my triple-chocolate cake.'

'Sold. We'll honeymoon in South America. You ever been white-water rafting or paragliding?'

She beamed at him. 'Neither, but I'd love to have a go.'

He lifted his coffee cup. 'To the perfect woman... well, if *half* of the chocolate were going, you'd be perfect.'

She rolled her eyes and snapped the bar in two.

Chapter Five

Q uite where the two-hour journey went, she had no
idea. Luke was her idea of perfect company:
funny, light-hearted, interesting, and although he
was talkative – that made two of them – he was also a good
listener. She got the impression that he would have been
able to repeat and remember everything she'd told him,
which in her book was a rare skill, especially in a man like
him. Usually confident, chatty types were too busy thinking
about what they wanted to say next about themselves.

Their conversation had batted backwards and forwards
with the ease of a gentle rally between Federer and Nadal,
and while she made friends easily, she couldn't remember
the last time she'd met someone and felt quite so instantly
at ease with them.

When the guard announced that the train would arrive
very soon at Brig, where they were both changing, she felt a
real pang of disappointment as Luke jumped to his feet and
gathered up his rucksack and suitcase.

'I'm afraid I've got a quick change here and I want to try and pick up my skis from the luggage office, so I'm going to love you and leave you.'

'Have a safe trip. Nice to meet you.' Her pulse tripped with regret. Asking for his phone number would be crazy. Two strangers on a train.

For a moment, the question hovered on her tongue and she very nearly asked him, but then that was the sort of impulsive behaviour that she was trying to avoid. It didn't fall within the remit of 'sorting herself out'.

'It was lovely to meet you,' he paused, his eyes skimming over her face, 'really lovely, Mina.' He gave her another one of his brilliant lopsided smiles, his gaze dropping with sudden shyness to her lips before he asked with a quick frown, 'Do you believe in serendipity?'

A couple of butterflies did a few star jumps in her stomach and something fizzed in her chest.

'I'm not sure,' she replied slowly, unable to tear her gaze away from his dancing blue eyes, that were now filled with mischief and challenge.

'Me neither, but sometimes you just know.' He leaned forward, his mouth inches from hers. 'If I kiss you maybe…' He lifted his shoulders in a shrug. She shrugged back, her heart skittering about in her chest. 'A kiss goodbye.'

His lips grazed hers in a barely-there kiss that seemed to crackle with electricity. Startled, she glanced up to find his eyes were as wide as hers, as if asking *did that really happen?* She gazed up at him, solemn-eyed, holding on to her breath and he frowned again as if puzzled. The train began to slow and his frown deepened as if he were trying to make up his mind. Then he leaned forward and slipped an arm around her waist, pulling her towards him. He paused again as if awaiting her permission. She rose on her toes to meet him as he lowered his mouth again. There was no time for a leisurely exploration – this was a once-in-a lifetime kiss that both embraced with enthusiasm. It was like stepping out into the sunshine, and warmth flooded every last bit of her, she never wanted it to stop.

Then Luke wrenched his mouth away. 'I've got to go. Maybe we'll meet again one day,' and with that he rushed away down the carriage to the door while she pressed her fingers against her mouth, smiling as she gathered her belongings together.

Everything still felt discombobulated, as if her whole system was on final spin cycle, when she boarded the next, considerably busier train. The two guys opposite, who had initially perked up like a pair of meerkats when she sat down, probably now thought she was a bit weird. For some reason she couldn't stop thinking about that kiss, and kept alternating between beaming dreamily to herself and frowning and screwing up her face in dismal self-analysis.

She didn't really know what to think. Part of her was in the thank-goodness-she-was-never going-to-see-him-again camp because he was so scarily right-but-wrong for her, and there was another part that almost grieved because she would never see him again and he was so scarily right-but-wrong for her. A pertinent reminder of why she'd come on this trip. She yanked *Moving Onwards and Upwards* out of her bag, opening it up and flattening it against her leg, glowering at the younger of the two men opposite, who craned his neck to read the title. Time to focus, and not think any more about serendipity and amazing kisses.

She forced herself to read the first page. It wasn't really her sort of thing, but then her sort of thing – jumping in with both feet and not considering consequences – was what had got her to this point in her life, so maybe she ought to make it her sort of thing.

Where are you on your journey in life?

- Waiting for a train
- Chasing a rainbow
- Lost in the forest
- Halfway across the bridge
- Stuck on the motorway

None of those things sounded the least bit appealing, in fact they all sounded depressing. Was she in one of these categories? With a sigh, she read on. Hannah disapproved of these self-help books on principle, she always said that they were written by masters of stating the bleeding obvious. Mina wondered for a minute if perhaps her sister had a point. But these books were written by experts, surely they knew what they were talking about? And shouldn't you be open to other people's perspectives on life?

She turned the page, forcing herself to focus. Apparently people who were 'waiting for a train' knew what they wanted to do, but were hampered by the belief that they just needed to wait for the right circumstances before they could achieve it. Well, *that* wasn't her. She believed you just got on and did things. If you waited for other people to make up their minds, sometimes, like with Derek and Miriam, you could wait forever.

'Rainbow chasers' also knew what they wanted, but were scuppered by their own lack of confidence. Again, not her. When she knew what she wanted, she went for it – although in hindsight that had been a big mistake with Simon. If she hadn't jumped the gun and proposed that night, would things have turned out differently? Although, she couldn't blame herself for his affair with Belinda.

With another sigh, which earned a further curious look from the guy opposite, she turned the page. According to the author, people 'lost in the forest' just didn't believe that what they wanted was achievable, and therefore gave up on their goals. That sounded a bit wishy-washy, decided Mina. Definitely not her. While reading 'halfway across the bridge', the light bulb went on. People who were in the middle of the bridge weren't sure whether to go forward or back; they didn't know what they *did* want, but they did know what they *didn't* want. Now that, sadly, did sound like her. Not all the time, but definitely now. Well, at least she wasn't alone.

With horrible awareness dawning, she reread the words. It *was* right. The events of the last few weeks had brought her to a crossroads, but none of the roads had helpful signposts on them. She had no idea what she wanted out of life. Her job, which she'd always thought was OK –

admittedly she'd been frustrated by the restrictions, but she'd always enjoyed it – now, thanks to Ian in HR pointing it out, wasn't what she wanted to do forever. It occurred to her, with rather depressing finality, that she wasn't even sure if she wanted to do it for the rest of this month. Following on from that unwelcome realisation came the next bit of awareness sliding perfectly into place: she didn't want to stay in Manchester forever.

Heedless of the other fascinated travellers, she let out a disgruntled huff. Darn it. If she were honest, she'd always known she wanted to live somewhere else, but this was the first time the thought had been brought out of hiding from its dusty shelf to be examined properly. But *where* would she go? You needed a job, a place to live, reasons to move.

And then there was the thorny issue of relationships. She wasn't built for solitude; she liked being with people and she certainly didn't want to be single forever, but after Simon, her confidence had been severely dented. She'd always thought she was good partner material. Fun, good company, caring. But Simon had made it clear he thought her personality and disposition weren't cut out for marriage at all, that being with her was wearing, irritating, and hard work – too much for a man to take on. His view had shocked and frightened her.

She swallowed, feeling uncharacteristically despondent. Her life was a bit of mess, really. At least, according to the book, she wasn't alone. If she were in the halfway-across-the-bridge category, it meant there were other people out there like her. Thank goodness she wasn't 'stuck on the motorway'. That sounded hideous. Apparently that was when you knew what you wanted, but there were too many things getting in the way. That would have driven her mad. She'd rather be a bulldozer and go straight over the top of obstacles. No, she was definitely halfway over the bridge.

To the curious amusement of the man opposite she let out a quick self-deprecating, 'Hnuh.' Meeting Luke on the train summed it all up – the perfect example of being halfway across the bridge. Fun, sexy, and spontaneous as he was, he epitomised all the things she didn't want in a man or a relationship. Ironic because he was so like her. They had so much in common. With awful irony, she realised that the type of guy that Luke was to her, was what she'd been to Simon.

'Ist dieser Platz besetzt?'

Mina glanced up at the fair-haired, slim woman in jeans and a sunshine-yellow anorak who'd clearly just boarded the train at the last stop. The rapid German defeated her schoolgirl knowledge, but from the way the other woman gestured towards the empty seat beside her, it didn't take a genius to work it out and she shook her head, giving the girl a welcoming smile. She couldn't stand those people who looked daggers at you as if they thought no one should sit next to them. 'All yours,' she said, indicating the empty seat.

'Great,' said the young woman, who was probably about Mina's age, flopping into the seat, immediately swapping to English in that easy way that so many Europeans did, and which always made Mina wish she'd tried a bit harder to learn a language at school. 'I thought I was going to have to stand. The train from Geneva was full to bursting.' She dug in her pocket and pulled out a packet of Jelly Beans. 'Would you like one?'

'I'd love one.' Mina shoved the book back into her bag and turned to give the new arrival her full attention. 'I haven't had any for ages and now you've given me a complete craving.'

The woman laughed. 'Me neither, I picked them up in the station shop.'

Over Jelly Beans, Mina bonded in the quick, easy way she frequently did with complete strangers. Hannah often complained she would talk to anyone, but Mina didn't think there was anything wrong with that. As far as she was concerned, everyone was a potential friend, and where was the harm in that? And once again it paid off, as twenty-seven-year-old Uta was also travelling to Reckingen to stay at a local hotel. Apparently she was meeting up with a party of friends who'd all used to work together in a bank in Zurich.

'We can take a taxi together,' said Mina.

'They go quickly from the station, so be ready to jump off quickly.'

Thanks to Uta's advice they hopped off the train sharply and made a quick dash to the taxi rank, and were first in the queue.

'Result,' said Mina, once again feeling that kick of excitement to be in a new place. She was impatient to see where she'd be staying for the next two weeks. Amelie had suggested she get a taxi, apologising profusely in her last email for this appalling welcome and dereliction of duty as a godmother, but explaining that Mina's expected arrival time coincided with the one of the busiest times at the ski chalet.

Once seated with Uta in the ancient Mercedes, glancing around at the scenery and the tiny village spread across the slopes, Mina wondered if she actually needed a taxi.

'The village is smaller than I expected,' she said to Uta.

'Yes, but it's deceptive, some of the houses are more spread out than they look, especially when you have a case, skis, and ski boots.'

Mina craned her neck to look around the driver, to see as much as she could.

The village seemed little more than a cluster of wooden buildings, spread out across the gentle, lower slopes of the valley between the rising mountains on either side. In the crisp winter sunshine, the thick layer of snow blanketing the uniform inverted V-shaped roofs glistened and sparkled like tiny diamonds. It was utterly enchanting and Mina clasped her hands and sighed with sheer pleasure at the pretty-as-a jigsaw-puzzle scenery surrounding her.

'It's so beautiful.'

'That's why we keep coming back, it's my favourite place in the whole of Switzerland but don't tell anyone I told you that. It would be lovely to live here, but there isn't so much work, not for a finance manager. The houses are very historic – see, they are all made of wood. It's a very traditional style in the Valais.'

Mina studied the big, dark, sturdy houses dotted across

the landscape. They seemed as if they'd been placed at random, with no discernible streets, or sense of the buildings facing the same way. She could probably count each one. She compared the scene to the view from her flat, where the houses and blocks of flats were so densely packed in, you had no idea what was in the next street, let alone on the other side of the valley.

The taxi drove past a few houses before crossing the main road, where she could see a small supermarket and a few shops, before starting to climb very slightly up the side of the valley.

'We'll stop at your hotel first. Mine is further on,' said Uta.

When at last they drew up outside a four-storey chalet, layered with balconies, Mina let out a small sigh of satisfaction. It looked every bit like a typical Swiss Chalet should.

'Some of my friends stay here. They rave about it,' said Uta, peering up at the signage by the steps. 'I keep meaning to stop by and check it out. Maybe I'll come by in a couple of days and we can have a drink?'

'Yes, do. You can give me some tips on what to do on the area.'

'Oh, that's easy. Ski, hike, and ski some more. Maybe I'll drop by on Sunday evening with a couple of the guys.'

'The more the merrier. See you then. Now, what do I owe you for the fare?'

Uta waved a hand. 'Pfff. Buy me a drink.'

As the taxi drove off, Uta waving from the back window, Mina stood for a moment just taking in the muffled silence, as if every sound had been dulled and diluted. The thick covering of snow had smoothed away the sharp edges of the buildings and softened out the contours of the land, like a freshly plumped-up feather duvet. She couldn't get over the whiteness of the pristine surface of the snow. At home, almost as soon as the snow fell it was blackened by the city's car exhaust fumes. Here, everything looked so clean, and as she breathed in, she felt the sharp hit of the freshness in the air. There was a purity and crispness to the atmosphere that she'd never experienced before. Was this what breathing pure oxygen was like, she wondered. She took in another deep breath, amused by the puffs of steam that drifted out of her mouth. The journey had cocooned her, and now it was like being thrust out into a jewel-bright world where all her senses were being retuned.

She turned to look at the building. Constructed entirely of wood, and pretty as it was, those great solid beams reminded her that it had been built to withstand the weather conditions in the winter. Although only four o'clock, the sun had dipped behind the mountains and the bright blue of the sky darkened at the edges like dampened blotting paper. She could feel the temperature dropping rapidly and was grateful for the golden glow that lit each of the windows on the front façade like welcoming beacons.

Lifting her case, she carefully walked up the snow-free steps and pushed open the big, heavy door. She found herself in a small, self-contained lobby area full of shelves and racks for boots and skis, with hanging rails that were already half full of ski jackets and that indefinable smell of the outdoors. Puddles and drips dotted the floor, particularly around the short, low benches on one side of the room where people obviously sat to discard their wet boots. There was a warm, fuggy atmosphere which she realised came from the pipes running around the edge of the room under the racks and rails, clearly designed to help everything dry out overnight. For a moment, she paused to examine the array of footwear, hiking boots, big plastic ski boots, and odd-looking, unfamiliar boots that looked like a cross between a slip-on trainer and an ankle boot. She felt another quick trip of excitement at the thought of getting out into the fresh air and skiing.

She pushed her way through another door and stepped into the most gorgeous light and airy open-plan room, clad with wood and open to the inverted, V-shaped, beamed ceiling. An open timber frame created a notional division between the reception room and the much bigger lounge beyond.

On her right, in the centre of the partition, embers glowed in a huge fireplace of rough-hewn stone built into a vast chimney breast, open on both sides to each room. On the other side the lounge area contained a few people quietly reading or chatting on the selection of sofas and chairs arranged around a big square coffee table facing the fireplace. The atmosphere was smart and elegant, but managing to be cosy and welcoming at the same time. There were two beautiful and expensive-looking, plump, fern-green velvet chairs side-by-side, just begging to be sunk into. They were separated by a small, highly polished table decorated with pretty china bowls, and a tall, long-necked lamp, and opposite, making up a right-angle, were two large, natural-linen, comfortable-looking sofas dotted with stylish cushions of velvet, silk and wool. Underfoot, the floor was made of rustic, wide-planked floorboards that looked as if they had a few stories to tell, and soft wool rugs were dotted here and there. Mina immediately felt as if she could go and take a seat and be at home with everyone else.

On this side of the fire, the reception room had a different feel, slightly more basic with several big squashy, battered, chestnut leather sofas that didn't look as if they'd quite earned their battle scars, and the coffee table here was a big rustic wooden affair pitted with knots and gnarls. Next to the fire was a huge wrought-iron log holder that was filled to the brim with chopped wood that scented the air.

As she was taking all this in, the cuckoo clock in front of her burst into action, a cuckoo popping out of its tiny door, narrowly missing being decapitated by the painted figure of a wood chopper, whose axe swung as the hands struck four. Mina laughed out loud with delight as she examined the clock with its detailed workmanship and elaborate carving. While it wasn't that big, it certainly made up for it in volume. Still smiling to herself, she turned and realised that people were appearing from all directions, as if the cuckoo had set off some secret signal, and everything began to happen in perfect sequence. It was like watching a set change at the theatre, as everyone settled into places. Guests who had been absorbed in their books suddenly began chatting to each other, and around corners more people began to appear, taking up seats in both rooms. The noise level rose to an all-round hum, and then a woman, carrying a large tray almost as big as she was, looking like an old-fashioned cigarette girl, burst through the doors at the back of the room, followed by two teenage girls carrying smaller trays. The hum rose and anticipation rippled through both rooms as the woman, beaming at everyone as she went, beat a determined path to the coffee table in the elegant lounge area.

With a hint of triumph, she placed the tray on the table and stood back to absorb the appreciative 'mmms' that filled the air. 'Tonight we have *Basler Kirschenbrottorte.*' Only the ta-dah was missing as she presented a dense, rustic-looking cake that perfumed the air with cherries and vanilla. The surface was pitted with craters of dark red, almost caramelised whole cherries. Mina's stomach rumbled in anticipation. With careful, attentive fussing, plates and mugs were dished out and the cake was sliced up and served.

Mina watched with a smile on her face as each of the guests, probably about twelve in total, were tended to. Cake was pressed upon one reluctant guest who was won over with quick, gentle chiding, a plate was presented with a flourish to another eager guest who clearly knew he was in for a treat, and a forkful-sized taster offered to one young lady who dared to refuse a slice. It was everything she loved to see, people coming together over food, and there at the centre of it was her godmother, Amelie, with a mile-wide smile on her face as she danced through the people, dishing out her little plates of joy. Then she looked up, her smile widening even more. She handed a plate over and, dusting down her hands on her flour-speckled apron, darted to the doorway and came rushing through.

'Mina, *liebling*. You're here,' she boomed in her deep, loud voice which was so out of keeping with her delicate frame, and grabbed her by the shoulders, kissing her soundly on both cheeks. She hugged Mina close to her. 'Beautiful girl. Although a little pale, I think.' She patted Mina's cheeks. 'But the good mountain air will bring the roses. Now come, come. Have some cake. Leave your things here.'

Mina found herself thrust into the other room. 'This is Mina, she's just arrived.' She waved at the people in the room as a plate with a slice of cake on it was pushed into her hands. 'They can introduce themselves. I must bring more coffee. More people are expected.

'After café and cake, I'll take you up to your room.' Amelie glanced up at the cuckoo clock and frowned. 'The new guests are late. They should be here. But your train was on time.'

'It was. The taxi rank was very busy.'

'Ah yes, and one of the taxis has broken down.' She walked over to the window, and whatever she saw relieved her. 'It's OK, they've just arrived.'

Mina found herself a seat, helped herself to one of the mugs of black coffee from one of the trays, and sat down on one of the sofas.

'You just arrived?' asked her nearest neighbour, an older man with the sort of serious, sophisticated, wireless-framed glasses she associated with Europeans, which didn't quite go with his extremely bushy eyebrows.

'Yes,' replied Mina, picking up her slice of cake and giving it a quick study, her eye caught by the unusual-looking ingredients. It reminded her of a rocky road slice, with unidentified layers among the cherries. 'This looks delicious.'

'It's a very traditional Swiss cake, but no one makes it quite like Amelie, that's why so many of us come back time and time again. She's full, you know, and she only started a year ago. I think it's the café and kuchen hour every day.'

'What, this?' Mina waved a hand around the room. Everyone was talking and eating. A symphony of harmony, all cemented together with the glue of cake.

'Yes, four o'clock. Complimentary cake. The only price is you have to stay and eat it around the fire, and talk to your neighbours.'

'Sounds very civilised to me.'

'Some of us have become resigned.' He gave her a long-suffering grimace. 'And now I find I can chat with my fellow men a little more easily, as long as I only have to do it once a day.'

Mina laughed. 'I'm sure it's good for you.'

'Hmm,' he muttered, 'that's exactly what Amelie said.'

'How long have you been coming here?'

'Since she opened the place last year. I was one of the naysayers. Led protests against it.'

Mina refrained from raising a 'really' eyebrow but she didn't manage to keep her face expressionless.

'I know. Now I come for cake at four a couple of times a week.'

'Are you staying here?'

'No, I live in the village, but we have a deal. I chop all her wood for her, and she feeds me cake once or twice a week. That's Amelie for you. Turns foes into friends – and then chokes up their arteries to get her revenge.' His weathered face, made golden by the sun, split into a goblin grin. 'I'm also a wine merchant, so I put together her wine list. We're good friends now.'

'I'm Kurt,' interrupted another man, leaning over and putting out his hand. 'I'm here for the weekend with my wife and daughter. I'm posted in Geneva but we come from Canada. We visit once a month for the hiking and to get out of the city. And...' He paused and held up his slice of cake. 'For this, like Johannes was saying.'

'Nice to meet you both.' Mina was amused and charmed by their easy friendliness. She certainly couldn't imagine this happening in a hotel in England. 'I'm Mina.' Out of the corner of her eye, she saw the door from the boot room open and some instinctive sixth sense made her turn and look at the three men crowding through, talking in loud, we're-really-pleased-to-see-each-other type voices. 'I'm here on holiday and I'm Amelie's—' The words died in her mouth as one of the men unwound a scarlet-red scarf, releasing a burst of familiar sun-streaked curls.

For a moment she thought she was imagining things, but when he turned around, the sight of him made her wonder if serendipity did exist after all.

Chapter Six

After a hot shower, which dispelled the travel fug, she put some fresh makeup on – hell, yes it was warpaint – and her favourite black trousers that made her legs look slimmer and longer than they really were (even Hannah cautiously agreed that she suffered from chunky thigh syndrome), and did good things to her bottom, which was disproportionately generous compared to other parts of her, but still cellulite-free. She added a soft, cashmere, pale pink jumper to the ensemble, knowing that it draped nicely over her boobs, enhancing her silhouette, and the colour brought out the blue of her eyes. Mina was more than happy with her body image; she was no stick insect, but she went in and out in all the right places, which counted more in her view, and she knew she was lucky with her striking colouring – the ice-white Nordic hair and the dark blue eyes which, with the right eye-shadow, looked almost indigo. She might have been a tiny bit vain about her hair, and spent a good half-hour blow-drying it into perfect shape.

Her pulse still hadn't settled from the shock of seeing the three new arrivals and the man in the midst of them. Thankfully, they'd all seemed to know what they were doing. They'd taken keys from the young girl at the desk and went straight upstairs.

Shortly after that, she followed in their tracks as Amelie brought her up three flights of stairs to her room. She wondered, as Amelie chattered away, reminiscing about trips to England, what on earth she would say to him if they bumped into him on the way.

Her godmother had always taken her godmotherly duties very seriously, and had visited at least once a year for as long as Mina could remember.

Impulsively Mina hugged her at the top of the stairs. 'I'm sorry I haven't been to visit since you've been here. It looks so beautiful.'

'I'm glad you're here now. Now, I hope you like your room, this is one of my favourites.'

Mina bit her lip as she followed Amelie down to the end of the corridor. 'Are you sure? I thought I'd be staying with you in the staff quarters or something.'

Amelie's eyes lit up with the naughty twinkle that Mina knew so well and was one of the many reasons why she adored her. 'You might have been, but this way I was able to truthfully tell Frau Müller that we were fully booked. And why shouldn't I give my goddaughter one of the best rooms in the house? If you were staying longer, then I might have given you the apartment next door to mine.'

'Apartment?'

'Yes, behind this building is another building, where

there are two apartments. I spend most of my time here in the kitchen, but in the summer it is lovely. I have a big balcony and a large living room with the most wonderful views. I keep meaning to offer the apartment for Airbnb, but it's just another thing to think about and administer, and to be honest, there is enough with the chalet.'

Amelie pushed open the door and Mina stepped inside. Outside the brilliant white of the snow highlighted the lines and shadows of the darkening valley. Lights twinkled in the distance and the mountains towered over the small village. The room, nestled into the apex of the roof, was warm and cosy. Soft light spilled from two bedside lamps on either side of the double bed cocooned in a pale blue, woollen blanket with a midnight-blue velvet throw across the end of the bed. Heavy curtains hung at either side of French windows that led out onto the balcony, and outside snow had drifted on one side of the balcony.

Mina, excited to see where she'd be staying for the next few weeks, strode across the room and straight over to the window looking out at the twilit sky and then back at the room. 'This is so cosy. I can imagine being tucked up in here while there's a snowstorm raging outside.'

Amelie laughed. 'Well, you won't have to imagine too hard. We get plenty of snow, although the forecast for this week is very good. Lots of sunshine. Now why don't you get settled and then come down? We serve wine from 6 p.m. in the lounge and then dinner is served in the dining room at seven.'

'But can't I do anything to help? I came to stay with you. Can't I help with dinner? Stay with you in the kitchen?'

Mina wasn't keen to see Luke until she was good and ready.

'There'll be plenty of time for that later,' said Amelie. 'You're my guest and this is my treat. And I'm also being a little bit selfish. I won't be able to give you my undivided attention before dinner and this stops me from feeling guilty that I'm not looking after your properly.'

'Don't be silly. I don't need to be looked after. I'm a big girl.'

'Yes, but I'm a stubborn, not-old-yet woman who is set in her ways. Come down at six, everyone is very friendly.' She gave Mina another of her mischievous grins. 'Unfriendly people aren't allowed to come back.'

Mina laughed, not quite sure whether Amelie was being serious. She wouldn't have put it past her godmother to have a list of names with black marks beside them.

Once Amelie had left her to unpack, she sank down in the downy embrace of the thick duvet on the bed and rubbed her eyes, still not quite able to believe that Luke was here in the same place. What were the chances – and more importantly, what on earth did you say to a man that you thought you were never going to see again, whose kiss had not so much blown your socks off as almost made them burst into flame? Her response still shocked her. She was impulsive – everyone knew that – but even she didn't go around kissing perfect strangers. And it wouldn't have been so bad if that kiss hadn't been so utterly, impossibly, damn perfect.

Now, an hour later, feeling a fizz of nerves at what she might meet downstairs, she stepped out of her room and into the corridor at the exact same moment as the guest in the room next door. As she lifted her head to say a friendly hello, all her senses tingled in sudden awareness. Her eyes met Luke's and it felt as if her heart had stopped. It was a huge consolation that he looked as shocked as she felt.

For a long electric moment, they simply stared at each other. She could almost feel the air around them crackle with static.

'Mina,' his voice came out as a croak.

'Hello,' she said but it came out as a whisper.

Then his face creased into a broad, delighted smile. 'How lovely to see you again. Serendipity?'

'It would certainly seem so.'

They both studied each other for a moment far longer than was polite, as if each of them knew that there was so much to say, but the enormity of it all had stolen their ability to speak.

Finally, and she saw the careful swallow before he spoke, Luke said, 'Would you care to accompany me downstairs for a glass of wine?' He bent his elbow in easy invitation and following his cue that they should pick up from where they'd left off, Mina slipped a hand into the crook of his arm. It seemed easier than unpicking the reality of them both ending up at the same place, and she didn't want to spoil the magic.

'That would be lovely.'

As her fingers closed around the textured cotton of his casual shirt, she could feel the warmth of his skin through the fabric. Her highly sensitive fingertips were aware of muscle, sinew, and bone beneath her light grasp, and with that awareness came a lightning strike of lust flashing through at the thought of his body. Hormones had a lot to answer for, she told herself sternly. They had no reason to get so carried away, even though she couldn't deny that he'd scooped the lottery when they were handing out the good-looking genes.

He escorted her down the corridor towards the stairs, and even their steps seemed to fall in line with each other's in perfect sync.

'Beautiful place, isn't it?' His free hand stroked the smooth polished wood of the bannister as they took the stairs side-by-side.

'Yes, it's lovely.' Amelie had clearly expended a lot of love on the place, it glowed with homeliness and welcome.

'Have you stayed before?'

'No, it's my first time. My ' she was about to explain that Amelie was her godmother, but he interrupted with a quick grin.

'It won't be your last. We're all like homing pigeons here. Keep coming back. It's like a home from home. How long are you here for? The weekend?'

'No, two weeks.'

His smile turned thoughtful. 'I usually just come for the weekend but this time I'm… I'm staying longer.' The slight pause made her think, again, like on the train, that there was something more to his words.

'Ah, Mina. You've met Luke, that's lovely.' Amelie greeted them at the bottom of the stairs, where she was carrying a tray of wine glasses into the lovely lounge area. There were a few other people there including the two men that had arrived with Luke.

'Hi guys. This is Mina.' He introduced her to the two men. 'Bernhardt and Kristian. They're here for the weekend.'

'How do you know each other?' she asked.

'Meeting here,' said Kristian, peering at her over his glasses with the solemnity of a shortsighted owl, which was at odds with his dapper appearance in a black rollneck jumper and black trousers, and highly polished black shoes. 'I'm from Lausanne. I work for the European Court of Justice.' The way that he lifted his chin ever so slightly made Mina think that she was supposed to be impressed with this.

'That sounds very interesting. You must do important work.' From the corner of her eye, she caught Bernhardt and Luke exchange quick glances.

Kristian eye's lit up with the holy glint of the fanatic. 'It is. We are at the heart of the legislative process. I am in a department where we draft policy for all the countries in the European Union.' Mina quickly realised her error as he droned on for another five minutes. At the end of it she still had no idea what he did apart from 'it was very important work', which he'd emphasised in every other sentence. Maybe it was the language difference. Luckily Amelie came by.

'Enough, Kristian. What have I told you about talking to young women? Mina, come meet Frank and Claudia.'

Despite his blush, Kristian looked pathetically grateful for Amelie's words.

'Sorry, I did it again. It's nerves when I meet—' he gave Mina an apologetic smile '—an attractive woman. My mind goes blank and I just talk. Was I very boring?'

'No, no.' She laughed at his clumsy but charming apology. No one should ever complain at being described as an attractive woman. 'I'm afraid I'm a bit tired. I've been travelling all day.' She gave him a gentle smile.

'Amelie has been trying to instruct me. I don't think I'm very good at talking to people. I expect most people think I'm quite dull.'

'Nonsense,' said Mina, whose heart cracked just a little at his defeated expression as she allowed herself to be herded across the room – Amelie would have made an excellent sheepdog – towards a middle-aged coupled who were standing looking out of the window. She'd never had a problem speaking to anyone in her life and couldn't imagine what it was like to find it difficult. Wherever she went she made new friends and found it easy, like chatting to Uta and Luke on the train earlier today. She resolved she would try and help Kristian while she was here. It wasn't as if she had any hard-and-fast plans. Now she was here, she was wondering what she was going to *do* for the whole two weeks on her own. It had sounded such a good idea when she was in England – going off on holiday for two weeks – but two weeks was a long time.

'Frank, Claudia. Let me introduce you to my goddaughter, Mina, who's here from England. You mentioned you were thinking about taking a trip to the Lake District.'

The couple were there from Basel for a week's hiking. They were keen walkers and after a few minutes chatting, Mina had to concede with a bright laugh, 'You know more about the Lake District than I do.' Despite that they fell into easy conversation and Mina enjoyed Claudia's dry sense of humour, but all the while she was conscious of Luke somewhere behind her. She was grateful she had her back to the rest of the room, the temptation to keep peeking at him would have been too much. It was weird how aware she was of him.

'You're going to have a lovely couple of weeks, although,' Claudia's cheeks dimpled, 'Amelie will keep you busy. She doesn't like to see anyone by themselves. Which is why we love to come here. It's very sociable, which is nice when you've had a day out with nature. Tomorrow we are skiing to Oberwald, it's about eleven kilometres.'

'And then we will take the train back,' said Frank with feeling. 'Do you ski?'

'I've done downhill,' she said, omitting to mention that it was only on an indoor ski slope, 'but I've never tried cross-country skiing. It looks a lot easier.'

Claudia snorted into her wine.

'Or maybe not?' Mina's eyes twinkled. 'That's what Luke said. Have I got it wrong?'

'I prefer it,' said Claudia, 'the boots are much more comfortable. But it's like running. You need to be fit.'

Mina liked to consider herself quite fit. She'd run a 10K in the autumn with little training, but admittedly that had been a spur of the moment thing. A friend had signed up and invited Mina to join her and before she knew it, it was October and she hadn't got around to doing any training apart from the odd 5K on the treadmill at the gym.

'It's less frenetic than downhill skiing,' said Frank. 'The slopes are always so crowded and you take your life in your hands with all the youngsters whizzing about like small, deadly missiles.'

'What he means is, it's a bit safer for us oldies,' said Claudia.

'You're not old,' exclaimed Mina, although they were probably the same age as Miriam and Derek, who seemed to have been middle-aged since they were in their teens.

'Well, we're planning to retire very soon,' said Frank, putting his arm around Claudia's shoulder. 'Which is why we come here so often. Our plan is to set up a cross-country ski-guide business and offer guided trips throughout Goms in the winter, and walking tours in the summer.'

'I can't wait,' said Claudia, her eyes shining and touching Frank's hand on her shoulder. 'We've been thinking and planning it for the last two years, and in a few months we'll be here. We're buying a place in the next village down the valley, Gluringen, which is just darling. The house, I mean.'

'Our daughter is going to do all the digital marketing for us,' explained Frank. 'And Amelie is going to let us use the chalet as a base.'

Claudia chipped in, 'So we can meet clients here, or bring them for coffee and cake at the end of the day as part of the package.'

The two of them were almost vibrating with enthusiasm and passion. Mina was swept up in their excitement and felt a touch of envy. How amazing must it be to know exactly what you wanted to do, and how you were going to do it? To be so sure. They definitely weren't 'lost in the forest' or 'halfway across a bridge'.

'It sounds as if you've got it all worked out.'

Claudia laughed. 'Frank has the most detailed business plan known to man. I think he bored the poor bank manager into submission. We needed to take out a loan to buy the house here, and next month we'll put ours on the market in Geneva. I can't wait.'

Despite that pernicious nudge of envy, Mina could have talked to them all night. Their excitement was infectious – but Amelie had other ideas. A dinner bell was rung at six-thirty by one of the pretty young waitresses and Amelie began directing people to the table. While she didn't lay down exactly where everyone should sit, she did steer people with decided intent. Definitely a sheepdog in another life, thought Mina, watching as she steered Kristian to sit with an older man and his daughter while Luke was teamed up with Claudia and Frank, and she found herself sitting next to Bernhardt.

'Impressive, isn't she?' he said in a dry voice.

'Yes,' said Mina with a laugh. 'She has an iron first in a velvet glove. It's fascinating to watch her in action.'

'We all do what we're told when Amelie's in charge. She's like a bossy head teacher with a class of unruly students, and we all love it.'

'So you've been here before then? Everyone seems to have been here before.'

Bernhardt nodded. 'It's becoming quite exclusive. I believe the chalet is fully booked this weekend.'

'I heard,' said Mina wryly, thinking of her luxurious bedroom.

'So what is it that you do for a living?'

In response to his very formal question which probably sounded more clipped due to his Swiss-German accent, she replied with her official job title.

'I'm a senior food technologist for the packaged division of a company.' It sounded scientific and dull when she said the words out loud. 'I develop new recipes for packaged meals and new formulations for food products.' Put like that, her job didn't sound very exciting at all.

'For Nestlé? You live in Vevey?'

'No, I'm here on holiday. I work in England.' She realised that Luke hadn't been kidding when he said that twenty per cent of the population were foreigners.

'I love London. I've been there many times, on business. Perhaps next time I come over I could take you out for dinner.'

Mina raised an eyebrow. 'That was smooth and quick.'

'Don't ask, don't get. And if you notice, there aren't many gorgeous single women here.'

With that sentence she realised that he was hedging his bets, staking an early claim because she was the only available woman. It amused rather than offended her.

'That would be lovely except I live in Manchester and

it's about two hundred miles from London. It sounds as if you may have been there more times than I have.'

'I'm sorry. I don't know why I made that assumption. Here in Switzerland we are much more federalist and we have the most direct democracy in the world. We don't even have one main language.'

'You don't? I thought it was German.'

'Shh,' he teased, putting his finger to his lips. 'And it's Swiss-German, if you please, and even then the cantons have their own local dialects. We have four official languages. French, Swiss-German, Italian and Romansh, but we're all very multi-lingual. And we have five official names for the country, Suisse, Schweiz, Svizzera, Svizra, and Helvetica, which comes from the Latin name Confoederatio Helvetica, which is where the CH you see on the car registration plates comes from.'

'Ah, I did wonder.'

'You'll see it shortened to Helvetia on stamps and coins.'

'And how do you know what language to speak?' It all sounded very confusing to Mina.

'Most of the country speaks Swiss-German, in the north, east, and central parts of the country. French is spoken in the western cantons, Geneva, Neuchatel, Vaud, and Jura. While Italian is spoken around the Italian border, in the canton of Ticino and Romansh—'

'I've never even heard of it before.'

'Not that many people speak it. Around 37,000 in the south-east in the canton of Graubünden. It dates back to Roman times. People who speak it are very proud of their language and the fact that it has survived so long.'

'And how many cantons are there?'

'I'm starting to feel like a tour guide.'

'Sorry, but it's interesting. It's so different.'

'We have twenty-six cantons and each one has its own government, laws, and constitutions. They also have their own distinct features, the food they grow, for example. Basel is famous for its cherries, hence Amelie's Basler Kirschbrotte.' Mina nodded making a mental note to ask her godmother about the recipe, she wanted to know how she'd achieved that unique texture. 'The population of each varies enormously from somewhere like Zurich, that has over a million people, to some of the small mountainous cantons, which might only have 16,000 people.'

'Give it a rest, Bernhardt. What are you trying to do, bore the poor girl into submission?' Luke sat down on the other side of Mina, bringing with him a bottle of wine. 'Would you like a glass? At least you can enjoy yourself as your eyes glaze over.' At her slight nod, he poured a generous glass.

Bernhardt laughed. 'I'm proud of my country. Sorry, I didn't mean to give a lecture.'

'Actually, it was really interesting. I didn't know any of that.' See: that's what happened when you went somewhere on a whim instead of thinking things through, and exactly why she needed to sort herself out. She smiled at Bernhardt. 'Thank you,' she said, before giving Luke a reproving glance – not that it abashed him in the slightest.

'It's alright, I forget Luke is a complete philistine. All he wants to do is hurl himself off mountains. Some of us have a better-developed sense of self-preservation.'

Mina winced a little at his stuffy tone, but Luke simply shrugged. 'Life is for living. You need to wring every last bit of pleasure out of it.'

And once upon a time she'd have agreed with him, but Simon's words of reproach were still ringing in her ears. *You can't base a marriage on fun.*

'But we also have responsibilities,' said Bernhardt. 'There is a time for fun and a time for being serious. You have to grow up sometime.'

Luke stared at him steadily, not responding, which surprised Mina. She'd have expected him to make some glib, flippant comment, but his eyes were filled with some quiet sadness.

She grabbed the printed sheet with a brief menu in front of her. 'I'm guessing if Amelie's cake is that good we're in for a treat. *Zürcher geschnetzeltes, rosti*, and *spargel*,' she read out loud. 'I wonder what that is.' While she was here, she was going to learn as much as she could about Swiss cooking. Amelie had told her in one of her many emails that there was more to it than cheese and chocolate.

'It's a very popular dish here; veal cooked in cream and white wine with rosti potato and asparagus,' translated Bernhardt. 'Apparently it's a favourite with Tina Turner and your football manager Roy Hodgson.'

'Sounds delicious,' said Mina, who had no idea who Roy Hodgson was. She was more interested in wondering how it was cooked, and smiling to herself. It was useful having an 'in' with the chef.

Talk turned to everyone's plans for the weekend.

'Kristian and I are going down to Fiesch by train to take

the ski lifts up to the slopes for a day's downhill skiing. What are you doing, Mina?'

'I've just got here, I'm not really sure what's on offer.' She didn't want to admit she had no plans at all, it made her sound a bit flaky. Coming here on a complete whim was all very well but she had two weeks to fill, and she hadn't thought things through that well. She didn't have any plans because she hadn't done any research.

'I can take you out one day,' offered Luke. 'Teach you to cross-country ski. How about this Sunday? You'll probably want to orientate yourself tomorrow.'

'That's for wimps and old people,' sneered Bernhard with a good-natured roll of his eyes. 'You could come with us for real skiing. What level are you?'

Mina wasn't about to admit that the sum total of her skiing experience was a dozen sessions at the Chill Factore in Trafford Quays. These guys were probably doing black runs before she'd even started nursery school.

'I'd love to. I'm probably... intermediate,' she said, crossing her fingers underneath her thighs. She wasn't about to pass up real skiing or the chance to get out in proper snow. Even if she couldn't keep up with them she was confident she could get down in one piece. A dozen ski lessons taught you quite a lot.

'Excellent,' said Bernhardt. 'It's very good skiing at Fiesch and there's been plenty of fresh snow this week.'

Kristian nodded enthusiastically, clearly including himself as one of the party. 'We leave early. Try to beat the crowds to the slopes. We like to go very early and ski for as long as possible. You coming, Luke?'

'No, too tame for me. I'm snowboarding tomorrow but I won't be leaving early. I want to enjoy the day at my own pace.'

Bernhardt shook his head. 'Snowboarding is for teenagers.'

'I can't win,' teased Luke, tossing his head of bouncing curls with a laugh. 'Old fogey and a wimp because I cross-country ski, and teenager because I snowboard. I just like being outside and making the most of everything there is to do. Variety is the spice of life and all that.'

'I'd rather master a skill, than be a jobber.'

'It's jack of all trades, master of none,' said Luke good-naturedly, not the least bit put out by Bernhardt's slight stuffy criticism.

'We're leaving at seven-thirty,' said Bernhardt.

Luke nudged Mina. 'And in Switzerland, seven-thirty means seven-thirty. The Swiss are possibly the promptest nation in the world.'

'It's efficient,' said Bernhardt with a reproving look at Luke before he turned to Mina with a gentler expression. 'If you come all this way, you need to maximise every minute.' Mina could imagine he was ruthlessly efficient in his time management. He seemed to be very precise about things.

'I can do seven-thirty,' she replied, jumping in with both feet as usual, ignoring the tiny voice trying to suggest that she might remind them she was only an intermediate skier. 'I can't wait to get out there. It's going to be great.'

Chapter Seven

Mina realised the next morning that half past seven really did mean half past seven, and she felt a touch guilty only saying a brief good morning to Amelie.

'Don't worry,' her godmother shushed her, with flapping hand movements in between making a large fresh pot of coffee and slicing up more cheese for the breakfast buffet.

'But we haven't even caught up yet,' said Mina. The previous night, Amelie, in between tidying up after dinner and laying the table for breakfast, had sorted Mina out with skis, poles, and the big clumpy, uncomfortable ski boots, which she didn't think she was ever going to get used to.

'We have two weeks.' Amelie patted her cheeks in a very godmotherly sort of gesture that had Mina smiling and resolving that tomorrow she would offer to help more. 'You'll be fed up with me.'

'I'll never be fed up with you. I should be helping.'

Amelie snorted and shook her head. 'You are on holiday.

I don't want you messing up my kitchen. Go have a lovely day. Have you got everything?'

'I think so.' Hearing Bernhardt's shouts that they were leaving and that the train left in fifteen minutes, she gave Amelie a quick hug and hurried out into the boot room, where it seemed the all the inhabitants of the chalet were gathering up their kit, rustling in ski jackets, knocking poles, and ducking skis. With everyone in their brightly coloured clothes, manoeuvring around each other with so much pent-up energy and enthusiasm to be off, it put Mina in mind of lots of electrons whizzing around an atom and she was happy to be swept along with them.

Bernhardt and Kristian were meeting up with some more friends at the station and on the train further down the line. 'We prefer staying here, although it is longer to travel,' explained Bernhardt as they walked down to the station. 'There are places where you can ski straight from your door but nowhere is quite like Amelie's.'

'That's what Luke said.' She recalled his words, *a home from home.*

'She makes very good cake,' said Kristian. 'And she tries to help me.' He pulled a face. 'I'm not very good at saying things.'

Bernhardt nudged him with a playful elbow. 'If you just kept quiet, it would help.'

Kristian nudged him back in that bantery way men do but Mina noticed his smile was pained. She linked her arm through his in a bid to cheer him up. 'Well, I think you do just fine when you're speaking English, and it's not even your native language.' She had noticed that during dinner last night he'd launched into a long monologue with one of his neighbours, totally unaware that she looked ready to stab herself with her own dessert spoon. The poor boy – even though he was probably a similar age to her – was harmless, but in that super-smart way of very clever people sometimes, he lacked self-awareness.

Despite the early hour on a Saturday, the train filled quickly, and Mina thanked her lucky stars that she'd teamed up with people who knew what they were doing in terms of buying train tickets and lift passes. She was delighted to see that Uta was part of the group.

'Hello again,' she said.

'Hey. How are you doing? I forgot the boys are staying at Amelie's.'

They fell into easy conversation as everyone produced piste maps and began a discussion in English, which was very kind of them all, as to which runs they planned to ski during the day, most of which involved the more advanced black runs as well as a number of red runs which even she, who never liked to back off from a challenge, decided she ought not to tackle. Not on day one. She would build up to them. After all, she had two whole weeks here.

'I think I'll stick to blue,' she said, wriggling her feet in the borrowed boots as they pulled into the station, aware that even her attempts at carrying her skis and poles looked amateur next to these snow addicts.

'Are you sure?' asked Bernhardt, looking a little disappointed, clearly torn between a desire to spend time with her and not wanting to spoil his own enjoyment. 'Shall we meet for lunch?'

'That would be great.'

As they queued for the ski lifts, there was a long debate as to where they should meet for lunch, which amused Mina because there really wasn't a huge amount of choice, but apparently it was a complex decision because of the distances some of the party intended to ski. It all sounded quite competitive and serious, while she was just keen to get out into the fresh air and ski on real snow.

She hung back, happy to leave it to them all as she didn't have a clue. Uta, standing next to her, rolled her eyes. 'I leave them to get on with it. If I'm nearby at one-thirty, I'll go there, but when I want a beer, I'll stop for one.'

'That sounds the best plan,' replied Mina as they took a couple of steps forward, getting nearer to the front of the queue. She was fully expecting to sit on the double chair lift with Uta and carry on chatting when, at the last minute, Bernhardt manoeuvred things so that he sat on the ski lift with her.

As the chair lift swooped upwards with a curious sway and jolt, she swung her legs, enjoying the feeling of freedom and flying. 'This is awesome. Actually I could probably just ride up and down on one of these all day. Look at the view.'

Bernhardt didn't say anything, and when she turned to look at him, he was gazing at her face with a somewhat cheesy smile on his face. 'I am. Do you know you look a bit like Cameron Diaz?'

'Mr Smooth again,' she said with a grin. It wasn't the

first time she'd had to deal with this sort of comment. She wasn't the least bit vain because, really, she wasn't that good-looking; it just seemed that having a zest for life and friendly attitude often made an instant impression. Luckily, once most men got to know her, they quickly preferred to settle for friendship. 'Don't you think it's amazing, or are you immune to it now? It's beautiful.' Her eyes scanned the dips and shadows of the slopes below, the almost uniform, dark green of the fir trees arranged in neat, contour-shaping rows.

'No, I don't think you can ever get immune to it, especially when you spend all week in the city.'

That was lovely to hear. Mina sat back in her seat and breathed in the fizziness of the pure, clear air, feeling that her lungs had never had such a treat. In that moment, the thought of going back to Manchester, to grey skies and drizzle, really didn't appeal. Being here was rather like being on top of the world, in a land above the clouds where the sun shone all the time.

With Bernhardt's help she worked out which run she planned to take, and she could see him wavering between old-fashioned manners, feeling he perhaps ought to escort her down the tame blue run, and the desire to hit the black run that zigzagged so enticingly across the mountain.

'I'll be fine. In fact, I think I'd rather be on my own when I make a complete fool of myself and wipe out. This way I can go at my own pace.' And, she thought, she could enjoy herself. Funnily enough, despite being such a sociable person – she loved the company of other people – she also loved the feeling of independence that being on her own brought her. These were perfect conditions. Plenty of time, no pressure, the beauty of her surroundings, and the most perfect weather. Even if she ended up walking down the mountain, how could she fail to enjoy this?

After a little fussing when they got off the ski lift, Bernhardt finally felt that he could go off on his black run, and she watched him skilfully ski away with the graceful, smooth ease of someone virtually born on skis. If she were entirely honest, she still felt a little bit awkward in the boots, managing the poles and the skis. But at last she was on her own. Kristian had given her an awkward, 'shall I stay, shall I go' sort of wave before he followed Bernhardt. Uta had given her a big thumbs up which did more for Mina's confidence than anything. This was easy. It was a blue run. She knew what she needed to do, and now she was on her own, sudden excitement fizzed in the base of her belly. There was no one to see her make a fool of herself, she could go at her own pace and she could practise all the techniques she'd been learning without constraint. *Blue run, here I come*. With a sudden burst of elation, she clipped on her skis and looked down the slope. There were plenty of other people taking things slowly, zig zagging in comfortable S-bends at their leisure, as well as those, their skis pointing straight downhill, with kamikaze keenness. Her aim was to be somewhere between the two.

Her skis felt uneven at first and she practised her turns and snowploughing as a quick reminder at the top of the slope, glad that it wasn't too busy yet. Gradually her confidence built and her turns became steeper as she allowed herself to face down the slope rather than cutting across. With that sudden moment of intuition, all her lessons, all the things the ski instructor had told her – bend the knees, lean forward, feel your skis – it all popped into her head and the instructions seemed to flow into her limbs. Her muscles responded and there she was, gliding over the snow, feeling her skis exactly like she'd been told and with that, she relaxed and the movements became even easier. Just think, if she hadn't proposed to Simon, she might never have graduated beyond an indoor slope. It was the only rushing in that hadn't turned out quite so badly after all. Everything else, she reflected, was in tatters but as she picked up speed, she felt her heart burst with happiness. She was skiing, proper skiing, and the feeling was just magical. A million times better than she'd ever imagined. To the moon and back better. This was heaven.

She met up with Uta at a restaurant at midday by chance. The mad, wonderful euphoria of skiing down real mountains, two runs in all, couldn't compensate for her increasingly wobbly legs and she desperately needed a rest. Following her nose rather than really understanding the map, which made no sense to her, she took a couple of ski lifts and found herself at the top of one of the peaks with the extremely welcome sight of Heidi's Hut.

'Hey Mina,' called Uta, who was at the terrace edge already enjoying a solitary beer.

'Hey.' She sank gratefully into a chair aware that her

thighs were more than a little shaky, her smile at least three miles wide. She couldn't remember the last time she'd felt so invigorated. 'I've had the most wonderful morning.'

'Perfect conditions. You ski a lot.'

'Mmm,' said Mina, taking a tactical sip of coffee, a touch envious of Uta's condensation-covered glass of beer.

They chatted for a little while before Uta rose to her feet. 'Might see you at lunchtime.'

Mina laughed. 'If I find the place.' She waved the map.

'Good luck, see you later.'

Mina enjoyed her coffee, pored over the map and decided that even though her legs had stopped trembling, she wasn't going to push it. She decided to ski gently down to the ski lift and then if she'd managed to follow the map correctly, she could take the ski lift up and then ski a little way to the cable car station where she'd take a cable car to Bergstation Eggishorn at the top of the mountain. Easy, she thought, clipping her skis back on and pushing off down the slope. She took it steadily, feeling the gentle protests of her thigh and calf muscles, but the views and the swish of her skis more than made up for the slight fatigue.

This time she shared the ski lift with chatty, seven-year-old, Tara – at least that's what she picked up from her limited German – who was on holiday, *urlaub* as she remembered from school, with her *familie*. Tara seemed content with her nods and smiles and her sole contribution to the conversation of *mein Name ist Mina*.

At the top, no sooner had the bar across the front of the chair lifted than Tara hopped off like a cheeky sparrow with a backhanded wave and swooshed off away without poles, looking as if her skis were part of her body. See: it was easy. Mina lifted herself off the seat, attempting to emulate the girl's confident departure. She did quite well at first, but then somehow one ski went one way and the other the opposite way, leaving her stuck in straddled position, bottom up and face down. At least she was no longer in the path of the ski lift, and hopefully no one would notice her here. Convinced her trousers might split at any second, if not something else, Mina tried to pull herself up with her ski poles, but her flabby muscles were in danger of giving way and her legs began to shake.

'Would you like a hand?' asked a cheery voice brimming with its usual laughter.

So much for hoping no one would see her.

Lifting her head to look up at him, she gave Luke a reluctant, self-deprecating smile. She must look completely ridiculous.

'Please. I seem to have got myself a bit stuck.'

He dropped the snowboard he carried and stood in front of her. 'What's it worth?' he asked with a teasing smile, those electric-blue eyes dancing with mischief.

She rolled her eyes. 'Seriously, you'd take advantage of a damsel in distress?'

'Every time.' He grinned, still standing there not making a move.

She groaned and tried to glare at him but it was impossible, he looked so stupidly cocky and cheerful. Instead she laughed. 'I'm glad you find this funny. I could split in two at any moment. I might never do gymnastics again.'

'Ouch,' he said, jumping forward and clasping her around the waist. With one quick, surprisingly strong jerk, he pulled her back upright. The momentum brought their bodies together and for a second their noses were almost touching. A quick sizzle fizzed through her body, and unable to help herself, she glanced at his lips and gave herself away. From the expression in Luke's eyes, she could tell he knew exactly what she was thinking.

Instead of pulling back he kept his hands on her waist, his blue eyes searching her face, which she could feel turning pink. Her knees were definitely wobbly now.

'Fancy bumping into you,' she said, pulling back, slightly embarrassed by her very obvious reaction to him. She'd never felt this instant attraction to anyone, and she wasn't sure how to handle it. It was all very well to spontaneously kiss a stranger you thought you'd never see again, but this, well, she had no idea how to play things.

'I keep telling you, it's serendipity. Meant to be.'

'Hmm, and there are only so many ski lifts on this mountain.' She seized gratefully on practical truths, and if she hadn't been laden down with her ski poles, she would have put her hands on her hips to emphasise the point.

'You're kidding. There are over 104 kilometres of piste up here. Definitely serendipity.'

She laughed at his dogged logic. 'Yes, Luke. Well, it will be serendipity if I manage to make it down to the cable car station.'

'You headed up to the top or down?'

'Up, or least I'm going to try.' She peered upwards to the mountain peak, squinting into the sunshine.

'Go for it. You've got to seize the moment. Life is too short for regrets, and I promise you if you don't go up there and see the view, you'll never know what you missed. Want some company? It's an easy route across to the cable station.'

'Sure.' Unable to help herself, she smiled back at him, knowing that she was unaccountably sparkly-eyed. It was as if, when he was around, her face took on a life of its own, reflecting the fizzy, washing machine feelings inside, even though she knew he was not the sort of man for her.

'Great.' He threw down his board and scooted it with one foot towards the slope. 'Ladies first.'

Feeling a little high inside, she pushed off and allowed the delicious sense of freedom and speed to overtake her, letting her body relax into the work. Already she was much more confident with her skis and felt that she was in control, but not so much that she felt able to look over her shoulder. Luke was somewhere behind her. Almost before she knew it, she'd skied underneath the twin sets of cables and she could see the big square gondola dangling further below in the valley them looking decidedly precarious.

Luke caught up with her when she slid to a halt near the cable station.

'That was easier than I expected,' she said, pulling off her helmet and goggles as they joined the queue to go up.

'It was a blue run. And you look pretty...' He paused deliberately, his eyes twinkling at her, before he finally added, 'Competent to me.'

She couldn't help roll her eyes at his terrible corny line. 'I bet you say that to all the girls.'

'Not all,' he said, tilting his head as if he were giving the matter serious consideration.

'I meant easier than I expected, in that following the map was simpler than I thought it would be. The markers are easy to spot. I was worried about getting lost.'

'I always figure as long as there are other people about you won't lose your way. Not in these conditions anyway. And if you do, head downhill.'

'Difficult to believe on a day like this that it's ever anything but sunny.'

'Where do you think all this white stuff comes from?'

'I know that but...' Mina lifted her shoulders and glanced up at the deep blue sky. There wasn't a cloud in sight.

Together they boarded the gondola, which clicked and whirred with mechanical efficiency as it lifted and swayed up out of the station. As it swung out away from the building, making her feel as if they were leaping out into mid-air, Mina's stomach lurched and dropped and she gripped the side bar.

Without saying anything, Luke dropped his hand on top of hers and gave it a reassuring squeeze, for which she was very grateful. Even though they began to climb smoothly upwards, the mesmerizing view made her feel a little dizzy and disorientated. The view emphasised just how high up they were, and although heights didn't normally bother her, she felt a certain sense of nature being so much mightier than mere humans, and it made her feel just a tiny bit vulnerable. Far below, the village looked like and reminded her of the model village her uncle had once taken her to. From this distance, the houses, dotted at random, looked as if you could tuck them in your pocket, and the dark ribbon of river cut through the white snow while row upon row of trees seemed to march up the wide expanse of the valley.

'The village looks tiny. Odd. When you're on the ground, you lose all sense of just how high up you are.'

'We're climbing to nearly three thousand metres,' said Luke.

'That doesn't mean much to me,' said Mina apologetically. 'Except it sounds high.'

'Everest is over eight thousand metres. There are fourteen mountains in the world over that height.'

'OK, that sort of puts it into perspective.'

'Wait until you get to the top. On a day like this it's spectacular. You can see a lot of the Aletsch Glacier, which is the longest in Switzerland.'

'Where do you learn all this stuff?'

Luke held up the map with a smirk. 'Most of it is on the back, here.'

'Cheat, I thought you were some kind of mastermind.'

'And I know about mountains.'

'Well, there are certainly plenty here.'

'When we get to the top you can see the Matterhorn, the Eiger, and the Jungfrau.'

'Only if you know what you're looking for. Good job I have a handy mountain expert guide.'

'It might cost you.' The devilment was back in his eyes.

'Not more chocolate,' she teased with a mock groan.

Luke pursed his mouth in quick consideration, screwing

his eyes up in thought before saying, his face alight with laughter, 'How about a kiss?'

Mina gave him an arch, reproving look, although inside it felt as if an army of frogs had taken up residence and were hopping up and down with mad excitement, saying yes, yes, yes. The memory of their one and only heart-stopping, ridiculously amazing, impromptu, never-should-have-happened kiss still had the power to make her toes curl. 'I don't give out kisses to just anyone, you know.'

'I'm not just anyone.' Luke raised his eyebrows playfully. 'Remember serendipity.'

'I think you've got serendipity on the brain.'

'Not me. I think it's trying to tell us something. Third time's a charm. This is the third time we've bumped into each other.'

'I think you talk a lot of nonsense,' said Mina, which was in fact her talking nonsense, because it turned out that 99.9 per cent of her seemed to find the thought kissing Luke an excellent idea. Her wistful smile belied her words and Luke's grin widened.

'See,' he said triumphantly, as if he could read her mind.

She rolled her eyes and ignored the dipping disappointment when he didn't kiss her. Instead he turned to the window and placed his gloved hand on the glass. 'Sometimes you can look down and the valley is full of clouds, and at this point we're above the clouds in sunshine and down in the valley it's a grey day. I always think that's a piece of magic. To be able to go higher than the clouds. I sometimes wonder what it must be like to be an airline pilot. Do they live in perpetual sunshine?'

Mina stared at him, a touch startled. It was the very thought she'd had on the way to Switzerland when the flight had left a grey, drizzly Manchester and climbed to a brilliant blue sky. No wonder pilots always wore aviator sunglasses or – duh! – why those sunglasses were called aviators.

'What?' asked Luke.

'I was just thinking about sunglasses and pilots.'

'Aviators.'

'Exactly.' The smile they exchanged this time was, Mina felt, was a bit deeper. An acknowledgement that they were actually on the same wavelength. Instead of reassuring her, it made her feel a little on edge.

Her innate honesty forced her to acknowledge that despite the sparkly feelings inside her, she needed to put a brake on things. She wasn't here for flirtation. She was here to sort herself out. To find what she wanted in life and to stop making impulsive decisions that caused chaos and created a wake of trouble. Luke, she decided, was not the type of person who was going to help her sort herself out.

He was a mirror image of herself. Like Simon had said, she was for fun not for permanence, just like her parents had been, and look where that had got them. They'd left behind the people they should have been taking care of. If she was going to sort herself out and move forward with her life, Luke was not the man for her. She needed someone who took life seriously. Someone who would rein in her impulsiveness, not encourage her with talk of serendipity and seizing the moment. Gorgeous and fun as Luke was, he wasn't what she needed right now, not when she was trying to create some firm footings and foundations in her life.

'Luke,' she said, knowing she had to say it now. 'That old cliché, I really like you but...' He raised an eyebrow as if to say, *I'm listening.*

'I'm just going to be honest.' She held up both hands. 'I'm here because I left a right old mess behind. I've buggered up my job and stuffed up a relationship, although admittedly it wasn't worth keeping, but I messed it up through jumping in without thinking. The reason I'm out here is to sort myself out, and that means making some changes, being more sensible about things, planning and not being impulsive. And not being impulsive means not kissing strange men on trains or believing in serendipity. I'm sorry. I am attracted to you but...' She smiled at him and exhaled heavily. 'We're too much alike and I can't be like that anymore.' She watched his face anxiously, already regretting the things she'd said, but it would be wrong to indulge in the flirtation that so clearly bubbled and fizzed between them.

'OK,' said Luke with a quick shrug and he turned to look up at the mountain peak looming into view.

'OK,' she echoed softly, knowing that it was contrary to feel that whisper of disappointment.

He turned back to her and gave her a cheerful smile. 'Yeah, you might not believe in serendipity but I do.'

'Luke, I'm serious. No more of...' She waved an inadequate hand that was supposed to indicate what she meant.

He took her hand and squeezed it. 'I understand, Mina.'

Then the infuriating creature lifted it to his lips and brushed his mouth across her knuckles. 'But there's nothing to stop us being friends.'

'No, not at all. I just wanted to be upfront with you.'

He grinned at her, seeming completely unperturbed. 'I can't imagine you being anything but, that's what I like about you. No games.' For a brief moment, he screwed up his eyes, 'I hate people trying to keep the truth from you.'

Mina wondered what he meant by that, but then the gondola swung into the station and everyone in the cable car began to crowd towards the door.

The view from the top of Eggishorn was like standing on top of the world. With the ranges of mountains spreading out around them and stretching as far as the eye could see, they could have been in Narnia or a Tolkien landscape.

Luke came to stand behind her, his breath grazing her cheek, and her heart did another of those inappropriate flips, but he didn't touch her. So why didn't she feel relieved? 'That's the Jungrau.' He pointed. 'And there's the Eiger. And that...'

'That's the Matterhorn,' said Mina, recognising the distinctive, crooked shape from photographs she'd seen, although from this angle it looked like a cresting wave.

'What about this?' He pointed to a wide sweep of what looked like an untouched highway cutting through the mountains.

'It looks like a road no one has ever used.' The thought

saddened her, but then perhaps that had a lot to do with the realisation that putting some distance between her and Luke was going to take quite a lot of effort on her part, because she genuinely liked being with him. With an internal wince, she realised he symbolised for her a road that would never be used, although it looked as if it headed to interesting places.

'It's the Aletsch Glacier, it's nearly fourteen miles long.'

'So underneath the snow it's ice.'

'Yes, about a kilometre deep.'

Mina's mind did a little of boggling at that.

'Sadly, it's in retreat, melting due to global warming. Research scientists reckon it's lost nearly a mile in length since 1980. Climate change. Deeply depressing, but it's what I do or rather what I did. Researcher for the UN Environment Programme in Geneva.' The downturn of his mouth suggested he didn't want to say more.

They both stared down at the glacier, lost in their own thoughts. Mina always thought it was incredible that things like this had been here for thousands of years before man, and that it was a terrible shame that man's advent on the world was causing so much destruction. It made her pesky problems seem fairly insignificant. All this would be here thousands of years after she'd gone. Life was short and she ought to make the most of it.

'This is wonderful, thanks for coming with me. I hope I'm not spoiling your skiing time.'

'You're kidding. I'm just happy being out here.'

Mina smiled. His attitude contrasted with Bernhardt and

Kristian's on the ski slope, they weren't going to let anyone hold them up or divert them from serious skiing.

'If you're sure.'

'Hell, yes. Mina. Just think of all the people stuck inside in their offices at this moment, staring at a computer screen or stirring pots over a stove or whatever it is you do at work.'

Mina thought about what a normal Tuesday morning would look like. An internal staff meeting. A packaging brief. Phone calls with marketing to tell them the design agency had missed an ingredient off the list. She'd far rather be here.

'We win. This is just stunning.'

'Fancy some lunch?'

'What, here?'

'No, I know a much nicer place further down the valley. Not so crowded.'

'Do I need to ski there?' asked Mina.

Luke shook his head. 'Straight down on the cable car all the way to the bottom.'

'Sold.' She had a feeling diehard skiers like Bernhardt and Kristian weren't going to miss her if she didn't make lunch. It was a fuel stop for them, whereas she fancied a leisurely lunch and then perhaps one more easy run before heading home. After all, she had two weeks to explore the slopes and give her muscles time to build up. She quite fancied the idea of still being able to walk tomorrow. It still amazed her that she was really here, out on the glorious slopes with what felt like the world at her feet, surrounded by timeless mountains.

It put so much in perspective and reinforced how small and limited she'd let her life become. This was her chance to do some hard thinking and consider how she was going to broaden her horizons and make some changes in her life. She'd done the right thing telling Luke that there couldn't be anything between them, even if annoyingly, it didn't feel quite as right as it should have done.

Chapter Eight

'I t's so good to have you here,' said Amelie the following morning, reaching across the table and laying a hand on Mina's wrist as they sat with coffee in the big kitchen tucked away behind the dining room.

It felt like the calm after the storm. Bernhardt, Kristian, and the rest of the guests had all been up early again, anxious to make the most of their last full day. Breakfast had been served and tidied away in an extremely slick operation. Everyone seemed anxious to eat and go, not that Mina blamed them. Despite the invitations to join the two men again, Mina had decided that she really ought to spend some time with her godmother, even though it was yet another glorious morning. Luke had casually invited her to go cross-country skiing later that day – and yes, she'd analysed his expression, the words, and the way he'd phrased it before coming to the conclusion that it was a purely friendly gesture and that he bore no grudge for her words the day before. She'd said she'd get back to him although she thought perhaps she should say no and avoid him.

Ignoring her aching legs, as soon as she'd woken she'd gone straight out onto the balcony where she'd had to shade her eyes against the dazzling white snow contrasting so beautifully against a pure azure sky. Even though there was a chill in the air, she'd stood in her pyjamas drinking in the view, drawing in great lungfuls of the crisp, clean air. As she looked out over the valley towards the giants towering from the horizons, it seemed that the air here had a different quality, clearer as well as cleaner. It made her feel alive and alert, and at the same time aware of how stifled she'd become at home and in her job, and how regimented life with Simon had started to feel. She and Hannah had always joked about Miriam and Derek's habitual routines but with hindsight she realised that she'd been in danger of falling into her own restrictive patterns. Not going out on Friday nights because Simon had football on Saturday morning, not doing much on Sunday evenings because they had work the next morning. In fact, she was surprised he'd found time in his fixed schedule to have an affair with Belinda.

Now, as she recalled that delicious hit of pure, clean air, which had brought home how far she'd come in just a few short days and how open to change she felt, she said earnestly, 'It's good to be here, it's so beautiful.'

'Yes. I'd been looking forward to coming back for a long time. My grandparents lived here when I was a little girl. This was their house. Oh, the fuss some of the villagers made when I came back and said I wanted to turn it into a guest house. You'd have thought I was opening a brothel.'

Mina laughed. 'I spoke to Johannes. He said he'd come round.'

'The power of cake,' said Amelie with a sultry grin.

'Oh, the cake yesterday! Delicious. What were the bits in it, apart from the cherries and the crispy base?' It was a good stodgy cake with a crumbly texture and nothing like she'd tasted before.

'You line the bottom of the cake tin with crushed cookies which give it that crisp base and soak pieces of old bread in vanilla milk, before you add them and ground almonds to the batter. It creates this wonderful rustic cake with lots of different flavours. It's one of my favourites, from an old recipe from Basel where they grow the best cherries. The literal translation is cherry bread cake.'

'I must get the recipe.'

'You're more than welcome. It's so good to see you, Mina. It's been such a long time.' Amelie hugged Mina again and then stepped back, to study Mina's face, cupping it with one warm hand. 'You look so like your mother.' She shook her head, her expression turning sombre. 'And I can't believe she's been gone for so long. Such a tragedy.'

Mina nodded, although to be honest, she had no recollection of her mother and never felt that she'd missed out. Miriam and Derek were wonderful, loving parents and sometimes in her more thoughtful moments, she suspected that they had probably done a better job than her real parents would have. From the photos she'd seen and, picking up on more of what Miriam didn't say when either she or Hannah asked about their real mum and dad, Mina suspected that Georgie and Stewart's adventures had come before their children. They had been reckless and impulsive, there was no denying that – what parents would go rally driving in unfamiliar, dangerous terrain when they had two small children at home? In her darkest moments, Mina worried that she might have inherited too many of her mother's genes, as Simon had accused.

'And how is Hannah?'

'She's good. Thinking about doing a cookery course at some place in Ireland.'

'Not the Ballygeary Cookery School?' Amelie's eyes widened with envy.

'Yes, that's the one.'

Amelie groaned. 'I'd love to go there. It sounds wonderful. I looked at doing one of their bread-making courses many years ago but with the flights, it was quite a price. I'm not surprised you two girls are interested in food, your Aunt Miriam, lovely as she is, is a dreadful cook.'

'Which is why I started baking.'

'Cake is the way to everyone's hearts.'

'Hmm,' said Mina, thinking of the convivial, warm atmosphere in the chalet the previous evening, everyone slightly weary but happy from their day's outdoor activity.

'And caring.' Amelie smiled gently at Mina. 'I really want all my guests to feel at home here. I hate those stuffy hotels where you go and everyone looks down their nose at you and you don't feel as if you should be there. People work so hard these days and a lot of them are so far from family, especially the expatriots, it's important to make them feel they can relax here. When my grandparents were alive, this was my refuge.' She gazed out of the window with a wistful smile and Mina wondered if there was a story there. 'They fixed me, every time I came. I want to extend that welcome to everyone who comes here.'

'What do you mean they fixed you?' Mina blurted out, curiosity getting the better of her.

Amelie laughed. 'You're so like your mother.'

'I'm not sure if that's a good thing or not. Sorry, you probably don't want to talk about it.'

'The reason we were such good friends was that we both lived hard and fast. Partying hard, working hard, earning lots of money and being frivolous with it. Money trickled through our hands, fancy restaurants, exotic holidays, always looking for the next thrill. We might have prided ourselves – we were smug about it – that we didn't do drugs, but we lived for the next adrenaline shot. I would fly to London. She would come to Zurich. We were both crazy, burning the candle at both ends. Every now and then I would run out of steam, and I'd come to see my grandmother, and she'd cook and look after me, without a word of reproach. Whereas if I'd gone to see my parents...' She lifted her hands in horror. 'Oh, the lectures I'd have got. They live in Geneva now.' She pulled the sort of face that suggested that as far as she was concerned, Geneva was the end of the line on the great railway of life.

'When your parents died, I'll be honest, it was a wake-up call. Georgie was spontaneous, but when she met your father, he was the daredevil. He encouraged her to go that bit further. It made me uncomfortable. And then...' Her face crumpled in sadness. 'They weren't there anymore. We all grew up that year, all the friends. I met my husband and got married and we were happy for twenty years, and then he died and the hole in my life came back.' She shook herself as if pulling herself out of the morass of memories. 'And I came here and... found something. I like looking after people, tending to them.' The words resonated with Mina and she thought of her Mexican dinner party. Although ultimately it had been a disaster, she'd looked forward to it with so much pleasure, anticipating her guests' tastes and cooking the most delicious dishes she could think of, to please them. She'd always loved cooking, but only now she realised that it stemmed from a desire to look after people, like Amelie, to tend to them. Simon had once accused her of using her cooking to show off, to be the centre of attention. At the time, he'd made her question her motives and it had knocked her confidence a little. Now she realised he'd been totally wrong.

'Did my mother cook?' she asked suddenly, wondering whether Georgie would have cooked to show off, or to look after people, realising there was so much she didn't know about her parents.

Amelie laughed sadly. 'No. That would be too boring. And too time-consuming. Life was to be lived at breakneck speed. She was always too busy looking for the next adventure.'

Mina blinked back tears. 'I don't really know that much about my mother. Part of me is mad at her that her adventures were more important than me and Hannah.' She put her hand over her mouth, shocked that she'd admitted as much out loud. Miriam, always fiercely loyal to her sister, had never said anything like that, but Mina had wondered if she thought it too.

Amelie frowned and looked away. She clearly didn't want to meet Mina's eyes.

'I knew her before she was a mother. I'm not sure I'd be the right person to comment on that.' Her eyes shifted again and Mina wondered if she really believed that. As she said herself, she liked tending to people, looking after them. Georgie and Stuart hadn't wanted to tend and look after Mina and her sister. They'd left that to Miriam and Derek.

Amelie brought her gaze back to Mina's face. 'But I do know she was enormous fun, generous to her friends, and had a huge capacity for love. I think she would have loved you very much.'

'We were loved.' Mina didn't mean to sound defensive but her adopted parents had been everything that she and Hannah had ever needed.

'I know. If I'm honest I think Georgie counted on that. It was her safety valve. She knew. I saw them two weeks before they died. They were going paragliding in Interlaken, but they stayed with me in Zurich before they went. Georgie had so many photos of you. I still have them somewhere.'

Uncomfortable with the conversation, Mina's gaze strayed to the series of lists and recipes pinned up on a pinboard, probably a metre square, on the opposite wall. Deep down, although she'd never voiced it, she didn't think that her parents had found their children enough. Babies weren't exciting enough. Looking after them hadn't been enough. Instead of voicing those dark, disloyal words she changed the subject. 'That all looks very organised.'

'I love a list. I like to plan each week, the cakes I'll make and what I plan to cook. I put the recipes up so that I can check whether I've got all the ingredients. It makes shopping so much easier, because the nearest wholesale and farmers' market is in Brig, which is about half an hour's drive away.'

Mina stood up and looked at the recipes: *zigercake, quark streuselkuchen, Solothurner torte, lozärner lebkuchen*. 'I've never heard of any of these. I'd love to know how to make them.' She never missed an opportunity to broaden her cooking repertoire.

'Of course, but you don't want to spend your whole time in the kitchen, do you? And I'm sorry, I'm busy this afternoon. What would you like to do? There's so much to do in the area. Did you see the leaflets in the lounge last night?' Amelie rose as if to go and fetch some.

'Don't worry. I'm sorted for today,' lied Mina. She still hadn't decided if she'd go out with Luke but she didn't want Amelie feeling guilty for abandoning her. 'Luke offered to take me out this afternoon and teach me how to cross-country ski. He said you hire out the skis, poles, and boots.' She felt guilty she'd taken the ski kit yesterday without even thinking about the hire charges. Amelie was already putting her up in a guest room without taking any money.

Amelie bristled for a moment. 'You can borrow them. Hire, indeed.'

'Sorry. It's just that… well, I wasn't expecting to be a

guest, but thank you,' said Mina, worried that she might have offended her.

'You are a guest in my own home, just a little more special than my other guests. And you will enjoy the cross-country skiing.'

'I'm really looking forward to trying something new.'

'Luke will be a good teacher. He's very patient. And—' she paused with a quick mischievous lift of her eyebrows '—easy on the eye.'

'I hadn't noticed,' said Mina mildly and they both burst out laughing. He was also kind and generous.

Once they'd finished their coffees, Amelie stood up. 'If you're really interested in our Swiss cakes, then today, if you want to stay in the kitchen all morning, I could show you how to make *Solothurner Torte*. It's a particular favourite of mine and a real treat for the guests. I always serve it on Sundays.'

'Of course I'd like to stay in the kitchen. I did come to see you, you know.' She crossed and gave Amelie a big hug. 'So what are we're making?'

'It's a delicious hazelnut meringue cake, which comes from the town of Solothurn in the North West of the country, not too far from Basel. It was invented by a baker in the town in 1915, and by the following morning was a sensation. People still make special trips to the bakery to buy it today.'

'Must be quite something. I've never heard of it.' In fact, aside from fondue and rosti, she couldn't actually think of any traditional Swiss dishes or cakes.

'Oh, it is.' Amelie took down the recipe and talked Mina

through the components of the three-layered cake before taking the biggest bag of hazelnuts Mina had ever seen out of the tall larder cupboard. As she weighed them out, she directed Mina to whip up egg whites and make the meringues.

They worked in diligent but noisy harmony as Amelie ground the hazelnuts which pinged and bounced in the food processor liked dozens of roulette balls, while Mina beat the eggs with an electric whisk.

'It's nice to have someone who knows what they're doing,' said Amelie, when Mina turned the bowl upside down to check the egg whites and sugar were stiff enough.

'It's nice to be doing something completely different for a change. This recipe sounds wonderful. I can't wait to try it.'

Once the meringue was made Amelie kept half an eye on her as Mina folded in the ground hazelnuts and she cut out four large grease paper circles. She then handed Mina a piping bag.

'Can you pipe four coiled circles onto the paper? While you're doing that I'm going to start making the hazelnut sponge, which goes in between the two meringue layers.'

Mina picked up the bag, filling it with mixture, determined to do the very best job she possibly could. She wanted her part of the cake to be perfect. At work her colleagues had always teased her that she was fiercely competitive when it came to cooking.

While the sponge was baking, Mina made the buttercream that would sandwich the whole sugary confection together. The amount of sugar in it had her fillings tingling.

By this time Amelie was assembling the ingredients for dinner.

'How many does the chalet sleep?' asked Mina, curious about to the day-to-day running of the chalet, which was a much bigger operation than she'd expected. 'I thought you were running a small bed and breakfast from what you said in your emails.'

Amelie let out a snort of laughter. 'That was the plan, but once I got here, it just grew. I started to build things around the needs of my guests – or rather, what I think they need.

'There are ten rooms in total, so officially twenty people is my maximum, but I take extra bookings for dinner and for coffee and cake by arrangement only. People have to book in advance so that I know how many to cater for. On Saturday and Sunday nights I tend to do a good hearty meal, because most of people have been out all day and are starving.' She laughed. 'Even though they have had cake. Tonight I'm making another very simple dish.'

Mina looked at the recipe on the pinboard. '*Benediktiner Eintopf.*'

'In English, you might call it monastery stew in one pot. Minced beef, with onions and leeks cooked in a vegetable broth, with Boursin added at the end, although any good-quality cream cheese will do. Couldn't be simpler or tastier, and it's served with rustic mashed potatoes and lots of bread to soak up the juices. Always goes down well. I can't bear those people who just put their heads down and eat,

eat like pigs at a trough or those fussy, picky people who don't really like food and just push it around their plate. They are not welcome to stay again.'

'You're making me hungry,' said Mina.

'That reminds me. Help yourself to anything in the fridge for lunch. I don't provide lunch for guests here, although they can order baguettes and some cheese and meat to take for a packed lunch. I always have plenty.'

'Thank you. You've thought of everything.'

'I try, although I'm worried I'm not being a terribly good hostess to you, not spending any time with you. But I promised Johannes I'd go over to his house later to choose some new wines. He was most insistent it had to be today.' She rolled her eyes but her mouth curved in a slight smile. 'I think he's quite lonely. He seems to like floating around here a lot. Unlike you. You've come for a break. I don't want you to be hanging around here with me, or expect you to be hanging on my apron strings.' She laughed. 'That's rather appropriate. I don't expect you to help in the kitchen. It's lovely having your company but you should be out there.' She pointed.

'But what if I want to? I'm having a lovely time. And there are some things that I *do* want to learn about.' Mina pointed to the fondue recipe.

'Ah, I quite often do a fondue or a raclette on a Monday, when it's much quieter. They're both good dishes for breaking the ice and making people talk to each other.'

As Mina helped Amelie clean up the kitchen, make the dinner, and assemble the cake, she realised how at home she felt. It was as if she and Amelie had worked alongside each other forever. There was a lot of work for one person. Amelie must have been up since at least six to have put out breakfast which was a help-yourself buffet of muesli and a typical continental breakfast of cheese, sliced meat, and bread, which had looked home-made to Mina.

'Don't you have any help?' she suddenly asked.

'Only to serve the food on Fridays, Saturdays, and Sundays, when we're full.' said Amelie. 'You wouldn't believe how many people catch the early train on Monday and go straight to work. Giselle and Franzi come in for a couple of hours in the mornings to make beds and clean the rooms, and in the evenings to serve dinner. They live in the village and are still at school. Gorgeous girls. But I do all the cooking.' She sighed. 'It's quite tiring. By Thursday evening I'm ready for bed straight after dinner. I love looking after everyone, and I'm afraid I'm too much of a perfectionist to let anyone else take over. Besides, I'm still getting things off the ground. Winter is OK but the summer… I still need to establish myself. I can't really afford to take anyone else on yet.'

'Well, I'm more than happy to help. I've really enjoyed this morning. I've missed cooking like this.'

Rather than eat on her own in the kitchen, Mina took her lunch up to her room so that she could enjoy the view while she ate. She wasn't meeting Luke until one-thirty, and with an hour to kill, she decided she might as well read a bit more of her book. Flicking through, she found her page again and tried to remember what the heck it had said. She remembered a moment of illumination on the train. That was it. She was halfway across the bridge – not knowing what she *did* want in life, but with an idea of what she *didn't*. So what did the book suggest she do about it?

Divide a page into two and on one side, make a list of all the things you instinctively know you don't want in life, no matter how big or small, but group them according to importance.

Mina frowned. That sounded quite easy in principle; she knew she didn't want to live in Outer Mongolia, eat raw fish every day, or become a supermodel. There were dozens of things she didn't want to do, and she couldn't see how that was supposed to help her. Luckily the book had a series of prompts.

- Think about your living arrangements. Do you still want to be where you are now in a six months, a year, five years?
- Think about where you are in a relationship. Where do you see it going in the next six months, a year, five years?
- Think about your job. Where do you want to be in six months, a year, five years?

Mina sucked on the end of her pen and gazed out of the window. People on skis in brightly coloured jackets whizzed along the trails with co-ordinated swishes of their poles, one behind the other like small, neat locomotives. In the far distance, on the other side of the valley, specks of people on an ant-like missions traversed the slopes. She wanted to be out there, doing fun stuff, not this navel-gazing. But she was supposed to be 'sorting herself out'. The words had become a sort of mantra in her head.

For the first time, it occurred to her that she'd been settling for a long time, just existing without really giving things much thought. What had happened to the high hopes and aspirations she'd had when she'd first started her job – her food crusade – where she'd introduce people to new flavours, different ingredients, and interesting dishes from around the world? She cringed. It didn't fit with the image she had of herself at all. She liked to think of herself as being outgoing, adventurous, positive, and forward-thinking. Ouch! The reality wasn't looking so great. What she'd really been doing was treading water in parts of her life.

With a sigh, she stared disconsolately at the blank page. A couple of weeks ago she'd have confidently told anyone she had all the answers: move in with Simon to a bigger place, get engaged, and apply for the next promotion at Freshfoods. Now she realised that none of those things had really excited her, or would have moved her life on to anything particularly different. She was a complete fraud, and the realisation hit her hard. There was a whole world out there.

She tossed the notebook aside, pushed open the French doors and stepped out onto the balcony, immediately blinking in the bright sunshine. Outdoors – that was where she wanted to be right now, instead of brooding over stupid self-help books which weren't helping at all. The damn book had just made her feel crap about her—

The snowball hit her right in the shoulder, sending a spray of ice crystals across her face and leaving her spluttering. She leaned over the balcony to find Luke laughing up at her and already patting a second snowball in his hands.

Without stopping to think, she ducked down to the drift in the corner of the balcony, scooped an armful of snow, and threw it down over him. The fine powder rained down like flour onto his upturned face.

'Gotcha!' she cried, pleased she'd hit her target.

'What are you doing up there, like Juliet?'

'Wishing I was outside.'

'Well, come on then, if you're free now. The day's a-wasting. I'll meet you in the boot room and we can get you kitted out. Be down in five otherwise I'm going without you.'

'I didn't say I was definitely coming,' she protested with a grin.

'But you know you want to. Look at this.' He threw out one arm to indicate the snow-covered landscape and shot her one of those disarming grins, of which he seemed to have a complete arsenal, before tramping through the snow towards the front door. And just like that the decision seemed so simple.

She dashed back inside, stripped off her jeans, and pulled on her thermals and a pair of black ski trousers over the top. After a quick detour to the bathroom, she grabbed a thick pair of socks, a fleece top and gloves, and jammed a pale blue cashmere hat on her head before racing down to the boot room.

'What kept you?' teased Luke, his eyes crinkling into his usual smile.

'That was a world record,' she said with mock outrage, still panting slightly from taking all three flights of stairs at a fast jog. She'd even managed a quick coat of mascara, which was probably still wet.

He looked at his watch. 'Five minutes and three seconds.'

'Oh, come on,' said Mina, whose competitive spirit was well and truly piqued.

'Just this once, I'll allow those three seconds. What shoe-size are you?'

It didn't take long for Luke to sort her out with the neat black ankle boots that reminded her of ice skates without the blade, and in less than fifteen minutes she was zipping up her ski jacket and carrying a set of skis and poles, very different from yesterday's, down the steps of the hotel.

'It's just a short walk to the track,' explained Luke.

'The track?' She'd envisioned gliding across the snow though the fir trees.

'Yes, it's a specially prepared trail for the skis, it makes it a lot easier especially when you're learning.'

'Where did you learn?' Mina was intrigued.

'My mother was Norwegian, so she taught me when I was younger. I think that was part of the attraction of coming to live in Switzerland. We always went to Norway in the winter on holiday to see my grandparents.'

'Are you Norwegian, then?' There was no trace of an accent in his voice, she'd assumed he was English.

'Half and half. My dad is English. My folks live in Surrey just outside Guildford. I've been living off and on in Geneva for the last few years. What about you?'

'English through and through. I feel a bit dull in comparison.' She'd always been the live wire at home, but here she was starting to realise that she really hadn't done that much with her life. 'Everyone here seems so cosmopolitan.'

'Doesn't necessarily make them interesting. I don't think you're the least bit dull.' His eyes held hers for a moment and she wondered if he was thinking of that impulsive kiss on the train. Then she *knew* he was as his gaze dropped to her lips and he gave her that warm lopsided smile. 'I know you have a sense of adventure.'

She felt the blush stain her cheeks and turned away.

'It's beautiful here, and these boots are so much more comfortable. I had a great time yesterday but I swear I've got bruises on my shins.' Hefting her skis onto her shoulder, she focused on watching where she was going as they crunched their way across the snow.

Here in the valley, the snow undulated gently across its surface, a heavy blanket curving and softening the landscape. The wide expanse of unmarked snow, except for the twin tracks that cut through the trees, made Mina feel as if they were the only people out here. There was an incredible silence, the sounds absorbed as much by the snow as by the thick layer of last year's golden pine needles beneath the closely planted firs. And there was the almost toothpaste freshness of the air, which she hoped she'd never take for granted while she was here.

'First thing you should know is that, unlike with downhill skis, only the toe of your boot clips into the ski, so you use your feet to propel yourself forward.'

'I feel like I could go dancing in these boots.' She did a quick pirouette, nearly taking him out with her poles and skis balanced across one shoulder.

'Oy,' he said, laughing as he ducked. 'No waltzing today. But I know what you mean. It's part of the attraction of cross-country. Don't get me wrong, I love the thrill of careering down a slope, but I like this because I have a sense of being in control. Once you get into a rhythm, it's a bit like running. It just feels as if I'm using my body. But then sometimes I think nothing beats snowboarding. I can never make up my mind.'

'How was the snow park yesterday? I'd quite like to have a go. I had lessons at the ski centre at home.' Much to Simon's disdain. Snowboarding apparently was for teenage boys and dropouts. In fact, what *had* she seen in Simon? He was a stuffy old man at times. She pushed him out of her thoughts. 'I used to be pretty good on a skateboard, though.'

Luke laughed. 'I could have guessed that about you. Did you hang about the skatepark with all the boys, looking cool in a beanie hat?'

'You must have been there.'

'It was the only cool thing to do when you were about fourteen, where I lived.'

Mina laughed. 'And boy, did we think we were cool,

talking trucks, wheels, decks, and bearings. Now I look back, I realise we were a bunch of four-wheeled nerds. Thank goodness I grew out of that. After that it was clubbing and partying. I bet you were one of the cool guys then, too.'

'Of course,' he said with a smile that didn't quite meet his eyes, but before Mina could explore the quick sense of unease she felt, he was nudging in her in the ribs, his usual cheeriness and enthusiasm radiating from him like an aura. 'Look, these are the tracks. There's an entire network of them through the Goms valley. And there are some specific trails, easy, middle, and difficult, so you can choose how far you go and how hard you want to push yourself. Today I'll just teach the basics.' He went on to explain the principles of movement, how to stop and how to use the lightweight poles.

Mina realised she'd unwittingly touched a raw nerve, even though he carried on talking in his usually friendly, open manner. If she hadn't been so in sync with him, she might not have picked up on it but she was – frighteningly so. It was as if all her senses were tuned into Luke frequency. In his presence she was so aware of him. The cold puffs of breath that came out of his mouth, the way that he'd tempered his long strides to match hers, and the path of his thoughts that seemed to run parallel to hers. Because they were similar, she told herself. He was like her. They would make great friends, but he was not the man for her. And she was not to think of *that* kiss. He was too like her. Too impulsive. Too spontaneous. Too much fun. She didn't want to be like that anymore. Couldn't be like that anymore. He could so easily derail her plans. When she returned to England she wanted to have everything worked out. She wanted to know where she was headed in life and how she was going to get there. They were big things to think about in only a week and a half.

Surprisingly, as Amelie had said, he was a very good teacher. Not once did he make her feel that he'd really rather be whizzing ahead and doing his own thing.

'That's it, poles in opposition to the legs. Yes. Nice rhythm.' After an hour, although her legs were beginning to feel tired, she felt she was getting the hang of it, and they were moving along the track smoothly, Luke slightly ahead of her but looking back frequently.

Every now and then he would hop off the track and let her pass him to watch her progress.

'You're doing brilliantly. You're a quick study.'

'Just concentrating.' She beamed at him. They got on so well and he was so easy to be with, it was difficult sometimes to remember that she was supposed to be keeping her distance. 'But when it comes together, it's great.'

'You've really got the hang of it. How are your legs? Especially after yesterday.'

They'd been out for just over an hour and a half now and she was starting to feel it in her thighs, but she said, 'Fine,' not prepared to admit to any weakness. Besides, she wanted to keep going and perfect her technique.

'OK, we'll take the trail up to the tree line and there's an intersection up there that takes us back to the village.'

For the next ten minutes she had to push hard as they

were going uphill. Although it wasn't steep, it was like running uphill and took a lot more effort and a lot more puff. She could feel herself breathing heavily but she was keeping up and from the clouds of steam up ahead, Luke was working just as hard.

'Not far now,' Luke called back. 'When we get into the trees, we're going to turn right onto a new trail and then it's downhill for a while before we level out. So you can have a bit of a rest.'

'Cool,' said Mina, keen to try out the technique for turning in the tracks that Luke had taught her. So far they'd been going in a straight line, which was great for practising, but she was ready for something new.

As they neared the trees, the incline got a little steeper and she focused on her skis rather than looking ahead. She could do this. It was just a question of willpower. Not looking how much further there was to go always helped when she ran. Digging in deeper, she forced herself to work harder to get up the last bit of the hill and completely failed to see that Luke was slowing down. Before she knew it she was almost on top of his skis.

'Oh no! Luke,' she called, realising that her momentum was such, she wasn't going to be able to stop in time, even if she could remember how.

He turned and saw her but there wasn't enough time for him to take evasive action and she caught one of his skis with hers. In a slow motion tangle of limbs, she pitched forward taking Luke with her, her boots snapping, as they were supposed to, out of her skis.

'Sor—' Her apology died as she grabbed him around the

waist and the two of them rolled to the side of the track. The icy touch of snow worked its way down her neck and her hat was wrenched off, and she found herself lying on top of Luke, her hair flopping into his face.

She drew in a quick breath. 'Oh God, I'm sorry. Are you OK?'

'We must stop meeting like this.' He grinned up at her. 'I think your knees are almost as pointy as you're elbows, and one of them is about to unman me.'

'Ouch, I'm sorry.' In her haste to roll off him, somehow she took him with her, so that they were now side-by-side facing each other in the snow, looking at each other. The silence pressed in on them and inexorably like a pair of magnets they gave in to the pull. Mina couldn't honestly have said who moved first, but she did know she sighed when his soft lips landed on hers with an unexpected but thrilling sense of familiarity.

Despite lying in the snow, her bones turned liquid, and inside her ski clothes she felt deliciously warm. Luke's mouth was gentle and unhurried as his lips explored hers and it was just like before, that gorgeous sensation of stepping into a sunbeam, all that golden warmth directed full on her.

When his tongue touched hers, a spark of electric lust shocked every bit of her, and she couldn't help the moan that escaped and sounded horribly loud in the snow-muffled landscape.

Luke groaned in response and deepened the kiss and they were lost for another few minutes before he finally pulled away and rested his head on her forehead.

He exhaled loudly. 'Wow, Mina, you pack a punch. I'm not sure which way is up at the moment.' With one hand he rubbed at his chest over his heart, the action as much as the hoarse words making her heart sing.

'Me neither.'

Luke's kisses had knocked her for six, but it was rather lovely to hear that he was as affected as she was. She felt as if she'd just been through an earthquake, did he feel the same?

When she looked into his eyes, she saw the same dazed expression. They stared at each other for a few moments longer and then Luke's cheeks dimpled. 'What is it with you throwing yourself at me? That's twice now. But I'm happy to avail. I've always fancied making out in the snow.'

'I thought you were worried about getting frostbite.' She arched a teasing eyebrow.

'That's the hiking. It all hangs out. I'm thinking warm caverns.' His eyes twinkled with sudden naughtiness.

She burst out laughing. 'That's terrible.'

Despite her laughter at his blatant innuendo, it didn't stop the dart of lust that hit right on the target, making her squirm discreetly. Damn, he wasn't supposed to be this irresistible and she really shouldn't be kissing him. This was halfway across the bridge, Luke was everything she didn't want.

Chapter Nine

'**R**eady?'

She shook her head.

'You hurt?'

'No, er… the kissing. We shouldn't.'

'We shouldn't?' Luke's voice held a note of surprise. 'Why not?'

'Why not?' she echoed. 'Remember what I said the other day?'

'I like kissing you. And there's no law against kissing, unless you're married with a dozen children to a guy that's going to hunt me down and cause me violence. And I'm kind of guessing that there is no man in your life.'

'And how do you come to that conclusion?' She raised an eyebrow, wondering what it was about her that said: single and recently rejected.

'Because if you had, there wouldn't have been that instant connection the first time we kissed. I would have known.'

'You'd have known from one kiss?' She was starting to sound like an echo chamber.

He gave her a cocky smile. 'Oh yes.'

She glowered at him feeling that she was losing control of this conversation. 'No more kissing.'

'OK,' he said with a loose shrug.

Again, like the other day, a contrary part of her was irritated by how easily he'd accepted it. He could at least have put up a bit of a fight. She rolled to one side to try and get up and fell back down, her skis sliding away before she could get to her feet. 'I mean it, Luke. We have to stop this.'

'OK,' he said again, a small smile tugging at that attractive lopsided mouth, as if he knew something she didn't. 'Here.' He held out a hand and reluctantly she let him haul her up, immediately making herself busy brushing herself down, dusting the snow from her ski jacket and shaking out her hat, before righting her skis and clipping her boots back into place with determined resolution.

'Thank you. Shall we go?' Her tone was brusque and back to business. She was desperate to avoid the return of the previous flirty vibes that had been buzzing like happy bees in high summer.

'Remember how to slow down? I don't want you taking me out again. I don't think my heart can take the strain.'

She let out a reluctant laugh in response to the cheerful expression on his face, relieved that Luke was able to carry on as normal and not sulk or be difficult about her putting the brakes on things.

'I promise I'll keep my hands off you in future,' she said with a teasing smile, although inside she meant every word.

'Yes, you with your pointy elbows and knees. You're a dangerous woman. I might not survive a full-blown assault. Anyone would think you didn't like me,' he said with the chirpy confidence of someone who knew the exact opposite.

She purposefully ignored him and fiddled with the zip on her ski jacket before adjusting her hat.

'Shall we go?' she asked with a brisk smile. Thankfully Luke switched back to being businesslike, which was a relief for her wayward pulse, which was still sputtering about with hormone-induced craziness.

'Right, from now on it's a lot easier. We're going downhill for most of the way with one little slope and then it's easy. Just remember to keep your body forward, and if you want to slow down take one of your skis out of the trail, roll your knee, and ankle inwards to turn the tip of your ski. It's a half snowplough, like you'd do in downhill. Want to practise before we really get going?'

Much as Mina wanted to say she'd be fine, for once sense overcame bravado. She didn't want to run him down. Twice was careless but a third time might look like an invitation. So she practised the manoeuvre a couple of times while Luke watched with no sign of itching to be off again.

'You're a very good teacher,' she said, feeling a lot more confident in her ability to control her skis. 'Very patient. I feel like I'm holding you up.'

'We're not in a hurry. This slope will still be here tomorrow, and the day after.' He looked around the scenery, his face lighting up with sheer pleasure. 'This is why I love cross-country skiing, there's no hurry. You can take your time. Appreciate all this.' He went quiet, lifting his head and staring at the view spread out before them. 'Appreciate being alive,' he added in a low voice.

She followed his gaze up at the majestic mountains crowned by rocky crags catching the sunlight and the two of them stood in the muffled silence of the valley looking up at a landscape that had been there for millennia. How much had this landscape changed in all that time, she wondered.

'Unfortunately, as wonderful as the view is, it won't keep body and soul together, and I'm starving.' He looked at his watch and tapped the face with a teasing twist to his mouth. 'I don't want to miss coffee-and-cake-time. I might have to abandon you, if you can't keep up. We've got an hour to get back.'

'An hour.' She pulled a face. 'It's taken an hour and a half to get here.'

'I promise you, going back is a lot easier and quicker.'

He was right, and the downhill journey was a real pleasure. The speed they achieved surprised her, as well as how much she enjoyed whizzing along, albeit more sedately than yesterday, with the cold wind biting at her cheeks with icy teeth. In contrast her body felt warm and fluid, responding to her skis with perfect co-ordination. There was much more of a sense of being at one with her environment and in charge of her body, and a very different sensation to yesterday's bursts of adrenaline and the constant awareness that one false move, bump, turn, or twist, and you could completely lose control and be at the total mercy of your fall. She grinned to herself, feeling an instant chill on her teeth but she didn't care. She hadn't felt this good for a long time.

As they crested a hill she saw Reckingen spread out below them, the lights starting to come on creating that already-familiar welcoming golden glow. Her heart missed a beat at the beauty of it. In just two days, she'd fallen in love with this serene, idyllic valley.

As they tipped over the edge of the hill it seemed to spur them both on, or maybe it was the lure of cake, and they sped up using their poles to push them faster and faster.

'Hop off here,' called Luke as they neared the place where they'd first started. With elegant ease that she wasn't sure she was going to emulate, he lifted one ski out of the track, and then the next, and gradually slowed to a halt. Her legs were tired now but she managed the manoeuvre, albeit with elephantine clumsiness that almost had her falling, but she managed to stay upright and with a triumphant yell drew to a wobbly halt next to Luke.

'That was awesome,' she cried, her cheeks flushed and her adrenaline racing, bubbling with enthusiasm and endorphins. 'Oh, I loved it. It was wonderful. Thank you, Luke, for taking me out.' She threw her arms around him in a spontaneous hug, because that was just the way she was made, and grinned up into his face.

He hugged her back and their eyes met in a brief frisson-filled second before he said, his eyes sparkling with laughter, 'There's nothing quite like it. Makes you feel glad to be alive.'

'Do you know, it really does.' She glanced back the way she'd come. She couldn't remember the last time she'd felt so energised and full of life. Yesterday had been too full of excitement and trepidation for her to fully enjoy the experience. 'I can't wait to have another go.'

'I'll take you out again, if you like.'

'That would be wonderful,' she said, before she had time to think. It was only as she picked her skis up and slung them over her shoulder to walk back to the chalet that she remembered she was supposed to be keeping her distance from Luke.

Up in her room, she examined her flushed cheeks and sparkling eyes. On the pretext of being desperate for the loo, she'd left Luke downstairs sorting out the skis and poles, which she didn't feel good about. She wasn't the sort of woman who left things to men. She'd heard him come back to his room about ten minutes after her.

Mountain air agreed with her, or maybe it was being with Luke. She sighed and frowned at her reflection. Luke's company was everything she enjoyed; they were so in tune. He was ideal friend material, except that kissing him was like drinking champagne, diving out of a plane, and coming home all at the same time. It made her feel alive and wild, safe and crazy. A bit like touching a live electric cable knowing you had wellington boots on.

With another heavy sigh, she changed quickly, spritzed with deodorant and perfume, and then sat on the bed waiting to hear Luke's door open and close. She didn't want to risk bumping into him in the corridor again. Eventually she heard his door click and close, and her heart began thumping as if aware of how close he was. She heard his footsteps pause. For some reason she held her breath. Was he going to knock for her? Her body seemed at odds with her brain, although that wasn't doing her any favours either. That sinfully, gorgeous kiss came flooding back into her mind.

She heard a shuffle and another step. Was he thinking of her? Was he about to raise a hand to rap on her door?

She imagined opening the door and seeing him in the doorway and her heart thudded. She wasn't sure she could trust herself with him. It was a relief when his footsteps picked up and padded away down the corridor to the staircase.

Giving herself a full five minutes, she gave another look at herself in the mirror and left the room.

'Just in time,' said Bernhardt, immediately crossing to her side as she walked into the lounge, as if he'd been looking out for her. She gave him a big smile, already aware of Luke in her peripheral vision.

'Don't worry, I wasn't going to miss this cake.' She reached for a plate and one of the delicate pastry forks. 'I helped Amelie make it this morning. Doesn't it look delicious? I'm dying to try it. You should have seen how light and fluffy the sponge was when Amelie took it out of the oven.' She was talking too much. She moved to sit down on one of the sofas, the slight ache of her thighs reminding her she'd had a good workout. Bernhardt took the seat next to her.

'Did you?' His eyebrows rose. 'Isn't that what you call a busman's holiday?'

Mina marvelled once more at how good everyone's English was, but Bernhardt shrugged. 'We're multilingual from a young age. So how come you're working in the kitchen when you're supposed to be on holiday?'

'I didn't get a chance to mention it yesterday, and I didn't get a chance to say thank you for taking me with you. I had a great time.'

'Yes. Sorry we lost you, but you know what it's like.'

'I didn't mind.' She grinned at him. 'It meant you didn't see how rubbish I am, but I definitely improved during the day.'

He laughed. 'We learn from a young age. I can't remember not being able to ski.'

'You do everything from a young age, it seems,' said Mina teasingly.

'Not everything,' he said it seriously but there was a sudden glint of humour in his eyes.

'Going back to your earlier question. You asked why I was in the kitchen. I was helping Amelie because I'm her goddaughter. I didn't expect to be a guest, I thought I'd be staying with her—' she lifted her shoulders '—in the staff quarters.'

'Instead you got the best room in the house,' chipped in Kristian, who had come to sit opposite them.

'Er… is it?' She was slightly perturbed by the fact that he knew exactly which room she was staying in.

'Kristian, you sound like a stalker.' Bernhardt rolled his

eyes and the other man blushed to the very roots of his pale blonde hair.

'Amelie said she'd saved the best room for her goddaughter. I know the rooms on the top floors are the best. Luke got one because he's staying and working here.'

'He's working here?'

She thought he'd told her he was between jobs.

Kristian waggled his eyebrows. 'No one knows what he does. We think he's a spy.'

'No, we don't,' said Bernhardt with an impatient huff. 'We don't think anything. I try not to think of him at all.' He turned back to Mina. 'So how was your day? I'm very impressed with the cake. It's a real speciality in Solothurn, but this is every bit as good as a real one from the Suteria bakery.'

Mina didn't want to laugh at his faint air of pomposity. She didn't think he was doing it on purpose, he was just rather serious, and in some ways it was rather cute. His dark eyes seemed to be narrowed in perpetual study, as if he wasn't sure whether he could take things at face value.

'I can't take any of the credit, I just helped Amelie, but it is a fantastic recipe. I'd love to introduce it to people at home.' She screwed up her face. There was no way she could persuade her bosses to create a dessert like this for the supermarket. It was such a shame, because she knew people would love it.

'Good evening, Mina.'

'Hello, Johannes.'

She watched him scan the room quickly, his eyes lingering on the door to the kitchen, before sitting down in the chair next to Kristian and studying the slice of cake on his plate. 'Another triumph from Amelie's kitchen, I think. She's a very talented woman.'

'Yes.' Kristian leaned forward, his blonde fringe flopping forward in his boyish enthusiasm. 'If she weren't so old, I'd ask her out.'

Bernhardt managed to refrain from rolling his eyes this time, but Mina got the impression he tolerated Kristian's inappropriate comments like one would a small, badly trained puppy. 'You should never mention a woman's age, and certainly not refer to her as old.'

'Really?' asked Kristian looking totally perplexed. 'Why not?'

Johannes patted him on the arm. 'You have a lot to learn, boy.'

Mina, enjoying the byplay between the three men, tried to focus on Bernhardt, aware that on the other side of the room, Luke was carrying on a lively conversation with Claudia and Frank. Although she tried not to look his way, it was as if she had developed some special radar for him, because she was constantly aware of exactly where he was in the room.

'Enjoy the skiing? I saw you come back.' asked Johannes.

'I loved it. It was so much fun.' Her eyes shone with the memory of the downhill trip back to the chalet.

He took a bite of the cake and closed his eyes in apparent bliss. 'This is exceptional.'

'Mina helped,' Kristian piped up.

Johannes opened his eyes and stared at her. 'Amelie

allowed you to brave her kitchen? You're very honoured. I've been trying to encourage her to take on some help, but she's very stubborn.'

'I guess she doesn't want to relinquish control,' Mina gave him a friendly shrug, getting the distinct impression that he felt a little put out. 'Not while she's still building the business.'

'Hmm. She's not very good at accepting help, although I did persuade her to accept my latest batch of chocolates to serve with coffee this evening.'

'You make chocolate?' Mina's eyes widened with sudden interest. 'I love chocolate.'

'Well, you've come to the right country. We make the best chocolate in the world,' declared Bernhardt.

'We do. For me, it started as a hobby, but now I sell everything I make.' There was definite touch of pride in the way Johannes straightened up in his seat as he finished the sentence.

'I'd love to see how you do it. Could I?'

Johannes frowned, his scraggy eyebrows drawing together like a pair of hairy caterpillars. 'Hmm, my recipes are a closely guarded secret. I never share them with anyone.'

'Oh,' said Mina, a little crestfallen and feeling that she'd overstepped some boundary. 'Not to worry. Perhaps you could tell me a little more, one day. I'd really love to know more about chocolate and how it's made.' She hoped her friendly smile might disarm him. While she knew there were some people who were very secretive about their recipes, it wasn't something she could relate to. Good food and lovely things were to be shared. Like this gorgeous cake. Just imagine if the bakery had kept the recipe to itself; all these people in this room, who were clearly loving it from the happy expressions on every single person's face, would never have tasted it. That would have been a terrible shame.

Johannes pursed his lips following her gaze and as if he knew what she were thinking, let out a small harrumphing noise. 'I'll think about it.'

She beamed at him but didn't say another word, instead just lifting another forkful of the delicious frothy confection of cake into her mouth. This was one recipe that she would definitely be taking home with her.

The room buzzed with that happy, low-key vibration of satisfied, contented people and as it started to get dark outside, Mina decided she would pop into the kitchen to check Amelie didn't need any help, before she went up to her room to have a soak in the bath before dinner.

Amelie was sitting with a cup of coffee on the table, looking as if she were about to fall asleep.

'Are you OK?' asked Mina, faintly alarmed at the weariness dragging at her godmother's eyes. 'Is there anything I can do to help?'

Amelie jumped up. 'Absolutely fine. Everything's under control. I'm just waiting for the potatoes to boil. And the girls will be here in half an hour to lay the tables in the dining room. Johannes has chopped some wood for me and is keeping an eye on the fire in the salon.'

She crossed to the oven and took off one of the lids over the big boiling pots. 'Yes, they're nearly done. Why don't you go up? There's a good two hours before dinner, I'm sure you'll want to freshen up and change after all that skiing this afternoon.'

'If you're sure you don't need any help.' The thought of a bath was extremely welcome.

'No, no. It's nearly all done the. I hope everyone is hungry, although I've made extra as there are another six coming in for dinner this evening.'

'Gosh, cooking for twenty-six. That's a lot of work.'

'Don't you start. I've got enough trouble with Johannes fussing. He's such an old woman.'

'He's a big fan of your cooking.'

'He's just in a good mood because I said yes to his chocolates.'

'What's wrong with them? Aren't they any good?'

'Good? They are wonderful. Stupid man is very stubborn about letting anyone know much about them.'

'I know,' sighed Mina. 'I asked him if I could see him at work.'

'And he said no.'

'Yes.'

'We'll have to see what we can do about that.' Amelie's eyes narrowed in quick thought. 'I guess he's like me, doesn't like anyone interfering in his kitchen.'

'You didn't mind me helping this morning.'

'You know what you're doing, and you are family,' said

Amelie placidly. 'It's not as if I have much, at least not interesting, family. You, my dear, are always interesting. Talking of which, have you any plans for tomorrow?'

'Not yet but I might go out and practise my cross-country skiing. I felt like I got the hang of it today. Luke was a good teacher.'

'Excellent.' Amelie beamed at her. 'He's such a lovely boy, and that was very kind of him to take you out.'

'It was, especially when I wiped him out earlier today.' Mina smiled, thinking of the moment they'd tumbled down together, and his easy smiles. Nothing seemed to faze him. 'But if you're doing something…'

'No. No. Tomorrow is an easy day. I'll be making bread tomorrow morning because we're having fondue for dinner, and I'm making *zigercake*. The ski bunnies will be off early to get the train back to the city. The girls come in and strip all the beds mid-morning and make up the new ones. Monday evening is very relaxed, so it's my rest day. and tomorrow I don't plan to do anything other than go for a nice walk, if you'd like to come with me. I can point out a few things help you get your bearings.'

Amelie looked like she needed a rest. There were dark purple smudges beneath her eyes and her shoulders sagged slightly as if they were weighed down by the enormous sacks of flour she kept in the larder.

'That would be lovely, and I can help before we go out.'

Amelie looked as if she were about to shake her head, and Mina laid a hand on her shoulder. 'Seriously, I don't mind, and I love learning new recipes. Cooking is my hobby.' It was a shame it had turned into her work as well, although that was a lot less satisfying. 'What's in a – what was it? – a *zigercake*?'

'*Ziger*,' said Amelie with a laugh. 'It's rather like a cheesecake, using a Swiss cheese similar to ricotta, although it's firmer and crumblier, so works really well in this recipe. It has no flour and is made with eggs, lemon, sugar, and garnished with toasted flaked almonds. And I'll teach you how to make it. In fact, I might take shameless advantage of you, and get you to help make the cakes in advance for Tuesday.'

'That's my very busy day. I take everything to the laundry in Brig, collect the new sheets, and go to the wholesalers for supplies. I need to get all that done before midday as I have a few people arriving, and they're staying until Friday.'

She glanced out of the window. 'In fact, if you help me tomorrow, we could do my favourite walk. It's a seven-kilometre trail up the valley, and then I can get the train back. To be honest, I haven't been out properly for a couple of weeks. Johannes keeps asking me, but there never seem to be enough hours in the day.'

'Gosh, don't you want to put your feet up?'

'And miss the mountains?' Amelie shook her head vehemently. 'I can rest plenty when I'm dead. Monday is the only real chance I get to take a good long walk and shake the cobwebs loose. There's no point living here if you don't experience the snow.'

After being out today and still feeling ruddy-cheeked, Mina could appreciate that.

Chapter Ten

Mina lowered herself into the warm pine-scented water in the rather wonderful freestanding, very contemporary bath, feeling her aching muscles immediately go 'aah' and relax. Much as she'd enjoyed it, the skiing was now making itself felt.

She was looking forward to dinner, trying Amelie's stew and enjoying the light-hearted camaraderie of the dining room, now that she knew a few people. There was something so welcoming about the chalet and she spent a while trying to analyse exactly how Amelie had achieved it. Good food, obviously. Amelie was a great cook, but there was more. Although there were a range of ages and people from different backgrounds, everyone seemed to get along and be happy to chat to each other. Even Johannes, who she suspected tended towards the irascible, seemed to mellow in the cosy lounge over cake. All the guests were so friendly. Surely Amelie didn't handpick them all. Clearly a lot of them came back. Over cake she'd discovered that both

Bernhardt and Kristian would be back the following weekend. She had a feeling that Amelie was like the soft delicious sponge in the Solothurner cake that held everything together. You couldn't see it, but you quickly realised it was there when you took the first delicious bite. Amelie was what made this place, she was a unique hostess and Mina doubted her hospitality could be replicated.

In danger of falling asleep, she hauled herself out of the bath into a sumptuous soft white bath sheet and padded through to the bedroom. Night had fallen now, and through the windows the glow of the lights was reflected on the snow. She would never get tired of this view, or the way the shadows fell on the soft, plump pillows of snow piled high on the roofs, walls, and ledges.

Dressing in her favourite black trousers, she spritzed some perfume and checked herself in the mirror, conscious of the muffled noises coming from next door. Her heart did that silly expanding thing at the thought of Luke. What was she going to do about that? Clearly there was serious chemistry between them. There was no denying he was gorgeous, had a great personality, and she'd enjoyed his company enormously, but she had no business starting a relationship with anyone, certainly not now when she was supposed to be focusing on getting her priorities sorted. But it was getting harder and harder to keep him out of his head, and to stop her body responding to the mere flipping sight of him. She glared at the book lying on her bed and with a sigh snatched it up. At least reading it, she felt as if she were doing *something* towards 'sorting herself out'. Ian's words had stung more than she'd realised at the time and she kept dwelling on them, going back over them like a tongue drawn to a jagged tooth. She had half an hour before dinner was served.

Know Yourself

Before you can truly understand what it is you want, you need to be true to yourself and identify those values at your very core. What are the things that are important to you?

Think about the things that:

- Excite and enthuse you
- Make you want to get out of bed in the morning
- Are the most precious to you
- Make you the person you are

Mina huffed out a sigh. Like Hannah said, stating the bleeding obvious. Pulling on her down coat, she opened the French doors and went out onto the balcony to what she now considered her thinking spot.

Food, adventure, travel, and chocolate – they all excited and enthused her. She narrowed her eyes. She really needed to butter Johannes up to see how chocolate was made. It would be crazy to come to what many people considered the home of chocolate and not learn more about it. If she couldn't persuade Johannes, she would have to visit one of the chocolate factories that the girl in the shop mentioned.

Perhaps there were some leaflets downstairs that she could investigate.

In fact, she'd go down now and take a look. Shrugging off her coat, she dumped it on the armchair and gave herself a quick once-over in the mirror. Her face, despite a liberal application of high-factor sunscreen, had taken on a golden hue which was enhanced with a quick slick of pink sparkly lipstick. OK, so she was being vain, but she was pleased with the wholesome, healthy reflection that smiled back at herself. She'd do.

She hadn't really taken much notice of the wooden rack of leaflets since she'd arrived, but one caught her eye immediately and she grabbed it. No! There couldn't be. A cheese and chocolate train? Cheese and chocolate, what was not to like? As she scanned the text, her excitement mounted and her tastebuds began to tingle. It sounded like her idea of heaven, especially as it took in Gruyère, one of her favourite cheeses, and then went on to one of the top chocolate factories in Switzerland, Maison Cailler. Not just that, the train was made up of vintage Pullman coaches, which looked wonderful and reminded her of pictures of the Orient Express.

'I've always fancied doing that.' She didn't need to turn around; at the sound of his voice, her stomach had done that familiar loop-the-loop.

'Luke.' As usual she couldn't help smiling back at him. 'It looks so much fun,' she said. 'The scenery is supposed to be spectacular. And I bet the cheese and chocolate aren't half bad either,' she added. 'I really want to know more about making chocolate. Let's go,' she said, impulsive as ever. She believed if you really wanted to do something you went for it. Wasn't that what the book was telling her? Find the things she did want to do. Did this count?

There was a wonderful Mark Twain quote that said you were more likely to regret the things you didn't do than those you did, and it was so true. She still regretted not going to see Green Day when she was offered tickets when she was eighteen. She should have fought a lot harder about not going to her cousin's wedding. They were only invited to the evening bit anyway. It still rankled all these years on. The more she thought about it, the more she wanted to go. 'I'm never going to get the chance to go on a cheese and chocolate train again. Or possibly travel in vintage Pullman carriages, which look lovely.' She paused and then asked, 'But I have no idea what they are. Is Pullman something special?'

Luke laughed. 'They were made in the early part of the twentieth century, and at the time were very luxurious. They still are. And I would love to go, it's one of the classic rail journeys in Switzerland. The only thing is, it would be quite complicated getting there. The train leaves Montreux at 8:44.' He pointed to the very precise time in the leaflet.

'And how far away is Montreux?'

'At least three hours by train.'

Her face fell. 'Hmm. I'll have to have a think.' The train trip itself was seven hours long. Even she had to accept that perhaps a thirteen-hour day wasn't completely practical.

'Fancy coming snowboarding on Tuesday, then? Test out your skateboarding skills. The slopes will be much quieter as the weekend crowd has left.'

Her face fell. 'I'd love to, but I said I'd go to Brig with Amelie.' And she really did feel that Amelie would appreciate the company as much as the help. This was quite an operation for one person.

'If you really fancy it, I could go on Wednesday or Thursday. My work is flexible, so I can rearrange easily.'

'I thought you said you were between posts.'

Luke frowned for a second before nodding. ' I am. But I also have a… a freelance job that I'm working on.' He paused studying her face for a moment. 'Would you like to see?'

'See?'

The familiar grin flashed back at her. 'See what I do. It's a sort of hobby.'

Now she was intrigued. 'OK.'

'You'd have to come up to my room.'

She raised an eyebrow.

He laughed. With a nod towards the stairs, he added, 'Come on then, we've just got time before dinner.'

Mina's curiosity worked overtime as they climbed the staircase. 'Can you give me any clues?'

'You'll never guess in a million years.' His expression was ever so slightly smug, but also filled with amusement. 'I make things.'

Never one to back down from a challenge, she narrowed her eyes. 'You knit,' she said remembering the chunky red scarf.

He shook his head.

'You paint.'

'Stick men, I'm afraid.'

'You… you make jigsaw puzzles.'

With a laugh, he shook his head. 'Where did that come from?'

She shrugged. 'You're a potter,' and she kept guessing with each shake of his head. 'You press flowers.' 'You make lederhosen.' That got another bark of laughter. 'You carve things.' 'You make jewellery.' By the time they reached the top floor, she'd run out of ideas and Luke was laughing so hard that he could barely open his door.

'Here you go.' He ushered her into the room, which was a little bigger than hers with a large work table in front of one of the big balcony doors. Her mouth curved instantly and she darted forward to examine the rolls of mod rock, tins of paint, paintbrushes, bottles of track magic, and a scattering of little trees strewn around the perimeter of the work surface.

She turned around and beamed.

'You're a modeller,' she said with delighted surprise, pleased to see she'd taken him unawares.

The items were as familiar to her as cooking ingredients, although the vintage suitcase in the middle of it all intrigued her. She picked up one of the tiny trees and twirled it between her fingers.

'How did you know? I was going to make you keep guessing.'

'Sorry,' she grinned at him unapologetically. 'My Uncle D spends hours making landscapes for his model railway. He has all this stuff.'

'Ah, but there's more.'

'Yes,' she said, turning back to the table. 'The suitcase. I remember seeing that on the train and wondering about it. Vintage. Cute. But and an odd choice for a man going skiing with a rucksack in the other hand.'

'Very good. You could give Sherlock a run for his money.'

He moved forward so that he was standing shoulder-to-shoulder with her and then leaned down to plug something into the mains and pulled the suitcase to the edge of the table.

With a touch of showmanship, he waited for a couple of seconds, heightening the anticipation. It was almost like waiting for a kiss, thought Mina, and immediately sneaked a glance at his mouth.

He caught her and his expression softened, as his eyes roved over her face. She swallowed and wished he would kiss her, despite telling him otherwise only a few hours ago. He made a tiny move towards her.

'So,' she said, over-bright, deliberately breaking eye-contact. 'What's in the case?'

With a knowing smile, as if he knew exactly what sort of a big fat coward she was, he lifted the lid.

Mina clapped her hands in delight. 'That is gorgeous. Oh Luke, it's beautiful.'

Inside the case was a miniature model village, every detail minutely captured, with a tiny train track wending its way around green fields, past thatched cottages and through a little station.

'It's not quite finished. I've got a couple of hours more work on it.'

'Oh my goodness, I've never seen anything so cute in my life. What a brilliant idea.'

He pressed a switch and she watched as a tiny train made its way along the track which ran around the very English village, drinking in all the details, from the little duck pond on the central green, the miniature bride and groom outside the church, the old-fashioned fire engine beside a singed haystack, through to the row of cottages beside the railway station.

'What gauge is it?' she asked in wonderment.

'Er...' Luke seemed surprised and gratified at the same time. 'It's an N gauge, nine millimetre. How did you...?'

'Uncle Derek. I told you. He used to go this big model railway show at the NEC every year, and when I was younger, I used to go with him. Someone had to make sure he'd get there in one piece, and the whole train thing bored Hannah rigid, and I didn't mind. It's amazing what you pick up.'

Luke laughed and hugged her. 'Mina, you are one in a million.'

'You're pretty special yourself.' She slipped her arms around his waist. 'This is just the most brilliant thing I've ever seen. Absolutely gorgeous.'

'Yes,' he said, looking down at her with that direct, uncompromising look that she'd come to know just a little too well, and she knew he wasn't talking about the train in the suitcase. Unlike her, Luke had no intention of hiding or fighting his attraction to her and unfortunately it made him all the more attractive.

Deliberately turning away, she reached out and touched

the tiny glossy fire engine. 'So what happens to it when it's finished? Do you sell it?'

'This one has been specially commissioned as a retirement present for someone. I work with a lady in the UK, a friend of my parents, she sources the vintage cases and the commissions, and I come up with the design and make the models.

'She set up a couple of years ago and it's growing slowly and surely. This one has to be finished by the end of this week. I'll take it into Brig and get it shipped. Then I have another one to start, this time they want the Scottish Highlands.' He pointed to another brown leather case under the table.

'I can't wait to tell Uncle Derek. Do you mind if I take some photos?'

'Er, would you mind waiting? The new owner hasn't even seen it yet; it seems a bit unfair on them if someone else gets to see it before them.'

'Oh, yes. Of course. That makes sense. Maybe I should buy one for him.' She'd already resolved to speak to Hannah. She could get her to take pictures of the family home before Derek and Miriam moved out and they could include a model of the house and give it to Derek as a retirement present or a moving house present. They could even have tiny figures of the four of them in the garden waving at the train. As always, her mind was leaping forward with seven-league boots.

Luke laughed. 'I can almost hear your brain racing, but I'm thrilled that you love the Suitcase Train as much as I do.'

'I do. No wonder you're such a patient teacher. You must have lots, to do this kind of painstaking, detailed work.'

'I had to learn it,' said Luke, just a touch enigmatically but she was still thinking of Derek's would-be reaction and didn't think about his odd response until much later.

———

A few minutes later, they followed their noses into the dining room, which was almost full. On the sideboard were three enormous, old-fashioned, steaming tureens filling the air with the scent of leeks and mince. Next to them were two breadboards with several French sticks.

'Ah, Mina, Luke. Just in time. Mina, would you like to sit between Claudia and Kristian and on the other side of Kristian?'

Mina nodded, pleased with her seating allocation; she'd really enjoyed talking to Claudia the previous night. She was amused to see that Luke looked a little mutinous as he made his way to the seat next-door-but-one to hers, with Kristian separating them.

As she sat down, she turned to Kristian and said good evening.

'You have lipstick on. It looks nice.'

'Thank you,' she said, trying to keep her amusement at the clumsy compliment.

'Yes. A nice colour. It makes your lips look...' He winced as he ran out of steam. 'Like lips.' There was a panicked expression in his eyes as he turned as red as a beetroot to the very tips of his ears.

She patted them. 'That's good then. That's what I was hoping for. I like this colour. Thank you.'

Kristian looked at her uncertainly, but seemed reassured by her straight face.

'*Guten Abend*,' he muttered, staring down at his place setting.

'Good evening, Mina.' Claudia greeted her with friendly charm and proceeded to ask her all about her virgin cross-country ski experience.

Once everyone was seated according to Amelie's directions, the two teenage servers started filling bowls with hearty portions of the *benediktiner eintopf* and she put baskets of the sliced baguettes in the middle of the table. There was very little conversation at first as everyone tucked in; everyone's earlier hunger, briefly quashed by cake, was well and truly back with a vengeance.

Amelie had a gift, thought Mina as she looked around the table. She was the fairy godmother of hostessing. With a simple wave of her wooden spoon, she'd managed to match each person up so that everyone had someone to talk to that they were comfortable with. Even Kristian next to her had gradually lost his nervousness and been able to address a couple of innocuous remarks to her without putting his foot in it or turning bright red again. Opposite her a young teenage girl was happily chatting away to Frank and just beyond her Luke and Bernhardt were indulging in playful banter, laughing and teasing each other with the familiarity of old friends. It was a convivial party, decided Mina, and even after coffee had been served and finished – Johannes's chocolates were amazing – everyone stayed at the table talking for another hour. Eventually people began to drift away in readiness for another early start in the morning.

'Look forward to seeing you later in the week, Mina,' said Bernhardt in a low voice, as he paused by her chair, putting what she suddenly realised was a proprietary hand on the back of the chair. 'And then we'll be back on Friday.' There was unexpected warmth in his dark eyes as he smiled down at her.

'Er… yes,' she said, having absolutely no idea what he meant. She knew he, Uta and Kristian were leaving the following morning but would be back at the weekend. It seemed a long way to come back for one night. Maybe she'd misheard. And maybe she'd misread the sudden interest he was showing. Where had that come from?

Chapter Eleven

'This is heaven,' said Mina as she surveyed the view. Little clumps of dark green fir dotted the landscape between the wooden chalets scattered across the slope dominated by a big two-storey white church with a black slate roof and domed clocked tower.

'And I thank God every day that I came back here,' said Amelie, leaning on one of her walking poles. They were both slightly out of breath and their pants came out in little puffs of steam in the crisp air. 'I love living in the mountains. And thank you for helping this morning. I feel like I've really got ahead of myself, especially with the cakes already made for tomorrow.'

'It's my pleasure. It's so interesting trying these recipes, they're very different to English cakes. Especially the way you separate out the egg whites and whip them up and fold them in at the end. It's inspiring me so much. What do you think of this? A fruity twist on the Solothurner cake. How about a cherry or raspberry version?'

'Hmm, I'm a bit of a traditionalist when it comes to recipes, but I could be persuaded. Sounds interesting.' Amelie tilted her head and broke off to point ahead with her walking pole. 'We're headed up there. Ready to go?'

Mina looked up at the slope towards a line of trees and nodded.

'So how would you adapt the recipe?' asked Amelie as they set off.

An hour later they were travelling back to the chalet on the train having talked non-stop during their walk about cakes, ingredients, and flavours. Mina's brain buzzed with ideas and her hands were jiggling up and down on her knee with that burning desire to get into the kitchen.

Amelie began to laugh. 'Why don't we buy you some ingredients tomorrow when we go to Brig and you can work in the kitchen?'

'Would you mind?' asked Mina, conscious that the kitchen was very much Amelie's domain. 'I'm dying to experiment. I feel really inspired by all your recipes. They're so different but there's so much scope to adapt them and I'm itching to have a go.'

Amelie laid a hand over Mina's knee. 'I can tell.' She laughed. 'You brim with enthusiasm and it's so invigorating to be around. You're making me think about my cooking. I'm looking forward to what you come up with. While I love baking, what motivates me is knowing that my guests will enjoy the results. I follow recipes that I know people will like. I'm not sure that I have the same passion for food and cooking that you do. Mine is more about pleasing people. Making them happy and comfortable.'

'I want to please people, and for them to enjoy my food, but I guess that I also want to challenge them, encourage them to try new foods and to fall in love with food.' Mina grinned at her. 'That doesn't necessarily make them comfortable, does it?'

Amelie laughed. 'Sometimes you have to push people. Like Kristian. A sweet boy but hopelessly clumsy, especially with women, and has a terrible tendency to say silly things. If he had his way, he'd hide in the corner all the time with Bernhardt and his other friends. Bernhardt is far too sure of himself. There's nothing I can do there, but he has a good heart. I'm trying to bring Kristian out of his shell and give him a bit more confidence in himself. He does get in a fluster and then he just talks.' She raised her eyes heavenward before adding with a touch of indulgent exasperation, 'Without thinking.'

'Ah, I did wonder.'

Amelie beamed at her. 'That's why it's lovely my guests keep coming back. He's much better than he used to be. I have a couple arriving tomorrow…' Her face clouded and her lips crimped together before she said, 'Well, I won't say anything until you've seen them in action. I'd be interested to see what you think. They're English. Both work in Geneva. They've been a couple of times before and this time are staying until Friday.' She paused. 'I did wonder about letting them book, especially as they want to come again for a couple of weekends. I've not confirmed those yet.'

Mina turned to her. 'Do you really choose who comes to stay?'

Amelie let out a light laugh. 'Not terribly good business

practice, is it? Dieter would have been horrified.' She smiled although there was a wistful look in her eye. Amelie didn't talk much about her husband, Dieter, who had been dead for two years. Mina could barely remember him. He'd never accompanied Amelie on her trips to the UK, and on the few visits to her apartment in Basel, he'd been a shy figure who kept himself to himself in the book-lined study. 'Dieter would have been interested in the practical elements, how to manage the energy, portion control, and the bottom line. Whereas I want my guests to be comfortable, and if other guests spoil that enjoyment for others, they're not welcome back.'

'And do you tell them that?' Mina asked, slightly curious.

'Goodness, no. I might just tell them I'm fully booked, like I did with Frau Müller.'

'What did she do wrong?'

Rolling her eyes, Amelie leaned forward. 'She's very negative. It's a drain on the other guests. Everything in life is wrong. She wasn't miserable, but she just didn't want to enjoy life. I suppose she enjoyed moaning more. But that sort of thing is wearing for the other guests. I don't want my guests to be wary, peering about like little bears when they come into the lounge, worrying about who they might have to sit next to at dinner. In a big hotel it doesn't matter so much, you can hide from people.'

'I get that. One year at our campsite, there was an awful couple who pitched their super deluxe ten-man tent with wine fridge, camp beds, and a Weber gas barbecue next to ours, and they had to tell us all the time how much bigger and better their equipment was.' Mina grinned at the memory. 'Derek was hilarious. For every boast they made, he deliberately downplayed things. Told them that our tent was from a skip, our barbecue came from a charity shop, and that he made me and my sister run down to the stream to collect the beer he'd left chilling in the water. On a campsite we could get away from them quite easily. They became the butt of our jokes. But I can see how people like that in close proximity could ruin your weekend.'

'Exactly. I shall have to see how Mr and Mrs Barnes behave this visit. Last time they were here, I nearly didn't let them book again.'

'What did they do wrong?'

Amelie considered the question with a frown before replying. 'I think I'll leave you to make up your own mind. You can tell me what you think.'

'That's not fair.'

'Mina my darling, always so impatient. But I would like your opinion.'

Mina was intrigued to meet the couple and wondered what Amelie meant.

'So, are you going to tell me what sent you hotfooting to Switzerland?'

Amelie's question took her by surprise, and when she didn't say anything, more out of shock than not wanting to confide, Amelie added, 'Of course, you don't have to tell me. I'm just wondering how I might be able to help you.'

'Fix me, you mean?' asked Mina with a sudden grin, realising that was what Amelie did with her guests. Her godmother's guileless smile or insouciant shrug didn't fool her for one minute. 'That's what you do for your guests, isn't it?'

'I'm not sure that I fix people, but I certainly do my best to make them happier.'

'I'm quite happy, really. I just took a wrong turn and it gave me a nasty wake up call.' In a light-hearted jokey way she told Amelie about Simon, the proposal, the public humiliation of discovering he was having an affair, and Smurfgate. Now with a bit of distance she was able to camp up the story and pretend that it was really quite funny even though Simon's words had stung.

Hiding her laughter behind a hand, Amelie shook her head, but tears were streaming down her face. 'That is... I shouldn't say it, but it's very funny, and what he and this Belinda girl deserved. And' her eyes narrowed with that no-one-hurts-mine gleam of loyalty '—they have both behaved very badly. I'm sorry, liebling.' She reached out and laid a hand on Mina's. 'He didn't deserve you, and he has lost something that he is too stupid to prize.'

And that was why Amelie was so special. She was always in Mina's corner, a hundred per cent. There was a special understanding there, and always had been, even when Mina was a little girl. Amelie *got* her.

Mina smiled sadly at her. 'You're right. His loss.' Amelie squeezed her hand again just as the train pulled into their station.

Standing up, they began to bundle back into their coats, hats, scarves, and gloves. As the cold air hit Mina's face when they stepped onto the platform, it sobered her for a moment and she turned to Amelie.

'It wasn't funny, really. He was right. Life should be more than just fun. Like he said, fun is not for keeps. I keep thinking of my parents. Look where being fun got them.'

'Oh, sweetheart.' Amelie laid a hand on her cheek. 'I'm sorry. They were very wrapped up in themselves.'

'Yes, but they egged each other on. Perhaps if one of them had been more sensible, then it might have put the brakes on things. They might still be around.'

'We'll never know,' said Amelie. 'And you can't change things. All you can do is live the best life you can.'

'Mm,' said Mina pensively, once again touching that metaphorical jagged tooth in her mind.

Lapsing into their own thoughts, neither spoke as they took a shortcut across the fields from the station to the chalet, their snowshoes crunch-crunching on the compacted snow. Mina wondered if Amelie still would have been friends with her parents all these years on, whether they would have changed as they got older, whether they might have tamed their ways.

When they arrived back at the chalet, it was almost time to serve the *zigercake* which she'd helped to make earlier that morning. It was completely different to any cake she'd baked before, and as always her tastebuds were salivating in anticipation. Good job she'd been out for a long walk today. Walking in the snow, even with the snowshoes clipped to hiking boots, was jolly hard work, but hopefully had burned a few calories – as at this rate, with all the cake she was consuming she'd be the size of an elephant.

The lounge that evening was much quieter as quite a few people had headed back to the cities for their working week. It meant there were vacant seats in front of the fire, which crackled and hissed in the vast grate. Mina tucked herself into a seat nearest the fire, curling her feet, toasty in heavy wool socks, around her, absently munching her slice of cake as she scribbled some notes in her notebook. After a few quick searches among some of her favourite recipe sites, she was now considering how she might tweak the hazelnut meringue recipe to create her very own *kirscher torte*.

'Problem?' asked Luke, taking possession of the chair next to her and breaking into her thoughts as she sat there frowning and sucking her pen.

'No,' she laughed, making a quick note on the page. 'Not at all. In fact I think I've just cracked it. It's going to need a fruit concentrate, otherwise the meringue will collapse.'

'And in English?'

'Sorry, I was thinking out loud. Working out a new recipe. It's what I do...' She gave a self-deprecating snort. 'Or what I'd like to do. Do you know it's actually in my job description? Recipe Development. Huh, chance would be a fine thing. That place doesn't want any new ideas. They just want the same-old same-old.' And then she slapped her hand over her mouth, horrified at what had spilled out. 'I'm sorry. I hate people who moan about their jobs. My motto is, do something about it. And...' Inside she was appalled at herself.

'I don't think you were moaning, more expressing frustration. But I do agree. I know that feeling, that's why I left my last post. No challenge. I hate seeing people stay in jobs that are gradually destroying their souls. I think you always need to keep moving, keep challenging yourself. And why stay somewhere if you're not enjoying it? There's more to life than work.'

'Yes, although I guess some people need the security. My adopted dad, Derek, has worked for the same company for forty-five years in the same office and I don't think he's ever thought about changing. In fact, I'm not really sure what he does. Work is that bit of the day between nine and five for him. But then again, I've never heard him complain once.'

Whereas if she was completely honest with herself, she'd had more and more doubts about her work in the last year. The mince pie debacle – quite frankly that slightly orange-flavoured pastry had been an absolute triumph, as was the touch of orange zest in the mincemeat – had been only one of several frustrations. The chicken and chorizo risotto, which had been much feted since it had become a top seller, had, in fact, been a very watered-down and bland affair compared to the recipe she'd initially come up with. She sat up straighter as the thought settled in hard and fast. It was time to move on. With crystal clarity, she knew what she *didn't* want to do. She didn't want to work at Freshfoods anymore. Which was fine and dandy. But what did she want to do?

'What?' asked Luke.

'I'm going to look for a new job.' She blurted the words out, surprising herself as much, she thought, as she had him.

He blinked at her. 'And you've just decided that now.'

'Yes,' she said with decided emphasis, the conviction in her gut growing stronger with each passing second. 'Cooking with Amelie in just two days has given me more pleasure than I've had at work in the last three months. I can't believe I didn't see it before. You know when you get on a treadmill and just keep walking. I got myself stuck in a rut. I need to do something different.'

'Any idea what?'

She lifted her hands palms upward. 'Now that is the fifty-million dollar question. I haven't a clue.' She thought of the self-help book lying abandoned upstairs – she was going to have to give the blasted thing some serious attention.

There were only four for dinner, or rather five once Mina had persuaded Amelie to join her, Luke, Claudia, and Frank. Everyone else had left to catch their trains to go back to the cities. For a fondue, it was the perfect number, as they were able to crowd around one of the smaller round tables near the glowing fire in the dining room, with the fondue pot in the middle.

'What do you call this?' asked Mina, keen to learn as always, pointing to the ceramic pan on top of the little burner.

'It's a *caquelon*,' explained Amelie. 'Do start.' She gestured to the two large bowls filled with cubes of bread. 'In the old days, this was a way of using up stale bread and making the cheese go a little further. These days it's quite a rich dish, as I use Gruyère and Vacherin Fribourgeois, which is a lovely semi-soft cheese and quite difficult to find, as it's still traditionally made by hand.'

Mina took one of the long forks and stabbed one of the cubes of bread, watching as Frank went first. With an expert twist of his wrist he managed to bring the bread to his mouth without dripping a drop. She wasn't sure she'd be that successful, but as her mouth watered, greed nudged table manners into second place and she dipped her bread into the rich yellow sauce. Unfortunately she didn't quite have Frank's knack, and the moment she took the bread out of the pot and started to bring it to her mouth, it fell off spattering the tablecloth. So near, so far. Everyone around the table paused.

'When I was a student, if you dropped the bread, you had to kiss the nearest person to you,' said Claudia with a sudden smile and flashing a quick knowing look at her husband.

'When I was a student, I remember certain women who might have be known to drop their bread for that very reason,' replied Frank, his eyes warming as they rested on Claudia.

She shrugged, a mischievous smile lighting her eyes. 'It worked.'

Mina smiled and said glibly, reaching for a fresh piece of bread, 'Poor Luke, I think this might be your unlucky night.' Although there was a sudden warmth inside her at the thought of kissing Luke again.

'I'll cope,' he said, laughing as she managed to scoop her second attempt into her mouth.

'Well, you'll be kissing a lot of people if you are tempted to use fresh bread,' said Amelie. 'I cut and cubed yesterday's bread this morning and left it to dry out. It keeps its shape much better, otherwise it does fall from the fork, often in the pot. I remember my mother doing that once. She thought it would be better to serve fresh bread, she was worried what people would think if she served stale bread to them.'

'Mmm, this is so delicious,' murmured Mina, already dipping another piece of bread. 'I'm going to have to buy myself a *caquelon* to take back.' She could already imagine setting it up on a winter's evening in her flat, with a few select friends that wouldn't include Belinda or Simon – except now the thought of going home didn't hold so much appeal.

'And easy,' sighed Amelie sitting back in her chair, stifling a yawn. Mina was glad they'd persuaded her to join them. She suspected Amelie might not have eaten this evening if she hadn't insisted she join them.

'Monday nights are my favourites,' said Luke. 'And Sundays actually.'

'Not school nights?' asked Mina, as she'd got teacher friends for whom Sunday nights were filled with dread.

'No.' Luke batted a hand as if pushing that idea away. 'You can chill after a good weekend. Reflect on how great it's been, and then you have the promise of a bright shiny new week ahead. A chance to start again, put things right, or just look forward to new experiences.'

'That's a lovely attitude, Luke,' said Claudia.

'Very positive,' said Mina, quite struck by what he'd said.

'As long as you've had a good weekend,' said Frank a little gloomily, although Claudia tapped him on the forearm in rebuke.

Luke shrugged. 'Bad things happen, but you can't let them scar you. You can't stop them, but you can choose how you react to them. You can choose to be positive or negative, happy or sad, angry or calm. None of us have any control over what life is going to throw at us, but if we respond in a positive manner we can make our lives so much better.' He paused as he realised that everyone was hanging on his words.

Mina wondered if perhaps she ought to be listening to him, rather than her self-help book.

'Sorry. Didn't mean to get on my soapbox.' He smiled at Mina, 'I'm really looking forward to the week ahead.'

She smiled back. Snowboarding. Going shopping with Amelie. Just being here in the mountains. Her week was looking pretty good too.

Chapter Twelve

M ina stood and stared. Her eyes scanned the broad shopping aisle, trying to take it in, every square inch of every single shelf devoted to chocolate. Never, in her entire life, had she seen so much chocolate in one place. Every variety, size, and type of bar possible was represented: chocolate bars with hazelnuts, rice crispies, honeycomb, and raisins; chocolate bars flavoured with orange, mint, and coffee; chocolate pralines; chocolate sticks; chocolate tiles; big bags, small bags; chunky bars, slim bars. The plethora of brands in rainbow colours was mind-boggling, some of which she'd never heard of, as well as the familiar; the purple packs of Milka, the boxes of Merci, and the airport favourite, Toblerone.

She turned open-mouthed to Amelie, unable to say a word.

'Why don't I leave you to explore for a while? I'll go and do some shopping.' Amelie gave her an amused smile.

They'd set off early, leaving breakfast out for the guests,

and Johannes on call if they needed anything, and driven to Brig in Amelie's big VW Passat estate to stock up for the week at the wholesalers, Prodega.

Visiting an overseas supermarket ranked high as Mina's idea of heaven as she loved seeing the different products. Coming back on the channel tunnel from the very occasional camping trip to Normandy, she'd always insisted that her parents stop at the big Carrefour just so that she could get her fix. They would sit patiently outside with a bottle of beer each while she prowled the supermarket, fascinated by different-shaped pastas, weird and wonderful tinned vegetables, incredible salamis and cheeses, bowled over by the sheer selection of yoghurts and desserts.

The sight of all that chocolate strengthened her resolve to talk to Johannes – she wanted to know more She had to persuade him to let her watch him making his products. There was nothing like first-hand experience when you wanted to learn about something. She'd been on dozens of courses, sourdough breadmaking, fish filleting, French patisserie, knife skills, as well as the more dull hygiene and environmental health courses – you name it, she'd done it. This was her chance to learn about chocolate.

She caught up with Amelie in the bakery section, which smelled tantalising. 'This place is amazing. Everything looks so good.' The shelves were packed with glistening loaves of *Zopf*, a soft egg-washed plaited bread that Amelie served for breakfast, along with seed-topped loaves, golden rolls and a range of flaky croissants and other pastries.

'It is. The quality is excellent and it makes my life easier.

I sometimes cheat and buy their fresh baked goods because their pastries are excellent, although I try not.'

'I don't think that's cheating. You can't do everything.'

Amelie lifted her shoulders but didn't say anything. Once again Mina thought she looked tired.

'Seriously, if the quality is good, you should give yourself a break sometimes. Why make life more difficult for yourself?'

Amelie laughed. 'You're quite right. I am my own worst enemy. Silly. I don't know why I can't let go, sometimes.'

'Because it's your pride and joy, and your reputation rests on it,' said Mina, inwardly sympathising. It was hard to let go when you'd worked hard at something.

'It was a dream for so long.' Amelie sighed and rubbed at the bar of the shopping trolley. 'One that I never really thought would come true, if I'm honest. Dieter and I talked about it, but I'm not sure we'd ever have left Basel or have been prepared to make the changes to make it happen. It was one of those "one day" ideas. When we were retired, or ready to retire. The truth is, I think if we'd retired we would have been less likely to move, to leave our friends, the life we knew. It makes me sad that Dieter never saw it, and that he died too soon. He was only fifty-seven.' She shook her head, her eyes glistening with tears. 'I do miss him. But then again, if he hadn't died when he did, I wouldn't be here. His dying was the impetus to make me move, open the guest house, and do the things we talked about, even if it took me a few years to make it happen.'

Mina put her arm around her godmother. 'I know he would have been very proud of what you've achieved. All the guests love the chalet. That's why they keep coming back.'

'Thank you. Right.' Mina almost felt Amelie girding her loins as the other woman glanced into the trolley which was already piled high with several boxes of eggs, a couple of large bags of sugar, icing sugar, and flour, as well as several packs of butter. 'Have you decided what ingredients you need for your recipes?'

Realising that the subject was closed, Mina took her cue. 'I need some sort of cherry purée, but it's probably best if I make it from whole cherries, which are clearly not yet in season.'

'No problem. You can either buy frozen, or there are some good-quality coulis.' They spent a little while debating the pros and cons before opting to buy extra frozen cherries, as Amelie used them in her *Kirschenbrottorte*.

They wrapped up the shopping trip with hot chocolate and pastries on the lively *Bahnhofstrasse*, where Mina learned a little bit about the busy town. Brig had grown and expanded thanks to its unique location at the head of the famous Simplon Pass, which cut through the mountains all the way to Italy.

By the time they returned to the chalet, the car was piled high with fresh sheets and towels that they'd picked up from the laundry and a week's supply of shopping.

'Hello ladies,' said Luke who greeted them at the foot of the stairs. He looked as if he were just going out. 'Successful trip?'

'Very,' said Mina, already thinking about her cherry-flavoured meringues.

Amelie hopped out of the car, opened up the boot, and took out the first bundle of towels.

Mina rushed to join her and Luke put down his skis and poles. 'Let me give you a hand.'

'Oh, it's fine. Don't you worry,' said Amelie. 'Where are you going this afternoon?'

Luke ignored her and was already moving around to the back of the car and lifting out the heaviest crate of shopping before saying. 'I'm taking it easy today, just taking the track to Münster. So I've got plenty time.'

'Alright for some,' said Johannes, stamping his way over, knocking snow from his hiking boots. Without another word, he lifted one of the boxes of shopping from the car and carried it inside.

From his timely appearance, Mia suspected that he'd been lying in wait and often helped Amelie with the shopping. She watched him navigate the path with the heavy box, shouldering his way through the front door ahead of Luke, before she picked up the plastic-wrapped stack of sheets from the back seat of the car. The slippery package was difficult to grasp and she was grateful when Luke met her at the top of the stairs and took it from her arms. Johannes pushed past, head down, ready to get the next load.

With Luke and Johannes helping, it didn't take too long to unload the car, although Mina built up a sheen of sweat with all three trips up the stairs into the chalet.

Johannes muttered, '*Das Alles*?' which she guessed meant, is that everything?

Amelie nodded but then reached out and grabbed his forearm. 'Thank you so much, Johannes. I don't know what I'd do with you.' Mina was struck by the quick glint of gratification in his eye.

'Right, well if you don't need any further help, I'm away,' said Luke. 'Mina, are you still up for snowboarding tomorrow?'

'Yes, if that's still OK?'

'Sure. About ten o'clock. I've got a Skype call first thing, but then I'm all yours.' His eyes sparkled in sudden flirtation.

'Make sure you are,' Mina replied, thinking that two could play that game. Flirting was like breathing to someone like Luke, he couldn't help himself.

He grinned at her and disappeared out of the door with a casual wave. 'See you later.'

Amelie watched him go. 'I think he likes you.'

'Of course he does,' said Mina with a quick jokey smile.

'You don't like him?' Amelie frowned.

'I do but he's… well, he's not someone you'd take seriously. But he is a lot of fun, and I enjoy his company.'

'There's a bit more to him than you realise.' Amelie shot her a sharp sidelong glance.

'Hmm,' said Mina. She knew Luke's type, she knew it inside out. He might as well have been her twin. They could have a lot of fun together, but it was never going to go any further than that. Before Simon, she'd had plenty of fun, and look at how those relationships had turned out. Jon owed her money, Jake stood her up more times than not, and Phil had abandoned her halfway up a Welsh mountain. Fun was not part of her future plans.

Once she and Amelie had put the shopping away, loaded up the linen cupboard with the bouncy, fresh-smelling towels and the crisp cotton sheets, and had a quick baguette with slices of Emmental and cured ham, Mina rolled up her sleeves and got out her notebook. She'd worked out the ratios of ingredients, but how much cherry purée she'd need to add to get enough flavour without wrecking the texture of the meringue was going to be down to trial and error. First of all she cooked up a pan of the frozen cherries to reduce them down, adding a little sugar, but not too much, as she wanted to retain the tartness of the fruit, which would balance against the sweetness of the meringue.

Amelie was fascinated by the process, and while she was making that evening's dinner, a pork and bean stew, would occasionally ask a question.

'Do you want some kirsch in there?'

Mina shook her head. 'No. I want sharp fruitiness. But I might try it the next time.'

'Next time?'

'I'll try lots of different variations of the purée once I'm happy with the ratio of purée to meringue.' She explained that she'd decided to make up one large batch of basic meringue mix and then divide it into four and add different amounts of purée so that she could work out which was going to work best. 'I'm going to need a couple of guinea pigs to do some taste-testing for me. Then I'm thinking about trying to make a chocolate mousse meringue.'

Amelie laughed. 'Well, you're not going to have to look very far. You can try them out on the guests at coffee and cake.'

'Are you sure? They might get sick of cherry meringue quite soon.'

'How many times will you make it?'

'It depends. I'm hopeful four batches will crack it. The main thing is to make sure I write down the exact quantities, so that I can remember what did work.'

Amelie studied her for a moment before saying with a gentle shake of her head, 'I'm surprised you have that much patience.'

'Surprises everyone,' replied Mina with a grin. 'When it comes to getting it right, I don't mind doing it over and over again. Ask me to do that with anything else and I know I'd get bored. Food is different. I love the science of it. And knowing that things respond in certain ways under certain conditions. Baking is very scientific and recipes have to be very precise.'

'You should write a recipe book.'

'I've thought about it but...' She shrugged. 'There are hundreds. What would be different about mine?'

'I don't know, but a resourceful girl like you could come up with something, I'm sure.'

Mina wasn't so sure. It was a crowded market, with celebrity chefs taking the lead. She'd often thought about starting a food blog, but then she needed something unique, a hook that would make it different. And did she have the discipline? Was it something she *really* wanted to do? It seemed she was really good at working out what she *didn't* want to do. Just not so good at identifying what she *did* want to do.

The afternoon passed quickly, and before she knew it, four o'clock was almost upon them.

'My new arrivals will be here any minute,' said Amelie. 'The ones I was telling you about.'

'The ones you want my opinion on,' said Mina, stretching and rolling her shoulders, which were complaining about her being hunched over the kitchen table for too long.

'Yes,' replied Amelie with a naughty twinkle in her bright eyes, tilting her head as if listening. 'And I think that might be them.'

She hurried out of the kitchen door into the reception area and Mina followed.

'David, watch where you're going.' A slight, dark-haired woman rolling her eyes stepped forward as her husband managed to bash one of his cases into the leather sofa, narrowly missing the German teenager sitting head-bent over her phone. 'So sorry,' she said to the girl who didn't so much as look up, before glowering back at the unfortunate David. 'You are useless.'

Mina caught Amelie's eye but Amelie had perfected her poker face and simply smiled.

'Sarah and David, welcome back. How lovely to see you.'

'Huh, are you sure? With David wrecking your furniture. I hope there isn't a tear in the leather. He's so clumsy.'

'I'm sure it will be fine. How was your journey?'

Sarah's mouth pursed. 'Fine. Except David had booked the early flight instead of the mid-morning one, so we had to get up at silly o'clock and now I feel exhausted.'

'Yes,' said Amelie, with a smile at poor old David, who was really getting in the neck, 'but if you'd got a later flight, you'd have missed coffee and cake, and you wouldn't have had time to relax before dinner. Come on, let's get you some cake and coffee.'

Before anyone could move, Luke came in through the door, shaking off his scarf and peeling a matching red beany hat from his head.

'Ah, Mina! I've been thinking—'

'Luke, isn't it?' The woman's sharp voice rang out, and before he could finish, she marched a few steps to meet him. 'We met last time we were here. Sarah McDonald.' She stabbed her hand out in a formal gesture that a robot might have been proud of.

'Oh, yes. Hi,' said Luke with one of his easy smiles, taking her hand and shaking it. 'And it's Dave, isn't it?'

Before the other man could respond, Sarah had chipped in again, 'Yes. We were here in November. Lovely weekend. And it's so lovely to be back, although I would have liked to come in January, but David's work was ridiculously busy, and for some reason—' she sighed heavily '—he couldn't get the time off work.'

'Well, you're here now,' said Amelie. 'And it's lovely to

see you. Your room is all ready for you. Why don't you go up and get settled? I'll make sure we save you some coffee and cake.'

'Oh that's fine,' said Sarah waving an airy hand. 'Dave, you take the cases up and I'll wait for you down here. I've been so looking forward to some of your delicious cake, dear Amelie. You have got such a wonderful light touch. Dave's the baker in our house.' Her mouth pursed. 'Of course he's nowhere near as good as you.'

Dave shrugged and his Eeyore face looked resigned.

'I'm sure that's not true,' said Amelie, tucking her arm into his and giving him a sparkling smile. 'I think it's lovely that he bakes at all. So many people don't bother these days. What's your favourite cake to make, Dave?'

The clouds on his face parted and the wrinkles fanning from his mouth cleared. 'I like making lemon drizzle cake. Lovely, moist sponge with nice, tart, sugary topping. Learned that one from my gran. Great woman.'

'I always think it's wonderful when recipes are handed down through the family.'

Sarah snorted. 'Dave's family are not that posh. His gran probably scribbled the recipe on the back of a pack of Benson & Hedges.'

'I remember cooking with my grandmother in this very house,' said Amelie as if she hadn't heard the dismissive comment. 'Cooking the same recipes brings back lovely memories. Leave the bags for now. Come have coffee, and I've made a lovely gingerbread cake which is just what you need after your journey. How was the train?'

Before Sarah, her mouth downturned in a crescent of

obvious displeasure, could voice her disagreement and reiterate her earlier demand that her husband take up the cases, Amelie had steered him through the archway into the lounge area and was guiding him to a spot next to Claudia.

Mina was about to catch Luke's eye, wondering what he'd been about to say, but Sarah beat her to it. 'So Luke, what have you been up to today?' Neatly elbowing Mina out of the way, the other woman fell into step beside him, and without allowing him to respond, began talking at him as they followed Amelie and Dave into the lounge.

With a grin, Mina shook her head to herself. It would be interesting to see what course Amelie intended in her attempt to fix the overbearing Sarah and her poor downtrodden husband.

Chapter Thirteen

The next few days passed quickly as Mina spent the mornings in the kitchen perfecting her *kirscher torte* recipe and the afternoons exploring the cross-country ski trails with Claudia and Amelie.

Her godmother continued to marvel over her uncharacteristic patience, as she tested several different variants of the recipe, making copious notes, but Mina was in her element. She loved this part of the process and it further reinforced how stifled she'd been at work and how little job satisfaction she'd derived in the last year.

On Friday, Amelie shooed her out of the kitchen and she spent a glorious day snowboarding with Luke, after admitting to herself that she had been avoiding him, something she regretted the minute she got out onto the slopes. Her misspent childhood in the skatepark came into its own and she found that snowboarding came more easily than she'd expected, although as always Luke proved to be an endlessly patient teacher.

They returned to the chalet having been wedged in on a packed train as the weekend skiers flocked in to the resorts.

'Thanks for taking me out,' said Mina, as she shook off her coat in the boot room and sat down to take her boots off. She'd had a wonderful day. A bit too wonderful. Luke had been a perfect gentleman, not one kiss or attempted kiss, and if he'd held her hand a couple of times, either helping her up or leading her up from the station, he just happened to be a very tactile person. He was also incredibly easy to be with. She couldn't remember the last time she'd laughed like she had today or enjoyed someone's company as much as his. Being with him was like drinking champagne all the time. She felt fizzy and sparkly, energised and excited. But, she told herself sternly, that wasn't real life. You couldn't drink champagne every day.

'My pleasure,' he said, giving her one of his broad smiles, his eyes twinkling, and she knew he meant it in the fullest sense of the word. She loved that he always seemed to be so happy and positive, embracing life with lively energy and enthusiasm. In some ways it was quite intoxicating and in others inspiring. It was also very attractive, and her heart chose to respond with one of its wayward flutters, but she managed to hold his gaze. It wasn't fair. He was so damn gorgeous.

'Not only did I have a great day but it helped clear my head. I'm starting a new train commission this week. A new suitcase is being couriered to me and I find getting out in the fresh air and exercise helps spark the old creativity.' He grinned and tugged down the zip of his coat. 'And I've come up with an idea. The client for the next commission wants a by-moonlight theme and I was racking my brains trying to think what that might look like.' He tugged off the coat and tossed it on the bench next them before sitting down next to her.

'Ooh, that sounds tough.' Mina was relieved the conversation had taken a less personal tack.

'The train track is going to run along the seafront and I'll have the moon reflected on the surface of the sea.' He circled the air with one finger as if tracing the route of his imagined train. 'And I'll have little pools of light under the lampposts and a blue wash over everything.'

'Clever.' At times like this, she realised there was more to him than met the eye. How did a man who was as vibrant and full of life as he was, have the painstaking patience to put together those intricate, beautiful models? She'd seen Uncle D at work and knew that the lifelike, miniature replica scenery took hours to create.

Having kicked off his boots, he rose and gave her a quick modest bow and took her coat and hung it up next to his.

'And I've had a result today,' she said, remembering her revelation at the top of one of the slopes. 'I'm going to make my *kirscher torte* a slightly different shape to the original that it's inspired by. I'm going to shape the meringue on top into little peaks, so that they look like the mountains at sunset. You know, when they turn slightly pink.'

'You had me at meringue. I've got a very sweet tooth.' He patted his extremely trim stomach and Mina's mind went where it shouldn't, imagining a smooth stomach and dark hair arrowing downward. Despite all her pep talks she couldn't deny the strong sexual attraction she felt for him. Who wouldn't? He was pretty perfect.

'Looks like we've both had a productive day. Although, I've had another brilliant idea as well.'

'What's that?' asked Mina, finally toeing off her boots. 'And what were you going to say the other evening?'

He looked down at her, a faint smile on his face as if considering telling her, and then shook his head. 'Same thing actually, but today I've decided to keep it a secret, but I think you'll like it.'

'I love surprises,' said Mina, realising that she was usually the one that did the surprising, although it hadn't worked out too well the last time she organised one, she thought, as she remembered Simon's shocked face and that quick side-long look at Belinda. The surprise had definitely been on her. Shaking the memory from her head, she stood up. 'I'm going to go and see if Amelie needs any help with dinner before she serves cake.' She didn't voice her concern, but her godmother was looking more and more tired.

'OK,' said Luke, seeming a little preoccupied. 'I'll see you in the lounge in a while.'

The kitchen, as always, brimmed with delicious smells and Amelie was hard at work putting the finishing touches to an enormous pastry-topped pie.

'That looks good.'

'It's *Churer fleischtorte*,' said Amelie with an impish smile.

'And you're going to tell me what that is,' said Mina, already curious as to what was in the pastry case.

'It comes from the city of Chur, of course, and it contains

ground pork, bacon, milk-soaked bread, and red wine. It won't win any beauty contests,' said Amelie with that incredible turn of English phrasing that never ceased to amaze Mina, 'but it tastes delicious.'

'I'll look forward to trying it. I came in to see if you needed any help.' Surreptitiously, she studied the purple shadows beneath Amelie's eyes.

'I'll enjoy your company if you'd like to stay, and you could peel some potatoes for me. And,' Amelie said with a teasing smile, 'tell me all about your snowboarding adventures.'

Mina laughed. 'I think I had more faceplants than adventures. I might have a few bruises. Luke says I want to run before I can walk, but I had a great time and I'm determined to master it.'

She peeled the potatoes quickly and asked for another job. 'You're supposed to be on holiday, not playing sous chef,' grumbled Amelie, although she still handed over a pile of carrots to peel and slice.

'Yes, but I came to see you as well.'

'You see me in the kitchen every morning and yesterday we had a lovely run out.'

'We did,' Mina agreed. They'd spent a couple of hours skiing along the valley to the village of Blitzingen where they'd stopped for hot chocolate in a pretty little café by the river. The route, which followed the River Rhone, had been a nice easy one and Mina was really starting to get the hang of cross-country skiing. On the couple of occasions she'd been out with Claudia, the other woman had helped her to improve her technique.

'And I'm quite capable of managing without you,' said Amelie, her face suddenly brightening with that naughty pixie smile of hers. 'Besides, I drafted in a helper this morning. Dave has made his lemon drizzle cake for everyone.'

'Has he now?' Mina made a thing of dropping her knife in mock surprise. 'I thought I was the only one you trusted in your kitchen, and more to the point, how on earth did you wangle that one?' Even after relatively short acquaintance over cake and coffee and dinners, Mina was very grateful that Amelie hadn't seated her next to the acerbic and opinionated Sarah. It was clear to everyone that Sarah liked to have Dave under her thumb, quite literally, at all times.

'Yes, and next week, he's going to make his legendary chocolate log.' Amelie grinned and looked over her shoulder before whispering, 'Sarah was complaining yesterday, over cake, about how she was desperate for a lie-in and to not have to do anything too strenuous today. I suggested that she sat by the fire and read a book, we have a good selection.' There was a bookshelf in the lounge on the back wall, with a variety of books of different genres in different languages, presumably left by previous guests. 'But she was worried that Dave would be bored as "he's not very resourceful" and then she would feel guilty, and then she wouldn't be able to read a book.'

Mina could imagine exactly how the conversation might have gone; she was only surprised she hadn't actually heard Sarah's complaints. No one would have described the woman as softly-spoken; her words boomed out like a foghorn with the volume turned to max.

'I said that she would be doing me an enormous favour if she would lend Dave to me.'

Mina marvelled at Amelie's clever psychology. By requesting Sarah's permission, she'd played to the woman's vanity and tendency to want to control her husband.

'Very clever.'

'I thought so,' replied Amelie with an insouciant grin.

Dave appeared in the kitchen at ten-to-four, and Mina smiled to herself at his barely concealed schoolboy pride.

'Have you seen my cake?' he asked.

'I have, it looks wonderful.'

'Amelie says I can carry it in.' His face fell for a second. 'I sound like a ten-year-old, don't I?'

'No,' said Amelie, suddenly stern. 'You sound like a man with a gift for baking, who wants to share his skill with new friends.'

As if by magic, his shoulders straightened and Mina mentally high-fived Amelie. Her godmother had an innate gift of understanding what made people tick. What a precious skill, and one she'd love to emulate. Perhaps if she'd been more mindful of what drove other people and what they wanted, she might have made things with Simon work. Then she shook her head. That was rubbish: she and Simon had been totally incompatible from day one, neither of them had wanted to recognise it, and for the first time, she understood he was as much at fault as her. It was a relief to realise that she wasn't the only one who had messed up.

She followed Dave into the lounge, carrying the tea plates and dessert forks. With the kindness she'd come to expect from the guests when they were all together, everyone oohed and aahed over the cake. The finish didn't quite have Amelie's professional precision, but the moist sponge glistened with lemon-soaked sugar and it smelled delicious. Mina noticed that Amelie watched Sarah's face like a hawk, almost as if she were preparing to jump to the defence of her chick.

This, she realised, was an important moment, and as soon as she was served her slice of cake, she took a forkful.

'Oh Dave,' she exclaimed, completely truthfully. 'This is amazing. You should go on *Bake Off*.' The sponge was light, fluffy, and moist, and the subtle flavour of lemon came through without being overpowering and was perfectly balanced by the sharp acidic hit of the lemon sugar drizzle topping.

Amelie shot her an approving smile and they exchanged a conspiratorial nod. Job done.

Sarah sat up and preened in Dave's reflected glory as the other guests began to congratulate him. Inside, Mina felt a warm glow, as he for once held court without his wife interrupting or putting him down. In fact she looked fondly on, with a definite touch of pride.

Mina wanted to laugh and wondered if they would be allowed to book a room here again.

As the chatter settled, she sank back into her seat, feeling the slight ache in her muscles, acutely aware that there was no sign of Luke, although she had no shortage of company. Benrhardt and Kristian had arrived, bringing with them Uta, who had popped in to say hello and sample Amelie's famous cake and coffee.

'I couldn't book to stay here, but I'm going to keep trying,' she said to Mina as they chatted by the fire. Mina resolved to introduce the other woman to Amelie when she next got the chance, feeling sure that Amelie would approve of the cheerful, friendly German.

The four of them were busy talking about the weekend plans when Luke appeared. He came straight over, waving a piece of paper, grinning from ear to ear.

'Hi guys,' he said, perching on the arm of the sofa next to Mina.

'You look like the rat that has taken the cream,' said Kristian.

'Yes,' said Luke, cutting across Bernhardt who was clearly about to correct his friend. 'I am and I have. Mina,' he announced grandly, 'I've booked tickets for the cheese and chocolate train. We're going on Wednesday.'

For a moment Mina was blindsided by surprise – but also a bolt of irritation. Wednesday was the day that Johannes was making his next batch of chocolate. She wasn't supposed to know, but Amelie had let slip, and she was really hoping to persuade him between now and then to let her observe or even help. It was her one opportunity. But Luke looked so delighted with himself, how could she disappoint him? Had Simon felt like this when she'd sprung the indoor skydiving on him when he was supposed to be playing an away match? Or when she'd booked out the whole bowling alley for his thirtieth birthday, when he'd been hoping for dinner at Ottolenghi in London.

Luckily the others unwittingly jumped into rescue her before she could say anything.

'I've always wanted to do that,' said Uta. 'What time does the train leave?'

'Me too,' said Kristian.

'The scenery is spectacular,' said Bernhardt. 'It is one of the great scenic railway trips and I really ought to do it one day.'

Mina realised she still hadn't said anything, and that Luke was watching her, a slight look of worry on his face.

'That's brilliant, thank you,' she said. And it was, really. She was being churlish. The trip would be fantastic. Actually, she told herself, she was being extremely churlish. Cheese and chocolate. A vintage train. What was not to like?

'I can't wait,' she said, smiling broadly at him as his face softened in relief while the others discussed the practicality of getting to Montreux, what time the train left, and what they'd be doing at work that day in their respective cities.

Luke winked at her and she recalled their conversation on the mountain. She'd far rather be here.

Chapter Fourteen

The train, waiting like a show pony on the platform, gleamed with old-fashioned patina; the vintage Pullman coaches were painted in smart cream and navy livery and decorated with flowing gold script. Along the length of the train, the open doors reminded her of a line of smart soldiers ready to welcome everyone onboard.

'Oh my goodness.' Mina whipped her phone out of her pocket. 'I need to get a picture of this for Uncle D. He would love it.' Taking a few snaps for the family WhatsApp group, she waited a minute, absorbing the atmosphere on the platform. It was both sedate and festive, an unusual combination – as if people wanted to respect the old-fashioned stateliness of the Pullman carriages at the same time as containing their excitement and anticipation for the forthcoming trip.

Luke linked his arm through hers, as always in complete accord.

'Wonderful, isn't it?'

'Yes,' she said, because it really was. 'I'm so glad you went ahead and booked.'

'I was a bit worried that perhaps I might have been a bit presumptuous.'

'Look at this.' She swept out an arm to indicate the train. 'Who would want to miss this?' She paused, remembering her brief moment of ingratitude, before adding, 'Thank you so much for organising this. It's a real treat.' Giving in to sudden impulse she rose on her toes and kissed him on the cheek. As soon as her lips touched his smooth skin and she smelled the fresh, clean-with-a hint-of-lemon scent of him, she wondered why she was fighting her attraction for him so hard. He was gorgeous, sexy, fun to be with, and made her heart beat faster every damn minute she was with him. Why not just give in and accept that there was something between them? Instead of focusing on worrying about what she didn't want, perhaps she should just live for the moment, like he seemed to do. She'd brought that stupid self-help book with her, which was no flipping help at all, because they'd be spending a long time on the train – but suddenly she was wondering whether it really was worth reading any more. But she wasn't going to worry about that now, instead she was going to take the day as it came, enjoy every minute – after all, cheese *and* chocolate, and a day with Luke sounded pretty perfect to her.

They boarded the train and found their reserved seats in one of the vintage coaches which immediately made Mina think of film sets and *Poirot*. She reached out to touch the plush, roomy, velvet seats, her foot scuffing real carpet on the floor.

'This is…' She stared at the polished brass luggage racks on the walls. 'Deluxe travel.' Each seat was more like an armchair, and as Mina sat down opposite Luke, she took out her phone again to take more pictures. Uncle D would just adore this, she had to persuade him and Auntie M to take a trip out here.

There was a palpable air of excitement as people boarded and found their seats.

'Thank you again, I can't believe, how gorgeous it is,' whispered Mina. 'I'm going to have to try and persuade my aunt and uncle to come. Uncle D would get such a kick out of this.' She beamed as she snapped away examining every inch of their seating area, running her hands over the glossy pull-up table, and rubbing her fingers against the nap of the velvet to darken it. Any moment she expected a troop of glamorous 1920s passengers to come gliding past, the women in elegant fashionable fur trimmed coats and cute cloche hats, and the men in smart tweed suits and trilbys.

'I feel like we should have dressed up,' she observed, picturing herself in a cherry-red bow-fronted hat.

'Yes,' said Luke. 'That would be fun. Providing it wasn't lederhosen.'

She laughed and nudged him. 'No, you idiot. I was thinking more *Murder on the Orient Express*.'

He laughed along with her.

'Well, this looks like fun,' said a cheery voice, and to Mina's surprise, Uta appeared.

'Hello! What are you doing here?' she asked.

'I had holiday time, and it sounded fun. Kristian and Bernhardt are coming too. It's one of the things you always think about doing and never do. So here we are.' Uta's sunny smile encompassed the two of them, and Mina found herself smiling back, although inside she felt a tug of disappointment. She didn't dare look at Luke. Had he felt the promise of the day shimmering in the air back on the platform?

'Here you are.' Bernhardt's hearty cry rang out. 'No sign of Kristian yet?'

Luke stood up, shook Bernhardt's hand, and subtly changed seats to sit down next to Mina while Uta was sorting herself out, taking off her coat and unravelling a very long scarf.

Just before the train was about to depart, Kristian came charging along the train and almost walked past them without seeing them. It was only Uta calling him that made him slow his flustered, agitated pace. He collapsed in the seat on the other side of the aisle, his chest heaving.

'Thought I wasn't going to make it. Tight connection.' He fanned his pink face, peeling his ski jacket off before grinning at everyone. 'Here we all are. Isn't this fun? My mum wanted to come. Good job she didn't I'm not sure she'd have made that run.'

Mina couldn't help but smile. There was something adorably dorkish about Kristian and she felt Luke nudge her knee as if in conspiratorial agreement. Bernhardt, on the other hand, rolled his eyes. Just then the train pulled out from the station and Uta clapped her hands. 'We're off.'

Mina laughed. 'It feels like we're on a school trip.' There was a definite sense of anticipation throughout the carriage.

They weren't the only ones excited by the thought of cheese and chocolate.

'I did go to a cheese factory on a trip once,' volunteered Kristian. 'It was really boring.' Everyone looked at him, Bernhardt rolled his eyes again, and Uta shook her head. 'I didn't like cheese then,' he protested, holding up his hands in surrender, realising that he'd said the wrong thing.

'I love cheese,' said Mina. 'But I love chocolate more.' They all laughed at her dreamy sigh. 'No, seriously. Chocolate has a magic about it, don't you think?'

Next to her, Luke tilted his head and raised an eyebrow.

'Er, hello. Who insisted on having half my chocolate bar, the very first time I met you?'

'I was hungry.' He nudged her thigh with his, but left it pressed against hers, as if wanting to remind her of the intimacy of that first train journey.

She tutted. 'How many people do you know who really don't like chocolate?'

Uta shook her head and so did Bernhardt, while Kristian screwed up his face in thought.

'I have a great-aunt who doesn't like coffee-flavoured chocolate,' he finally announced.

'That doesn't count,' said Bernhardt, quick to depress his comment. 'I think most people do like chocolate.' He gave Mina a charming smile. 'Does that make it magic?'

'It's the theobromide,' said Luke, as if producing a rabbit from a hat.

Mina chuckled. 'Theobromine, but nice try. Actually that's a stimulant like caffeine, but there are a number of chemicals in chocolate, including a neurotransmitter, anandamide, which comes from the Sanskrit for joy or bliss. It stimulates the brain in a similar way to cannabis.'

'Not just a pretty face,' said Bernhardt, with an admiring look at her. 'I'm very impressed.'

From the seat opposite, Uta did a very bad job of hiding her smirk at his slightly pompous words.

'I'm a food scientist. Lots of chemicals in foods. Although to be honest, the ones in chocolate are mere traces, you'd have to eat a hell of a lot of chocolate to get high. It's the sugar that people are really tasting. But there's something about the smooth texture of chocolate and the smell.'

'We get it, you're a chocolate junkie,' said Uta. 'Talking of which, look what's headed our way.' She nodded towards the very smiley lady bringing coffee and croissants through the carriage pushing a trolley.

'You can't possibly eat another croissant,' teased Mina, as Luke selected a pain au chocolat. They'd had two on the journey here from Brig, although admittedly they had left at five in the morning. Poor Johannes had been co-opted into driving them to the station.

'Watch me. I'm a growing boy.'

'I guess I burned a million calories yesterday,' said Mina, selecting one for herself.

'Were you skiing?' asked Bernhardt. 'I was at a desk all day.'

'Sorry, yes. It was a gorgeous day. The air here feels so fresh, I just want to be outdoors all the time.'

'You've been lucky with the weather so far,' said Luke. 'There are days when it's a white-out and you can't get out.

Too many of those days and people start getting cabin fever, especially people who have come up just to ski.'

Mina glanced up at the bright blue sky, realising that she'd been extremely lucky with the weather since she'd been here. All that snow, piled inches deep on the roofs of the houses, looking so picturesque and harmless, had to have come from somewhere. Would it snow while she was still here? Although everyone at the ski chalet discussed the weather for the coming day almost obsessively, she hadn't once thought about checking the forecast while she was here. She wondered if the village ever got snowed in.

She looked out of the train window; they'd left the snow behind today. As their train from Brig had travelled nearer to Montreux, the snow had gradually melted away. Funny, in just a short space of time she'd forgotten what green fields looked like. The train moved at a steady speed and they all quietened as they munched their croissants and drank hot milky chocolate. Leaning back in her seat, she watched the beautiful countryside, feeling a delicious lassitude and sense of peace.

The track edged along the side of a steep hill and across the valley, dramatic tree-covered peaks, with lines of dark firs clinging to the contours of the landscape, bordered the skyline. The sharp points of the trees were crowded together like indomitable battalions of centurions standing on guard. Mina craned her neck a little to take in the pretty village that came into view, struck by the vibrant colours of the day. The orange terracotta tiles covering the familiar inverted V-shaped roofs, contrasted beautifully with the rich green of the fields and, above, the brilliant blue of the sky. A single church like a benign angel dominated the village, its whitewashed walls with their long, tall windows towering over the nearby houses, the impressive large square tower topped with a black dome which looked as if it were watching over the village and all who lived there.

A few fawn, doe-eyed cows grazed in the field alongside the track, some looking up, although with marked disinterest. The colours suggested spring was on its way. What would Reckingen be like in the spring, in the summer? Mina frowned for a moment. She didn't want to go home. She'd completely fallen in love with this country. The sudden realisation stabbed right through her with such intensity that she actually gasped out loud.

'You OK?' asked Luke. The others busy chatting hadn't noticed.

'Yes. No. I'm not sure,' she said, a little discombobulated by the absolute conviction that filled her. She wanted to stay in Switzerland. In Reckingen. She wanted to see the seasons change, be outside as much as she could, ski, walk and cook.

'That sounds confusing.' He put a hand over hers, hidden from sight between them.

She gave him a brilliant smile. 'No, it's not confusing at all. It's…' She paused. 'Perfect. I know what I want to do.' And suddenly all the reasons for keeping him at arm's length didn't seem quite so important now.

'Always good,' said Luke, clearly not understanding – and why should he? He hadn't been trying to make sense of that bloody book for the last few days.

She pulled it out of her bag. 'This. I've identified all the things I *don't* want to do, but I was having a hard time deciding what I *did* want to do.'

Luke looked thoroughly confused. 'Why do you need a book to do that? Isn't it simple? You do the things that make you happy. That make you feel glad to be alive. And avoid the things that don't. If you're not happy, you change things. Only you can do that.'

She stared at him. She'd spent far too much time thinking about what she didn't want to do, because she hadn't known what really made her happy. Suddenly it all seemed so obvious. She just had to work out how she was going to accomplish it – but she was a great believer in where-there's-a will-there's-a way.

'Excuse me, I need to go to the loo.' She stood up, pushed the book into her bag, and strode down the carriage with a sense of purpose. A few carriages down, by one of the doors, she pushed down the window and took in several deep breaths. Funny, it seemed so simple. She didn't have to go back to Manchester. That was her starting point, everything else would come to her. She pulled the book from her bag and stared at it, before lifting it towards the window. The breeze riffled the pages but then the words of an old anti-litter campaign popped into her head – 'don't be a tosser' – and much as she wanted rid of the book, she couldn't bring herself to do it. Instead she walked to the far end of the train and left it on a table in an empty section of one of the modern carriages at the end of the train. Maybe someone else might find a use for it.

Mina was quite surprised when the train began to slow and everyone began to gather their things together.

'I thought we'd be on here for hours,' she said.

'No, we transfer here onto a coach which takes up to the village of Gruyères,' Bernhardt informed her. He had done his homework, of course he had. She, as usual, had decided to go with the flow and enjoy the day. It was rather nice not being in charge for once. She was the one that normally planned trips – or, as Hannah said, 'she was the bossy one'.

Everyone on the coach was all smiles and as she walked along the aisle, Mina heard snippets of Canadian English, Australian English, Italian, Spanish, and German. It all felt rather jolly, with everyone united in a common goal, to go forth and discover cheese and chocolate. Funny how the little things united people.

'It's all so beautiful,' she said with a contented sigh as the coach wound up the hill, the road spliced with shards of sunshine that cut through the trees.

'It sure beats being at work,' agreed Uta from the seat in front of her.

'If you look up there you can see Cape au Moine, it's in the regional nature park.' Bernhardt, who'd snagged the seat next to her, leaned over her and pointed at a jagged, tree-clad peak.

'Right,' said Mina, a little bemused and amused. Bernhardt seemed determined to entertain and impress her. She'd noticed a couple of times, that he'd tried to enlighten her in his earnest way. Unfortunately, despite his genuine desire to please, it came across as ever so slightly patronising.

Luke, sitting with Kristian on the seats opposite, smiled but didn't comment, and a small part of Mina wished for about the fifth time that it was just the two of them today.

Mina had done many factory trips in her time, it was part of her job to visit the places from where they sourced ingredients, but she had to admit that the Gruyère factory was extremely slick and efficient as well as astounding.

'I love it when a food product has real provenence,' commented Mina, as they began the tour.

'What do you mean?' asked Uta.

'Well, they've been making this cheese since 1115 and it's only made here. I think in this day and age, that's really amazing. A lot of cheese, like cheddar in England, is produced all over the place in factories. But this has to be made here because the cow's milk is unique to the local area, because they eat grasses and herbs that grow high up in the alpine meadows. And it's been made for nearly a thousand years. How incredible is that?'

'Incredible,' agreed Uta with a smirk. 'You're really into all this.'

'How can you not be?' Mina wrinkled her nose. 'I know, it's just my thing.'

Despite the others teasing her, Mina's favourite fact of the day was that the staff who turned the wheels in the vast storeroom talked to the cheese Apparently it was tradition for people, rather than robots, as in other factories, to turn the cheese because, as a living thing, it needed that human touch.

'That has tickled me,' said Mina. 'I will never think of Gruyère in the same way again. Do you think people offload their problems? "My wife's left me. My daughter's pregnant." Do you think the flavour is a little bit influenced by what they've heard?'

Luke slung a casual arm around her shoulder. 'I have no idea, but it's one of the best stories I've heard in a long time, and I love that it appeals so much to you. You really are a bit of a nerd about food.'

Pleased that he got it, she leaned into him, allowing herself the treat of being close to him. 'Hell, yes. Derek says I'm the trainspotting equivalent. I don't think I'm *that* dull, do you?' She winked at him.

'No,' said Luke, giving her a quick squeeze. 'Definitely not that dull at all. Although I happen to like trains a lot.' In that moment, as their eyes met in complete understanding, she really regretted the presence of the others.

Once the tour was done, they piled back into the bus, each of them sporting a bag of cheese – although Luke had been a lot more restrained. 'I'll share yours,' he joked to Mina, this time making sure he bagged the seat next to her. Bernhardt narrowed his eyes and quickly sat down next to Uta, leaving Kristian on his own, although he'd buttonholed a young Australian couple and was chatting away to them. Mina watched out of the corner of her eye, hoping that some of Amelie's training might have rubbed off. As both were smiling, she decided he was talking cheese rather than the principles of European patent law.

The sudden competitiveness of Bernhardt worried her as much as it amused Uta, who'd murmured, 'I think he likes you,' when they stepped off the bus into the village of Gruyères.

'Mm,' said Mina not wanting to dwell upon it. Luckily the group was stopped in their tracks by the first glimpse of the village proper.

It was, decided Mina, quite possibly the most picturesque place she had ever seen. There was even a walled castle perched on the side of the mountain overlooking the village. The main cobbled street was lined with white-painted medieval buildings protected bywide overhanging tiled roofs. Each of them was immaculate; some with neat shutters flanking the windows and others with precision-planted window boxes filled with spring daffodils and crocuses, their heads dancing in the light breeze. A couple of the houses had well-trained and - trimmed broad-leaved ivy climbing the walls, the spring green contrasting against the whitewashed walls.

Almost everyone had their cameras out, Mina included. Miriam would love this, she liked everything to be neat and tidy.

The wide cobbled street was quiet and spotlessly clean, and led up to a tiny, beautifully maintained church, with a tiled triangular peaked roof. The whole place exuded old-world charm and just invited people to come and meander through the streets, to explore and admire at their own gentle pace. It was completely enchanting, decided Mina, wondering which of the many traditional-looking restaurants with their rustic doors and windows they would chose for lunch. There was quite a choice, all offering authentic fondues.

'There's a place I'd quite like to visit,' said Bernhardt turning to Mina. 'I think you'll like it.' He checked the map on his phone. 'It's the Giger Bar. I've heard it's like nothing you'll ever see anywhere else.'

'OK,' said Mina always interested in something new and different. 'What's special about it?'

'Wait and see.' Bernhardt looked as if he were harbouring a particularly juicy secret, although halfway up a mountain in the shadow of a fairytale castle that looked as if it might have inspired Disney's Cinderella's castle, she couldn't imagine what it could possibly be.

They followed the little blue dot on his phone and eventually came to the Giger Museum, and turned into the bar adjacent. It took a moment for Mina's eyes to adjust from the brilliant sunshine outside to the dim interior, and then in a decidedly girly, horror film moment, she grabbed Luke's arm.

'Oh my god,' she hissed quietly, as Bernhardt strutted in as proud as a peacock in full display.

Luke stared round, wide-eyed, and reached for her hand, giving it a quick squeeze under the cover of the gloom.

As they grew accustomed to the light they both stared around them in amazement, Mina's gaze was drawn to the vaulted roof that looked as if it were supported by alien spines, with intricate rows of odd-shaped bones. At the bar, vast otherworldly chairs looked as if they'd been beamed straight from a gothic

Star Trek set. The effect was both macabre and fascinating at the same time.

Bernhardt was extolling the virtues of the designer, Giger, who'd created what Mina considered the monstrous interior.

'Not what I was expecting at all,' she said, trying to take in the odd-shaped furniture and not-quite-human features of a set of skulls decorating a booth. Instinctively she edged closer to Luke. 'It's like the insides of a fossilised dinosaur,' she whispered with a quick shudder.

Over by the bar, Bernhardt was holding court with Kristian and Uta listening intently. 'Giger is an artist, but he's probably most famous for his work on the film *Alien* and lots of famous album covers. He has quite a cult following.'

'I'm afraid I'm not joining.' Mina spoke in an undertone. Maybe it was a European thing but she really didn't like it in here. 'Can you imagine what his dreams must have been like?' She shuddered, quite creeped out by the place.

'You OK?'

'No, I really don't like it in here.'

'Hey Bernhardt, we're just going back outside. Mina's feeling a bit warm.' Without waiting for a response, Luke guided her out of the bar, back into the light spring sunshine.

As soon as they got outside he put his arm around her and gave her a hug, and without thinking she leaned into him and he enfolded her to his chest, looking down at her with a warm smile in his eyes.

Her heart did that funny miss-a beat thing and she

swallowed. Don't look at his lips, she told herself, but she wanted him to kiss her more than anything else at that moment.

'Better?' he asked, looking down at her.

'Much, thank you.' She hugged him back, loathe to relinquish her hold on him. 'I'm not normally that squeamish, but that wasn't for me.'

'Don't apologise. I'm glad to have you to myself for a while. Being part of a tour group wasn't quite what I had in mind when I planned this trip.' His smile was rueful. 'I know you said you weren't interested in a relationship, but I can't stop thinking about you or wanting to spend time with you. I'm not very good at giving up on what I want. I'm of the opinion life's too short not to keep trying.'

Mina took a deep breath. 'What if I told you I'd had a change of heart, which is crazy because I'm only here for a couple more days.'

'England's not so far away,' he said, lowering his face nearer to hers. 'And I could be posted anywhere. It doesn't have to be Switzerland.'

'Funny,' she said tilting her head up. 'I'd just decided I'd quite like to stay here.'

His mouth was mere inches from hers and she wasn't sure who closed the gap first.

Excitement like a thousand bees buzzed through her as his lips touched hers. How could she have forgotten this exhilaration?

Luke pulled back first. 'Shall we go and find somewhere for lunch?'

'Yes. What about the others?'

'What about them?' asked Luke with a grin. 'Every man for himself. We'll see them back on the bus at two.'

He held her hand as they wandered along the street trying to decide which of the charming-looking restaurants did the best fondue in the world. They finally settled on a traditional, rustic place doing a roaring trade.

Mina let out a sigh. 'This is more like it. I think I'm quite a simple creature at heart. That place should be in New York or a trendy part of London.'

'Bernhardt is obviously a fan. I think he's rather proud that Switzerland could produce something of that ilk.'

'Bernhardt can keep it. Not my thing at all. I can appreciate it's clever and unique, but it made me feel quite uncomfortable. If I ate in somewhere like that, I'd spend the whole time looking over my shoulder convinced something nasty and bony was going to jump out at me. Restaurants and bars should be welcoming and homely, making you relax, not feel stressed. The lighting should be just right to give a glow, like a beacon guiding you home, the furniture comfortable but not too fussy so that you worry about spilling things on it, and the menu appealing without too much pretentious nonsense about it. You know, include those things that you don't realise are exactly what you fancy. Things that are hearty but a treat as well. And of course it should be all about quality. Locally sourced ingredients and authentic overseas specialities.'

'It sounds as if you've given it a lot of thought.'

'Sorry, my sister Hannah would say I've gone off on one.' Mina paused. 'It's my hobby horse, the perfect restaurant, although I don't have any desire to open one of my own. I just know exactly what I want in a restaurant, but that's not the sort of cooking I want to do. I prefer sweet treats, desserts, chocolates.' Something glimmered at the back of her mind, an elusive idea that floated just out of reach. She knew from experience it was best to let things to percolate and come to her when they were ready, although she could do with the idea speeding up because, as she'd told Luke, she only had a few more days here.

They were just about to enter the restaurant when Kristian's voice hailed them. 'There you are. I've left Uta and Bernhardt because I wanted fondue. This place looks nice.'

Mina and Luke avoided looking at each other.

'That'll be a table for three then,' said Luke dryly.

———

The others caught up with them on the coach, having opted to stay and eat at the Giger Bar. Mina hoped the food was more appealing than the avant garde décor. Next stop was the Maison Cailler in Broc, a five-minute bus ride away. According to Bernahrdt, who had done his research, Cailler was the first and oldest brand of chocolate in Switzerland.

The rich delicious smell of chocolate reached them before they even disembarked from the bus. Mina closed her eyes and inhaled, the air redolent with the sinfully decadent scent.

'This could be the closest thing to heaven,' she murmured with a little moan.

'You're not going to have a *When Harry Met Sally* moment, are you?' asked Luke, amusement at the expression on her face sparkling in his eyes.

'There's a distinct possibility.' Mina linked an arm through his, ignoring the narrowing of Bernhardt's eyes 'Come on, you.'

Everyone from the coach crowded in, milling about in the foyer before being funnelled onto the tour, which did feel very much like a school trip. Informative and educational, with typical Swiss efficiency, the well-designed displays gave considerable insight into the origins of chocolate, where the beans were grown, how they were harvested and treated on the way to being made into chocolate. Mina, keen to learn as much as she could, paid attention to how chocolate was made and how solid chocolate as eaten today came into being. Bernhardt chipped in plenty of additional facts. Apparently, before a chap called Daniel Peter added milk to chocolate, it was a gritty bitter paste. His use of condensed milk produced by the Nestlé factory next door created the product now known the world over as chocolate.

As the tour progressed, Mina's hunger to know more grew keener, but the tour kept them at arm's length during the actual processes, much of it mechanised behind huge plate-glass windows, and there was no one around to answer the questions she had.

When they reached the end of the tour, Mina felt a little

edgy and irritated, and even more determined to press Johannes to let her go and see his operation.

'You look like you're planning something,' commented Luke as they made their way out. 'Are you planning to go into production?'

'Not yet. But I am going to bombard Johannes with a gazillion questions. He can't possibly have all that machinery. And I know lots of smaller, artisan producers who don't have that level of production, so how do they do it? That's what I'm really interested in.'

'If Johannes won't help, I have a friend in Vevey who has a cousin who runs a chocolate shop. Perhaps I could arrange a visit for you?' Bernhardt offered.

'That's very kind, but I'm running short of time, and Johannes is on the doorstep. It's alright, I'll come up with something.' A sweetener perhaps, like telling him what Amelie's favourite flowers were, or when her birthday was.

The end of the tour led them into an all-you-can-eat chocolate extravaganza with a huge selection of different chocolates.

'Willy Wonka eat your heart out,' murmured Mina, watching the delight on two children's faces as they double-checked with their parents that they really could eat the chocolate. The company had done a great job in designing the tasting room, and she studied the various stations which had been arranged to display both the chocolates and their ingredients. She nodded with approval, already thinking about the chocolate shop she'd been to in Zurich and how she would set things up. There was plenty of room here, which was probably just as well, as there were a lot of excitable children zipping about, unable to believe their luck, but it lacked the style of the shop. Although, much as she'd liked it, it had been a bit *too* stylish, making you feel a little self-conscious about tasting there, whereas here there was absolutely no concept of self-restraint. If it were up to her, she'd come up with a happy medium. Something a lot more cosy, perhaps small, beautifully decorated, round tables with room around them for people to gather, but with plenty of other things on display to draw the eye.

Mina shook her head and winced as a little girl careered past, holding a chocolate in either sticky hand, her eyes alight with happiness, calling to her mother. 'And the trick is not too eat too much,' she said to herself, her mind still buzzing with ideas.

Uta and Kristian had already tucked in, while Bernhardt was wandering around each station, his hands behind his back, perusing each carefully as if working out his tasting strategy.

It look far too restrained for Mina. She wanted to try everything.

She turned to Luke, who'd caught up with her having been caught in conversation with one of a group of women from their coach. She hadn't missed how their eyes lit up when they'd seen him the first time they boarded the coach.

'Funny,' she said to him, 'that this is the most famous brand in Switzerland, and the oldest, and yet in the UK we've never heard of it.'

'The Swiss like to keep the good stuff for themselves,' said Luke. 'Where shall we start?'

'At the beginning, of course,' said Mina primly. 'We have to do this properly.'

'Is there a proper way to taste chocolate?' teased Luke, following her to the first station, where cone-shaped swirls of glossy brown chocolate were arranged in uniform rows, like a small battalion of sweetness. He picked one up and popped it straight into his mouth. 'Mmm.' With dancing eyes he signalled that it was good as he savoured the chocolate.

'Philistine,' said Mina picking one up and delicately holding it under her nose. 'You should smell it first; it heightens the experience.' She inhaled the delicious scent, closing her eyes. It smelled of comfort, of warm kitchens, heaven. When she opened her eyes, Luke was watching her, a smile playing around his mouth.

'What?' she asked, feeling her breath catch just a little at the expression on his face.

'You just make me smile, Mina. You have such a passion for life.'

He continued to watch as she carefully put the chocolate in her mouth and bit through the crisp hard shell, which gave way to silken praline inside, flavoured with hazelnuts, which made her squirm with pleasure. She savoured the smooth texture in her mouth, feeling the sensual pleasure which was heightened under Luke's steady gaze.

'Good?' he asked.

'Very.'

'Here,' Luke picked up the little cup-shaped chocolate and held it up to her nose, the rest of his fingers lightly grazing her chin with a tiny touch that sent a frisson racing across her skin in hair-raising ripples.

'Caramel,' she murmured, as he lifted the chocolate to her mouth. Their eyes locked as she took it from his fingers and put it into her mouth. The intensity of his gaze as she tasted the rich sweetness of sugar made her pulse hiccough.

'Here.' She picked up one of the chocolates and with clumsy fingers shoved it towards him, without an ounce of finesse, but he was making her feel a touch jittery as well as hot and definitely bothered.

He opened his mouth expectantly and she stared at his lips, feeling a ridiculously ill-placed spark of lust shoot through her. Hastily she popped the chocolate in with the urgency of a basketball player shooting a hoop in the dying seconds of a game. Feeling a flush racing along her cheeks, she moved along without waiting for him. She busied herself, studying the case of ingredients rather than picking up one of the rounds of chocolate with a coffee bean on the top, waiting for her heart to stop playing silly buggers and return to an acceptable rate. Did Luke have any idea of the effect he was having on her? She prayed she wasn't giving herself away.

'Want to try a piece of this?' she asked, moving on to a display of white chocolate in large bars, even though she wasn't a fan. She always found that it had a cloying texture and left a greasy mouthfeel. She preferred milk chocolate to any other.

Luke shook his head. 'That's not proper chocolate. It sticks to the roof of your mouth.'

'I think we might be twins separated at birth,' she said

with a laugh. 'That's exactly how I feel about it. Largely decorative.'

The next station was much more appealing: tiny rounds of dark chocolate flavoured with orange. They both nodded in shared appreciation.

'That's good. The best yet,' said Luke, his hand already reaching for a second piece.

'You missed a bit.' Without thinking she reached up to away the smear left just below his lip, and as soon as she did, a big klaxon went off in her head – a few seconds too late, because the damage was done. At the same moment his tongue slipped out to lick away the streak of chocolate and touched her fingertip. A thousand volts rocketed through her at the unexpected intimate contact and she gave a startled gasp at the same time as Luke's eyes widened.

'Sorry,' she said hurriedly.

'I'm not,' said Luke, holding her gaze and smiling down at her with a look in his eyes that was hard to resist. It held sincerity and tenderness rather than cocky confidence, and it made her yearn for things that she had no business yearning for in a busy tasting room.

Unable to help herself, she smiled back up at him. She couldn't fight off the pent-up longing, and when he lowered his head, she lifted hers...

'What's your favourite?' asked Bernhardt, suddenly appearing behind her with Kristian and Uta in tow. 'Uta likes the pralines best. Kristian can't make up his mind. What's this one? Chocolate and orange?'

'Er... I...' Mina gave Luke a panicked look, flushing

bright red before turning to face Bernhardt, hoping that he hadn't just seen what had happened. A second later and they'd have been kissing. Luckily he seemed to be more interested in the decorative display behind her of dried orange slices and little hessian sacks of dark cocoa nibs.

'Mm, these are good,' said Uta, trying one of the orange-flavoured chocolates and making room for Kristian to step forward and try one.

Mina nodded, trying to appear normal, while her system still pumped with adrenaline and excitement, her pulse rocketing along like a runaway train. It felt as if her hormones were in revolt, so close and yet so far, sending a hot flash through her as if to say, how could you do this to us?

Luke shot her a quick, rueful smile as the others fell into to step with them, and she wondered if he was suffering from the same sort of hormonal fallout. The others began talking about which they thought was the best chocolate and Mina tried to join in, biting back keen disappointment. What might have happened if the others hadn't joined them at that moment? She shot a sidelong glance at Luke, now engaged in conversation with Uta, and sighed softly to herself.

Kristian and Bernhardt began a lively debate as to whether milk or dark chocolate was better, which continued on into the obligatory end-of-tour shop, which rang with as much excitable noise and chatter as the monkey enclosure at a zoo. Children darted this way and that, tugging on their parents' hands like small explorers making huge new discoveries with each new shelf of goodies.

There was a coach tour of Japanese people ahead of them, who were buying chocolate like it was going out of style, with huge smiles on their faces, and they weren't alone: everyone seemed to have shopping baskets piled high. It was like a horde of locusts whipping through, as if this was the last chocolate on the planet, but the thing that struck Mina was that everyone was smiling. Despite the niggly sense of frustration at wanting to be with Luke on her own, she couldn't help smiling too. It was the simplest equation. Chocolate = happiness. The whole shop was filled with joy. Even now she was thinking about the people in her life that she wanted to buy chocolate for, because she cared about them and wanted to show she was thinking of them. Chocolate did all that and more. Suddenly she knew what she *did* want. She wanted to do something with chocolate. Bring joy to people.

Already she was thinking of who she wanted to buy gifts for: Hannah, Miriam, and Derek, obviously; and then Ian at work, because although he was the HR bod, he'd also been kind and supportive and on her side about the blue hair-thing; and then there were the two Georges, because she still loved them, despite their Facebook faux pas; and Patsy and James. Before she knew it, her basket was full too, but she didn't care, because she was already imagining her friends and family savouring each bite of deliciousness. Once upon a time she'd have bought something for Belinda; she loved white chocolate, which figured. Mina ignored the pang of sadness she felt. Belinda hadn't even tried to apologise or explain. Not one text message or call. Some friend. Twenty-odd years down the drain. And yet here was

Luke next to her – who of course didn't like white chocolate – and she knew whatever happened, after knowing him for less than two weeks, he would always be a friend. Ever since that kiss on the train there'd been something between them.

'Have you got some in there to share with me on the train?' murmured Luke in her ear as she stood in the queue to pay for her goodies. There was no sign of the others who'd moved on out of the shop.

She laughed at him, studying his handsome face brimming with amusement and that ever-present readiness to smile. There was just something infectious about him, as if there was always a candle burning bright inside him. It was time to stop fighting the attraction between them and enjoy being with him for the next few days. Her normal modus operandi was to throw caution to the wind. She'd been overthinking this 'sorting herself out' business. And after today, she had an idea about what she wanted to do.

'I think this time—' she turned to face him '—it's your turn to buy the chocolate.'

'To be truthful, I'm all chocolated out. I fancy something nice and savoury like a packet of crisps.'

Mina laughed, although she knew exactly what he meant. 'And a can of coke. All this chocolate makes you thirsty.'

'Now who's the philistine?'

Everyone on the bus travelling back to pick the train up was in high spirits, and the earlier reserve between different nationalities and ages dissolved as a loud discussion commenced about where everyone had eaten at lunchtime and what they'd had. This moved onto the best cheese, the best chocolate, and then the best train journeys in Switzerland. There was no doubt that every single person was completely smitten with the country. There wasn't a single complaint from anyone and by the time the rain rolled into Montreux all the passengers were firm friends, calling goodbye as they all clutched their bulging bags of cheese and chocolate. Mina almost felt sorry to be saying goodbye to Bernhardt, Kristian, and Uta.

'We'll see you on Friday,' said Kristian. 'Don't miss us too much.'

'I'll do my best,' said Mina, shooting a stern glance at Uta laughing over his shoulder.

'See you Friday,' said Bernhardt, stepping forward to kiss her on either cheek. Although the gesture was quite formal, it still discomfited her slightly, especially when Uta raised her eyebrows and smirked.

'Have a safe trip back,' said Uta, giving her a quick hug adding in a quick whisper, 'I bet you'll be glad to be on your own. See you Friday.'

Mina hugged her back and gave her a reproachful smile. 'See you Friday.'

With all their goodbyes said, Luke and Mina made their way to the platform for the train to Brig.

'Phew, peace and quiet,' said Luke.

'Everyone was so friendly. It was fun, though.'

'It was but...' Luke's hand found Mina's and he threaded her fingers through hers, leaving the sentence unfinished. She looked up at him and smiled, knowing exactly what he meant. It was nice to be just the two of them again and she enjoyed the simple feel of his hand in hers. The unspoken connection and the quiet simplicity of standing side-by-side without having to say a word. When the train to Brig arrived and they sat next to each other, thigh-to-thigh, it seemed totally natural for Luke to put his arm around her, and for her to rest her head on his shoulders. It had been a lovely day, and one she was going to remember for a long time, especially as she was finally closer to finding something she wanted to do. She didn't know what it was yet, but she knew it had to involve chocolate.

Chapter Fifteen

As they walked, weary but happy, up to the chalet, Mina felt a sense of homecoming and serenity at the sight of the light spilling out from the first-floor window of the lounge, golden and warm, enticing them in. It might also have had something to do with the way Luke's gloved hand casually took hers again as they stepped off the train.

Although her body sagged with the travel-stained weariness of a long day, Mina felt a little catherine wheel of excitement and anticipation fizzing in her chest, one that could be examined later. Despite having eaten her fill of cheese and chocolate over the course of the day, she was ready for something hearty and savoury.

'Luke, Mina,' called Amelie as soon they appeared in the doorway of the chalet. 'Just in time. How was your day? Come, come. Sit down.'

They exchanged reluctant smiles. Mina wanted a quiet, private moment to further explore that almost-kiss, to savour what it might feel like to be held in Luke's arms. It felt like they'd been thwarted again, although admittedly at that present moment, Mina was too tired to do anything other than peel off her coat and drop her bags onto one of the sofas in the lounge. Before she walked through, Luke caught her arm and very gently stroked the inside of her wrist as if to remind her he was still there. It boosted her spirits and she gave him a shy smile. Amelie, doing her usual sheepdog impersonation, ushered them into two seats at the end of the table, next to Dave and Claudia. Within minutes Amelie had placed big plates of fragrant golden risotto in front of her and Luke. Inhaling the lovely scent Mina felt herself perk up almost immediately. She could see tiny strands of saffron colouring the rice, and the lovely unctuous, glossiness of melted cheese.

'Perfect, exactly what I need,' said Mina, sinking back into the chair, already comforted by the prospect of good food and the thought of not having to move for a while.

'You mean you're not full?' asked Claudia.

Mina beamed at her. 'I was a grown-up today. I was sensible with the chocolate.' Luke caught her eye and then ducked his head, concentrating hard on his meal. With her foot, she nudged at his ankle under the table, feeling a little thrill when he rested his foot against hers. 'But it was wonderful. My suitcase when I go home is going to stink though, because I couldn't resist the aged Gruyère, or the Appenzeller cheese. Why haven't I had that before?'

Claudia patted her hand. 'We like to keep the good stuff here. Appenzeller is my favourite too.'

'Basically, Mina could probably open her own cheese shop,' chipped in Luke. 'And probably a chocolate shop too.'

Mina gave him an outraged poke. 'And you didn't buy anything,' she teased him back.

'I'm a growing boy. Besides,' he added with a lofty grin, 'I'm always willing to share my chocolate.'

'Just the once, and I didn't even know you then. Honestly, talk about bearing a grudge.'

The rest of the table had gone silent and everyone, without exception, watched the pair of them with indulgent smiles. Mina blushed and suddenly applied herself to her risotto, and Dave, who she could have hugged, said, 'Shame you missed my legendary chocolate log today.'

'It was wonderful,' said Amelie jumping in quickly. 'I might have to retire and let Dave take over.'

Dave seemed to have grown an inch taller and Mina smiled at him before realising that there was no sign of Sarah. 'Where's your wife?'

'She's not feeling too good. Migraine. So she went to bed early.'

'That's a shame,' said Mina, although she couldn't help thinking that Dave seemed much happier this evening. She shot a suspicious look at Amelie who was standing by the side table opening a bottle of wine and wondered what had wrought the change. Amelie gave her a guileless smile back.

After a glass of wine, Mina felt herself flagging.

Out of sight under the table, Luke took her hand, whispering in her ear. 'Are you OK?'

'Just knackered,' she said, feeling his thumb trace a tiny circle on her palm. She held her breath at the intimate, secretive touch and clenched her knees together, suddenly flustered. 'I think I'm…' He did it again and inside she softened, longing for the moment they could be alone. 'I'm ready for my bed. I think I'll go up now.' She squeezed his hand, sure he would follow her lead.

'Me too. Funny how travelling makes you so tired.'

'Yes, we've sat on our backsides most of the day or…' She couldn't stifle the yawn that broke free. 'Or done nothing but eat.' Now she'd started yawning she couldn't stop.

'Sorry folks, I'm done in.' She pulled back from the table. 'Goodnight.'

Luke stayed put and nodded at her, and she felt the plummet of disappointment in her stomach. Swallowing down her frustration, she left to a chorus of goodnights from everyone at the table, including Luke. Just as she reached the stairs, she realised she'd forgotten to collect her coat and bag from where she'd abandoned them on the sofa in the lounge. It felt like far too much effort. She eyed the stairs, already a mountain to climb. The coat and bag could wait until morning.

She was halfway up the flight when Luke came up behind, clutching both.

'You forgot these.' His face lit up with a slow smile.

'Thank you.' She was cooler with him, still not sure where she stood with him. 'I was too lazy to go back for them.'

Luke reached up and touched her face. 'I didn't want

everyone to put two and two together if I left at the same time as you. I was worried it might look too obvious.'

'Too obvious.'

'How desperate I am to kiss you again.'

Mina laughed. 'Subtlety doesn't really work with me. I'm easily confused by it.'

He fell into step with her as they climbed the last flights in silent accord.

When they reached the corridor with their rooms, they paused outside his bedroom door in that slightly so-what-happens-now moment. It shimmered between them for a second before he took her bag and coat from her with gentle hands. She thought it rather gentlemanly until he dropped them on the floor with a thud and a rustle of feathers, and placed his hands on her hips, pulling her towards him with determined intent in his eyes that made her heart miss a beat.

'I have been waiting all day to do this, but if you don't want me to kiss you...' His eyes flashing with sincerity moved over her face with a desperate urgency. 'Speak now or forever hold your peace.'

'Who needs peace?' she said with involuntary huskiness, heady with anticipation, as butterflies stirred in her stomach and her pulse thudded so hard she felt as if her entire body was vibrating. 'I want you to kiss me. I want to kiss you.' She slipped her arms around his neck, her fingers playing across the warm skin, tangling slightly in the long curls. The anticipation and desire had been simmering between them all the way back from Broc, and now she felt positively light-headed.

'Skiing? Tomorrow? Afternoon?' asked Luke, as if anxious to get that said and done before more important matters. She nodded, and she wasn't sure who kissed who first, but she did know that she could die a happy woman. His lips were soft as they made a leisurely exploration of her mouth with slow, careful movements that made her feel as if he was savouring her like fine chocolate.

Eventually both of them had to come up for air, and all she could do was stare at him, a little dazed and most definitely discombobulated.

'Wow,' she murmured.

'Wow, indeed.'

Bemused they stared at each other. 'I think I probably need to say goodnight.' Mina found trying to gather her thoughts together was like knitting with mist.

'Yes,' said Luke gravely before grinning at her. 'I'm trying to be sensible here, but I think you might have just fried all my circuits. I'm not sure I'm capable of stringing a sentence together and I think I'd better go to bed before I make a total tit of myself and say something embarrassing.'

'Glad it's not just me then.' She gave him a goofy grin, unable to stop her mouth acting on its own.

'It's definitely not just you.'

For a moment both of them stood encircled in each other's arms just looking at each other. Then Luke pulled her close and pressed tiny kisses to her temple, reverent and almost thankful, as she sank against his chest. She closed her eyes and savoured the feeling of coming home.

The fizz of passion and anticipation still raced through

her system but it was overlaid by an overwhelming sense of peace and of being in the right place.

She sighed and lifted her face to Luke. He kissed her and although neither of them spoke, she knew that he felt it too. He smiled and laid a finger on her lips. 'Goodnight, Mina.'

'Night, Luke. See you in the morning.'

Chapter Sixteen

'Just the person,' said Mina, coming down the stairs and jumping off the bottom step just as Johannes was conducting his usual early morning task of bringing in a sack of logs. His scraggy eyebrows drew together in bird's wings of suspicion, and although he acknowledged her with a brief nod, he carried on through to the reception area and began to unload the wood into one of the alcoves on either side of the fireplace.

Mina followed him, undeterred. 'I'd really like to see your chocolate production. Yesterday was... well, it wasn't enough.'

'You went to Maison Cailler,' he said shortly, continuing to empty the sack, piling each log neatly on the stack next to the fire.

'Yes but that's like eating a shop-bought cake instead of a home-made one. I want authenticity, artisan. Chocolate magic.' She didn't quite flutter her llama eyelashes at him, but it was a close-run thing. There was no point being subtle with someone like Johannes.

He made a grumbling sound first before he turned and focused sharp blue eyes on her. 'It's a serious business, you know.'

'I know and I'm seriously interested. Food, any kind of food, is part of my job, and I'm genuinely interested. Yesterday was interesting, but I didn't learn that much about actual hands-on making of chocolate.'

'You could come today,' he said grudgingly. 'There'll be something to see.'

'Today?' She almost skipped on the spot. 'That would be awesome.'

He glared at her as if the word offended him. 'Fantastic,' she amended, 'I just need to check with Amelie whether she'd like some help in the kitchen first.'

'She's in there now.' He inclined his head towards the door. 'Been up since five, I think, crazy woman.'

Mina crossed to the doorway and slipped into the kitchen.

'Morning,' she called, and Amelie whirled around her apron already covered in flour.

'Good morning, *liebling*. Did you sleep well?'

'Oh, like a rock. I don't think I moved all night.' She laughed. 'Probably weighted down by all the cheese and chocolate.'

'Coffee?' Amelie's hand was already on the jug on the stove.

'Yes, please,' growled Johannes who had followed Mina into the kitchen and was leaning against the counter making himself at home. 'Mina wants to come over this morning.'

'Oh lovely,' said Amelie. 'It's fascinating, and the chocolate is amazing, although—' her mouth puckered with an amused little smile '—just imagine how much better it would taste if it were made with love.'

Johannes glowered at her. 'It's chocolate, it doesn't need love. It needs a firm hand, attention to detail, and a watchful eye on the thermometer.'

Amelie sighed and handed a steaming mug of coffee to him. Mina noticed she'd already put two sugars in it without asking. 'Johannes, where's the poetry in your soul?'

'I don't need poetry, or fanciful women.' He smelled his coffee and a very faint smile lifted his face. 'Thank you.'

Mina wondered if they realised they were like an old married couple who'd settled into a groove of familiarity. She suspected that Johannes burrowed into that very spot most mornings when he'd delivered his logs, and that Amelie stirred in his sugar without even thinking about it.

'I thought I could give you some help straight after breakfast, and then maybe go over to Johannes about eleven.' Hopefully that would give her a couple of hours before she met up with Luke to go skiing. Who knew that her timetable would end up being so full?

'That's very kind of you, but Dave is going to help again this morning. Yesterday I discovered the man has the lightest touch with pastry, and tonight I'm making *chäschüechli*, individual cheese tarts. I shall put him to work, and then I shall ask him to make some apple strudel that I can freeze.'

Mina raised an eyebrow. For a woman who didn't like people in her kitchen, she suddenly seemed rather accommodating. 'Sounds like you have a full itinerary planned for him.'

Amelie's eyes twinkled. 'I do. His wife can't decide whether she's irritated that he's not going skiing with their group, or proud that he's so useful. I intend to take advantage of him without shame.'

'And will that include lots of praise and encouragement?' asked Mina, suddenly understanding the other woman's strategy.

'He just needs to remember that he has qualities, and get some of his self-esteem back. His wife is very quick to point out his flaws, and he is very quick to bend like a branch under the weight of them.' Amelie suddenly took a few paces imitating Dave's shambling gate, her shoulders bowed and her demeanour defeated before straightening with a fox-like sharpness to her face. 'I think there's hope there.'

'And I think you shouldn't meddle,' said Johannes, his mouth pursing.

Amelie simply peered at him as if she were looking over a pair of glasses, and sniffed before turning back to the large piece of cheese she was chopping. Mina looked at it again.

'That's the longest piece of cheese I've ever seen.'

'A quarter of a metre long,' said Amelie. 'I bought it from a local dairy where they make half-metre rounds of cheese. Here, try some,' She handed over a chunk from the pile she was cutting. 'Emmental is a metre long, that's why you always buy it in squares, a slice would be half a metre long.'

Mina munched thoughtfully on the cheese. It looked as if Amelie had everything under control for the day. She agreed with Johannes that she would come straight over after breakfast had been tidied away and she'd had coffee with Amelie, which would give her time in the afternoon to go for a cross-country ski with Luke for an hour or two. It looked like her day was panning out perfectly.

———————

Breakfast, unlike the other leisurely meals in the chalet, reminded Mina of being at a petrol station. Sitting at a table by the window, she watched with amusement. People basically served themselves as quickly as possible, ate, and left. As people reached across each other for another croissant, a slice of rustic bread, or a seeded roll, there were a few exchanges about the weather forecast – excellent today and for the following day – and an occasional nod and acknowledgement of where people were headed, as they helped themselves to coffee, with the occasional reference to the previous evening's discussions about the best cross-country trails, which had been discussed exhaustively over dinner.

Mina watched Sarah bustling about in an all-in-one pink ski-suit, amused to see that she was just as bossy with her two friends as she was with Dave. They were part of a group of seven, who were very keen cross-country skiers; thankfully the other three were staying elsewhere as Mina had decided they were rather boring about it. They held court over their breakfast in loud voices, declaring with overbearing certainty and a certain amount of dogmatic confidence which were the best trails.

'Morning,' murmured Luke in a husky voice that immediately brought her nerve endings to attention as he slid into the chair next to her with a plate piled with bread, ham, cheese, and a couple of croissants.

In a black roll-neck and black ski pants, he once again looked like a broad-shouldered, slim-hipped action hero, ready to ski off into the breach, and for a minute she wished she was going out with him right now.

'Morning.' She smiled back at him, and for a minute just drank in his handsome loveliness in a soppy, star-struck sort of way before she pulled herself together. It was considerable consolation that he looked just as dazed. 'I've sorted everything out, so if you're still available this afternoon we can go out then. Amelie's drafted Dave in for the morning, so I'm going to Johannes on a chocolate mission.' She sat back feeling rather pleased with herself.

'You have been busy.'

'The early bird catches the worm and all that. I didn't like to disturb you.' Although she had heard him moving about next door.

'I was up early, but I did some work on my new commission, made a start anyway. Like you, I didn't want to waste a minute, and it's such a gorgeous morning I can't bear to be inside. I'm going to ski over to Oberwald with Claudia and Frank. I'll be back about one-thirty, and I'll just need to check in with work, and then we can go out this afternoon when you're done with Johannes, if that's still OK with you.'

'Perfect.' She rubbed her hands together. 'I do like it when a plan comes together.'

As Luke ploughed through his huge breakfast they were joined by Claudia and Frank, and Mina was happy to leave Luke as they began to discuss this morning's trip.

They were very impressed that Johannes was prepared to show her his chocolate production.

'You're very honoured,' said Claudia, her mouth turning down with mock disappointment. 'I've asked him many times.'

'I'm worried he'll change his mind.'

'He's not going to change his mind,' said Luke. 'Now he's said, "yes" you have the golden ticket to Willy Wonka's chocolate palace.'

Mina grinned. 'I don't think by any stretch of the imagination you could compare Johannes with Willy Wonka. If the Grinch made chocolate however…'

———

Johannes was surprisingly businesslike when she turned up at his house at eleven o'clock later that day, and insisted on giving her a hairnet, a white coat, blue plastic overshoes, and an apron to match his own, before leading her down into his basement. She realised within a matter of minutes that he took his chocolate business very seriously.

'This used to be the barn,' explained Johannes as they came to the bottom of the stairs. 'This place belonged to my grandfather's brother, he lived here all his life, and his grandfather before him. In those days, the cattle were kept here in the winter, and then in the spring they would go up to the alpine meadows for the whole summer and stay there until late autumn.'

'So your great-uncle,' Mina worked out that's who it would have been, 'must have known Amelie's grandparents.'

'Yes, this was a very tight-knit community. Amelie and I played together as children for a couple of summers. We used to swim at the lake, Geschinersee.'

'I didn't realised you'd known each other for that long.'

His eyes suddenly twinkled. 'We were seven or eight then. I don't think that counts as knowing each other.'

'Do people change so much?'

'Huh. Not in some ways, I realise. Amelie was always rescuing small creatures back then. Although when I met her in my late twenties, she had changed a lot. Quite the party girl. Like every man, I was completely entranced by her. She was like a comet bursting through the sky at a hundred miles an hour. And like a pompous prig, I blew it. Expected to cut her wings and have her dance to my tune. I had a job in Zurich. I gave her an ultimatum. Come with me or...'

Mina stared. 'I had no idea.' Amelie had never given any indication that there'd been anything between her and Johannes.

'Why would you? It clearly didn't mean that much to Amelie, whereas...' He paused and leaned forward to open the door at the foot of the stairs. 'I made the biggest mistake of my life. I never met another woman who could match her.'

He suddenly gave Mina a shrewd look.

With guarded eyes she looked back, but he didn't say anything more.

'Now I'm trying to make up for lost time. I worry she doesn't look after herself properly, yes. She needs more help in that place. It's too much for one person, but she's so stubborn.' That, Mina suspected, was the kettle calling the pot black, and he seemed to do quite a bit of helping whether Amelie wanted it or not.

'I think she wants to prove she can do it.'

'Hmm,' growled Johannes leading Mina into a bright, airy space with whitewashed stone walls. Surprised, she blinked at the blue-white brightness of the room lit by stark LED lights.

'It looked very different in here when I started. Of course, I've done a lot of work to insulate it now. There are still plenty of barns in the villages throughout this valley who still farm the old way.' His craggy face broke into a smile. 'And a good job, too. It's their milk that makes all the difference, although every damn cheese producer and artisan chocolate maker claims the same.'

Having heard this in detail at La Maison de Gruyère, Mina ginned back at him. 'And what do you think?'

'Actually, old cynic that I am, there might be something in it. Why shouldn't the grasses, wild flowers, and herbs the cows eat create character in their milk? It's certainly a good marketing angle.'

The room was far more modern than she'd expected,

and Mina was impressed with the amount of machinery he had, completely dousing her expectation that it would look homespun and small-scale. This had more in common with a craft beer micro-brewery, with its gleaming stainless steel vats and shiny silver pipes running overhead from one to another. She looked at him, surprise in her eyes.

'This is why I don't let people come in here very often. One, hygiene is very important, and two—' his eyes suddenly twinkled '—I prefer to let them imagine it's all magic, pure alchemy, rather than the hard, scientific work that needs to be put in to make the alchemy happen. And while there is a lot of science involved, there's also a certain amount of magic.'

Mina recognised in the sudden upbeat lift of his voice, the passion for his subject. 'Have you ever seen a raw cacao bean? Damn ugly things. They remind me of some sightless sea creature that lives at the bottom of the Marianas Trench.'

Mina didn't think anything lived at the bottom of the Marianas Trench, but she got the idea, having seen the display at the factory tour the day before. Chocolate definitely came from humble origins.

'To get from that to this—' he held up a cellophane-wrapped bar of chocolate that he produced from his pocket '—is pretty incredible.'

Once Johannes started talking, she found it fascinating, and the two of them chatted happily as equals. He was clearly a little flattered by her interest, but also equally impressed by her knowledge. Although she hadn't made chocolate herself, she knew enough about food production processes to ask plenty of in-depth questions.

Chocolate was complex stuff, she learned, and making it like this was very time-consuming. The main process that was responsible for the texture and consistency of the chocolate, and which made the difference between high-quality and low-quality chocolate, was the conching process.

Johannes patted the top of stainless steel piece of kit, which was making a regular hum with a rhythmic whirring noise.

'Take a look inside.' He lifted the lid.

'Oh, the smell. That's delicious.' She peered into the large container at the smooth liquid chocolate churning away inside in elegant, sinuous movements.

'This is conching. It's a kneading and smoothing process that ensures all the particles in chocolate face the same way. Imagine the nap of a fabric or a piece of velvet. If you stroke it the wrong way, you rough up the surface or the pile.' He paused and gave her a very stern look. 'I think relationships are like that. If you find someone where the particles all face the same way, where you don't rub each other the wrong way, it's a good match. Understand.'

She nodded, surprised but also intrigued and a little bit charmed at likening finding love to a type of food processing. It seemed rather appropriate.

'Finding that without having to go through the conching process – which I see as negotiation and compromise, which I had to do with my first wife – is a rare thing.' He said the latter with considerable warmth and stared at her intently.

There was silence in the room apart from the whirring

and churning of the machine next to him, which seemed to emphasise his meaning.

Mina was too surprised by his directness to say anything at first, but then she said. 'Are you talking about Luke?'

'Ah, you do understand, then. I've seen the two of you. I know you think I'm a grumpy old unromantic, but I see more than you think. Bernhardt's keen, you know, but that's practicality over anything else. You're a good-looking girl, know how to behave in company, so he's decided you might be a suitable candidate – and also there's a little bit of competition there, so he's prepared to throw his hat into the ring.'

Mina burst out laughing because he'd summed it up perfectly.

'Whereas Luke...' He tilted his head. 'Most people never find that.'

'Did Amelie tell you what happened before I came here?'

'No, she wouldn't betray your confidence, but I can see that you're trying to find your direction.'

'Exactly, and I'm not sure Luke is part of that direction. Not at the moment.'

'Don't make the mistake of waiting for the right moment. If I were you, I'd seize it, everything else can work around you.'

Mina shook her head. 'I'm not sure it's that simple. And I'm going home in four days' time.'

'That doesn't have to be the end, does it? There are planes and trains. Jobs in Switzerland. Jobs in England. Jobs all over the world.'

She suddenly gave him a brilliant smile. 'You're right.' Plenty of people survived long-distance relationships.

She looked down at the moving mass, slightly beguiled by the silken chestnut river swirling in the giant mixer, savouring the rich, sweet smell rising up. 'So what do you do with the chocolate once it's made?'

He stared at her for a moment, his deep set eyes narrowing with thought, and then he laughed, a deep, throaty belly laugh which stopped just short of him slapping his knee. 'I sell it, of course... When I was made redundant, put out to pasture like a good Swiss cow, I sulked for a little while. Then I looked for another marketing job, and started work for a small packaging company, specialising in confectionery. They produced very high-class designs, works of art, and I enjoyed the work, but I realised that a lot of the products didn't actually live up to the packaging. Felt it was a missed opportunity, and I had a redundancy cheque burning a hole in my pocket. I invested my redundancy money and here I am.'

'In secret.'

'It's not such a secret, but I don't want to be disturbed every five minutes by people. I'm not sure I really like them.'

Mina pulled a sceptical face. 'I'm not sure you're really as curmudgeonly as you like to make out.'

'And how do you come by that conclusion?'

'You come for cake most days.'

'I like cake.'

She raised an eyebrow.

'And Amelie chooses her guests with care,' he added

grudgingly. 'Although I'm not sure she's ever going to knock young Kristian into shape. I think that one was born under the klutz star.'

Mina giggled, remembering that he'd been quite kind to the young man in question.

'Now I suppose you'd like to try some,' said Johannes with a mock weary sigh.

'Well, if you don't mind. Let's see if it lives up to the hype.'

'Come upstairs, I have a little tasting room, although it's more trouble than it's worth and I could do with the space for storage.' He scowled. 'Sometimes these dumb fool executives want to visit...' He paused and the scowl deepened. '...*The site* and they want to talk to me. Amelie suggested I set it up. I can ill afford the space or the time. But she was right, I've sold far more chocolate that way. I really need a retail outlet but I don't have the time or the resources to run one.'

He led the way back upstairs and in the hallway turned left into a tiny showroom. Mina hid a grimace. The room was dark and the shelves crammed with boxes of chocolate, none of which displayed the pretty packaging to its best effect. Johannes yanked out a box and handed her a bar.

'This is made with candied rose petals and the beans are from Sur de Lago in Venezuela. I made them for a hotel chain that specialises in unique properties, they wanted something unique to them. Try some.'

She unwrapped the matt cream wrapper, embossed with pale pink roses – the design really was stunning, it sold itself – and bit into the tiny block. Immediately she sighed with pure pleasure at the subtle rose flavour offset by the smooth dark richness of the chocolate. 'Oh, that is lovely.'

'Should be, took a lot of work that one. But they can't get enough of it. They want me to come up with something for their after-dinner coffee. I'm thinking a single estate in the Esmeraldas in Ecuador with a very light peppermint oil.

'And here…' He pulled out an attractive orange box decorated with maple leaves and handed her a cellophane bag. 'An American company wanted some high-end chocolate for Halloween. Crazy, but that's a big sale time for them.' He ripped open another bag and thrust it at her. 'Smell this. Flavoured with gingerbread spices. And now taste.'

At the first bite, the hint of ginger, nutmeg, and cinnamon immediately reminded her of autumn evenings kicking through russet leaves, the bright orange of pumpkins, and the sweet, dark intensity of home-baked parkin. 'Oh that's wonderful. If I were cooking with it, it would make a lovely sauce on ginger ice cream.'

'Hmph,' muttered Johannes as if insulted that she would use it for cooking.

As Mina moved around the cramped room, she couldn't help feeling dismayed that the wonderful selection of chocolate, flavoured with everything from roasted coconut, candied rose petals, and cranberries through to chillies and passion fruit hadn't been given the chance to shine.

'I had no idea of the scale of this. It's amazing. You must be really proud.' It really was quite some achievement, and it sounded as if he was far more successful than he was taking credit for, but she felt he could do so much more.

Johannes shrugged modestly. 'It's taken a while to get this point. And I do have some help. I send the finished items to two women in Brig who I employ, and they do all the packaging, hand-tie the bows, and put on the flowers and stickers. They pretty it up. Then there it goes to the distributor. I'm expanding quickly. Like I said I need a retail outlet. I'm going to have find premises and get an apprentice. Staff.' His lip curled at the very idea.

Mina whirled around. 'Would you employ me?'

Johannes looked taken aback at first and then a slow, cunning smile lit up his face. 'Now that would create a lot of solutions, wouldn't it?' He nodded before looking out of the window over her shoulder at the ski chalet. 'And I think I know just the place. Let's go and discuss it over a coffee with Amelie.'

They walked across the crisp expanse of snow over to Amelie's house, their breath rising in plumes of steam in the cold, sharp air, both of them lost in thought. Palpable excitement hummed between them. All of her ideas from the previous day coalesced in Mina's head. She could already envisage the perfect tasting room and if, as she got the impression, Johannes had a local site in mind, she might be able to run a coffee and cake shop, operating at lunchtimes. During all her walks and trips throughout the valley, she'd realised that there was nowhere to go for a quick coffee or a snack and that Amelie had to provide packed lunches for walkers, hikers, and skiers.

'Have you seen the barn downstairs?' asked Johannes as they skirted the big wooden chalet, and he pointed to the ground floor with its heavily shuttered windows.

'No,' replied Mina.

'Hmm,' said Johannes thougtfully as he led the way up the steps to the back door into the kitchen, pushing at the handle as he turned back to Mina. 'I hope there's fresh coffee.'

Mina looked at her watch. 'We might even scrounge some baguettes and cheese from the fridge. I had no idea it was so late.' Right on cue, her stomach rumbled, reiterating that it was twenty-to-three.

Johannes pushed at the door but it didn't open. Instead it stopped, blocked by something just in front of the door.

'Amelie?' he called and pushed harder. The door moved another inch to reveal a bolster of bright blue blocking the doorway. It took both of them a moment to recognise the pretty fabric of Amelie's dress.

'Amelie!' Johannes tried to insert himself into the gap but her body was a dead weight against the door.

'Don't, you might hurt her.' Mina was already backing down the steps. 'I'll go round to the front.' Slipping and sliding on the frozen surface of the snow, she floundered around the building, realising that Johannes followed right behind. Despite the difficult conditions, she didn't think she'd ever run so fast or been so scared in her life.

They thundered up the front steps, almost ploughing Dave down as they burst through the door.

'Hey guys,' he said, backing up.

Johannes pushed past, almost barging the other man into the cloakroom pegs.

'How long ago did you see Amelie?' panted Mina, slowing briefly.

'I left her in the kitchen ten minutes ago.'

'Thanks,' she gasped and shot after him.

'What's going on?' Dave called after her, but she was too anxious to get to the kitchen to reply.

'Amelie. Amelie.' Johannes clumsily crashed into one of the kitchen chairs as he skirted the table to fall on his knees by her side. She lay limp and pale on the floor in front of the back door, surrounded by spilled peas.

Mina dropped to her knees beside him as he patted her face, calling her name. She reached for her godmother's wrist to try and find a pulse. 'Is she breathing?' Years of being designated first-aider finally paid off, but no one had warned her that her own heart rate would skyrocket so high that she thought her pulse might explode out of her ears.

'I can't tell.'

'Hold a hand in front of her nose and mouth.'

She was still trying to find a pulse and was starting to panic. Amelie's skin was clammy and her slack face looked grey.

'We need to call an ambulance!' Johannes turned to face her, looking vague. Did they even have ambulances out here? Where was the nearest hospital? 'Johannes. Now!' Her sharp snap penetrated and he jumped to his feet, crossing to the telephone handset on the counter.

She moved into his place and put her hand on Amelie's chest. Her breaths were very shallow and her pulse, now Mina had finally located it, was thready and feeble.

'Amelie, can you hear me?' She tapped her godmother's face gently, as she'd been taught on one course. 'Amelie?' There was no response and Mina felt her chest constrict with fear. Johannes was talking in rapid German down the phone and she had no idea what he was saying.

Then Dave appeared in the doorway, his eyes widening as he took in the scene, but he stayed put, clearly aware that unless he could do something he would be in the way.

'Can you go and grab a blanket and a cushion?'

Suddenly she remembered the recovery position and squeezed her eyes shut trying to picture exactly what that entailed. She'd done training with a life-size dummy called Herbert on the floor of the staff room in training. Now all the giggling and silliness didn't seem quite so funny, but the process popped into her head. She leaned over Amelie and pushed one leg up, bent at the knee, pulled out her right arm and gently rolled her body onto her side. That looked about right, although the bluish tinge around Amelie's face worried her. Did that mean lack of oxygen or something? God, she wished she knew more. She hated being so useless. Sitting back on her haunches, she stared down at her lifeless body, praying that the ambulance could get here quickly.

Johannes hung up the phone. 'They're on their way.'

'How long will it be?'

'Not long, there's a paramedic station not so far away.' He patted her shoulder, looking worriedly at Amelie.

'Not so far away' could mean anything round here. Mina blinked back a tear, grateful that he was there, and that he was his usual gruff self. Other people might have panicked and been ineffectual.

He picked up Amelie's hand stroking it. 'She's cold.'

'Dave's getting a blanket.' And no sooner were the

words out of her mouth than he appeared with one of the soft wool blankets that were normally piled in a corner of the lounge for guests to help themselves to.

They draped the blanket around her, and even though Mina wasn't sure it was the right thing to do they wedged the cushion under Amelie's head. She hadn't stirred at all, which was the most frightening thing of all. Mina had never seen anyone so pale and still before, and terror drove her to keep checking Amelie's pulse, her fear ratcheting up each time it took her a while to find its feeble beat, scared that it might stop at any minute.

Dave stood back, his hands clasped over his stomach in respectful silence.

'How was she when you left?' asked Mina.

He frowned. 'She was... actually she was quiet, and now I realise she'd slowed down in the last half-hour. Yesterday she was busy, busy. Here and there. Today, not so much, and when I left she sat down at the table. She looked tired.' He winced and screwed up his mouth. 'She kept rubbing her chest.'

Johannes and Mina exchanged a grave look. They both knew Amelie worked too hard.

'She never sits,' said Johannes. 'Always has to do everything.' He stroked a loose, dark curl from Amelie's face. 'I kept telling her.' He shook his head and Mina could see that his hand was shaking. She laid a hand on his shoulder, wanting the touch of another person as much as to comfort him. 'She's a stubborn one. Thinks she can run the world on her own.'

There were so many platitudes to be mouthed in

situations like this, thought Mina, and she couldn't bring herself to say a single one.

At last they heard the sound of a siren approaching, but it sounded a long way in the distance.

'Shall I go out to the front?' asked Dave.

'Yes,' said Mina and Johannes at the same moment. Clearly, like her, he didn't want to leave Amelie's side.

With Dave's departure they sat in silence as Mina once again took Amelie's pulse, to give herself something to do as much as to reassure herself that she'd done everything she possibly could.

Her fingers moved along the edge of Amelie's wrist, inching across the skin. There was no pulse. Trying to fight the rising panic, she pressed her fingers down harder. Still no pulse.

'I think her heart's stopped. The pulse. It's gone.' Her mouth dried. CPR. That's what she needed to do. She remembered that annoying dummy and how hard you had to press. How many compressions? Was it two per second? Interlock the hands. In her head she pictured the rhythm of the trainer. One. Two. One. Two.

She shoved Johannes out of the way and pushed Amelie onto her back, placing both hands in the centre of her breastbone. Pressing down with all her body weight, she began. One. Two. One. Two.

'Pulse.' One, two. 'Check.' One, two. 'It.'

One. Two. One. Two. The siren still sounded a long way off.

She heard Luke's voice come from somewhere behind her. One. Two. One. Two.

He spoke to Johannes but quietly as not wanting to disturb her concentration. She focused everything on each compression.

'One. Two. One. Two.'

Luke came to kneel beside her.

'Keep going, you doing a great job. They'll be here soon.' He counted with her. One. Two.

Her arms were starting to tire but she forced herself to keep going.

'Let me know when you need me to take over. I know it's exhausting. You're doing brilliantly.'

There was a burning sensation in her shoulders and biceps, her own chest ached.

She kept it up as long as she could, listening hard for the siren, which mercifully sounded much closer, but she wasn't sure she could keep going.

'Luke.'

'Yes, it's OK. Want me to take over?'

'One. In a sec. Two.' She was worried she wasn't pressing hard enough but she was too scared to stop. Luke shuffled closer and closer, so that they were thigh-to-thigh. 'On my count of three, move along and I'll take over.'

She nodded and she put her all in the final depressions as Luke counted down and without missing the beat, took over.

She sat back on her heels, her arms aching and her knees throbbing, watching Luke's curls dance as he steadily pumped his arms over Amelie's chest. Thank God he was here, she couldn't have kept that up for much longer –

although who knew what you could achieve when you absolutely had to?

The phrase heart-in-the-mouth had never meant as much as it did just then, as she watched Luke working over her godmother's inert body. *Please let her be alright*, she prayed. Next to her, Johannes was rigid, his hand gripping one of the kitchen tables, the knuckles as white and proud as a mountain range and his mouth a straight, flat line that radiated tension.

There was nothing as welcome as the sound of heavy, determined boots filling the air, and automatically Mina and Johannes stepped back out of the way, leaving Luke still working hard. The paramedics in navy blue uniforms came in and went straight to Amelie's side with brisk efficiency, one of them taking over from Luke with professional ease, the other immediately trying to find a pulse. They asked lots of questions in German which Johannes answered. Mina managed to pick up that they were asking her age and how long she'd been there.

'How long had you been doing the CPR before I came in?' asked Luke, forwarding the paramedic's question.

'Two minutes,' she said, grateful for the digital clock on the cooker. It had been the longest two minutes of her life.

While the main paramedic continued to pump Amelie's chest with professional vigour, the other with calm speed unpacked a defibrillator and within seconds the paramedic had attached the pads to Amelie's chest. The punch of power lifted her body with a jolt that looked every inch as painful and dramatic as the images Mina had seen before. She winced and caught her lip between her teeth.

There was a sudden flurry, a nod as the second paramedic found a pulse. A thumbs up, although the first paramedic continued with the CPR while the second knelt and took out a blood pressure cuff and began calling Amelie's name. They asked Johannes more questions to which he could only answer, 'Nein.'

Mina was aware of a slight relaxation between the two paramedics, their movements were smoother and slower as if the immediate crisis was over, although they were still completely focused on their patient, talking to each other in low undertones.

Luke came to stand next to her and she found herself leaning against him. His fingers interlocked with hers and he gave her a hand a gentle squeeze. No one, it seemed, dare speak in case they broke the spell of dedicated treatment. At last the paramedic completed his last compression and gave his colleague a nod of satisfaction that signalled to the whole room that things were under control.

There was a brief conversation and Luke translated as one of them disappeared to bring in a stretcher.

'They're going to take her to hospital in Brig. They think she might have had a heart attack.'

Mina swallowed and felt tears gathering in her eyes. She was not going to fall apart now. Amelie needed her.

'Do you want to go to the hospital with her?' he asked. 'One person can go in the ambulance.'

She nodded and turned to the older man. It was obvious to anyone that he was in love with her, even if perhaps he'd only just realised quite how deeply in the last half-hour. 'Johannes?'

'I can drive,' he said gruffly. 'I'll follow the ambulance. You'll need to get home somehow.'

Luke's eyes met Mina's; they were shadowed and full of concern but also something else. 'Do you want me to come with you?' The words were slightly stiff as if it cost him dear to say them.

It was rare for her to rely on anyone else or to let her lean on anyone else but in that moment, she really wanted to be with him. She needed his perpetual positivity, that sunny outlook, and that calm, unflustered demeanour. 'Yes, please,' she said.

He swallowed. 'OK. I'll go with Johannes. I'll see you at the hospital.'

Chapter Seventeen

Inside the ambulance the siren wasn't as loud as she'd feared, and Mina perched on a side-seat watching with fearful eyes every move the paramedic made as he kept up the careful monitoring of his patient. Regular pulse checks. Another blood pressure check. And reassuring smiles to Mina.

Amelie didn't so much as flicker her eyes.

'She is stable,' said Torsten, as per his name badge.

'Is she going to be OK?'

'The hospital will look after her. Her heartbeat is good.' He nodded as his fingers sought out Amelie's pulse, and again there was that sense of satisfaction of a job well done – but he hadn't answered her question.

Mina hated feeling so bloody helpless and useless. Being a paramedic was a proper job. This man seemed so calm and utterly competent. He knew exactly what he was doing and it made Mina's panic start to recede. All she was able to do was hold Amelie's free hand and stroke the pale skin, saying the same prayer over and over in her head. *Please let her be alright. Please let her be alright.*

Now she had time to think, she realised that she'd completely abandoned the hotel to poor Dave, who had stood in the doorway watching the proceedings with quiet, stolid patience. Just as she was about to follow the stretcher out, she'd stopped in sudden alarm, realising that there was still a hotel to be run, and he'd stepped up to her, patted her arm and said, 'Don't worry, Mina. I'll sort dinner out.'

All she'd been able to say was, 'Thank you,' because there was no other option.

Johannes had had a little more presence of mind. 'I'll phone Franzi and Giselle, see if they can come and help. They know what they're doing.'

Grateful for that, Mina had scooped up her bag and grabbed her coat, and scrambled into the ambulance.

Once they reached the hospital things started to blur as Amelie was whisked away, surrounded by doctors and nurses, leaving Mina alone in a corridor. For a little while she paced, trying to get rid of that edgy, itchy feeling of being surplus to requirements, until Torsten came back down the corridor about fifteen minutes later.

She looked hopefully at him. 'Any news?'

'She is with the doctor. They will come to you.' He smiled at her, kind and reassuring. 'When they have news.'

'Thank you,' said Mina, realising that he probably didn't know any more at that moment.

Feeling lost and in limbo, she slumped into her seat, for once her natural positivity subdued by the enormity of things. What if Amelie died? There were so many things she'd never asked her. If she was honest with herself, she'd shied away from asking questions about her mother. There was that deep-buried nugget of resentment that her parents had been unable to give up their reckless lifestyle for the sake of their small daughters. And she hadn't spent enough time with Amelie. Not nearly enough. She'd been a constant in the background of Mina's life, but always there like some exotic fairy godmother who was on her side no matter what, and Mina had taken that for granted.

She dropped her head into her hands and focused on her breathing. Amelie was young. She was fit. They'd walked a couple of kilometres the other day and she'd been fine. She looked healthy, if a little tired, and she wasn't overweight. Too much rushing about in the chalet for that. What caused heart attacks? Furred arteries. Mina's mind raced down different corridors, coming to dead ends constantly, wishing she was more knowledgeable about such things.

She spotted the heavy boots first, and looked up. Torsten stood in front of her with a take-out cup of coffee.

'For you.'

For a stupid second, tears swam into her eyes at his kindness. 'That's… very kind. *Danke schön.*'

His quick smile – with a touch of male appreciation – and her first tentative sip of coffee made her feel a lot better and she smiled back at him.

'I hope she will be OK.' With a quick, shy goodbye gesture he turned and walked away down the corridor, leaving Mina feeling heartened by his kind sympathy. There were always good people in the world to brighten things, no matter how bleak the situation appeared. The quick episode restored Mina's natural faith in the world and that things would turn out well.

As she drained her coffee cup, Johannes and Luke appeared. The older man looked grey and drawn, and Luke anxious like a nervous rabbit, constantly checking for danger.

'Any news?' asked Luke.

She shook her head. 'I haven't seen anyone. She's through there.' She pointed to the double doors with their big red circle with a line through it, which clearly read 'no admittance' in any language.

Luke and Johannes both sat down on either side of her.

'Do you want a coffee?' she asked, suddenly needing to do something.

Luke shook his head. 'I'm OK.'

Johannes did the same.

The three of them sat in silence, although Mina noticed that Luke fidgeted constantly. His foot tapped, his kneed jigged, and he seemed to have shrunk into his chair, as if he didn't want to be there or to touch anything.

At last, over an hour later, a doctor came out of the double doors, a mask across his face, which he pulled down.

All three of them jumped to their feet in perfect unison and the doctor's mouth twitched.

He held up a hand and began to speak. Luke interrupted

in quick German. '*Sprechen sie Englisch. Sie ist eine familie und Englisch.*'

'The lady, she's your…'

'My godmother. I'm staying with her. There is no other family. Her name is Amelie,' Mina added the last a little fiercely.

'Your godmother has had a heart attack. She will recover, but we need to insert a stent to enlarge an artery bringing blood to the heart. It's a simple procedure. We shall do it tomorrow.'

'Is she conscious?'

He shook his head. 'Not yet. She's going into a room on her own, and will be monitored overnight.'

'Can I… we see her?'

'Yes, once she has been settled. Half an hour.'

'She's not going to die?'

The doctor, his eyes glinting behind his glasses, gave her a stern look. 'Not if I can help it.' Then he gave her a grave smile. 'Modern medicine means that her condition will not be so serious once we have done the procedure. Until then we will be watching her very carefully. But it will be important for her to avoid stress and anxiety.'

'Let's hope the woman will see some sense now and let other people help her,' Johannes grumbled as soon as the doctor left. 'I've been telling her.'

Mina smiled at him. 'If you know what's best for you, I wouldn't tell her you told her so. It might not endear you to her.'

His mouth shut abruptly and for a second his moustache

bristled, before he regarded her with a steady glance. 'Perhaps not.'

'Amelie doesn't like being told what to do.'

'Well, she might have to learn to put up with it,' he said, folding his arms and looking recalcitrant, clearly a man who didn't like being told what to do either.

'Perhaps you need to tell her why it's so important to you,' said Mina, trying to suppress a smile.

He glowered at her. 'Hmmph.'

Mina rolled her eyes. 'The two of you are as bad as one another. I think you need to tell her how you feel.'

She almost felt sorry for him as he coloured. 'Hmph.'

'In words of more than one grunt,' she teased.

'I've tried to show her.'

'Maybe she thinks you're being neighbourly.'

'Foolish woman.'

'Hearts and flowers,' interrupted Luke, suddenly appearing a little more lifelike. 'A romantic gesture.' For a while he'd been looking like some kind of graveyard effigy. 'That's what you need.'

It took longer than the predicted half-hour, nearer an hour and a half, before they were led through several corridors to a ward with several private rooms.

'I'll wait outside,' said Luke, seeming uncharacteristically on edge.

'Are you sure?'

'Yes. Probably only allowed two visitors.'

Mina guessed he was right. This was actually the first time she'd ever been inside any part of a hospital apart from A&E. There'd been plenty of trips there – like the time she'd fallen out of a tree, when she'd bounced too high off the trampoline, and taken a tumble off her bike from a home-made ramp across the garden bench; she really did break her wrist that time, but the previous excursions had been false alarms. She felt now as if she should be tiptoeing, and wasn't sure if it was alright to speak above a whisper. Glancing at Johannes, she tentatively pushed open the door.

Amelie was wired up to a beeping monitor made familiar by endless episodes of *Casualty*, thanks to Hannah, who'd once thought she'd like to be a nurse, an idea scuppered by her aversion to blood and a couple of spectacular faints. Mina felt a little bit like fainting now, at the sight of her godmother lying so still. The insistent sounds, the green waves oscillating on screen. This was serious. How did someone go from being alive and well in the morning to this, silent and lifeless? Nothing in her experience had prepared her for this. The enormity of everything hit her hard. Amelie wasn't going anywhere for a while. The chalet. The guests. Someone needed to run the place. Amelie would worry. Worry was bad for the heart. Mina stared down at her godmother making a silent resolution. Her godmother had given her so much security over the years and she knew how important the chalet and the guests were to her.

She touched her godmother's hand, while Johannes hung back a little, a look of blatant longing on his face. Mina beckoned him over.

'Talk to her. I'm sure whatever we say will register in her subconscious.' That's what they always said on the television.

271

He swallowed as if too self-conscious, so she took pity on him and started.

'Hey Amelie, it's Mina. You gave us quite a scare but the doctors say you're going to be fine. And don't worry about anything at the chalet. I'll sort everything out. Johannes and Franzi and Giselle and Dave are all helping. And I promise I'll look after the chalet as if it was my own home and all your guests were staying with me. You don't need to worry about anything.'

Johannes stepped forward and Mina patted his arm, she could see his throat working as he tried to find the words.

'No, you mustn't worry about anything. We're all here to help you. I… we love you. Just get better and come back to us.'

Her breath caught in her throat at seeing the usually-so-forthright man lost for words, and the emotion came flooding back. She'd been trying so hard to be pragmatic; seeing Johannes's pain was more than she could bear herself.

Leaving him with Amelie, she stumbled out in the corridor, the heavy lump in her chest almost suffocating her. Luke leaned against the wall, his arms folded, looking detached and closed-off, as if this was the last place in the world he wanted to be. When he saw her his face softened and he dropped the aloof stance and held out his arms. She went straight into his embrace and buried her face in his warm neck, determined not to cry but just to lean into the comfort he was offering. His arms enfolded her hugging her to him, both hands clasped against her back.

'I've got you,' he murmured into her hair. 'It's OK.'

She sucked in several determined breaths; she wasn't going to cry. It wouldn't help. Instead she clung to Luke, relishing the feel of his body, warm and strong, stalwart and steady. Instinctively she knew she could rely on him. He was hers. In that moment, the truth of it imprinted itself onto her brain. He was hers.

Neither of them said a word for a few minutes. Eventually she peeled her head away and looked up at him. He bent his head to lay a soft kiss on her lips. She pushed up on her toes to deepen the contact, needing that human connection, needing Luke's unspoken calm. He responded briefly before pulling back and lifting a hand to stroke her face.

'Thank you,' she whispered, stretching up and kissing the corner of his mouth. 'For being here.'

She was overwhelmed by the feeling that bloomed, warm and heartfelt in her chest. It had been hopeless from the moment she'd met him. Remembering what Johannes had said, she knew she shouldn't waste any more time. As much as she'd tried to deny it, she couldn't now. She was in love with Luke. She looked up at him with tremulous smile, everything she felt shining out of her eyes. 'Luke?'

'And finally,' he said, stroking a tender thumb over her mouth. 'She gets it.'

'You?' She couldn't bring herself the ask the question in full, she was still getting used to the idea that she was totally, head-over-heels, lightning-bolt, in love with him.

'Always. From the very first day I met you. I told you, it was serendipity. Love at pointy elbows.' Despite everything she managed a shaky laugh.

'I'm never going to live those elbows down, am I?'

He shook his head, the familiar lopsided smile lighting up his face.

By the time they left the hospital it was just after seven and growing dark. The journey back to Reckingen was completed in silence, and just as they drove through Fiesch a few snowflakes tumbled out of the sky. Mina stared at them, a kaleidoscope of icy white against the pitch-black sky. Every now and then Luke would look back from the passenger seat, almost as if she checking she was still there, and send her a quiet smile.

At one point Johannes tutted and muttered something to himself in German. Luke laughed and turned around to Mina. 'He's complaining about us distracting him. That was German for "get a room".'

'I'm not doing anything,' she replied demurely, raising her eyebrows at him in the rear-view mirror.

'You don't need to do anything,' Luke said, his eyes radiating gentle sincerity and intimacy.

She tucked the comment away in that little warm glow radiating quiet joy inside her. As always when with him, all her senses were attuned to Luke frequency, and in the dark of the car it seemed to have intensified.

Ten minutes on, when Mina looked up at the dark night sky, it had filled quickly with whirling flakes, spinning down like autumn leaves toyed with by a gale. She was surprised by the speed at which it was settling.

The road ahead, lit up by the headlights, had a cotton wool-bobbled surface in no time at all. Johannes slowed his driving, and although they moved at a steady pace, the last bit of the journey took a good ten minutes longer than usual.

When at last they pulled up outside the chalet, defeat overwhelmed Mina. Returning without Amelie felt wrong and she tramped up the steps, bashing the snow with irritable kicks from her boots as she went. Inside she shook off the flakes clinging to her hair, left her things in the boot room and opened the door into the reception. Subdued voices murmured in the dining room beyond the lounge and she crossed the room to find a few people still seated at the dining table, including Dave, Frank, and Claudia. Their heads all turned in quick succession.

Mina dredged up a smile, although she felt totally drained. Until now she hadn't realised how taut and tense she'd been in the hospital. They all jumped, firing questions over each other. She held up a hand to silence them. 'She's fine. Amelie's had a small heart attack, but she's in the right place.' She explained about tomorrow's operation and the planned stent and then turned to Dave.

'How was dinner? Did you manage?'

'It was fine... thanks to Franzi who was able to come and help, but I know where the cutlery and tableware is kept now.' He grinned. 'Claudia helped lay the tables and Frank opened the wine.'

'Bless them.' She pulled a small grimace. 'I hope they didn't mind. They are paying guests.'

'They're also good friends of Amelie's. They don't mind

at all.' Dave shot her a sympathetic glance. 'I can help again tomorrow.'

'Can you?' Mina wasn't in a position to turn any help down. 'Are you sure? What about Sarah?'

For a moment he almost looked cocky. 'She doesn't mind sleeping with the chef.'

Mina laughed. 'Well, that's excellent news. But you are on holiday.'

'As long as I can get out in the afternoons, I'll be happy. Franzi did say that she and Giselle will help where they can, but they've got exams coming up at school so can't do any extra hours. Franzi helped tonight because it was an emergency.'

'It will be fine,' said Mina, already starting to make lists in her head. She could do this. She had to.

'Have you eaten? There are some cheese pies left.'

'Do you know what? I'm starving, and I bet Luke and Johannes are too.' She looked around and both men were talking, warming their hands in front of the fire, although Johannes still had his coat on.

'Johannes, stay for something to eat,' she said, making it more of an order than a request. His face still looked grey and exhausted, and if he felt anything like she did, he was probably worn out and depleted. She guessed that the last thing he wanted to do was go home on his own.

The three of them retreated to the kitchen. Mina needed that barrier between herself and the guests, in part because she didn't want to impose her worry and concern on them, but also needing that separation, because although they might care about Amelie, it wasn't really their problem.

Trying not to think about Amelie mixing dough, flouring the surfaces, beating eggs, and baking her gorgeous cakes, Mina laid the table at one end and put the pies in the oven to heat, while Johannes made coffee.

The silent group ate mechanically to the hum of the dishwasher. Franzi had clearly stayed to tidy up the plates and cutlery from the dining table, although there were still a few glasses and the dirty tablecloths to be removed. Mina wasn't sure if either Johannes or Luke actually tasted the little cheese pies. When Johannes finally laid down his knife and fork he rubbed a weary hand over his forehead. 'I should go. I'll come across early in the morning to clean the fire. You'll need to put the guards in front before you close up for the night.' Mina nodded. Tiredness tugged at her but she realised she couldn't go to bed until she'd switched out lights, locked doors, and cleared the dining table. She really ought to lay it as well for breakfast, it would be one less job in the morning. As it was, she was going to have to get up very early. Could she go to bed before the guests?

Johannes took his leave and Mina rose to give him a quick hug.

'I'll ring the hospital in the morning.'

'Thank you. Goodnight.'

As soon as he'd gone, she looked at Luke as she tried and failed to stifle a yawn.

'You look bushed.' He stood up and ran a thumb under her eyes, the gentle touch taking any insult out of his words.

'Just what every girl wants to hear,' she replied with a wan smile, reaching up to touch the fine lines fanning from his mouth thinking that he still looked quite tense. She stroked her hand down his jawline to the warm skin between his neck and shoulder, not wanting to relinquish the touch. He laid his hand over hers and squeezed. Seconds passed as they stood facing each other, each of them studying the other. It would have been easy, thought Mina, in a moment of uncharacteristic weakness, to step forward, sink into his arms, and stay there. There was the flicker of understanding in his eyes when instead she said, 'I can't go to bed yet.' And part of her didn't want to. She didn't want to be on her own, weighed down by thoughts in the dark. 'I need to lay the table for breakfast.'

'Do it in the morning. I'll help.'

'I want to say you don't need to do that, but I think, being practical, I'm going to need all the help I can get. Ever run a hotel before?' Although she said it with a positive wrinkle of her nose, her concern was not running the place, but running it to Amelie's standards.

'Can't say I have, but I do know things always look better after a good night's sleep.'

'You're right. I'll just do the dining table.'

'I'll do the fire guards for you.'

Teamwork, she thought as they headed toward to the dining room and the lounge. Luke would always be on her team and she wasn't sure how she knew that – she just did. All the guests had disappeared, for which she was grateful, although not surprised; people tended to go to up to their rooms early after a hard day's skiing and hiking. While Luke locked the doors, raked the fire, and put fire guards on both sides of the open fireplace, she put a fresh cloth on the main dining table, cleared the evening's condiments from the sideboard, and put out the large jars of cereal and muesli. She'd put out the fresh bits in the morning.

Feeling that at least she knew what she was doing tomorrow morning, she clicked out the light with a relieved sigh. Elephants, she thought. One bite at a time.

Luke met her at the bottom of the stairs and they climbed them together. Tread by tread. There was a funny fizz in the bottom of her stomach as she listened to their synchronised steps. Was being in step another form of serendipity?

What a day. She'd never have dreamed this morning, when she'd ambushed Johannes by jumping off the bottom step, that it would turn out quite like this. For a brief second the germ of the idea that had been fluttering at the back of her head since she'd visited his chocolate den flitted through her mind like an elusive wisp of mist. She made an inarticulate noise of frustration. It would come back when her body didn't feel as limp as a water-deprived daisy.

Luke took her hand as her steps slowed. 'Come on.'

She relished the touch of the contact and squeezed his hand, knowing that she couldn't let go. Not tonight – but it felt right, not needy and pathetic. Just right.

When Luke led her to her door she opened the door and tugged at his hand.

'Mina,' he whispered.

'I don't want you to go.'

He rested his forehead on hers and they stood in the doorway, the small creaks and sighs of the building settling for the night around them, like comforting ghosts.

Pulling him in, she closed the door and led him to the bed.

'Stay with me,' she said. 'Just hold me.'

He lifted a hand and stroked along her cheekbones and kissed her gently on the mouth, one hand resting with a featherlight touch on her thigh. Although she wanted his comfort, that touch sent a tiny electric current of awareness.

'I'll hold you,' he whispered. 'Always.' Her heart turned a slow, weighted somersault in her chest. How had she fallen in love with him? At the same time, how could she not?

She slipped off her jeans and padded in her thick socks to the bathroom to clean her teeth. When she came back, Luke was lying on the far side of the bed on top of the bedclothes, the cover on her side turned back in waiting. She ignored it and climbed onto the bed, where he held out an arm. She lay next to him on her side as he pulled her into his chest.

'You'll get cold,' he whispered.

She didn't care, she wanted to be close to him. Hooking one leg over his, she nestled in closer. 'You'll keep me warm.'

They lay in the golden glow of the bedside lamp, their breathing quiet, Luke rubbing soothing strokes up and down her neck, as if trying to massage her to sleep, but now she was in bed, her brain didn't want to shut down.

'I hope she's going to be OK,' she murmured as much to reassure herself as to seek reassurance.

'The human body is an amazing thing, but the human

spirit, human resilience, is far greater. Amelie won't give up. Sometimes it's about temperament.'

'You sound as if you know a lot about it,' said Mina, surprised. Luke hadn't struck her as particularly spiritual before, always so positive and practical.

'I do.' The pause, weighted with significance, seemed to hang heavy in the night air. 'I spent a lot of time in hospital. When I was nineteen I was very… ill.' Mina heard the import in the word. 'You see a lot from a hospital bed when you're there for that long.'

Mina swallowed. She had the sense that he was steeling himself to say more and she didn't want to be that person shaking things loose when they might be better left unsaid.

'You learn who's going to die and who isn't.'

Awareness prickled and ran across her skin at the soft words. She spread her hand out across his chest, her fingers splaying across his ribs under his T-shirt as if to anchor him to her. It seemed impossible to imagine Luke as anything other than vibrant, strong, and energetic.

'That sounds tough.'

She felt his shoulders shrug. 'Other people lost, I survived. I'm still here.' He let out a mirthless laugh. 'Sorry, I bottled it at the hospital. I had leukaemia. Two years of treatment. Too many memories. I hate the bloody places. It's the first time I've been in one for… a while. It's triggered a lot of emotions that I thought I'd got over.'

'I'm sorry.'

'Don't be. It made me who I am now – although I hate anyone else saying that to me, as if they're trying to find a positive or make a virtue of having had a blood cancer.

There are no positives. It's shit. Or rather, it was shit and now I'm through the other side. But those two years were the worst of my life – not so much for me, but for my parents, my sister, my cousins, grandparents, friends. Watching them suffer. Bloody shit. I never want to put anyone through that again. You can bear it for yourself. You know if you stick with the treatment, there might be some let-up for your body at some stage. You stand to gain, but it's a sod watching other people going through it. My mum always trying not to cry. My dad trying not to let her see him cry. My sister crying and feeling guilty that she was crying. That grief, fear – it screws everyone up. I'd have done anything for them not to have suffered like that.'

She laid a hand on his chest, wanting to comfort him. The raw pain in his voice moving her to silent tears. 'It must have been tough for all of you. I had no idea. Are you OK now?'

'If I wasn't, I wouldn't be here with you. I don't normally talk about it. It's only because of today...'

'Then thank you for coming with me. It made a difference.' She kissed him on the neck, appreciating that he really didn't want to talk about it anymore, her lips pressing into the pulse flickering there.

He nodded and pulled her closer, and she shivered a little as goose bumps rose on her legs.

'You're cold, you should get under the cover.'

'Only if you do.'

He turned onto his side and his eyes swept her face before locking onto hers. She stared back at him. Without saying anything he slipped off the bed, removed his trousers, and slid back under the covers. She joined him under the heavy feather duvet, feeling it settle, cocooning the pair of them as one. Her bare legs touched the soft silkiness of the hair on his legs and every nerve-ending pinged to attention. She slipped a hand around his waist, her fingers brushing the warm skin under his T-shirt.

He turned and kissed her forehead. 'Go to sleep.'

'I'm not sure I can. My brain keeps darting off in different directions. What will I cook for dinner? When will Amelie be home? What happens if it keeps snowing?'

He huffed out a laugh. 'Count sheep.'

'They'll get lost in the snow.'

'Amelie will be fine. Cooking is the least of your worries. If it keeps snowing, people will stay inside and entertain themselves.'

'I love a man who has all the answers.'

'And I love a woman who throws herself at my feet, shares her chocolate, and is always ready for the next adventure. It's going to be fine.'

'I almost believe you.'

'What, that I love you?' It wasn't what she meant at all but now he'd asked…

'Do you?'

His eyes locked on hers and she could see it shining in them before he uttered the quiet, heartfelt, 'I do.'

Fizzy catherine wheels of happiness exploded in her heart. She slipped her leg over his and settled herself onto his chest, taking his face in her hands. 'I'm not supposed to fall in love with you. You're all wrong for me.'

'I don't think serendipity gives you any choice, does it? I

didn't plan on falling in love either. It just happened, and now I can't imagine it not happening.'

She drew in a shaky breath. 'I know how you feel.'

He held her close. 'Sleep. It's been a tough day.'

They woke to a snow-blanketed world of silence. Everything outside was soft and curved, and blurred by the whirling flakes that continued to stream past the window. Mina lay looking out of the window, watching the dancing snow swirl and eddy in the downdrafts like tiny feathers riding the thermals as she thought about what she needed to do today. Then she allowed herself to turn over and look at Luke, who she found was awake and looking back at her.

'Morning,' he said, reaching forward and smoothing her hair from her face. She reached up to touch the fine blonde fuzz she knew she'd find there. She always woke with serious bed-head. 'You think loudly.'

'I do?' she asked with a perplexed smile.

'Mmm. I can hear the cogs whirring, and you fidget a lot with your hands when you're thinking.'

She laughed and tucked her hands under the covers. 'That's my tell, is it?'

'One of them. You also get this really cute little furrow just here.' He touched her eyebrow.

'Smooth pillow talk, mister,' she teased.

'I was a late starter.' A tiny frown darkened his face. 'I missed out on a lot in my late teens.'

'Well, I can tell you there are definitely a few

departments you've caught up in quite nicely. Although I might need to check on the kissing again.' She leaned forward and pressed her lips on his before she could let her sympathy show. Knowing Luke, he wouldn't welcome it, but being that ill when you were nineteen and twenty must have been hellish, especially if he'd been in hospital for most of that time. At nineteen, she was at university in Leeds having some of the best times of her life. That was when she'd really discovered who she was and what life was about. Much as she loved Miriam and Derek, they led a sheltered and quite restricted life. Living in a big city had opened so many doors for Mina. New friends, new ideas, new places. She'd become a lot more worldly.

Luke's hand slid around her waist, his fingers soothing over her skin as he pulled her towards him to deepen the kiss. She relaxed into his body, her senses humming, amazed that this felt so natural and easy.

'I'm sorry,' she said with a sultry twist to her lips, 'much as I'd like to stay here all morning and see what pops up, I'm afraid—'

'What pops up?' Luke spluttered and lifted the covers, looking down. 'This is as popped as it gets, in all its morning glory.'

She grazed his earlobe with her teeth and shot him a wicked grin, but couldn't resist squirming up against him. There was something life-affirming and – to be quite honest, very flattering – about that physical manifestation of his desire for her. 'Good, perhaps you can remind me another time. Sadly, some of us have work to do.' She threw back the covers but before she could get out of bed, he snagged an arm around her waist, pulled her back against his chest, and kissed the nape of her neck, while lazily caressing her breast with his other hand, his fingers unerringly homing in on her over-sensitive nipple. The moan of pleasure slipped out and he let go.

'Payback's a bitch.' He grinned.

She turned to face him, hooked a hand around his neck and they met in the middle with a frantic, hot kiss.

'Now that's how you start the day,' said Luke with a cocky smile. 'None of this, "much as I'd like to stay here all morning" malarkey. Kissing is a much under-rated pastime in my view.'

Mina sighed, fizzing with pleasure and happiness. 'No argument here. But I do need to get up.'

'Into the shower with you. I'll clean you up.'

'If you do that, we'll never get out of here. And breakfast is due to be served in twenty-two minutes.'

She gave him one last kiss and got out of bed.

'I'll go shower next door.' Luke swung his legs out of bed and stood up, his back to her, and for a distinctly male-objectification moment she took in his lean lines and muscles, powerful shoulders, narrow waist, and rather fine gluteus maximus. God, he really was rather gorgeous – and she needed to stop staring and get on with the day.

Chapter Eighteen

The falling snow changed the dynamic that morning, which was just as well, as Mina struggled to get breakfast out in time. Thankfully, most people decided to take advantage of the white-out to have a lie-in, and very few people emerged before seven-thirty. It took her a while to work out where everything was, which slowed her down a lot; cutlery, plates, tablecloths, and then remembering everything; pickles, boiling the eggs, putting the right knives out. Each omission she added to a list she was creating on a new page in her notebook.

Lists were about to become her best friend. By the time everyone had had breakfast, she was hoping to have created a checklist for the next day, so that tomorrow she would do better. The list was growing rapidly, and as she was adding, *heat croissants* and *check muesli supplies*, Johannes stomped into the kitchen in heavy boots. 'No news from the hospital. Too early to speak to anyone. I've filled up the log baskets and I've lit the fire.' The strain around his eyes touched

Mina; he didn't look as if he'd had much sleep. It made her doubly grateful she hadn't been on her own. The night with Luke had lit a small, warming glow inside her that she carried like her own personal beacon.

'Thank you. Would you like a coffee?' That was one thing she had managed to get right this morning. She'd kept the coffee pot full and regularly replenished as everyone seemed quite happy to dally over breakfast. Normally guests would all have been up and off – today Frank and Claudia lingered over three cups of coffee, and the couple who normally skied with Sarah had come back for second and third helpings of breakfast.

'Yes, please.' He looked with longing at the coffee pot, and she realised that he'd probably come straight over this morning without stopping for breakfast. She poured him a large mug and put the two sugars in.

His mouth twisted in a wry smile. 'Thank you. Not good for my waistline, but I can't drink it without.' He took a sip and sighed. 'I think people will be staying inside this morning. Visibility is not good for skiing, although you always get some idiots who think they're invincible. The steps need clearing.'

'I can do that,' said Luke, appearing like some sort of ghost in the doorway. 'Sorry Mina, I got held up with a couple of phone calls.' He shot her a bright smile, just that tiny bit too bright. Almost brittle. 'I'll get right onto it.'

She turned, her eyes softening at the sight of him. Last night had changed everything. Now she could see a future for them. It didn't matter that they were so similar. Johannes was right, the nap of their fabric was perfectly aligned, and for the life of her now she couldn't understand why she'd been fighting it for so long. They were ideally suited. Just looking at him now, broad-shouldered, leaning lazily in the doorway, his blue eyes thoughtful for once, she couldn't help but sigh, and her heart did another one those funny little bunny hops.

'Have some coffee first,' she insisted. 'And breakfast. You too, Johannes. I bet you haven't eaten.' Both of them turned to her with the exact same expression, which she called hopeful dog-eyes.

She grinned. 'See, I'm stepping into Amelie's shoes already.' With that she pulled two plates from the cupboard and put a basket of bread on the table before nipping into the breakfast room, which was now empty, and bringing back the remains of the plates of salami and cheese and the basket of bread and bread rolls.

Both men tucked in with hearty appetites and the sort of single-minded attention to food that didn't require any kind of verbal communication, which meant she could start looking at the planned menus on the walls as she dried the cutlery from the dishwasher. Thank goodness for Amelie's superb organisational skills, and that Mina had taken that trip to Brig with her. As a result, she had a good understanding of how Amelie managed her food resources. She knew that for the rest of this week, the food was all planned and had been shopped for. Next week was where it would get interesting. With a sudden start, Mina dropped the spoon she was polishing. Next week.

'What?' Luke's head shot up, immediately studying her face.

'I've just realised. I'm supposed to be back at work next week.' Funny how things like that faded into insignificance in the face of something really important.

Johannes's forehead furrowed into one of his stern frowns and Luke stared at her in horror. Now they quivered with worry like dogs whose food bowls could be moved at any second.

'Don't worry. I'm not leaving. I'll just have to tell them I've had a family emergency.' Hopefully, Ian would be understanding. They had policies for that sort of thing, didn't they?

As soon as they finished eating, Johannes phoned the hospital again for an update on Amelie. This time he was able to speak to a nurse on the ward. Amelie had had a restful night and was stable. They were planning to do the procedure later in the day, at two, and she could have visitors in the late afternoon, although looking at the snow still bucketing down outside the window, Mina wondered if that was possible.

'What about the weather?' she asked.

Johannes shrugged. 'We'll have to see. The forecast says there will be snow off and on for the next twenty four hours. They're expecting thirty centimetres. But the snow plough will come through again soon and I can get to Brig later, or I can take the train.' Mina couldn't hide her scepticism when she looked out of the window again. At home the whole country ground to a halt if there was so much as an inch of snow. 'Really?'

A very slight smile lifted his face. 'This is Switzerland. We are used to snow. Here we get maybe twenty centimetres of snow every couple of days in the winter months. The road will be open.'

Mina looked around the kitchen. What was more important? Seeing Amelie, or ensuring that she didn't need to worry about the chalet? 'Do you think we could speak to her?' Mina frowned, trying to figure out what part of the day she could get away to visit. 'There are probably things she needs, and she'll want her mobile.'

'I'll call the hospital again and find out,' said Johannes in his usual gruff manner.

Luke rose, frowning at his phone, which he seemed to be checking every five minutes all of a sudden. 'I'm going to clear the steps,' he said, distractedly tugging on his ski jacket.

'Great.' Something wasn't right. Luke had retreated. No one would ever accuse her of being high maintenance or clingy, but there was a slight distance between them that hadn't been there before – but right now she had other things to worry about. Food. Timings. The comfort of guests. With the snow falling so heavily, it looked as if she was going to have the additional headache of supplying lunch.

A thought struck her. 'Do you need to do the steps when it's still snowing?'

'Yes,' interjected Johannes. 'In case any guests do go outside. You don't want any accidents. There's a sack of grit in the barn. I'll show you.'

The men headed for the door, Johannes leading the way.

'You any good at peeling vegetables?' she asked Luke, wondering if she was imagining things. As if he read her mind, his face brightened and he strode over and kissed her on the lips, completely ignoring Johannes's superior smirk.

'As soon as I've cleared the steps, I will be at your beck and call. Promise.' He tucked the phone firmly in his pocket and drew up the zip of his ski jacket.

'Good, because you're on soup-making duty,' she called out to his departing back, already planning what needed to be done next. If she started some bread dough now, fresh bread combined with a hearty vegetable soup would feed plenty of people without too much effort. That was lunch taken care of. One step at a time, she told herself, as the number of jobs and tasks started to unravel in her head.

'Want a cake-maker?' asked a cheerful voice.

She could have kissed Dave as well. His timing was impeccable. Everything was possible. She needed to utilise all the help she could get. How on earth had Amelie done all this on her own? No wonder she'd had a heart attack.

'Dave, just the man. How do you fancy making a *zuger kirschtorte*?' She pointed to the recipe on the wall.

Dave pulled a doubtful face. 'Not sure about that. Never made one of those before.' He made no move to read the laminated sheet of paper. Mina brightened her smile, hiding an inward sigh. How difficult was following a recipe? It took her a second to curb her instinct to chivvy him along and tell him it would be easy. Poor Dave was standing there full of indecision and uncertainty when she really needed him just to crack on. Mina chewed at her lip. What would Amelie do?

She thought of the conversations she'd shared with her godmother. Amelie wouldn't push him; she was trying to build his confidence. Mina's personal view was that if he made it and it was a success, it would be a triumph; if it wasn't, it wasn't the end of the world. And that was the difference between her and Dave. She was a risk-taker while he was not. He preferred to follow rather than lead. She needed to keep things within his comfort zone. Not everyone wanted to experiment all the time. Some people liked to stick with the tried and tested, like her adopted parents. Guilt pinched at her. Sometimes she wasn't as patient as she could be with people, didn't always accept their differences. She'd been quite impatient with Simon sometimes. He took forever to make a decision, and if she were honest, she'd quite often made them for him.

And today she needed some certainty. She couldn't afford to have to find an alternative cake if this one didn't bake to plan.

'OK, plan B. How do you fancy making a Victoria sponge?'

His lugubrious heavy set face lifted immediately. 'My nan loved a Victoria sponge. Swore by a recipe in her old Be-Ro book. I tell you, that thing was falling apart.'

'Excellent.' Mina smiled. Now to push him a little – she couldn't quite help herself. 'And what about doing it with a bit of a Swiss twist?' She deliberately nodded her head in encouragement, which she seemed to remember was a psychological trick to get people to agree to do things.

'What do you mean?' His words radiated suspicion which made her laugh out loud.

'Nothing too wild, I promise. But I'd quite like to keep things a little bit Swiss for Amelie's sake. I was thinking of a filling made with cream and cherries. What do you think? There are loads of frozen cherries in the freezer.'

The careful ruminations of his mind were reflected in the movement and twitches of his mouth. Dave would never make a poker player.

'Hmm, I suppose I could make a sort of cherry jam. Nan was a great jam-maker too.'

'Perfect.' She gave Dave her best encouraging we've-got-this smile.

Now all she had to do was sort out dinner. She glanced outside at the snow. It was still falling. Would they get to the hospital today? And if they did, she needed to get a message to Amelie before then to let her know that everything was under control and that Mina wasn't leaving any time soon. Which reminded her she needed to make a few personal calls of her own.

Hannah answered almost immediately, and before Mina could say a word, said, 'I've done it, Mina. I've done it.'

'Done what?'

'Booked my trip to Ireland. I'm going in September.'

'Wow, and what about work?'

'I'm taking a sabbatical. I wasn't quite brave enough to jack it all in. That's the sort of thing you'd do.'

'Ha! Funny you should say that. I might be just about to commit career suicide.'

'Why? What have you done?' Why was it that everyone always assumed it was Mina that had done something?

'*I* haven't done anything. Not yet anyway but...' She paused, trying to find the right words so as not to alarm Hannah unduly. 'Amelie's had a health scare. She's in hospital. But she's going to be OK.' Mina crossed her fingers on both hands so as not to tempt providence. 'She's had a heart attack, but the doctor said she should make a full recovery. She's just going to need to rest and recuperate for a while.'

'Oh no, poor Amelie. Is she OK? Have you seen her?'

'I think so. And I haven't seen her today. The nearest hospital is half an hour away, and it's chucking down with snow, I've never seen anything like it.'

'You are in the Alps,' Hannah pointed out with dry amusement.

'Yeah, even so, it's really coming down. It would bring Manchester to a grinding halt, I can tell you.'

'You might have to wait until tomorrow,' mused Hannah.

Mina realised that her sister hadn't yet picked up on the most salient point. 'I'm going to have to stay out here for a bit longer. There's no one to look after the chalet.'

'But doesn't Amelie have any staff?'

Mina explained the situation, and by the end of the lengthy call, Hannah had offered to come out and help as well. 'I'll call in the cavalry, if I need to,' Mina promised before saying goodbye. Right now she needed to get to grips with running the place, having a non-cook to train would complicate matters.

While Dave made the Victoria sponge, she gathered together the ingredients to make a hearty soup and studied Amelie's recipes. Spaghetti di Ascona. Now that sounded the perfect comfort dish: chicken, prosciutto, mushrooms, and garlic, which were combined to make a rich tomato sauce poured over spaghetti. Mina read the notes. Apparently Ascona was on the shores of the Swiss side of Lake Maggiore. More importantly, it was quick and easy, which would leave her time to do everything else – although she had yet to figure out quite what everything else was.

As she chopped the chicken, Luke returned looking ruddy but smiling. 'All done.' He grinned and looked out of the window. 'For the time being. Have you seen the barn underneath here? It's huge.'

'No, but I guess it would have to be big for the cows. Johannes has converted his into the…' She suddenly remembered what Johannes had been saying before they'd found Amelie lying on the floor. With an inward shudder she tried to shake the awful image of her prone body from her head.

Luke carried on talking but she was still thinking about what might have happened if she and Johannes hadn't come back when they did. It didn't bear thinking about; instead she needed to focus on making sure Amelie's hotel ran smoothly.

'It's wasted space. Honestly you should see it. I'm surprised Amelie hasn't turned it into a games room or something. Or more bedrooms.'

'Maybe she just hasn't had time,' said Mina a touch distractedly, thinking of what she needed to do next. 'And sorry, I should have said, thank you.'

'No problem.'

'Have many people gone out this morning? I haven't even looked in the lounge.'

'A few have braved the elements, and there are a couple of people sitting reading. The German family are playing cards, and Sarah and her friends are chatting.'

'Do you think I ought to offer them coffee?' asked Mina worriedly. What would Amelie do on a day like this? Would she serve cake at eleven?

'I think Amelie normally leaves out a couple of those big flasks so that people can help themselves.'

'That's a good idea.' Another job. She hadn't even seen any flasks. Maybe they were in the pantry. 'I'll put those out at ten-thirty.'

'Good shout. Right, what do you want me to do?'

She got him set up with a pile of carrots, having decided to offer a warming carrot and ginger soup for lunch. With Luke peeling, Dave beating butter and sugar together, the spaghetti sauce almost made, and the Kitchen Aid kneading dough for bread, she felt a little more on top of things. Reassured by the familiar sounds, she put the coffee machine on and found the flasks in the pantry, which were as per Amelie's usual efficiency easy enough to find. Unfortunately they were next to a large tin of cocoa which managed to lose its lid and fall off the shelf, spilling it's load down her front as she pulled them down.

Dark brown powder engulfed her leaving her blinking and gasping. She emerged from the pantry feeling a complete fool and when both men burst into laughter, she burst into tears. It was all too much.

'Hey,' said Luke, ignoring the cocoa powder and drawing her into his arms. 'It's OK. Sorry, we shouldn't have laughed.'

With a sniff and a gulp she said, 'I–It's OK.'

'No, it isn't. You need to take five. Come on. Let's sort you out.'

For once she let someone else take charge and allowed Luke to lead her upstairs. It was only when she saw the rumpled bed that she realised what everything else entailed. She had bedrooms and bathrooms to set to rights.

Her face began to crumple again.

'What?'

'I've got all the rooms to clean.'

'Don't worry. We'll sort it. Between us.'

He took her into the bathroom, stripped off her cocoa dusted clothes and then settled her on the edge of the bath. They'd both agreed that getting it wet would probably make even more mess.

'You're just going to smell delicious all day,' he teased gently cleaning down her face, neck and arms with a bath towel. He then spent the most blissful five minutes rubbing his hand through her scalp before brushing the powder out of her hair with firm, gentle strokes. All the while he watched her in the mirror and she felt a well of tenderness rise up and bloom in her chest, warming her whole body. Tears pricked at her eyes again but they were tears of gratitude and joy.

'Right, you'll do.'

She rose, unselfconscious in her bra and knickers, and pulled on fresh clothes, ready to go back to the kitchen, but Luke stopped her outside the door.

'Come into my room for a minute. I want you to see something.'

He led her to the table. 'Sit.' He opened the suitcase. The model was now finished. 'Just sit and watch the train, and take five.'

She looked up at him in puzzlement. He gave her a mock stern frown. 'Five minutes.'

With a grumbly sigh, she decided to humour him. even though she had a million things to do.

He switched on the little train and she studied the new additions to the scene. There were now tiny ducks on the pond, a smattering of confetti around the bride and groom, and flowers trailing up the sides of the cottages. The train circled the route, its familiar whirring noise bringing back happy memories of her uncle. Smiling, she sat and watched, feeling herself relax. He stood behind, both hands on her shoulders, gently kneading at the knots there.

'This is what I did when I was convalescing. When everyone else was out at the skatepark being cool.' His mouth twisted. 'In some ways it saved my life. Not literally, but my mental health. It helped me cope with what was going on. Having to pay attention to the minutest details takes your mind off other things. Doing this helped me to learn to be patient. Not something that, at that age, came naturally. Now when I get wound up, I find modelling or watching the train takes my mind off things.'

She leaned back into his gentle hands. No one had ever looked after her quite this well, taking the trouble to force her to just sit for five minutes. With a self-deprecating laugh, she realised that no one had ever been quite her match before.

'What?' asked Luke. 'Not feeling it?' She stood up and

turned around, sliding her arms around his neck, smiling up at him.

'Luke, no one has soothed, seduced, and cared for me with a model train before. It's ridiculously sexy and attractive, and I have no idea why.' But she did. There was nothing quite so attractive as man who was prepared to share how much something meant to him.

Chapter Nineteen

By lunchtime, Mina wished she'd brought her fitbit. Running up and down the stairs, she'd probably racked up at least ten thousand steps. Thank goodness the chalet was only half-full at the moment.

At ten-past-twelve, she served the soup and bread – thank you Luke, he'd been an exceptional chopper of vegetables. By twelve-thirty, there was nothing left but crumbs and empty bowls. Mina smiled to herself as she collected up the empty bowls. Of course the speed with which it was despatched had everything to do with the fact that the snow had stopped, and miraculously the sun had appeared. Everyone was keen to get out. 'Powder hounds,' Luke explained as they all dashed off as soon as they'd laid down their soup spoons. 'Perfect ski conditions. But there's more snow forecast, so it's a small window.'

'Do you want to go?'

'No, I'm...' He pulled his phone out of his pocket, 'I'm

waiting for an urgent call.' Tiny lines appeared around his mouth.

'Is everything alright?'

'Yeah, sure. Fine.' His quick smile didn't convince her. 'What can I do to help? I'm really good at cleaning bathrooms.'

She shot him a sceptical glance, but was grateful that he was so willing to do anything to help. She gave a quick glance around the kitchen. There were a good couple of hours before round two, and at the moment the road through the valley was closed. Johannes was on fire duty and kept popping in to check the fire was banked properly, for which she was grateful (it seemed that fire management required particular man skills).

'Show me the storeroom below. I'm running low on cleaning supplies and I remember Amelie bought a case of toilet cleaner when we went to the wholesalers, and I can't find it anywhere.'

'You'll need a coat. Unless there's a secret passage down there, we have to go round to the side to get in.'

Being out in the fresh air boosted Mina's senses as she breathed in the crisp, cold air. It also cleared her head, which had become a bit foggy trying to juggle so many things this morning. The new snow was soft and powdery, and had that delicious squeaky crunch as she left footprints on the surface. Underneath the house, which she realised was built on giant stilts resting on stone pedestals, there was a whole floor, just like Johannes's place. This was a little more basic, and there was a small storeroom just off to the right as they went in. Intrigued by the open space, she ignored the storeroom and went straight in to explore.

'Wow, this is great,' said Mina. 'Bigger than I expected.' In the gloomy light she could just make out that work had been started. Two of the walls had been plasterboarded and she could see bales of insulation on the floor.

'Looks like someone had plans for in here,' said Luke, nodding towards the building supplies, but Mina was already making a thoughtful circuit of the barn space.

This was it. This was what Johannes had been going to show her. She could see it so clearly.

A table here, a kitchen there.

'Mina?'

'Mm,' she said vaguely, now studying the large solid wooden doors that once must have opened to let the cattle in and out. On either side, were two large windows shielded by wooden shutters to keep the weather out. They would let lots of light in. And the view.

It was perfect. She could invest her own money to make the necessary alterations. Rent the spare apartment from Amelie.

'Mina? Are you listening?'

'Sorry, what did you say?'

'Do you want to check the storeroom?'

'In a minute.' She waved an abstracted hand, utterly absorbed in thought. She prowled around the room.

'Look: stairs.' There was a small wooden staircase leading up to a trapdoor in the roof. 'This must lead up into the kitchen somewhere. Hmm.' She could hardly quell her rising excitement. There was space for a tasting room, an area for tables and chairs. She walked over to shuttered windows and peered through the gaps.

'Wow.' For a second she fiddled with the catches, opened the window, and pushed open the shutters to reveal the full extent of the view of the snow-clad village, the layers of snow like puff pastry on the nearby roofs, and the towering mountains opposite. Leaving the shutters open, she closed the window and turned around. The light flooding in brightened the room, and as she surveyed the floor space, synapses suddenly started firing in her brain. Everything fell into place. She whirled and clapped her hands. 'It's perfect. I can't believe it.' Suddenly she had all the answers and knew exactly what she wanted to do. She'd stay in Switzerland, work for Johannes, set up his retail outlet, and serve snacks and cakes here.

'Perfect for what?'

Luke's forehead wrinkled for a second but he followed her excited gaze.

'For my chocolate shop,' she replied. 'And a café serving cake and coffee, and perhaps lunch.' She spun around, fizzing with enthusiasm, and pointed to the front of the building. 'Look, you could have the tables here, looking out at that fabulous view. There might be even be room for a little terrace in the summer.' With another turn, she pointed to the back of the room. 'There's access to the kitchen upstairs, but you could put a small kitchen area in over there. It would be perfect. And we're right in the middle of all the trails. There's nowhere for lunch locally. This would be a perfect halfway point and stopping-off place for a lot of the trails.' The more she thought about it, the more perfect it was. 'Amelie says people often want lunch but she can't cater for them because she doesn't have time. Johannes needs a bigger space to sell and sample chocolate. I could make a big thing of it being locally made and sell it to the tourists. There'd be room for a tasting area.' Her brain raced with ideas, she could picture it so clearly.

Luke stood and watched, his lopsided smile turning into a laugh.

'What?'

'You. Your enthusiasm. You've lit up inside.'

'But can't you see it?' Mina waved an expansive hand, her breath coming out in tiny white puffs. 'Wooden tables, little tub chairs. Cakes on pretty china cake stands. A shiny espresso machine. A wood-burning stove in the winter, the doors open in the summer.' She paused and did a quick twirl throwing her arms out. 'I'd source old-fashioned china tea cups and plates, or rather, get Hannah to send mine over.' She'd amassed quite a collection and often lent them out to friends for vintage events. 'And it's ripe for some bunting.'

Everything crystallised in her head, like a flower opening up to the sun. She'd crossed that damn bridge, and had reached happy island. 'I want to open a little café here. I want to make cakes. Develop chocolate recipes. I want to experiment. Create new cakes. I want to live in Switzerland.' She paused, the next sentence too impulsive even for her – as she realised she wanted to be with him – and instead she said, 'I'd call it serendipity.'

Luke raised an eyebrow, and if she hadn't known him so well or be so attuned to him, in the way that she had since the very first day they'd met, she would have missed that tiny, imperceptible stiffening.

Ignoring the tiny dart of disappointment that slipped straight and sure into her heart, she launched into logic. 'It makes perfect sense. I could make the cakes for Amelie, which would lighten her load. That would save her loads of time in the mornings. I could provide lunches which would also save her work and I could help her in the chalet, so that she could have more time off. And it would cut down on the amount of shopping she had to do, because she wouldn't need so much. I could pay her rent and she could use that to pay for more help as well.'

'You've got it all worked out.' He glanced at his watch. 'In all of five minutes.'

'Someone once said to me, "sometimes you just know".' Luke walked over to the window and studied the view, shoving his hands in his pockets. Mina felt a flicker of foreboding. Something wasn't right. What had changed? The hunch of his shoulders made him appear distant and isolated, as if he were shutting the world out. Normally he welcomed the world in. It was one of things she'd noticed straight away about him. One of the things she'd liked most about him. That open, prepared-to-be-friends-with-everyone readiness. Mina often thought there were two types of people in the world, those that thought everyone was a potential foe, and those that believed everyone was a potential friend.

'What about Amelie?' he asked quietly. 'She might not like you making these unilateral decisions on her behalf. Just because she's ill doesn't mean she'll be happy with *you* deciding what's best for her and her business.' She flinched at the soft insistence in his voice. 'People have a tendency to do that.' His head shot up and gave her a sad smile. 'They like to assume that they know better than you. That they know what you can and can't cope with, without even doing you the courtesy of asking.'

'Was that what people did to you?' She swallowed.

'Yes. Cancelled my university place, although in hindsight I would have been too ill to go. Moved house because it was closer to the hospital. Things were just done. No one ever thought to ask me what I thought. I know they were trying to do the right thing, and that makes it harder because then you look like an ungrateful, whinging, adolescent, hormonal sod.'

Mina winced. She had made assumptions about Amelie, although it wasn't because she thought she knew best. What she'd been trying to do was put forward a logical argument for her sudden impulsive idea. One that, now she'd come up with it, she desperately wanted to make happen. Maybe she should have slowed down and not let her enthusiasm and imagination get the better of her.

'You're right,' she acquiesced quietly, a little bit ashamed of herself. He was right in one way; she was still too impulsive. She hadn't thought before she spoke, just run her mouth off letting her enthusiasm race away with her like bolting horses. 'But if I can't do it here, then... then I'll find somewhere else. Johannes already said that he'd employ me. Well,' she qualified, 'we were going to talk about it.'

'Sorry, I was being a bit harsh.' He moved across the room and took her in his arms and kissed the tip of her nose. 'I love that you have this positive, can-do attitude. It is a great idea. You've described it perfectly. I can imagine sitting here with one of those glass mugs of hot chocolate piled with whipped cream and marshmallows and a big slab of chocolate cake. I'm just a bit off-balance today. Ignore me. Something has come up.'

'I'm not sure I could ever ignore you,' said Mina, reaching up and kissing him on the mouth. 'But I think, now that I've calmed down a bit, Amelie might already have plans for this place. Someone's made a start on insulating it.'

Luke's phone chose to beep at that moment and he pulled it out of his pocket wrinkling his nose. 'Sorry, I need to return this call. I also need to make arrangements to get the Suitcase Train shipped. I'll probably have to take it into Brig tomorrow. Do you mind if I leave you to it?'

'No, problem. I'll see you later.'

She closed the shutter and listened to his receding steps. Now that she knew about his illness, a lot of comments over the last two weeks made sense. His positive, live-life-to-the-full attitude. She guessed if you'd had your life severely curtailed for a couple of years, you would want to make the most of every moment and every opportunity. It's certainly what she would have done. Yesterday's hospital visit must have triggered unpleasant memories. No wonder he was a bit sensitive – and if she was honest, she had been totally *in*sensitive about poor Amelie. For all she knew, her godmother might want to sell up and take life more easily.

But despite her resolution that she wouldn't let herself

get carried away before she'd spoken to Amelie, she couldn't help thinking that this was the answer to everything she'd been looking for. She knew exactly what she wanted to do.

At three o'clock she stood beside Johannes while he rang the hospital again.

Halfway through the conversation with the nurse, he suddenly brightened. 'We can speak to her. They've done the procedure and she's sitting up in bed.'

Suddenly he was shy and he handed the phone to Mina, his face turning pink.

'Amelie?'

'Mina. How are you?'

'How am *I*? How are you?'

'I'm fine. Stupid really. They put this stent thing in to widen an artery. Do you know they put it in through a vein in my wrist? Quite astonishing. And now I feel so much better. It's like magic. And how is everything? How are the guests?'

'Everything is fine. The guests all send their love.'

'I'm so worried, they should have had lunch today. Not many would have gone out. And coffee.'

'Amelie, it's all fine. They had soup and bread for lunch. And I made coffee at eleven.'

Her sigh of relief echoed down the phone and even Johannes, standing a foot to her right, smiled.

'And I've done the bedrooms. Dave has made a

wonderful cake. And I'm about to start cooking dinner. You mustn't worry. Everything is under control.'

'You are a treasure, Mina. And remember the guests. They need looking after. How are Dave and Sarah?'

Mina laughed. 'They are fine.'

'Hmm,' said Amelie. 'And what about the new arrivals?'

Mina gulped. 'Yes. The new arrivals.' Shit, they would be arriving in… she glanced at her watch. Oh shit, two hours.

'Remember Kristian needs keeping an eye on, and the Italian family are back, and of course you know Bernhardt. It's all in the book.'

'Don't worry. It's all under control. Now do you need anything? Johannes is going to come visit this evening. I'm sorry, I'm not sure I can cook dinner and come see you. Will you mind?'

'No, no. I am happier knowing that my guests will be fed. You can call Franzi and Giselle.'

'Yes, I'll do that.' Mina had never been more grateful that it was Saturday tomorrow, they couldn't possibly have an exam.

'Good. So Johannes is coming. Is he terribly worried?' There was a tiny ripple of amusement in her voice.

'Terribly,' said Mina. 'Although I'm not sure I can spare him, he's been on fire duty.'

Amelie laughed. 'He does love looking after my fire.'

Mina bit back a snigger at the unintentional double entendre, at least she thought it was unintentional – her godmother's English was so good, it might not have been.

'I'll hand you over,' she said, giving the phone to

Johannes, who immediately seemed to be tongue-tied. She patted him on the shoulder. 'I'll leave you to it.'

Slipping out of the kitchen she went into the dining room, which promptly reminded her that the table needed laying for dinner. When she returned to the kitchen Johannes sat with a dazed expression on his face.

Biting back a smile, Mina asked him what Amelie needed to be taken to the hospital, and had to laugh when he couldn't remember a single thing she'd asked for.

'Do you know where she keeps the keys for her apartment?'

'There.' He pointed to a bunch of keys hanging on the hook on the end of the dresser.

'Would you like me to go and get some things for her?'

He responded, nodding enthusiastically. 'That would be... appropriate.'

Dust motes leapt into the air, scared into action by the keys rattling in the lock, as Mina stepped into the silent apartment. It felt wrong to be entering Amelie's space without her, even though she had permission. Of course, Mina's curiosity couldn't be contained, so she took a peep into the living room. With a small two-seater sofa, a solitary coffee table, and a virtually empty bookshelf, the room created a stark contrast with the cosy lounge in the chalet. Not a single picture hung on the walls, no cushions, no throws, which surprised Mina; it didn't feel like Amelie at all. Puzzled, she walked into the centre of the room. It had the potential to be a beautiful room, with the lovely rosy wood-clad walls, the polished floorboards, and the wide windows.

Then she realised Amelie had put all her energy into the chalet. That was her true home. Mina realised that her godmother probably never spent any time here. It strengthened her resolve to try and help. But mindful of Luke's comments, she would approach it diplomatically. He'd clearly had a rough ride as a teenager, and the more she thought about it, the more she sympathised.

When she moved into the bedroom, she immediately felt more comfortable when she spotted the selection of photographs on the dressing table, which included a couple of pictures of Mina and Hannah when they were younger, and a more recent one of Mina taken when she'd just completed a mini triathlon. In the picture she grinned up at the camera, holding her medal. Mina laughed out loud at her own image – a typical example of triumph over adversity. Despite never having done a triathlon in her life, or even attempted an open water swim, she signed up to the charity event because it sounded fun. She'd finished it, and wasn't last. Next to that picture was a much larger silver frame with a photograph of her mother and Amelie, their arms slung around each other in a restaurant somewhere, huge smiles on faces lit up with genuine affection for each other. Mina wondered for the thousandth time how different her life might have been if her parents hadn't been killed in that accident. Amelie had been good to her and Hannah. What would Miriam and Derek say if she decided to stay in Switzerland? Although set in their ways, they'd never held her or Hannah back. They'd always given them free reign, and gentle, understated support.

Quickly and methodically, Mina gathered up clothes, a dressing gown, and toiletries, putting them all in a stylish navy leather holdall. On impulse, as she was locking up, she darted across the hallway to the other apartment. It was completely different from Amelie's; the lounge and kitchen were open-plan with a small wood burner in the corner. Wide French windows opened on to a wide balcony filled with empty window boxes. The two first-floor apartments had been built into the slope just above the chalet, and so looked out over the roof of its neighbours, affording another wonderful view. Mina could immediately imagine living here, and wondered where the nearest Ikea was. With cushions, throws, and lights, it would be easy to make this room look really homely. The kitchen was a decent size and already contained a fridge, cooker, and microwave. But she needed to stop getting her hopes up: she had to speak to Amelie first.

———

By the time Dave's delicious Victoria sponge, sitting in lofty splendour on a cake stand, was ready to be served at four o'clock, Mina had got dinner under control, and couldn't believe where the day had gone. She was a little nervous about the rosti potatoes because the only time she'd made them before at home, they'd been a little raw. Hopefully Amelie's method using potatoes cooked the day before would be foolproof. Now all she had to do was greet the new arrivals and make sure they all felt welcome. Whether she could encourage everyone to mix over coffee and cake the way that Amelie did was another matter, but she was determined to do her best. There'd still been no word from Johannes, which was worrying her, and she wished she'd thought to ask for his mobile number or for the name of the hospital.

She let Dave carry his latest masterpiece out from the kitchen, because quite frankly anyone whose sponge rose quite like that deserved every last bit of praise.

Its arrival in the dining room was perfectly timed, as Sarah and her friends had just returned.

'Wow, Dave, that's a big one,' said one of them.

'Isn't it just?' said the other with a roguish snigger.

Sarah, who was quite prudish, blushed and exchanged a private look with Dave that made everyone take a second look at him.

Dave, quite unperturbed, grinned. 'That's what all my women say.' He winked at Sarah, who ducked her head shyly and didn't say another word.

Mina hide a wry smile at the unexpected rise in Dave's status. As the skiers shed their layers, she left him to serve the cake and coffee while she went to the little cubby hole in the reception area where Amelie did her admin. Thankfully she relied on pen and paper, and there was a good old-fashioned A4 desk diary with neat pencilled lines splitting each page into eleven sections, ten of which were the room numbers. To Mina's utter relief the system was *almost* foolproof, and she could see exactly which rooms had been allocated to today's new arrivals – thankfully all the rooms had been cleaned and made ready when people had departed earlier in the week. She could also see who was arriving and how long they were staying. The bookings for the weekend included Bernhardt and Kristian, who were sharing a room, a couple and their two children – who Mina thought must be the Italian family with the two teenagers, who'd been here last weekend – and one other couple. All that was quite straightforward. What wasn't obvious was the annotations next to each name. AT, U, LC. Mina didn't have a clue what they signified, least of all because they were probably in Swiss-German. There was no point even trying to fathom them out. She'd have to ask Amelie.

Taking the keys for the rooms, she ran up the stairs and double-checked, just as Amelie always did, that they were clean and ready. To her relief they all looked pristine, and she sauntered down the stairs to find the Italian family group she'd met the previous weekend arriving.

'Hello,' she said, greeting them with a big smile. 'Nice to see you again.' She said a silent prayer in thanks for the way in which Amelie ensured everyone was introduced to each other during their stays. She was able to greet them with perfect friendliness.

'Hello, Mina,' said the father of the group. 'Where's Amelie?'

'I'm afraid she's not very well, so I'm standing in for her this evening.' Before they could make any comment, she added, 'Your rooms are all ready for you, and you have your usual ones, if that's OK? Can I just ask you to sign in?'

As they were regulars, they happily took their keys and headed up the stairs.

Mina glanced at the desk diary and the initials and numbers next to the names. She'd worked out that the numbers related to how many times the guests had been before. Luke had stayed here a grand total of ten times, making him the most frequent guest. Bernhardt and Kristian six times. As for the initials, she suspected, given Amelie's fussiness about who she allowed to stay, that they might be ratings on the guests themselves. What did they translate as? Next to Dave and Sarah's names were the initials. BSH. Next to Kristian's, BVH. And next to Luke's, FM. A fanciful thought crossed her mind. For Mina?

As she was studying the diary, the door opened, bringing in a fresh set of faces, two of which were reassuringly familiar.

'Mina,' cried Kristian, and gave her a gangly wave, his long arm almost side-swiping Bernhardt next to him. 'You're still here.' Like a small lumbering elephant, he dropped his boot bag and his overnight bag with a crash, making heads in the lounge on the other side of the fire turn.

'Hello, Mina,' said Bernhardt, a lot more calmly and smoothly, giving her a warm, appreciative smile. 'Lovely to see you again.'

They'd shared a taxi with the last of the arrivals, an English girl, Jane, and her French friend, Matilde. It was their third visit, and they were very sorry to hear about Amelie's absence, as were the two men. Once they'd completed the paperwork, they all opted to leave their bags by the desk and join the others for cake. Jane and Matilde seemed, like most of the guests, quite happy to dive right in and join everyone in the lounge. Mina nodded to herself; Amelie had got the right recipe for success. She chose her guests well. How many visits were allowed before someone was accepted or blacklisted? It wasn't exactly a sensible way to run a hospitality business but then, Mina realised with a sudden flash of insight, this was also Amelie's home. She clearly didn't use the apartment apart from for sleeping in. The chalet was her whole world. No wonder she only wanted nice people staying here.

With everyone checked in, she joined everyone in the lounge and immediately noticed that Kristian was standing awkwardly with a plate of cake, eyeing it as if he were contemplating mounting an expedition to climb Everest. As well he might: Dave servings went beyond generous, and with the cherry filling oozing out, they definitely needed a dessert fork, as well as firm foundations for the bottom. He was on his own, as the French girl Matilde was happily chatting to Frank and Claudia, along with the Italian family, and Bernhardt talked to Dave and Sarah. Jane, the new arrival, had tucked herself into the corner nursing a cup of coffee.

'Kristian, why don't you come sit here,' said Mina indicating the seat next to Jane. 'And I'll get you a fork for that cake.'

'Jane, would you like some cake?'

'Er... um, yes. Not so big.' She looked at Kristian's towering slice.

'Would you like some of mine?' With puppy like enthusiasm, he shoved his plate towards her and almost stuffed the cake up her nose. She reared back looking slightly terrified.

'I'll get you a slice,' interrupted Mina, wondering how on earth Amelie made her interventions look so smooth. 'Just sit, Kristian.' He looked grateful to be told what to do.

Now that the room was full, and dessert forks had been handed out, it was easier to guide people into seats and offer more coffee, and soon the room was humming with quiet chatter, and everyone had someone to talk to.

'Well done,' murmured Luke, coming up behind her. Immediately she was grateful for his presence, even though everything appeared to be running smoothly.

'Thank you. Amelie makes it look so easy, you're not even aware she's doing it. She must have eyes in the back of her head.'

'She also knows her guests well.'

'You would know. I see you've stayed here ten times.'

'What can I say? I'm a creature of habit.'

'Are you?' That didn't quite fit with her image of him at all.

He shrugged in answer and forked up a large mouthful of cake. She glanced over at Dave and gave him a thumbs up. As she crossed to speak to him, his wife gave her a brilliant, twinkly-eyed smile which was a long way from the fretful, naggy creature of last week.

'I think this cake is a triumph,' said Mina. 'Especially the cherry filling. I don't suppose you could make up another batch? I've got an idea for a meringue dish, and this would be perfect.'

'No problem. If you don't mind, darling.' He turned to his wife. 'I can join you in the afternoon.'

'Not at all. It's quite nice in the morning. I can go at my own pace. I don't have to try and keep up with you out on the tracks all the time,' she confessed almost shyly.

'I didn't know that,' said Dave, looking horrified.

She lifted her shoulder in a small shrug. 'I didn't like to... and it made me a bit resentful. I'm sorry.'

'Darling, you should have said.'

'You know me.' She shared a rueful smile with Mina. 'I like to be in charge, but I don't like to admit that I can't do anything, or keep up with you.'

He nudged her and kissed her on her neck. 'You daft thing. I just enjoy being out there. I don't care how far we go, or how fast.' He put his plate down on the big coffee table and slipped his hand into hers.

Mina smiled. This might just be one of Amelie's success stories. Although she wasn't so sure about Kristian. Jane had a pained expression on her face, and when Mina crossed to speak to them, she could understand why. Kristian was delivering a lengthy lecture about a point of law that was enough to bore a retired judge, let alone a complete layperson.

'Jane,' said Mina. 'You've been here before. What are your plans for the weekend?'

'We want to ski, downhill, but we're not sure the best place to go?'

'Kristian, you went downhill skiing last weekend. Where did you go? That sounded as if it had plenty of runs and ski lifts.'

'Ah, yes.' Kristian's eyes filled with gratitude as he gave himself a smart self-deprecating slap on the top of the head as if to say, *Why didn't I think of that?* Bless him, he really was quite hopeless.

Satisfied that she'd done her best to oil the social wheels, Mina returned to the kitchen with a pile of plates and empty coffee cups and started loading the dishwasher, already working out her plan of action for the rest of the evening, and mentally trying to work out where she would seat everyone for dinner. Now she understood how important it was to get it right. Perhaps she'd give Jane a respite and seat her next to Frank, who was very easy to talk to. No wonder everyone loved coming here, Amelie looked after every aspect of their stay. All Mina had to do was follow suit.

Chapter Twenty

Given the sparsity of Amelie's apartment, Mina decided to put the bunch of yellow roses on the table in the kitchen, although getting them had been quite a palaver, as she'd had to ask Johannes to pick them up in Brig for her.

Mina had become obsessed with the thought of opening her chocolate shop. What she'd stock. The cakes she'd make. How she'd merchandise things. Not that she'd discussed her plans with anyone, they just seemed to keep growing in her head.

At last, in the early afternoon, Johannes ushered Amelie into the kitchen. 'I'll just check the fire,' he said to no one in particular, and to Mina's delight pecked Amelie quickly on the cheek like a sparrow at a breadcrumb before hurrying away. Mina raised her eyebrows and Amelie blushed like a schoolgirl on prom night. Rather than say anything, although she was dying to tease her, Mina enfolded her godmother into a gentle hug. 'It's so good to have you back,' she said.

'It's so good to be back.' Amelie squeezed her tight. 'I've missed you.'

'I'm sorry, I couldn't get to the hospital. There was, well, you know.' Mina waved a feeble hand around the kitchen. 'But you look so well,' she said, amazed by the rosy glow on her godmother's cheeks.

'I feel wonderful. All that extra blood pumping to my heart. No wonder I felt tired all the time.' Amelie's mouth in her pixie face was pursed. 'I'm supposed to rest, but I do feel so well.'

Mina gave her a reproving look and Amelie held her hands up in quick surrender. 'Don't worry, I will do as I'm told…' Her eyes twinkled. 'As much as I can.'

'I'm not above tying you to a chair,' warned Mina. 'You gave us a terrible scare.' Now was not the time to sit her godmother down and tell her just how scary it had been, and how she really did need to slow down and organise things to make her life easier. Mina suddenly felt the weight of responsibility and that the tables at been well and truly turned. Amelie had been her mentor, supporter, and fairy godmother for so long. Now Mina felt that she was the one that should be looking out for Amelie.

'Would you like a coffee?'

'I would love one. The stuff in the hospital was awful. I kept sneaking out to the machine in the canteen, although it was still dreadful.'

'Here you go' she said, handing a cup to Amelie, who sipped at it with an appreciative sigh.

Amelie picked up her phone. 'The grapevine has been busy. I think I must have had a message from everyone in the village. It's going to take me all day to respond. It's so good to be home.

'So how have things been? How are Dave and Sarah?'

Mina began to laugh. 'So you're not worried whether your guests have been fed and watered properly, you just want to know whether your marriage guidance tactics have been working.'

'Well, of course. Then you can tell me everything else.'

'You'll be pleased to hear that I think Sarah has turned a corner and is suddenly a lot more appreciative of her husband's talents… and not just in the kitchen.'

'Really?' Amelie's eyes widened in delighted surprise. 'You have done well.'

'And I think Kristian and Jane are getting on like the proverbial house on fire, although perhaps we're talking a small barbeque in the garden at the moment rather than full conflagration.'

'Excellent.' Amelie gave a regal nod.

'You're going to have to explain your secret code notes.'

Amelie's cheeks dimpled. 'You mean you haven't worked them out.'

'I know that you count how many times they've stayed before, and that you have some sort of traffic light system for guests. Dave and Sarah were on their last chance? What does BH mean or BVH.'

'*Braucht Hilfe*. Needs help. *Bracht viel Hilfe*. Needs a lot of help.'

Mina laughed. 'Poor old Kristian, although I do think he's getting better.'

'Good. With every guest you have to look behind the façade. People put them up to hide their own anxieties. You only have to look at Luke. On the surface, he's ready for anything and everything, adventurous, happy go lucky. Inside he's weighing things up. He's not nearly as impulsive as he first seems.'

'No, I've realised that,' agreed Mina not wanting to give too much away. He'd been noticeably absent today even before he disappeared mid-afternoon telling her he was taking the Suitcase Train to be shipped. She felt a little hurt that he hadn't sought her out, especially when they'd spent the previous night together again – although now she thought about it, he had been a little preoccupied. But then she'd been so tired, she'd flaked out as soon as she lay down, and he'd been gone when she'd woken this morning. If she were honest, that piqued her a little, but common sense asserted itself: there was probably a good reason. After all, she herself had to hit the ground running.

Once she and Amelie had finished coffee, she rolled up her sleeves. 'You sit there while I start making dinner.'

'Yes, boss.' Amelie put her elbows on table and rested her chin in her hands, looking to all the world completely obedient.

'I've cancelled my flight home on Monday.'

Amelie thankfully didn't object, instead she said, 'Thank you, *liebling*.'

'I'll stay for... well, I'd like to talk to you about that.'

With a heavy sigh, Amelie pulled a face. 'I'm going to

have to make a few changes around here for the next few weeks.'

'And beyond that. This is all too much for one person.' Mina sat down again and cupped her hands around her coffee. 'Or at least, the way you're running it is.'

Amelie's face crumpled. 'But the personal touch is so important. I wanted it to be different. I want people to feel like it's a home from home. I don't want to change things.' She held up her hand. 'And before you say anything: I know, I need to. Johannes has already given me a lecture on the way home... a kind lecture, but a lecture all the same. He thinks I need to employ more staff... and I know I will have to, but getting the right person is so important. At least I have the spare apartment, so I can offer free board and lodgings, because I certainly can't afford to pay very much, and even then...' She lifted her shoulders. 'Johannes is talking about helping, and says he has an idea, but I don't want it to be like that. Whatever happens between us, I don't want to be beholden to him. I want to be equal. This is my business.' A faint sheen in her eyes tugged at Mina's heart.

Mina took a deep breath, now or never. 'I have a suggestion.'

'I know you're going to offer to stay and help, but you have a job.'

'When I came here, I told you I needed some time out, some time to figure out what I wanted to do.' She paused.

'And?'

'I know what I want to do. I want to set up a chocolate shop, with a café. I've already asked Johannes if he would employ me to run a retail outlet for him. We haven't had a chance to talk details.'

'Go on.' Amelie leaned back in her chair, her eyes bright with interest.

'The barn, below here. That could be turned into a café and shop…'

Amelie jumped up and clapped her hands. 'And you could live in the other apartment. That would be wonderful.'

Mina laughed. 'But I haven't even—'

'I've been wanting to do something with the barn. It would be perfect.' Amelie fidgeted in her seat and looked around the kitchen before leaning back and pulling open a drawer of the dresser to find a notepad and pen.

'I was thinking I could offer lunches and cake.' Mina didn't need to worry about being tentative or offending Amelie like Luke had suggested. 'Maybe make the cakes for you to save you a job.'

'Even better. Oh, this is such a good idea.' She flicked open the notepad. 'Now, what do we need to do?'

'But…' said Mina having expected to have to do some persuading.

'But…' Amelie teased. 'What are we waiting for?'

By the end of the afternoon they had a long list of action points. Mina still had to argue the toss about paying rent on the apartment and helping more in the chalet, but for the most part they had a plan.

'And I will pay for the renovation work to the barn,' insisted Mina. 'I'll be able to rent my flat out in Manchester and pay you rent here.'

'We'll worry about that later, but paying for the renovations would be a big help, because I don't have much capital. That's why I've left it for the time being.'

Mina was pleased that she'd managed to win that concession, although she wasn't happy about Amelie insisting she had the apartment rent free. 'But you'll be working and making a difference,' argued Amelie. 'And if you keep on fighting me on this,' she clutched her chest, 'it might cause me more stress.'

'Not fair,' growled Mina.

'I know, but there have to be some benefits to having a heart attack.' Amelie shot her an unrepentant grin. 'It will be lovely to have the company, and you'll have plenty of entertainment and friends. Bernhardt, Kristian, and Luke are all regular visitors, and Frank and Claudia will be moving here soon. In fact, their tour groups could meet for breakfast or coffee at the café.'

'The benefits just keep piling up,' said Mina with a happy smile, not quite able to believe that her idea was working out so easily. Surely there had to be some pitfalls, but when Johannes, by far the more astute businessman, joined them later, he was in full agreement and offered to call his cousin, who had done the work on his barn, to come and give a quote the very next day. He even talked about her becoming an apprentice chocolate-maker as well.

'Now I need to get on top of dinner,' said Mina. 'And I think you need to rest.' She thought of Amelie's bare apartment but Johannes must have had the same idea.

'Why don't you come to my house?' asked Johannes.

'The wood burner is glowing nicely and you can lay on one of the sofas.'

'That would be lovely,' agreed Amelie. 'I'm too tired to argue, and I think if I tried the two of you would gang up on me.'

'We just want to look after you,' said Mina, giving her a quick hug.

'Thank you, I appreciate it, and you looking after my guests.'

Johannes, hovering like a broody hen, saw Amelie out of the back door and took her arm once they were down the stairs. Mina watched him guide her back to his house, grateful that he would be looking after her. Despite his gruff exterior, inside lurked an extremely kind man. For a moment she felt a brief pang. Only two days ago she felt as if she'd fallen through a rainbow and the pot of gold had landed at her feet. Now she wasn't sure where she stood. Since she'd talked with so much enthusiasm in the barn, Luke had been withdrawing. Had she frightened him off by announcing she was staying in Switzerland? She refused to believe that, but she did need to speak to him, especially now that her plans were firming up so quickly.

Chapter Twenty-One

S he hadn't seen Luke since breakfast. With the two girls working and Amelie 'overseeing' things, Dave setting to work on a chocolate fudge cake, and Johannes hovering in the background, the kitchen was a little crowded, so when he'd bobbed his head in and ducked it out again, Mina hadn't blamed him one bit – but that was an hour ago. The snow was still falling steadily and many of the guests had gravitated to the lounge and the pile of board games that Amelie had put out.

Leaving everyone in the kitchen, she'd been able to set to on her chambermaiding duties – her least favourite part of her new job She rapped soundly on Luke's door, as she did at every guest's door. It still worried her that she might barge in on one of them naked, or see something she really didn't want to see. She waited for a second but there was no answer, and she was just about to insert the master key in the lock when it opened.

'Hi, housekeeping,' said Mina with a teasing grin. 'Here to service your room.'

'Ah, yes. Come in.' Luke frowned and looked preoccupied.

'Sorry, have I interrupted? Are you working?' She looked towards the table. It was bare, and all the modelling materials were piled into a new vintage suitcase on the floor. A sense of foreboding closed around her heart, like a cold hand. 'Shall I come back later?'

'No.' He sighed. 'I need to talk to you.' He took her hand and led her to the end of the bed, and sat, pulling her down next to him. 'I hear your plans are gathering pace.'

'Yes. I can't believe it. Everything is falling into place and it's...' She lifted her shoulders, still not able to believe everything was coming together so perfectly.

'That's fantastic, Mina. I'm so pleased for you.'

She frowned, her pleasure checked by the odd note of formality.

'You sound like a teacher, or my boss, or a colleague. As if it's a platitude or something.'

He lifted a hand and rubbed at his forehead. 'Sorry, I am genuinely pleased. I know what this means to you. In some ways it makes things easier.' He lifted the same hand to her face. 'You're fairly sparkling with it. I thought you crackled with life and energy the first time I saw you, but now... you're positively incandescent.' His smile, filled with sadness, tugged at her heart.

'What's wrong, Luke?' she asked, putting a hand on his thigh.

'I've been offered a new posting.'

'And it's not in Switzerland?' She looked up into his eyes, which shone with apology and regret. The sense of foreboding deepened.

'No, it's not in Switzerland.'

'Ah,' she said, as inside everything began to unravel.

'Ah, indeed.'

They held each other's gaze. She swallowed. It was worse this time. A thousand times worse. It hurt even more when you knew that the other person was going to hurt too. Knowing they cared as much as you.

'I'd ask you to come but... that wouldn't be fair.'

She closed her eyes. He understood. She'd found what she wanted to do, and it was everything and more. She loved him even more for his understanding and sensitivity.'

'Where's the posting?'

He scrunched up his face. 'On a research ship heading to the Galapagos. It will allow us to see first-hand the environmental work they're doing, and it will help inform the future environmental agenda. That's the official line, but it is an incredible opportunity.'

'Oh my God, Luke.' Her eyes widened, once again realising that there was so much more to Luke than his modest exterior let on. 'That is amazing. If I Google you, are you quite a big deal?'

He shrugged. 'Not really.'

She raised an eyebrow.

'I'm quite well-respected in my field.'

'So when you said you were between postings...'

'I knew this was a possibility, but it's such a competitive field, and it's a major expedition. Part of me is chuffed to be offered...' He winced and cupped her face with both hands. 'But another part wishes they'd picked someone else.' His shoulders shifted again and she saw in the tiny movement the weight of his unhappiness. 'I could turn it down.'

'No! No you couldn't.' She grabbed his forearms. 'You absolutely couldn't.'

His face softened. 'Being honest. No, I can't.' He closed his eyes.

She reached for his hand and squeezed it, trying to comfort him. It hurt more than she could have imagined, watching Luke fighting his own pain, and her stomach tightened in knots.

'When I was ill, I promised myself that if I ever got better, I would make the most of every minute of my life. There was a time when I thought I would die. I made a pact. If I lived, I would take every opportunity. Live life to the full. So although this will do amazing things for my career, it's also an adventure, a chance I might never get again.'

'Oh God, Luke. You couldn't turn that down. I completely get that.' Part of her was humbled that he'd even considered it. She felt a touch of guilt. Would she consider giving up what was so close at hand? They were, as she'd always known, two of a kind. Ready for new adventures, but also the type of people that needed challenge and motivation to lead fulfilling lives.

It hurt. Playing fair was too hard.

'Luke, you don't need to feel bad. You can't turn something like this down.'

'But...'

'There are no buts. I wouldn't expect you to ask me to give up my plans, and I know you wouldn't.'

'I couldn't, not when I see how much they mean to you but...' He slapped a frustrated a hand. 'Timing, eh? It's shit. You know I love you.'

'I know. And I love you. More than anyone before.'

'Sucks, doesn't it? I knew, that first time on the train.' His mouth scrunched into a grim line. 'And that makes it worse.' He reached for her hand. 'But I still believe in serendipity. That we met for a reason.'

Mina smiled at him. 'I've found what I was looking for here. I think some of that is thanks to you. Your positive attitude has made me see that you need to embrace life and go for what you want. How long will you be gone for?'

'I have to go back to the UK for an orientation period of between four and six weeks, and then it's weather-dependent when we set off. It sounds pretty intensive. We'll be away for anywhere between a year and eighteen months.'

She nodded. Who knew what could happen in that length of time? Look how much her life had changed in two short weeks.

'I can't make any promises, and I don't want to.' He waved a hand at the mobile phone on the side. With a flash of insight, she realised. No contact. No texts. No messages. And she understood, completely. They both had to get on with their lives. A cruel double-edged sword.

'What will be, will be. Let's leave it in the hands of serendipity,' said Mina, attempting a smile. Ironic, really, that in Luke she had found her kindred spirit and a shared passion for life, enthusiasm for adventure, and suddenly the positive outlook that had fuelled their initial attraction had to be dialled back and squashed. Now she understood what Simon had meant: sometimes, fun wasn't enough.

His fingers finally curled around hers and squeezed her hand.

'Thank you.' Luke kissed her on the cheek, their eyes meeting and a thousand unsaid things passed between them making her heart fizz with sorrow. 'Shall we just tell ourselves we'll leave things to fate?'

'To serendipity?' she asked with a lift of one eyebrow.

He kissed her on the lips and put his arm around her shoulders.

Together they sat in silence watching the snow fall.

Chapter Twenty-Two

L ater that night, invited by Mina, Luke came to her bed and they said goodbye under the cover of darkness.

The following morning, she watched dry-eyed from the balcony as he walked down to the station, rucksack on his back, vintage suitcase in hand, without a backward glance.

Part Three

Chapter Twenty-Three

'I'm sure this wasn't what you signed up for this weekend,' teased Mina, pushing her roller through the paint in the paint tray, ready to apply the final touches the to the wall she was working on.

'Not quite, but when it's snowing like this I'd rather be doing something,' replied Bernhardt, who was filling in the tricky masking-taped bits around the big pine skirting boards and the light switches. 'After all,' he added in his usual dry way, 'it's better than sitting by a roaring log fire with a good book.'

Mina grinned at him. 'I'm very grateful.'

'And don't forget we get extra cake rations,' said Kristian, who was applying the final coat of cream paint to the walls in the kitchen area.

'There is that,' said Bernhardt with a wry smile.

Mina wasn't sure that extra cake really made up for helping with painting, it seemed above and beyond the call of duty as a guest, but when they'd offered to help, Amelie had encouraged them, sending Johannes off for extra rollers and paint trays, and Mina wasn't going to turn down a spare pair of hands or two. Kristian had actually turned out to be quite skilled.

She stepped back to study the paint colour for the fiftieth time. She really did love this forest green feature wall; it added an extra *je ne sais quoi* to the room.

'It's looking great already,' said Bernhardt, coming to stand next to her. 'I can't believe how much you've achieved since we were last here, four weeks ago. You're a human whirlwind.' He shot her an admiring glance.

'I'm not sure about that. It helps that Johannes knows every tradesman for fifty miles around, and that they all seem to owe him favours.'

'You do know that it's mainly curiosity.'

'Curiosity?' Mina frowned while Bernhardt gave a superior teasing smirk.

'They want to see the woman who felled him. Johannes has been famously single for years. They're also partial to cake.'

'Tell me about it.' She giggled. Her version of *Solothurner torte* had been rechristened *Reckingener torte* and had become a huge hit, especially with the plumber who'd put in the new cloakroom and the electrician that had rewired the barn and put up the most wonderful bronze dome pendant lights throughout the café area. She'd spent a lot of time perfecting that recipe and several others because she was going to need to a full repertoire when she opened the café, and because it used up her spare time and stopped her thinking about Luke.

He'd been gone for four weeks and he haunted her thoughts constantly. It wasn't supposed to feel like this. They'd both agreed to go their separate ways. It had been the right thing to do, but now she bitterly regretted that they'd never exchanged mobile numbers in that stupid pact that they'd try to make it easier by not sharing details.

To her shame, despite her promise to him, she'd looked through Amelie's records but Luke's details had been shredded along with everyone else's passport details once they checked out. It had become a habit to scan through the bookings each week, in the vague hope that he might come before he set sail.

Lifting her chin, she smiled at Bernhardt, determined to hide the dull ache that dogged her. 'One more wall and then we're done. The kitchen goes in on Monday and the last few snagging bits are due to be done by the flooring guy, the builder, and the tiler next week. She had no doubt they would all turn up on time because Johannes was rather fearsome with his clipboard and checklist. He'd been an excellent project manager. Although she knew what she wanted, she'd never managed any building work before.

'Are you really going to open next week?'

'I don't see why not. Providing the kitchen is in.'

'It will be quiet here soon,' observed Bernhardt, as he went back to his painting. 'What will you do then, when the ski season finishes?'

Mina frowned. 'Johannes says there are lots of hikers and tourists. And I think the chalet will be busy. Amelie already has bookings for May, June, and July.'

'Yes, but what about April? Won't you be lonely?'

'I'm sure there will be lots to do.' She deliberately made her voice bright and cheerful, as if being lonely had never entered her lexicon of emotions.

'You might like to come to Zurich for a visit. I can show you round the city.'

'That's kind. I'm going next week actually.'

'You are?'

'An Ikea trip. I'm moving into an apartment in the building behind.'

Bernhardt nodded as if that was completely normal, which of course it was. Amelie had thought nothing of suggesting the five-hour round trip. They were borrowing a van from someone in the village and making the trip together.

Mina applied more paint, listening to the satisfying *sh-sh* of the roller over the wall. She only had a tiny bit more to do and Bernhardt had almost finished the final section of skirting board.

'Nearly there,' she said, stretching her back, already looking forward to a long hot soak in the bath.

'Yes.' Bernhardt looked out of the window with a hopeful expression on his face which made Mina pat him on the arm.

'Yes, you can go back to the slopes tomorrow.'

'Come with us. There won't be many more chances, and this is nearly done.'

Mina bit her lip, tempted by the offer. This last week she'd barely left the chalet and if she was honest, she was a bit sick of her own company. When Luke had first left, she'd thrown herself into helping to run the chalet and getting as much skiing in as she could, even if it was just a quick hour cross-country skiing in the afternoons, but Amelie had quickly re-established control over the kitchen, insisting that she would die of boredom if she weren't allowed to cook. Under Johannes's watchful eye, Amelie spent most evenings toasting her toes in front of his wood burner with one of his wonderful bottles of red wine, and although they often invited her, Mina didn't want to cramp their style.

God, it was tempting. Maybe it would do her some good. Stop her being so bloody miserable. There: she'd said it. Who knew she was such a fantastic actress? While on the outside she greeted the world with her typical everything-is-wonderful attitude, inside the world felt dull and brown, curling up at the edges, and she found it harder and harder to keep up. A day out might lift her out of this annoyingly persistent fug.

What was stopping her, really?

Amelie wouldn't mind. Franzi and Giselle worked on Sundays doing the housekeeping in the mornings and serving in the dining room in the evenings, and Amelie would cook, and tomorrow night's plans for dinner included a hearty stew, which would be easy, and an apple strudel, one of the ones Dave had made and frozen a few weeks before. If Mina got up a little bit earlier, she could bake the lovely squidgy chocolate *Gotthelftorte* for afternoon tea, which she'd perfected last week.

'OK,' she said, feeling a sudden release of tension. It would be good to get out for a change, and she'd just go to bed a bit earlier this evening; it would relieve the loneliness that she hated having to admit to, even if it was only to herself.

──────────────

After a dull cloudy week, the sun blessed them with a magnificently brilliant appearance, chasing away the sense of gloom that had settled upon her over the last few days. Serendipity, she thought, the word flitting annoyingly into her brain. Ignoring it, she sucked in a deep breath and looked down the mountain, already anticipating the swish and bump of her skis over the fresh snow.

'Perfect conditions. You ready?' asked Bernhardt, pulling down his googles and rearranging the poles into his hands.

'Yes,' she said, confident that she'd be able to keep up this time. She had pent-up energy to burn. She pushed off first, immediately feeling the adrenaline firing through, along with a burst of relief. The swish of skis on snow soothed her and she quickly relaxed into a smooth rhythm, gliding over the surface, her body in sync. Even the boots seemed almost comfortable today. She couldn't imagine going back to Manchester again. Ian had accepted her resignation, and the very next day booked a trip out to the chalet in June which had tickled her. She'd obviously done a good sales job on him.

Even Miriam and Derek, to her absolute astonishment, had agreed that it was a good move.

'You've always needed to spread your wings,' said

Miriam in a tearful phone conversation, 'But we'll always be here for you. And we've sold the house.'

Derek, chipping in on speaker phone, told her all about the bungalow they'd found with the loft space for his trains and the most wonderful cottage garden. Their excitement about their own change of circumstances made her feel a lot less guilty about moving away.

Bernhardt came racing past her and she laughed out loud. Clearly his patience with her pace had run out. She watched his elegant competence, wondering if she'd ever be that good, although just being out here was enough. She'd never get used to the spring freshness of the air, that was for sure.

The slopes teemed with people in high spirits, all anxious to get as much skiing done as they could before the season ended. By the time Mina reached the bottom, to find Bernhardt waiting for her, she felt exhilarated.

'You ski much better now,' he commented as they skied across the flat towards the ski lifts.

'Practice,' she said, still a little breathless.

'You'll be Swiss soon,' he teased. 'Would you like a beer?'

'That would be great. What about Kristian?'

Bernhardt shrugged. 'He'll find us. There is a nice bar if we get this ski lift, and then there is a run over towards the west.'

'OK, lead on.'

They took the chair lift together.

'Having a good time?' he asked, smiling at her.

'Yes, it's good to be outside and away from the paint fumes.'

'How long do you think you will run the café for?'

'I don't know,' replied Mina honestly, a little surprised by the question.

'What about your career? Back in England.'

'Time for a new one. I realise now that I wasn't that happy.'

'But will this be enough? Do you want to stay in a tiny village forever? You lived in a big city, with a good job.'

Mina bristled at the implication of what he was saying, but realised that in his precise, formal way, it must have seemed strange.

'I came here to try and sort out my life. Yes, I had a good job, a flat of my own, and nearly a fiancé. But when he didn't want to marry me, it made me see things differently. My job wasn't making me happy, my flat was just a place to live, and I didn't know what was really important to me.'

'And now you do?' Scepticism laced his voice, and it forced her to think hard about the answer.

'Yes,' she said firmly, realising that this was everything she'd been trying to find a way towards with that bloody book. 'I want to cook. To experiment. To create recipes. Learn how to make chocolate. Sell chocolate. To feed people. To look after them. It might not look much, but it makes me happy. I've been happier here than I have in my whole working life.'

'You have?'

She beamed at him, the knowledge lighting her up inside. 'Yes.'

Bernhardt gave her a thoughtful nod, followed by a slow smile. 'Then, that is good.'

She smiled. She could almost see him mentally casting her off. She couldn't resist teasing him. 'So, not the woman for you?'

He had the grace to blush. 'Compatibility is important, no?'

'It is, and we're not.' Never were, thought Mina, but all the same patted his hand. Keeping friends was far preferable to creating enemies. Part of her wished she could have liked him more. Bernhardt was the sort of man she should have been looking for. A balance to her. Someone who would sort her out, stop her making rash decisions like deciding to open a chocolate café in the middle of nowhere in another country. She laughed at herself – and that wasn't the sort of person she wanted at all.

The ski chair dipped and Bernhardt raised the bar readying himself for the off, which he did with enviably smooth control. Mina still found disembarking chair lifts a hit or miss affair. Thankfully today she managed it with some dignity.

'This way,' called Bernhardt, already champing at the bit to be off. Before she could catch up with him he'd already disappeared from view. She followed and reached the start of the run, looking down at the steep, narrow path through an outcrop of rocks on one side and a long drop away to the valley far below on the other. No margin for error, she thought, a shiver of fear clutching the base of her spine.

With a swallow and a deep breath, she gingerly inched forward. Eeek, that looked steep. Really, really steep. None of the previous runs she'd ever done had been anything like as challenging as this. She might be impulsive and always ready to try things, but she also had a healthy sense of self-preservation.

But there was only one way down and Bernhardt, already a bright blue speck, was about to disappear from sight. Grasping her poles, she edged forward, her skis already in snowplough position. Behind her she heard voices and then a group of six appeared. With excited shouts and whoops they hurled themselves over the edge, one of them bumping into her with his arm. Although it only knocked her a tiny bit off balance, it was enough to startle her and she drew her skis together, and before she could stop herself she'd begun moving down the slope. In an undignified scramble she gathered her poles and tried to stay upright. By some miracle she managed, but her skis were in control, not her. She leaned back instead of forwards, which made things worse, and quickly righted herself. Her skis were picking up speed far quicker than she could have imagined. Don't panic, she told herself. Don't panic. But she was going too fast now. The wind whipped in her face and it took all her concentration to steer along the narrow path and not look towards the drop on her right. One of her skis scraped over a rock, sending her careering off course, making her heart pound in fear. *Stay upright, Mina. Stay upright.* She tucked her poles close to her sides, bent her knees, and tried to keep her balance as she hurtled downwards, everything in her peripheral vision a blur of white. Inside her roll-neck top, she felt the sweat breaking out as she tried to focus.

As the track widened ahead, she tried to push her legs out to snowplough but was going at such a speed she was terrified she was going to end up doing the splits. A small whimper of fear escaped and she clamped her mouth shut, her mind desperately trying to think. Attempting a turn here would be impossible, there wasn't enough room, and if she tried to ski parallel across the slope, she'd either end up in the rocks or career off the run to tumble down the steep mountain side. All she could do was stay upright and pray like crazy that the run would end soon but glancing ahead that didn't look very likely. Every jolt and bump of her skis made her pulse jerk and her heart jump in her chest. Her hands cramped, gripping the poles so tightly as she fought the temptation to try and slow herself down with them.

At last the run came into an open section although it curved sharply away to the right and then over a swell and down even more steeply. Her stomach churned and she sucked in a terrified breath. *Now or never…* She remembered everything she'd been taught about turning. *Turn your feet, but not your body. Feet not body. Feet not body. Face forwards.* She kept chickening out. Then she did it. Screwing her eyes tight shut probably wasn't the smartest move. One of her skis scraped over something hard, the edge catching. She flew rather than fell, her legs tangling with the skis, and she hit the snow with a resounding wallop that thudded through her ski helmet. Her body carried on scudding down the slope and she scrabbled for purchase, feeling a sharp pain in her knee as her ski caught. Like a grappling iron it thankfully anchored her momentarily, until her boot unclipped from the ski and she came to a merciful, crumpled halt.

For a moment she lay winded and disorientated, and it took her a minute to realise she must have flipped at some point as her head faced down the slope. Giving into an almost welcome sense of defeat she stayed put, a little scared by the thundering beat of her heart. Perhaps if she just lay here, she could pretend that everything was fine, and that she didn't still have to get down the rest of this awful slope. Self-pitying tears welled up in her eyes that she couldn't even dash away without taking off gloves, goggles, and helmet. Maybe if she just stayed put someone would find her. And then she'd look a complete idiot, because clearly this run was far too difficult for someone who'd only done a couple of weeks' real skiing. *Come on, pull yourself together and stop being such a wuss*, she finally told herself, and carefully hauled herself up, feeling an ache in one her arms where she'd wrenched it. Her knee hurt too, where it had been twisted when her leg went one way and the ski the other. But on the plus side, as she gingerly tested each limb, nothing had broken – although everything seemed to hurt, especially her head.

Forcing herself to her feet, she unclipped the other ski and trudged a few metres back up the slope to collect the other one. After weighing up all her options she decided that there was nothing for it but to walk down this bit and through the mogul field that she could now see ahead. If the run got easier in places she put her skis back on, but up here with that treacherous drop to her right she refused to take any chances.

Once she started moving, the aches and pains receded. Although her head still thumped, some of her natural optimism reasserted itself. It could be a lot worse. She could walk, the sun was shining, and now that her heart no longer threatened to pump its way out of her chest, she could appreciate the wonderful view. No wonder Luke loved it up here; these mountains made you aware of your own insignificance at the same time as inspiring you to live life to the full. Mina couldn't imagine a more life-affirming sight. Hoisting her skis higher onto her shoulder and gripping her poles in one hand, she trudged down the hill, tilting her face up to the sun, and tried not to think about where Luke might be right now, and what he was doing. Instead she just said a heartfelt prayer, focusing on the mountain tops. Please let him be safe and happy. It had been a month now. Had he set sail yet?

A skier shushed by and then swerved to a flashy stop.

'Mina.' Kristian pushed up his goggles, his kind eyes anxiously surveying her. 'Are you alright?'

'Took a tumble. This is a bit advanced for me. My pride is bruised and a few other bits of me, but I'm OK.'

'I'm sorry.' He bent and unclipped his skis. 'I will walk with you.'

'You don't need to do that.'

With a boyish grin, he shrugged. 'I can ski anytime. I like talking to you.'

'Thank you. I appreciate it.' She felt pathetically grateful to him. 'I thought I'd wait for an easier bit and maybe have another go.'

'Yes, otherwise it is a long walk.' A thought struck him,

so obviously that it made Mina chuckle. 'Where is Bernhardt?'

'Long gone,' she said.

Kristian frowned but didn't say anything.

'Not very gentlemanly,' she teased, trying to make light of it with a laugh. 'He was testing my mettle.' She paused, before saying, more to herself than Kristian, 'He failed.'

His frown deepened. 'I thought he liked you.'

'He did.' Mina grinned which clearly puzzled the poor man.

'You didn't like him?'

'As a friend,' she said to keep things simple. Actually Bernhardt had opened her eyes to something she'd missed. Luke would never have left her on the mountain, he would have made sure she was safe. He would have made it his responsibility to know what she was capable of before he took her anywhere. It struck her that Luke might be fun and impulsive, but at the same time he thought things through, planned, and weighed up the risks. She'd been an idiot to let him go. She should have fought harder to keep him. He was the perfect match for her. Now all she had was hope that one day serendipity would deliver and bring him back to her.

Chapter Twenty-Four

She and Kristian skied to the end of the run, which traversed the mountain going across instead of down, which meant that the slope flattened out a lot and lower down became, thankfully, a lot easier. Even so Mina's leg's felt decidedly wobbly, and she was even more grateful to see the two-way lines of the cable cars and the station up ahead.

As always she took a moment to take in the view, the craggy mountain tops, greyed-out against the white, the sun casting secretive shadows in the rough-hewn, granite faces. They made her think of sleeping giants keeping a watchful, and possibly despairing, guard over the planet. And such thoughts led her to Luke, and him taking her to the viewpoint of Eggishorn.

Another overnight fall of snow had created fresh pristine vistas with only a few ski tracks marring the surface, and crystals of ice sparkled in the sun like half buried diamonds. The clouds had rolled back and edged the mountains leaving a crater of blue above them and the sun's rays felt warm on her face. This was what was important. Life, being alive, and enjoying what you had. She forced away the melancholy that crept in, like a stray dog, whenever it got the chance.

'What kept you?' asked Bernhardt with a Cheshire cat grin when they pulled level with him at the bottom, where he was chatting to another group. 'Are you ready for that beer?'

'Sure,' said Mina with a wink at Kristian.

Kristian rolled his eyes, but didn't say anything about their painful progress down the mountain. He'd actually been a patient and kind coach once they'd got back on their skis, guiding her down some of the more difficult bits, breaking them up into small achievable sections. Underneath all that social awkwardness, lurked a very kind, gentle, and surprisingly thoughtful man, and Mina could see exactly why Amelie was so determined to nurture him.

As they queued in the busy bar, delayed shock began to set in, and the sweat on her body had cooled now making her a little chilly.

'Why don't we sit inside?' suggested Kristian.

'No,' said Bernhardt. 'Why would you want to? It's a lovely day.'

'I'm feeling a bit cold,' insisted Kristian.

'I'll stay inside with you,' said Mina shooting him a grateful glance.

'Beer?' asked Bernhardt with an impatient huff, as the girl serving approached them.

'I think I'm going to have hot chocolate. Mina?'

'That's a good idea.' she replied, doubly grateful to him – having alcohol on top of the shock probably wasn't very sensible. She still had to get down the mountain, and although the cable car was there, she wasn't sure where it went to and how much more skiing she would have to do from there. She had a sudden memory of Luke poring over the ski map with her, explaining exactly where they were and how to get back from Eggishorn.

Having placed and received their orders, they made their way to a table, Mina and Kristian both protectively cupping the tall glasses of whipped creamed and chocolate shavings as if to shield them from harm.

'How do you find that run?' asked Bernhardt.

'Terrifying.' Mina grinned.

'Well done for getting down. It's quite challenging.'

'Hmm,' said Mina, keeping the fixed grin in place. She could see Kristian about to say something, but before she could nudge him under the table, he decided against it and applied himself to the cream on his drink. She smiled: he was learning.

After a sandwich, she excused herself. 'There are a few things I could do in the café and they're preying on my mind.'

'Do you need any help?' asked Kristian.

'No, I'm fine.' There wasn't actually anything to do, she just wanted to go and potter in the café and revel in being there. Her boxes of china were due to arrive any day, thanks to Hannah painstakingly packing it all up, and she couldn't wait to be reunited with them and see them in situ.

'All work and no play,' said Bernhardt, once again showing off his command of English.

'I guess I don't really think of it as work, and that's when you know you've made the right decision,' and as she said it, Mina felt a satisfying sense of contentment settle over her.

———————

To her delight the china had arrived while she was out, and one of Amelie's neighbours had kindly collected it from the depot to save the driver a job.

'Isn't it pretty?' cried Amelie in delight as they knelt on the pretty new cushions on the floor of the café, unwrapping sheet after sheet of newspaper to reveal tea plates, cups, saucers, and cake stands. Mina stroked the gilt pattern of one of the plates, relieved that it had all made it in one piece.

'Yes, I've been collecting it for a couple of years, although I'm not quite sure I'm going to have quite enough.' As a last resort she'd have to buy some of the very plain white china that was sold in the wholesalers, but in the short term she could be borrow plates and cups from Amelie.

They stacked the china in haphazard piles on one of the rustic tables, one of eight that Johannes's cousin, Pieter, had provided. He made furniture, and these were unsold pieces that he'd let Mina have at a heavily discounted price. She'd ordered spindle backed chairs and cushions in shades of green, yellow, and white, embroidered with traditional

Swiss cross-stich patterns to create a fresh bright colour scheme.

Mina stepped back to survey the room, which despite being full, still looked huge. The big barn doors had been replaced with a large picture window, and on either side were heavy double-glazed bi-fold doors, which would fold back in the summer to give access to a terrace. The groundwork for that couldn't start until the spring thaw, but in the meantime customers had a wonderful view from behind the glass. The café area with the kitchen and the chairs and tables took up three quarters of the space, but the final quarter was partitioned off with one of the original rustic wooden walls that would have penned in the cattle. Here Mina, with Amelie's artistic direction, had created an improved tasting and display room for Johannes's chocolate range, with further space for other local products which Mina still needed to source. She just hadn't had time.

'Now I have a surprise for you. My opening gift for the café.' From behind the counter where the kitchen would be installed, Amelie pulled – or rather dragged – out a huge parcel, nearly two metres long. 'I have a friend in Gluringen who works with wood.'

Mina fought her way through the brown paper and yet more layers of bubble wrap to reveal the carved swirling letters painted in green to match her feature wall.

Tears sprang to her eyes. 'Oh Amelie, you didn't have to do this. It's beautiful.'

'I hope it's alright, but I didn't place the order with the signwriter like you asked me to. As soon as you said what you wanted to call the café, I thought of Gregor.'

Mina traced the S at the front of the sign. 'It's perfect.'

'I'm still curious why you've called it that.'

Mina's gave her a tearful smile. 'One day, I'll tell you.'

Rather than plague her for an answer like some people would have done, Amelie nodded. 'When you're ready.'

Mina prayed that the day would come. Until then she could only hope.

'It's nearly time for cake and coffee, do you want to choose a cake stand for the *Gotthelftorte*?'

'That's easy. The one there with the gilt edges and the tiny pink flowers and green trailing ivy design. It will go perfectly with the raspberries. That is one beautiful chocolate cake, I think you make it better than me.'

'I'm sure I don't.'

Amelie shook her head. 'Either way, the guests are going to have a treat this afternoon, although now the evenings are growing long, more of them will stay out a little later.'

'Johannes will appreciate it,' teased Mina.

'Johannes is rapidly becoming a cake connoisseur, among other things.' Her godmother's mouth twitched and there was a dreamy look in her eye that Mina really didn't want to think too much about.

'Well, he'd better like this one, as I used his chocolate.' The recipe using melted chocolate made the most delicious squidgy moist sponge and Mina had already decided that it would be one of the signature dishes in the café. She would ring the seasonal changes with different fruit garnishes.

'He's also...' Amelie paused and blushed. 'He's about to take on a new role.'

'He is?'

'We're getting married.'

Mina squealed. 'Oh my God!' She threw her arms around her godmother. 'That's amazing.'

'I wanted you to be the first to know.'

'When? How?'

Amelie laughed. 'You don't think it's too soon?'

Mina stopped, hit by a sudden wave of grief. 'No, not when you know.'

It had taken one kiss for her and Luke, although it had taken her another two weeks to appreciate it, and now when it was far too late, she knew that there'd never be anyone quite as perfect as him.

'It was quite romantic,' Amelie laughed. 'I'd never have thought it of Johannes, he's always been such a gruff bear.'

'The love of a good woman, you see.'

'Hmm, or maybe mellowing with age.'

'So how did he propose?'

'He asked me to look at a new wine list for the chalet that he'd put together, because he had a few new additions from a new supplier that he thought I might like.' Amelie's eyes sparkled as she recalled the memory. 'When I read the list, there was a wine *Will You Marry Me* from the vineyard of Johannes Metterhorn. "A loyal, faithful grape variety, occasionally short-tempered but always good-hearted."'

'Ah, that's lovely.'

'But you don't think people will think it's very sudden?'

'No, people will think you've finally taken pity on the poor man. It was obvious the first day I arrived that he adored you.'

Amelie giggled. 'You wouldn't think so if you knew

what a hard time he gave me when I first opened the chalet.'

'That's just his way, he likes to challenge things. I suspect he was worried that you might not stay the course.'

With a sigh Amelie pulled Mina closer and put her arm across her shoulder. 'I probably wouldn't have done, without you. I was already thinking about giving up my dream before you came. You were right: it is too much work for one person on their own, and I was too stubborn to let go. Then having a heart attack forced me to. When I lay in that hospital bed, thinking of all the bother I was causing, I very nearly decided to put it on the market and go back to Basel. And then you, my wonderful girl, gave me all the solutions. I'm so grateful to you. I wish I could do something to make you happy.' Her smile held a hint of sadness and sympathy. 'I think that's the way of the newly engaged: they want everyone to be as happy as they are.'

'I'm happy,' said Mina, indignation tinging her voice. 'Perfectly happy. I've found what I want to do. And I've also decided to set up a blog about Swiss food, talking about the origins of the recipes, the regional foods, and the seasonal dishes. Maybe try and write a recipe book or two. I'd quite like to do one all about chocolate. There's so much I want do. It's exciting.' And true, she'd found her place here, and the time and space to do the things that she really wanted to do. Only one thing was missing, and it wouldn't kill her.

'That's surface happy. Anyone can be happy like that, but you deserve more.'

'Don't be nice to me. I'm trying to be brave.'

'Is it Luke?'

'Yes.'

'Is he coming back?'

'No,' she said with a finality that inside she couldn't quite accept. For some crazy, stupid reason, she had a secret, romantic hope that he would turn up for the opening of the café, which was why she'd blasted it all over the café's new Facebook page and Instagram account, although if he was in the middle of the Atlantic, it was hardly likely.

Amelie raised both eyebrows.

'He isn't, no matter how much I wish it. Let's talk about you.' She hugged her. 'Congratulations. I am so so so pleased for you.'

'I think I'm still in shock. At my age, I didn't expect anyone to fall in love with me, never mind me fall in love with them.'

'What, you always have men chopping wood for you?'

'Always.' Her eyes danced with impish amusement.

Mina jumped up. 'I know, we can have a joint celebration – an engagement party combined with the dry run opening of the café, and invite all your friends in the village as well as the guests. I was wondering about a theme. I'll do everything with love hearts and flowers.'

'That's a wonderful idea, but you should also invite local hotel owners and other businesspeople in the area so that they'll recommend it to people.'

'Brilliant, and I was going to have a laptop open and ask people to leave Tripadvisor reviews. I've been taking pictures of cakes for social media, and I've already got tons of followers. People seem to love cake!'

'And why wouldn't they? But a joint party sounds a very good idea, and I'm sure Johannes would like to contribute some champagne.'

'That's not necessary.'

'Oh, I think it is,' Amelie said with an irrepressible smile.

Chapter Twenty-Five

M ina woke, her brain springing into action as soon as her eyes opened, racing through her checklist. *Breathe*, she told herself. Everything was done that could be done in advance. She'd baked all the cakes in advance, iced the biscuits yesterday, Johannes had brought the specially made chocolate love-hearts over last night, the paper napkins she'd ordered at the last minute had turned up, and she'd ironed her favourite dress, which she'd had poor Hannah – 'Your Post Office bitch' – send over not long after her china.

Rolling out of bed, she opened the balcony doors and wrapped the throw from the bed around her shoulders. She would never tire of this view. It still held the same magic for her, the mighty guardianship of the mountains, the clear, brilliant sky, and the pretty village with its sturdy buildings, nestling in the valley. It spoke of longevity, tradition, and steadiness, which she found reassuring. All this would be here long after she was gone.

She traced the path of the river Rhone. Although out of sight here, it had shaped the long valley with its collection of twelve villages from Biel to Oberwald. Soon summer would arrive, and she couldn't wait to see the mountain meadows, the wild flowers, and walk along the scenic hiking trails and show the place off to Derek and Miriam, whom she'd persuaded to come out in June. They'd love it here, she was sure they would, and Derek would be enthralled with the train journeys he could plan. The thought of train journeys brought unwelcome memories.

Enough daydreaming, she told herself, and marched back into the room, getting straight into the shower to wash her hair. She took her time blow-drying it, and decided to come back to do her makeup later when she put her dress on. Even as she skipped down the stairs, she knew she'd take a detour to check the guest register, just in case. She skimmed a finger across the diary page for that day, and then over the next and raised an eyebrow – Frau Müller, it appeared, had been given a reprieve. Pausing for a moment, she closed her eyes and forced a cheerful smile on her face. What will be, will be. Straightening up, she strode into the kitchen.

'Morning, Amelie.'

'Good morning, you're full of beans.'

'Big day.'

'It is. Would you like some breakfast?'

'Not just now, thank you.' Her appetite had taken a hike. Probably nerves.

For the rest of the morning, she and Amelie put the

finishing touches to the cakes, and prepared a selection of canapes including several Swiss favourites that Mina had not come across before: avocado slices and horseradish mousse rolled in smoked salmon; tiny rounds of bread topped by toasted cheese and a dressing of honey, vinegar, mustard, garlic, and rosemary; and tiny pinched dumplings of pastry containing spicy sausage meat. The official opening was due to take place at one o'clock, and they both kept a careful eye on the time. Mina also kept an ear out for noises in reception and a couple of times lifted her head at the sound of the front door to the boot room opening and closing. Once, hearing low male tones, she even went out on the pretext of needing to go to the loo.

'Hey, Mina.'

Kristian carrying a heavy box was holding open the door for Johannes who was carrying a second box.

'Kristian. Lovely to see you. Do you think you have enough champagne there?' she asked with a laugh.

'Wouldn't miss the grand opening. And Jane's coming this weekend.' He frowned down at the box. 'Don't you think this is enough?'

Johannes rolled his eyes and shouldered his way through the kitchen door. 'It's plenty. People only need one glass.'

'It's a party.' Amelie's eyes twinkled as she gave him a quick kiss on the cheek as he put the case of champagne down on the table.

'Hmm,' he grumbled, and winked at Mina. 'There's plenty more, *if* we need it. Thanks Kristian.'

'Can I leave you in charge of flutes?' asked Amelie, peeling off her apron. 'Some of us need to go and get ready for a party.'

'These are all chilled. The buckets are downstairs, along with the flutes, and I'll leave the spare bottles outside on the terrace.'

'Would you like me to check Kristian in, and then I'll go straight up and change?' asked Mina.

'If you don't mind. I need to find a nice shirt for Johannes,' said Amelie with a steely glint in her eye.

'What's wrong with this one?'

Mina and Kristian left them discussing the matter.

Mina slipped her favourite dress from its hanger. The shirt-style, with buttons all way down the front, had a flared midi-length skirt, and felt feminine and floaty when she wore it. Vanity had elevated it to favourite because the rich blue silky fabric seemed to accentuate her eyes and turn them almost royal blue. Only her pensive smile as she studied herself in the mirror gave any hint of her feelings.

'Showtime,' she said to her reflection, gathered up her wrap in case it got colder later and her bag, and left the hotel room, grateful that Amelie had insisted that, with room to spare, she stay put for the time being. With a foolish gesture she stroked the door to what had once been Luke's room and told herself off for being fanciful.

As soon as she came down the stairs to the café from the

kitchen, Johannes handed her a glass of champagne. 'This will calm your nerves,' he said.

'Thank you.' She took the glass with a steady hand; her nerves had nothing to do with the opening.

'You look beautiful,' said Amelie, and raised her glass. 'To Mina, for bringing everything together.'

To her surprise, Johannes kissed her on the cheek before adding a hearty, 'To Mina.' He actually looked a little emotional.

'It looks wonderful, doesn't it?' she said, taking a sip of the champagne. 'You know some great craftsmen.'

'A team effort, but it would not have been possible without your enthusiasm and determination, Mina. You had the vision. Is it how you saw it?' he asked.

'Better.' Mina sighed, utterly thrilled with how it all turned out. 'I think I might cry.'

'Don't do that, *liebling*.' Amelie hugged her which brought the tears closer. 'This is a celebration. You can cry at the wedding. Which reminds me, do you think that you could make our wedding cake?'

Mina's eyes widened and she threw her arms around her godmother. 'I'd be honoured. Ooh, I've got loads of ideas for wedding cakes.'

Amelie patted her. 'There's plenty of time. Well, a few weeks.'

'A few weeks!'

'Don't tell everyone, but we don't want a lot of fuss, and why wait? We're both old enough to know what we want. It will be a small wedding, only ten or so people, but we'll have a party afterwards for everyone.'

'A wedding cake.' Ideas were already flooding into her head.

'Why don't you concentrate on today first?' Amelie patted her cheek. 'One thing at a time.'

'You know me. Always onto the next thing.'

'Well not today, this is your day too. Look its nearly time.'

In the way that she'd learned was typically Swiss, many of the invited guests, especially the older people, arrived at exactly one o'clock, with none of the fashionably-late rubbish that so often characterised things at home. Even though she knew by now to expect it, she was still surprised to see the orderly prompt queue waiting outside the new door, which had been painted forest-green to match the inside wall. In no time at all the café filled with noise, cheerful chatter bouncing off the walls. Claudia and Frank turned up with a beautiful potted plant and insisted on being given a guided tour of every inch of the kitchen, tasting room and café area.

'You've done an amazing job. This is beautiful,' exclaimed Claudia. 'I can't wait to bring our first tour here. We've planned a really interesting route so that we can stop here for lunch.'

Mina felt a little overcome by their support. 'That's so kind of you.'

'It's business,' said Frank. 'If we show our customers a good time and take them to nice places, they'll recommend us to their friends and family. Word of mouth is one of the best ways of advertising.' Then he winked. 'And there is nothing like cake to keep tired hikers going.'

As she laughed with him, she noticed some newcomers arrive at the door. 'Excuse me, I ought to go and say hello.' Throughout the next hour, people kept arriving and Mina found her attention constantly straying to the door.

Kristian arrived with Jane, the Italian family popped in, and various villagers as well as guests from a neighbouring hotel.

'I very much like this.' Mrs Huber, one of Amelie's neighbours, spoke in stilted English and pointed to the tea plate she held in her plump hands.

'The *Gotthelftorte*?'

'*Nein, der Teller*.' She chinked the plate between her finger and thumb.

'Ah, the plate. Thank you, I brought them from England.'

'Very good.' She nodded approvingly and beckoned another older woman over. The two of them compared their plates and started a lively conversation in German, little of which Mina understood, despite her German improving over the last month. Now she'd decided to stay there was no excuse not to speak the language instead of relying on other people to translate all the time. Her eyes slid, yet again, to the doorway.

She noticed Johannes circulating topping up everyone's glasses and steeled herself for the official bit coming up.

Ting. Ting. When Johannes tapped his glass everyone, with extreme politeness and notable deference, stopped talking.

'Welcome everyone, and thank you all for coming to this wonderful occasion. Today we have two celebrations, and my fiancé and I...' He paused as a ripple of laughter ran through the room. 'We would especially like to thank Mina for allowing us to hijack her grand opening. Mina.' He beckoned her forward.

She swallowed and checked the door once more. With an inward sigh, she wound her way through the gathered crowd to Johannes and Amelie's side. She'd really hoped.

Schooling her face into a serene smile, which hid the wrenching disappointment inside, she turned and faced everyone, touched by the warmth of the smiling faces reflected towards her.

'Thank you all for coming, and for being so welcoming. I'm looking forward to living here and getting to know all of you in the coming months. Starting up a small business in a small community is both daunting and exciting. You've all seen me setting up, I hope that you'll all see me thrive. At the same time, I know how important it is for us to support each other, so I'm open to any ideas or ways that I can help your businesses, too.' She beamed at everyone. 'Now that's the boring bit over, more important is the celebration. I'd like you all to join in with me and congratulate Amelie and Johannes on their engagement.' She raised a glass. 'To Amelie and Johannes.'

Everyone cheered and raised their glasses.

Johannes made an extremely, pink-faced, brief speech about how wonderful Amelie was and how happy he was, and then extorted everyone to leave five-star reviews on Tripadvisor, pointing to the laptop in the corner of the room.

The rest of the afternoon passed in a happy haze, and finally people drifted away, many of them leaving fulsome comments, until only Kristian, Jane, Mina, and the happy couple were left.

Mina gave the door one last forlorn look. She'd been so hopeful, so convinced, although she didn't know why.

'Well, that was a triumph,' said Amelie starting to collect up plates.

'It was great,' said Jane, picking up glasses, and nudging Kristian to do the same. 'I'm sure it's going to be a huge success.'

'Thank you.' She heard the door and whirled around, her heart suddenly in her mouth.

Frau Huber poked her head around. 'Still here. Good. I have something for you.' She walked in with a slow, rolling gait, followed by her son carrying a large box. He placed it carefully on one of the tables. 'Come. Come.' The older woman pointed to the cardboard flaps. Puzzled, Mina opened the box. Inside were lots of paper-wrapped odd-shaped parcels. She unwrapped one of the parcels. Inside were six china tea plates with a delicate pale-blue design, edged with white.

'This is beautiful.'

'My grandmother's china. And my aunt's. And my sister's mother-in-law.'

'My goodness.' Mina unwrapped another bundle of tea plates and a couple of cups with elegantly shaped china handles.

'No good to me.' She spoke in rapid German, with a few

clucks of disparagement, and Mina only picked up a few words. She glanced towards Amelie for translation.

'Frau Huber says you can have it. She has no use for it, and would rather it was being used.' Amelie laughed. 'She says there's no point giving it to her son, Franz, he is too clumsy and his fingers don't fit the cups.'

Frau Huber's eyes gleamed with amusement and she patted her son on the arm. Mina smiled back.

'That's incredibly kind of you. *Danke schön*, Frau Huber. Would you like some money for it?' Although she'd spent most of budget already, once her flat was let out more money was coming, and of course the money from her parents' house would be coming soon.

'*Nein, nein.*' Frau Huber waved her hand. 'I have another box for Franz to bring later.'

Mina laughed, unable to believe the other woman's generosity. 'Are you sure?'

'Look at him,' she said in her heavy accent.

Franz rolled his eyes. 'I don't want it. I'm too scared to even look at it.'

Mina laughed again. 'Well, that's extraordinarily generous of you. I would love to have it. Thank you. Perhaps Franz would like to be paid in cake occasionally?' Mina knew there would be times when cake needed eating up, it was good to know grateful recipients in advance.

His eyes lit up and he nodded enthusiastically.

The Hubers left and the tidying up was done remarkably quickly. As they said, many hands made light work, but Mina's heart was heavy. She'd really thought that Luke would come.

'I'll just stay a minute,' she said as the others prepared to leave.

Amelie gave her a fond smile. 'See you upstairs.'

Switching out all but one small lamp, she sank into a chair, her arm resting on the table and checked her phone. She'd posted the time of the opening on Facebook and Instagram, on both her personal and business pages. In her heart of hearts she'd honestly believed that Luke would turn up. She'd believed in serendipity.

'And that's what you get, Mina Campbell, for believing in superstitious, romantic rubbish. This is real life, not a flipping film. You're a scientist, for goodness' sake. You of all people know that cakes are made with chemical reactions, not magic. The correct quantities of x and y equal z.' She spoke out loud, cursing herself for being such an idiot. 'It stops here and now.' Luke wasn't coming. He'd really gone. How could she blame him? She hadn't expected to miss him so much, or for it to hurt like this, or for him to sidle into her thoughts each and every sodding day. She'd lost count of the number of times she had would-be conversations in her head with him, imagining telling him about the triumphs of her day and the funny things that had gone wrong. Did he feel the same way?

Probably not. He knew where she was, he could have sent her a message for today. He knew how much it meant to her.

She had to accept he wasn't coming back. It bloody sucked, and went against the grain for someone who always found a way, for someone who didn't give up. It really bloody sucked. She realised she didn't do defeat awfully well. No matter how hard she tried to focus on the future and all the positives, the heaviness of loss grated.

It was over and she had the face the fact that serendipity didn't exist.

Chapter Twenty-Six

Minds were bloody contrary things, decided Mina, thumping her pillow. Why didn't they do what you wanted them to do? Instead of letting her relish the triumph of her opening party, hers now insisted on coming up with a-gazillion-and-one ideas for Amelie and Johannes's wedding cake, and refused to let sleeping Lukes lie.

Wedding cake, that was what she would focus on today. Amelie might think that a few weeks allowed plenty of time but Mina knew better. She needed a design. To practise. Get the couple's approval. As this weekend was probably going to be her last free one before the café opened officially on Monday, she decided to get a head start and catch the train to Brig to visit the wholesalers to look at ingredients and cake-decorating supplies to find out what was on offer. There was no point coming up with a dozen ideas if she then couldn't make them happen.

Throwing the covers off, she dived into the shower and

dressed quickly in jeans, sweater, and a scarf, without even bothering to look in the mirror, and dragged a quick comb through her hair because she didn't need to see her reflection to know she'd be sporting a halo of bed-head frizz.

The shy tendrils of spring, with early green shoots poking through the snow, extended to the temperature, and it definitely felt a few degrees warmer as she walked down to the station pulling along a small cabin bag. She knew herself too well, she was bound to end up buying supplies today, and this seemed eminently practical if, as she was bound to, she got carried away and bought more than she could carry.

The train, although busy today, was full of local people going shopping with far fewer tourists than usual, and she got the sense of the winter season starting to ebb away. Part of her felt sad about that, but another part excited to see what summer would bring. She wondered if there was a twilight period between seasons where the local people existed in a quiet lull before the storm.

More people clambered on with shopping bags at each station, and by the time the train pulled into Brig it was packed. As soon as she walked from the station to the town centre she quickly realised why. Market stalls lined the cobbled streets, their colourful awnings bright in the morning sunshine. Foodie heaven, decided Mina, quickening her steps as she crossed to the nearest stall, which was filled with cured meats in every shape and size as well as traditional Swiss Cervelat sausage. For a moment she marvelled at the selection, wishing she knew more about what they all were, before moving on to the next straw-covered stall offering an amazing array of cheese. A giant round of Emmental sat upright on its side, surrounded by small, different-coloured, round cheeses, like babies that had spilled out of the nest. Baskets containing thick wedges of every shade of golden, cream, and white cheeses were arranged along the front of the stall, and in the middle were tubs of soft cheese with big wooden spoons.

'Want to try some?' asked the good-looking man behind the stall in perfect English. Wearing a black down jacket and a wool hat, his blue eyes gave her a quick once-over.

'I'd love to.' Mina smiled at him, part friendliness and part amusement at his obvious interest. 'What's that one?'

Before long she'd tried half the cheeses stall and found herself chatting away (and flirting just a little) to Hans, who ran the stall for his father, who made cheese in Biel, not far from Reckingen.

'I'd love to stock your cheese, if it's of interest,' she said, having told him about the café, which he already knew all about – apparently it was the hot topic of gossip in the villages.

'I wish you luck.' He gave her a card. 'Speak to my father.'

'Thank you, that's brilliant. I was wondering how to go about finding local suppliers.'

'Ah, wait. Hey, Walter,' he called to the meat stall holder and spoke quick-fire German.

Twenty minutes later she had a handful of cards and a bag full of samples of cheese and salamis, and two new friends, both of whom promised to visit when they next went out hiking, and to send all their friends and neighbours. She wished she had a card to press on them.

'Thanks so much, Hans,' she said the cheese stallholder. 'You've been so helpful.'

'No problem. Perhaps we could have a coffee sometime? My number's on the card.'

Mina paused for a moment. There had to be life after Luke. 'That would be nice,' she said, smiling back at him. She had to start somewhere.

'Great,' he beamed at her.

Leaving them, she skirted a stall full of fresh bread, the scent filling the air, making her stomach rumble. Moving on, she ambled the streets, basking in the sunshine until she decided to treat herself to a coffee. She rather enjoyed being on her own. This last few weeks had been frenetic with so much to do, and hopefully the café would have plenty of customers, even though Reckingen was such a small place. According to faithful Google, it was a good walk to the wholesalers, and although the sun shone, the ground temperature was still quite cold, so she took a taxi, asking him in her best German to return in an hour and a half to take her back to the station.

After a very successful shopping trip to the wholesalers, the taxi driver deposited her right outside the station, and she realised if she hurried she could just make the next train, which left in five minutes. Rushing through the barrier, she found the platform and made a mad dash to the train, pulling the now quite heavy case along behind her. Thank goodness she'd brought it – although perhaps if she hadn't, she wouldn't have been quite so tempted. She had a ton of ideas for Amelie and Johannes's wedding cake, and had bought ready-roll icing, a selection of bottles of colour, a roll of fancy ribbon, and some delicate sprays of moulded-icing roses, as well some speciality flour, some cake bases, dowelling, and a tiny bride and groom. If Luke had been here, she might have asked him to help make a bride and groom – with his modelling skills, he'd have been invaluable. And there she was bloody thinking about him again.

With a minute to spare, she jumped onto the train, and was about to slam the door behind her when a voice shouted urgently, 'Wait!' She left the door and moved a step forward. Two seconds later someone hurled themselves through the door, knocked her flying – and to add insult to injury, landed on top of her.

Blue eyes appeared as a hand pushed a shaggy mop of hair from his face.

Completely winded by the fall, it took her a second to try and catch her breath, but that failed as everything went haywire. Her pulse exploded into hyper-speed and her breath caught in her chest as she stared into the familiar face.

He grinned down at her.

Finally, she managed to haul air into her deprived lungs as the train smoothly moved off.

'Do you think you could move your pointy elbow out of

my ribs?' she asked with a gasp, pushing at his arm uncomfortably wedged into her side.

'Oh, sorry.' He sat up and then reached for her, pulling her up to a sitting position. 'We really must stop meeting like this.'

For a moment she glared at him and then thumped him hard on the arm. 'Is that all you can say?' she asked indignantly, although every nerve-ending in every last bit of her jumped up and down with happiness.

'I love you. I missed you. I'm sorry.'

'I should think so too. What kept you?'

'Well, apparently it's quite difficult getting off a boat when you're halfway across the Irish Sea.'

'Luke, I was joking. Why are you here?'

'Because it turns out the opportunity of a lifetime doesn't mean much when you're missing someone so much you want to gnaw your own arm off.'

Mina laughed. 'That's not terribly romantic.'

'I know, but that's how I felt. It was awful. I couldn't stop thinking about you. I thought perhaps when we set off, it might get better, but it was worse and the sea sickness didn't help. Luckily I was so ill that they let me bail in Dublin.'

'Oh, Luke.'

He gave her a naughty grin. 'I'm also, it turns out, quite a good actor. I might have exaggerated my symptoms somewhat. It was that or jump overboard.'

'I think jumping overboard would have been a little drastic.'

He shrugged his shoulders, those blue eyes dancing,

'You're worth it.'

'Seriously, Luke. It was a big deal.'

'Not when I was on a boat heading in the opposite direction from you.' His tone might have been jokey, but his eyes were deadly serious.

'But what about your career?' Mina spluttered, still not quite able to believe he was really here. 'The adventure?'

'I want to try a new adventure. One with you by my side. And I hate to say it—' his mouth quirked in what she assumed was an attempt at modesty '—but I've already been offered two other jobs, both of which are based in Geneva.'

'Well, that's handy.'

'I thought so. I think if you're going to start an adventure with the love of your life, being in the same country is a good start.' He let out a laugh. 'You know I love you, Mina Campbell.'

'And I love you Luke… whatever your bloody surname is.'

'You're not going to believe this but it's… Love.'

'What?'

'Whatever my parents named me, it was going to be problematic with a surname like that. It's derived from "luiff", which meant wolf, and there are ten thousand of us in the UK, so it's not completely weird.'

'No, it's completely perfect.' Mina began to laugh because underneath those facts, he sounded ever so slightly defensive.

Luke smiled. 'Remember the first time I kissed you?'

'I don't think I'll ever forget it. I never believed in love at first sight, or first kiss, or serendipity.'

'And do you now?'

'Yes, I do,' she said, smiling up at his handsome face. 'We had no idea whether we would ever see each other again. On that train either of us could have been headed anywhere in Europe. You couldn't possibly have known that we were both going to end up at the same ski chalet, could you?'

There was a tiny glimmer of something in Luke's eyes but he shook his head, his hand straying to flick something from her cabin bag.

'And if it wasn't for that chance meeting again at Amelie's, I wouldn't have always believed in here—' she held a hand over her heart '—that one day you'd come back.'

'I knew the first time we kissed that you were the girl for me.' Luke stared at her with an indecipherable expression on his face.

'You know what I named the café?'

'I saw. You left no stone unturned on Facebook or Instagram.'

'I needed you to know.'

'I knew alright. I'm sorry I didn't make it to the party yesterday. I did try, but I wasn't ill enough to be airlifted off the boat. Apparent you need to be in a near-coma for that. I wasn't sure… I made you something.' From behind his back he pulled a battered leather case.

Mina looked at his face and smiled at the small boy excitement lurking there. She flicked open the catches and flipped back the lid.

Inside was a perfect alpine scene, with a train running through a valley, and perched on the side of the valley was an exact replica of the ski chalet, complete with a tiny terrace with tables and chairs, and above the barn doors was an identical copy of the swirling Serendipity sign.

'I didn't think hearts and flowers were enough. I'd already decided I'd come back one day and bring it with me.'

'Oh Luke, it's beautiful.' The intricate detail spoke of a labour of love.

'I never stopped thinking about you, and I was determined to give you this in person.'

Luke leaned forward and kissed her. As soon as his lips touched hers, her body responded, every cell attuned to that wonderful sensation of coming home, as well as that nerve-tingling deliciousness of a first kiss in a long time.

The kiss developed into something that really wasn't very suitable for a train corridor, but at that moment in time, neither of them cared. And if Luke fingered the *Harry Potter* luggage tag hanging from her bag behind her back, no one would ever need to know that he'd always known, the first time they met, that he'd see her again, but sheer willpower and determination had been responsible for him coming back to her for the second…

THE END

Don't miss *The Cosy Cottage in Ireland*, the next heartwarming instalment in the Romantic Escapes series by Julie Caplin.

Acknowledgments

My biggest thanks go to the extraordinarily generous Andie Pilot, creator of the Helvetic Kitchen website, whose passionate writing about Swiss food and her wonderful curation of Swiss recipes has inspired and taught me all about the food of the region. I have shamelessly plundered her treasure chest of Swiss recipes and if you're interested in finding out more about any of the dishes and delicious cakes featured in the book, I would urge you to head over to www.helvetickitchen.com for all the recipes and to learn about the history and tradition of the dishes.

As always I have to thank my wonderful writing buddies, Donna Ashcroft, Bella Osborne, Darcie Boleyn, Philippa Ashley and Sarah Bennett – a woman could not have a better bunch of cheerleaders, friends and supporters. Even during lockdown we've managed to have virtual drinks via Zoom or in the case of Donna, Prosecco in the garden by the fire pit.

During the last year when travel has been difficult if not

impossible, I'm hugely grateful to all the readers that have written, messaged and Instagrammed to let me know that through my books they've been able to escape to another place for a couple of hours. Those messages make my day every single time!

Special thanks to my much loved agent, Broo Doherty, and my brilliant editor, Charlotte, who can spot a flabby middle at a hundred paces but knows just what to do about it. Thanks also go to the whole team at One More Chapter, who make all the magic happen behind the scenes and the fabulous unsung heroines, the HarperCollins Rights team, who are nothing short of amazing, especially the lovely Emily Yolland, who goes out and buys my books!

Life this year has been challenging for so many people, so I think not being able to go back to Switzerland is a very minor problem in the scheme of things. However, I hope that my memories have served me well. Any mistakes and I'm blaming Google! I hope that you've enjoyed your trip with Mina and Luke and Amelie and Johannes and that you'll be ready to join me on the next adventure with Mina's sister Hannah.

Recipe: Basler Kirschenbrottorte

500 g leftover bread
400 ml milk
1 tsp vanilla paste or extract
800 g to 1 kg cherries
100 g cookie crumbs
120 g butter, soft
200 g sugar
pinch of salt
7 eggs, separated
100 g ground almonds
20 g flour
2 tsp baking powder
2 tsp cinnamon
a shot kirsch

Cube the bread and put it in a big bowl. Heat the milk and vanilla in a pot over the stove or in a microwave. When it's bubbling, add it to the bread. Press the bread down with a fork so it soaks up the liquid. Let this cool a little.

While you're waiting, pit the cherries.

Preheat oven to 180 C / 350 F / gas mark 4.

Line a 26 cm (10 inch) springform pan with parchment. Butter the sides, then sprinkle about half of the cookie crumbs over the bottom of the pan. Set aside.

Once the bread has absorbed the milk, use a fork (or your fingers) to mash it all together.

In a large bowl, cream together the butter and sugar. Add the salt and vanilla. Beat in the egg yolks a little at a time until everything is incorporated.

In a separate bowl, whisk together the rest of the cookie crumbs, ground almonds, flour, baking powder, and cinnamon.

Using another separate, clean bowl and whisk or mixer, whisk the egg whites until stiff and glossy.

Mix the soaked bread into the butter and egg mixture. Add the flour mixture. Stir in the cherries and kirsch. Fold in the egg whites.

Pour into your prepared pan.

Bake in the oven for 1 to 1¼ hours, until the top has browned and the centre is no longer jiggly.

YOUR NUMBER ONE STOP

ONE MORE CHAPTER

FOR PAGETURNING BOOKS

One More Chapter is an
award-winning global
division of HarperCollins.

Sign up to our newsletter to get our
latest eBook deals and stay up to date
with our weekly Book Club!
<u>Subscribe here</u>.

Meet the team at
<u>www.onemorechapter.com</u>

Follow us!

 @OneMoreChapter_
 @OneMoreChapter
 @onemorechapterhc

Do you write unputdownable fiction?
We love to hear from new voices.
Find out how to submit your novel at
<u>www.onemorechapter.com/submissions</u>